DOORS

ר

Other works by Deena Metzger:

FICTION

Skin Shadows / Silence
The Woman Who Slept With Men to Take the War Out of Them
What Dinah Thought
The Other Hand

Non-fiction

Entering the Ghost River
Writing for Your Life
Tree Essays and Pieces
Intimate Nature The Bond Between Women and Animals
(with Brenda Peterson and Linda Hogan)

POETRY

Dark Milk
The Axis Mundi Poems
Looking for the Faces of God
A Sabbath Among the Ruins

PLAYS

The Book of Hags
Not As Sleepwalkers
Dreams Against The State

Doors

A Fiction for Jazz Horn

ד

Deena Metzger

Red Hen Press ◆ Los Angeles

Cover photo of Julio Cortázar
Copyright © Anne de Brunnhof
Courtesy of Agencia Literaria Carmen Balcells

Author photo by Ayelet Berman-Cohen
Book and cover design by Mark E. Cull
Production assistant Gina Gagliano

ISBN 1-888996-99-4
Library of Congress Catalog Card Number 2004095865

The City of Los Angeles Cultural Affairs Department,
Los Angeles County Arts Commission, California Arts Council
and the National Endowment for the Arts
partially support Red Hen Press.

Published by
Red Hen Press

FIRST PRINTING

First Edition

In Memoriam J. C.

Doors

ד

PART I

ר

how vain to believe
we're born
or we die
when all that's real is the hole left in the page[1]
Julio Cortázar

This is the story. It occurred in August 1974. More than nineteen years ago. Ten years later he died: the second story. The two stories became points on a trajectory that lead here to this moment. From this vista, we can look back to try to understand what occurred and forward to discern what might be. A story is a little world. I have said this so many times but now I am in it, in the world of the story. Its laws and possibilities. Everything we need to know is here. This bindu point is the first story. There is another bindu point that is the second story. Each story is, itself, a little world but, also, a larger universe is projected from the way they intermingle when they meet and traverse the timeline that emanates from them both. The shortest distance is the straight line between two points. And then the distance from these two points to this moment— the third point. The composite line forms the diameter of a circle and the circle revolves to become a sphere and the sphere is the entire larger world that we are entering together.

The first story occurs *Here*. *Here* means planet Earth, Europe, the United States, Latin America, and so on, the last quarter of the 20th century and onwards. A timeline from hell. They were *Here* together, the two of them. The second story occurs *Here* but emanates from what he calls *On this side* and what she calls *Over there*. He is no longer *Here*. He is *Over there*. He can't speak of it as *Here*. For him *Here* has become *There*. Every story has a geography, a location that is intrinsic to its nature. A change in location at the core of the story determines its music. What occurs when these two stories intercept each other and what occurs when they intersect?

One story leads to another story. One world leads to another world.

The first story is a small story. It took place over a few hours. An event that could have been easily forgotten, but wasn't. With each passing day, instead of fading, it became more vivid. First it was an incident that became in the telling an amusing anecdote. Then it became an event and then an important story. Then it became a primary story, an origins story that determined the nature of the universe in which she was living. A cosmology developed from it. There was always the possibility that it was all in her imagination, but what if it wasn't? From the perspective of *Here* it can all be dismissed as fantasy or obsession. But when she steps over the line to the place where *Here* and *Over there* commingle, then every such event has to be taken most seriously. We can't be certain about any of this; we are simply speculating. Speculating on the possible forms through which the apparent meeting could occur. Two stories, two themes, two people, two worlds meeting the way two sound waves meet and form a third and then travel together through time, round and full.

The first dissonant notes of *Here* meeting the first notes of *Over there* and a third sound beginning that neither of them ever heard before but captivating them. Becoming the theme they develop together.

Were I a composer, I would write this piece of music and it would be sufficient. The horn, his voice, as is its metaphysical purpose, to open the way. The trumpet speaking the details of the world they were fated to share together, the universal grief. A flute, her voice meeting his. Drums. The crucial, if implausible, constant heartbeat. And a drone, a bass, probably, or Keith Jarrett on the piano, carrying the unremitting continuous agony of The woman in the cellar whose cries never cease, whose anguish is unremitting, whose reality must never be ignored. Perhaps you will be able to hear it, the music, that they never expected to play together. Without knowing it, she dreamed of it, pined for it, wanted nothing but it, while feeling entirely incapable of such a duet. It wasn't a partner she longed for, it was such an activity and he was by far the best candidate. As for him, he never thought of it or at least not with her. At least as far she knows. When he knew her, *Here*, she was far too young, and they were both preoccupied with their own separate lives. That is what they thought. Such is the nature of living in hell. There is rarely time, space or means to emerge cleanly from its preoccupations and engulfment. But once he was *Over there*, everything shifted and he looked back toward *Here* to see what was possible. He kept getting pulled toward the first story because she had kept it alive and instilled it with such vitality. A story can have a life of its own, its own eternal vortex, spinning, spinning.

Once he was *Over there*, he wasn't obligated to a single story, but could enter many at the same time and in different ways. Why not this one too? He had become by his new nature, polyphonic. He was making his own music, simultaneously blowing a thousand different horns in a thousand different places according to different musical themes. A 21st century phenomenon. Though they share a world together, they do not share all worlds. She knows nothing of the other worlds he is inhabiting at this time.

What follows then is the first story.

He blew a horn and she had just learned to carry a tune. He liked jazz, Charlie Parker especially, and she wasn't sure. His name was Rio. Because he was born—no, was to die—under Pisces, his mother named him for that one of the elements. He liked the name; liked rivers; he studied them, their movement and flow, became an expert on shifts and changeability. Secretly she called him Hermes, St. Hermes' fire, for his mercurial quality, that will-o'-the-wisp phantom fire, into which she knew, even before she met him, that he could/would vanish and from which he would appear again in her life without warning. And he knew her secret; that she saw him. In this you might say they ultimately became one, St. Elmo's fire, the siblings. Castor and Pollux, in the underworld one day, and here on this side, the next. He was smart and she was just as smart as he was. He knew he was smart and he knew she was smart, but she didn't know about herself. When he received her letter of introduction which swept into his life on the great cold winds of the mistral, he shivered. Her name was Iris and he thought of *el aire* and sometimes *los aires* but not necessarily of *los buenos aires* among which he might have been born on the Río de la Plata. He also knew that Iris, the sweet one, had been the servant of Hera, was the one without enemies, the one sent down into the underworld for the bitter waters by which the gods swore their oaths and so, inevitably, he was in for it. From the beginning, she looked at him and her eyes demanded, "Swear!" In his eyes, it was because she was so young, and American, that she could assume it was easy to do. She was the kind of young woman who was so full of passion that she couldn't tally cost. She lived by challenge, an energy that blinded her to the consequences of her insistence. Within the challenge, she believed she could do anything and demanded the same from the men she loved. Clearly, she wanted something from him even if she didn't know it and he / they would never escape it.

She was with her lover when they met and he was with his and so they examined each other through that clear lens we imagine ourselves, as a third party, to be. Her lover, Vito, prided himself upon being conceived and born in Italy when his parents were visiting the old country, and then they stayed longer than they had ever intended until his mother refused to have her baby anywhere but in the farmhouse where she, herself, had been born. His mother credited Vito's birth with keeping his father from joining the Lincoln Brigade and fighting the fascists in Spain (instead of in their neighborhood where, she claimed, they were just as rampant if hidden), because she refused to raise her son herself even if they were living in Brooklyn; she always crossed herself when she told this part of the story and even so the father agreed with her. This history, Vito seemed to think, gave him permission to comment on all manner of subjects and to wear odd colors, pink, purple, wine, and magenta while viewing the world through a rosy Marxist perspective. Rio didn't understand why she was with this bull of a man any more than Iris understood why he had chosen Hélène, who in Iris' eyes was tall and soft and broad as a cow, to be his lover. Whenever Iris looked at Rio, Hélène was in the way in the manner of cows covering a landscape. Or it was something like shadow dancing. If he was the wall, Hélène was the shadow that moved over him. As if the light were elsewhere, as if he weren't the light. One looked for him and there was Hélène—though she hadn't seemed to move and was relatively silent—there she was. Hélène, herself a designer of scarves or buildings or books—Iris couldn't remember which—couldn't, in Iris' view, have been afraid that Iris had designs on him. First of all, there was Vito and second of all she had only come for dinner and might never return to France and then Rio had a toothache and would have been happier to read a book or make notes for a story than to broil lamb chops for two American citizens who had searched him out in his hiding place in Saignon overlooking the Mediterranean. More pointedly, Iris was young and naïve and enthusiastic in ways Hélène was certain would/should irritate Rio. But even if according to Iris, Hélène didn't see her at all, this was not to say that Hélène should or shouldn't have been wary.

Vito and Hélène are distractions. Let's not pay attention to them. That is exactly what Iris was thinking after being with Rio for half an hour. Something is wrong here, she thought. She wanted to speak with him about everything that was unspeakable. There was a world between them and it was at war. Not one of those great wars that killed millions but a dreadful small and personal national slaughter that pretended to be an isolated skirmish even though it was clearly aided and abetted from afar and didn't seem to perturb most people, but was every bit a war for those who were suffering it. Her friends. His friends. He was older than she and wearier. He could see that she was readying herself for a fight that would make her breasts knot and swell while it took the marrow out of him.

She was aware of a fundamental cognitive disturbance in the atmosphere. Six or seven thousand miles away some people they knew in common were in prison. She tried to imagine it over the paté. There was no way to escape the paté. She wanted the paté, delighted in its smoky flavor. If it was not paté, it would have been something else. The doorbell rings. One answers it. There are the guests. One invites them in. One offers them something. They are or will be hungry. There is no escape from the twins—distraction and courtesy.

A smear of paté on a hexagonal cracker puffed up around tiny holes that were gleaming with a few shimmering grains of salt. The white wine was from the neighboring vineyard and so the bottle had no label. It was a young wine, bright and scented with herbs, not quite as pronounced as the pine pitch in *retsina* but still cold and pungent with spices. Every week or so when he and his guests had finished a dozen bottles or so, Rio would wash them out carefully scrubbing them with a thin brush on a long wooden handle that he dipped in hot soapy water, a labor he enjoyed, and returned them to the vineyard and took another dozen back home and placed them in the cool earth cellar.

There was a room they took you to down a flight of stairs; after the door closed behind you, no one heard the screams. But he was hearing the screams of a woman in the cellar. He was never out of range of the screams. Iris knew this because she heard them as well. Not as well as he heard them as he was a musician attuned to all the registers, upper and lower, and the half tones and the quarter tones in-between. He heard the audible as well as anyone but he also listened to the inaudible, studying its gradations and differentiations as if it were the holy grail which it is.

. . . the prisoner tied to a post, the faces of the people around . . . some American or Danish ethnologist . . . a bad camera . . . the choice of knives indicated work on the right ear and the rest of the naked body . . . one could see the victim was alive . . . his head thrown back, his mouth still open . . . but one could see in the seventh that a decisive cut had been made because the shape of the thighs which had been turned outward . . . the change was

not in the thighs but in the groin . . . something pouring out of a hole,
something like a little girl who had been raped, with blood flowing down her
thighs . . . the eighth picture the victim could not have been alive any more . . .
"According to what I have been told, the whole operation took an hour and a
half," Wong observed . . . "Of course, Peking is not what it used to be . . . I'm
sorry I showed you something so primitive, but one cannot carry certain other
documents in his billfold, there have to be explanations, an initiation . . . [2]

"How do you live with it?" This was one of the questions she had come to ask him and so silently mouthed it in her mind both in English and in her barely adequate Spanish and long forgotten high school French. Tears welled up in her eyes. And so in his. He shook his great leonine head.

A paper, folded in four, small enough to fit into a wallet. Had Rio actually been there when the one he called Wong extracted it from his wallet and showed it to the men in the room, reviewing the scene in which he had shown it to women in a café, complaining that "they didn't understand it at all." And did he suspect when he wrote about it that he would know such stories from his own time and about his own people, his kin, those he loved? Looking into Rio's eyes, Iris was seeing the future. She had only read *Hopscotch* once. She didn't know what he knew. She was too young to know what he knew and whether, if he were able or willing to love her, he would want to spare her what he knew, what he was always seeing/hearing. What Wong had heard but claimed had been the past although Iris knew it wasn't the past even if she didn't know what it was yet. It was now. In the moment. There beneath their feet. She could feel it. She insisted upon feeling it because, if he would love her, she would not let him spare her. She wanted to know and this is why she imagined loving him.

From the moment she had read his work, she had imagined loving him. Immediately, she abandoned all the ideas she had held about romance and chemistry. She wanted to love him because she wanted to walk alongside him, to walk alongside such a one as he—not that she wanted to walk alongside him because she loved him.

There were doors. He knew how to open them and step across the threshold. He knew what was beneath his feet because he knew how to enter *Over there*. It wasn't from *Here* it was from *Over there* that he knew about the woman in the cellar. About her and about other things. Things Iris suspected existed. Things she dreamed about. Ways of knowing. She had always dreamed of *Over there*. She wanted to walk over there too. And so with him.

Here she was on the deck overlooking the Mediterranean, seated at a simple peasant table on a wooden kitchen chair that demanded that she sit straight and be alert. She'd been seated next to him and had been given the best view of the sea and the late dying afternoon light so they each had to choose to turn to one or another when they began speaking, otherwise their words were uttered to the view. Before them were the tiny scattered roofs of the villages and their early lights like first stars scattered as if they had fallen down when Coyote, on the continent where she lived, had flung the Milky Way into the sky with such complete abandon. Or to the contrary, the stars had been placed there, exactly, with purpose, the way sacred pollen is strewn during morning prayers from the top of the hills down toward that sea that blends into the heavens and so leaving the question open as to whether magic is haphazard or intentional. Sky blue, sky purple, sky gray. A French sky that was reluctant to imagine torture except as it might be occurring elsewhere. Under this sky, only beauty was possible, but only of a certain kind— this beauty, infiltrated with the gestures of the human hand, a domestic beauty, not wild, nor of the wilderness. Iris didn't know yet how far she was going to go from the cities she thought she admired. But two nights previous, she and Vito had been offered a restaurant table covered with a fine linen cloth, placed among several others in a line down the center of a wretched street. The waiters scampered out of the restaurants on both sides, swerving tight-assed, not unlike bullfighters, to avoid the hot breath and horns of the cars and motorcycles passing through. After waiting forty minutes they were brought their soups, tepid water and one golden onion the size of a marble in fine china. Vito had insisted that they leave without tasting or paying. If they were going to be hungry, Vito insisted, it was going to be alongside the hungry and not in an overpriced French restaurant that had been awarded too many stars. Anyway, they were close enough to Italy to consider ordering spaghetti.

Yes, here he was. His broad, curved forehead, his unruly beard, his smile and laughter interrupted by his toothache, his swollen jaw. She had never experienced the vertigo of such a moment when the real and the possible begin to whirl about each other so fast that each partakes of the other, and in this process of irisation, one shining color blends into another, until they are one spectrum and so definitively altered as to be another entity altogether; one she had imagined, but, inevitably, quite imperfectly. The great danger, she understood, of setting out to create a golem: one got what one asked for but it was never what one had imagined, even though it came directly out of the action of the self. Accordingly—the danger.

Canapés. Chardonnay. Café. The difference between what was being said and what was unsaid, or said only under the breath, was palpable to her. And to him. For otherwise she would not be so certain that they were involved in a private and urgent conversation that she, privately, supposed would never end. No, it would never end. She accepted this fact as a death, no, as a life sentence and even though they were speaking politics, that is, of the present, she was suspended—perhaps it was the night sky which had turned burgundy and then black and so carried the visual fragrance of eternity—she was suspended elsewhere, in their future, which had become a great maw containing everything, past and present, the intimation of continuity which would, however, she equally understood, never be realized in the ways men and women habitually enacted their connections to each other. More like a breath under language, a continuous undercurrent so far below the surface of the sea as to be virtually undetectable, both sacred and invisible. She only thought she knew something about the sacred. In each moment, one thinks one knows something, but then, later, if one is fortunate, one knows more or differently and laments the earlier, now understood to be inevitable, naiveté. But she did know something about the invisible. Even then. As did he. That's what she had seen and so had written.

There are so many possibilities, all cogent, all true. There is the story of the young naïve American girl—not entirely young except in the ways even Iris regretted that American women—and she was no exception—insist upon remaining young forever—who had fallen for the charismatic great man because of his writerly skills, his politics, his craggy, rough, broken (brokenhearted) face that resembled all the giants of Greek and Nordic literature. He had been named for water, as if he already was or would be Pisces, in the form of Poseidon, the sea and the earth shaker at once, earthquake and tidal wave. She saw the stone of the sea floor in his body, the way giants are always mountains and the earth rumbles when they walk. Or he was some kind of lightning rod, the mast of a sailing ship, the blue green lights of the spectral fires fluorescent around him. That's one story. The most familiar, the most plausible, the one Hélène imagined as she had had to endure its occurrence so many times before. There were so many moments in that evening when Iris wanted to reach out to Hélène and make an alliance that would honor her, each other, the woman in the cellar but she didn't know how. Some days later, she would be sitting on a balcony overlooking the sea again, in Vito's grandmother's moldy miniature palacio wrapped in the sweater Rio had insisted she take back with her—*his* sweater—which meant he was with her like an odor—and speaking with Vito's sister-in-law, Rosanna, and suddenly Iris would know how to speak to a woman again, as if the woman had come out of the cellar with her eyes open, her voice intact and her mind whole. But in the meantime, the story Iris thought that Hélène was imagining did not invite a conversation between Hélène and Iris even if in the end, it was not *the* story.

Or the story of the woman who was cutting her own path as a writer and wanted and needed encouragement to see how a pathfinder manifested in the flesh. Or the story of an adventurer. Or the story of a woman who had the outrageous intention of creating an alliance of language and vision with a man twenty-two years older than she, experienced, recognized, erudite, talented, established and who was, inevitably, also very busy, occupied and pre-occupied. Any of these familiar and predictable scenarios could serve to describe this moment between them. In a sense, they are all accurate but, ultimately, we hope, understood as inaccurate.

There was another story. A story not known then or later, really. Not known until this moment. This moment when a woman named I■, or, alternatively, I, is writing the story or when someone is reading it and able to learn the entire history, what is future here but will be past soon enough in the reader's mind. Enacted then but remaining potential, unborn so to speak. Or occurring outside of time but no less accurate than the stories that could have been enacted then. But weren't because this is the story that occurred in that moment. It was the moment.

The story. Fleeting as a wink. They were together at last and there was nothing to be said about it. It would never be different than it was in this moment. It was fate. Fate, she knew, was invisible and inaudible. But the terrible and awesome Fates, the Moerae, Clotho, Lachesis and Atropos, were the great gods that even Zeus dared not oppose. Those three women who spin and weave and snip. She and he, Vito and Hélène had fallen into their domain and all it had taken was a letter and a knock at the door for the story to begin.

· · ·

"There are doors which can be opened," he was saying, "they take a long time, but they can be opened."
. . . Sure, every once in a while the door opens a little bit.[3]

She had missed exactly what she had wanted to hear, what she had expected he would say only to her and what he would never say only to her because it would mean something different, entirely, within such a context. It would imply the camaraderie of possibility which lay outside of them. Her mind began to wander until it seemed she could recall each incident in which a man had held a door open for her and each incident in which she had, deliberately, stepped forward and opened the door herself, her entire posture changing as she led, arm outstretched, palm raised or tilted and forward, aware of a certain bravura or audacity that announced to the world that she was and would remain an independent woman. There were other possibilities: a man as tall as Rio pulled the door open toward him and placed his other arm high on the doorjamb to survey what lay ahead of them but/and she slipped under his raised arm and entered the other territory first, then turned toward him and beckoned.

She was severely, unconscionably distracted. This was not about her. The door that needed to be opened was not only the door before Iris. There was another door. It was locked. Behind it was a woman in a cellar. The woman in the cellar. This was the door that needed to be opened. There was no difference between opening that door and opening the door for herself.

The woman in the cellar was not and did not become an object of erotic exchange between them. Iris didn't/couldn't know what the woman was thinking, if thought was even possible when one was suffering so extremely and without expectation of cessation, without even the possibility of willing her death, of fainting away into oblivion, and so would have to hold on to the hope that someone would not be able to bear her affliction, even as they could only imagine it, and the woman would welcome even this leisurely moment among the four of them, this routine of camaraderie, as long as none of them became oblivious to her extreme torture, as long as someone remembered, as long as some activity on behalf of the woman would be taken. Now. Before the next blow.

The Chinese man had not been so fortunate. What remained of him was a ragged newspaper clipping folded into a wallet, taken out in a moment of bravery or drunkenness and returned there except that Rio had remembered it and recorded it and Iris, and others, had read it, remembered it. But this had done nothing for the Chinese man. He was, finally, blissfully, given what had gone before, dead.

The woman in the cellar had been brought without her agreement to what is sought as the gift—call it being present—call it martyrdom—but in this instance was only the torture of the incessant present. Pain has neither past nor future. Pain is the undiluted pristine present moment.

For Iris who felt equally hopeful and despairing, powerless and encouraged by the fact of this meeting—they had, hadn't they, driven across France to accomplish it?—the world teetered between two possibilities, each equally untenable; there was some core remedy that could/would be accomplished; the door would be opened; the woman would be freed; such circumstances, as she was suffering, would not be repeated; she would not be re-arrested; no one would be arrested in her place; the cell to which she was confined would not be used again; the woman's body would be her body, and her body alone, from this moment hence. Iris had constructed her psyche and, she hoped, her life around the full realization of this possibility at least for other men and women as Iris wasn't being tortured, had never been tortured and was careful not to use such a metaphor for her own suffering—and so scrutinized every action and reaction in herself and others because she wanted to be certain that the essential causes of such agonies as the woman in the cellar was experiencing now, not on celluloid or videotape, mind you, but in her own body, would be attended wisely, that is, halted.

But/and also, Iris feared the other possibility: that they could do nothing except congratulate themselves for trying, that they would devote their lives and still it would come to nothing, that all the words they spoke or wrote would come to nothing, that one of them might also someday be trapped in the terrible isolation of suffering because what they had attempted had come to nothing. The fact of how much each of them cared had made them candidates for the very agony they protested and when *les jeux sont fait* she would be helpless to alter his reality. She would be a witness to his agony and then death from afar and without hope or possibility. 'I will not be able to bear his suffering,' she thought and pulled herself back from the mire of these thoughts, listened listlessly to the familiar music of such a quartet as they had become, what they were daring among themselves and what was being denied.

Making love with Vito, and before him with so many other men, distinctly different, as men are from each other but also, in such instances, so similar, she had never been convinced that the exquisite but equally studied tenderness of his gestures rendered torture unthinkable. But, still she imagined, there could exist a variant of fierce tenderness that, by its nature, eradicated cruelty.

When she was with Vito, they each sought their own pleasure and were grateful when it occurred in each other's presence and through each other's activities. Yes, it was that remote, their love making. Not a biological imperative so much as a psychological imperative enacted through the skill of their hands, mouths and organs. With eyes closed they enacted a fantasy: hers that he loved *her*; his that she *yielded* to him completely. He wanted her . . . when he wanted her . . . how he wanted her . . . wanted her to fit his wanting. . . . At this moment, she was not interested in Vito, certainly not in the ways some lovers focus on each other out of pride or embarrassment when they are with others. But in the dark, when his hands probed her, or, worse, in the dark, when he turned away from her and placed his hands beneath his pillow, then she could not bear to be separate from him. And when he finally touched her but from such a great distance, with arms seemingly miles long, and whispered to her with a voice that issued commands as though hissing through a megaphone, she was infused with need and could barely contain her lust to turn on the light, to stand up before him, to say, "This body, can't you see, I am this body. Love this body." If she ever would do so, he would leave her. That was certain and that was why, she understood, he demanded she close her eyes while he also put a flannel hand over her mouth so as to silence any sound she might make. It was as if she were in a shroud of Mussolini leather, perfectly fit to her face, a small slit only so she could breathe, the skin of the animal molded to her skin and laced behind and her dark hair falling around this blank face that could countenance everything or nothing. It was only because she was, in those

all—according to the most prominent democracy, that other country that had enjoyed, prospered from its dependency. So it mounted an attack while the far less democratic countries who had supported her independence wholeheartedly, stood by helplessly. She was quickly down on her knees, the mother country, a gun at her head. Everyone claimed the conflict was internal, a civil war, the self divided against itself. But this wasn't true. The mother country was being taught, as any newly independent country must learn, to say, "Uncle."

Iris knew this not in her bones alone, but in fact. She knew who and when and where and how. Even though it was a secret. A secret occurs when the perpetrator has the power to deny what he is doing in broad daylight while everyone is watching. Iris had known what she hadn't wanted to know as soon as ten days after *el golpe* and she had worked hard with others to make a documentary about it that made its small rounds without influencing anyone sufficiently to end it. It had taken ten years for some of what she had known to become public knowledge; after ten years such truths hardly disturb the U.S. or international tranquility. After ten years some of the truth—but laundered of its most devastating and incriminating revelations—had become a movie, *Missing*, with a movie star, Jack Lemmon. Iris had gone to the movie alone one afternoon. She had sat in the very center of the almost empty movie theatre and watched as the truth emerged and dissolved. She had held that story in her hands. It had been a living story and now it was a story that moved among the shades. The movie had gone the way of most films of concern—to oblivion. By that time, Rio was dying.

At this moment, ten years earlier, though, looking over the Mediterranean, Vito knew what Iris knew and Rio knew it and, yes, Hélène knew it as well. This is what had brought them together—these unbearable truths. And the name of the woman in the cellar who had probably been pushed to her knees at the same time. And even the names of some of the others who were with her there, sharing her fate and those imposing it.

Iris knew that her idea of independence did not accord with the ideas of independence held by those who had subjugated the likes of her for millennia. Even those who seemed to applaud her independence or, in their ways, profited from it, nevertheless they had ideas about how it should manifest itself—to accord with them.

At this point, she didn't believe in God or divinity, in spirit or spirits, nothing supernatural, but she did believe in natural law, her particular cosmology, and so postulated a gesture so tender in its intent, so full of kindness and mercy, that an entire universe might flow from it which could not by its nature co-exist with or encompass cruelty. Because of this, she looked at Rio and wanted to touch him, wanted him to touch her.

She had been struck in love-making. Who hadn't? She had been tied down, restrained. She had felt pain. She had been implored to advocate such freedom and explorations. She had been told to close her eyes; she had been told to keep them open. She had accorded to the demand that she be blind to and also that she not fail to observe, the faint twist of her lover's mouth as he skillfully bent her to his will and, simultaneously, eluded her so that she was always longing for him.

After a time, it came to this: In her body, she couldn't live without Vito or whomever; she could no longer live without him/them not because of anything that transpired between them but exactly because of what was not between them, the nothing that could not be traversed. Her fists tightly clenched about the shining coils of black hair; she pulled them and she wailed. It was that banal.

Torture as an institution develops from such moments. She had always known it even though she had seen that her own lover, Vito, would not have gone in that direction because he feared his own pain and was devoted to beauty and hated distortion, and so his eyes would turn even blacker with fear of the reality he could not avoid and exulted in imagining. In college, she had made love once with a poet studying history with whom she had spent many hours drinking black coffee and arguing about the possible. Afterwards, they had risen from the dingy sheets on his single bed, finished the last of last night's pizza in the stained cardboard box in the refrigerator and had gone to the movies where he blindly followed the fight on the screen with his own clenched fists—"Take that. Take that!" Her arm was no longer entwined with his though he gave no indication that he had felt hers slide away from him; she had never wanted to return to his bed and he had never invited her back. When she saw him in class, she was ashamed to be the carrier of his guilty secret, that she had seen what no woman should see, the small boy completely lost in the movie theater, fists clenched, one striking the air after another, duking it out with the stars.

It was Vito who had taught her how to be a modern lover, how to come forward in pain, how to open when it would be instinctual to withhold, how to shout with ecstasy in a moment of torment, and how to turn what she had previously thought would be intolerable into something she hungered for and which, her body learned, could/would/must now be called pleasure.

He had convinced her that her freedom lay in this direction. Such trust as he imagined between them could only come of her own free will. He would never force himself upon her. But she had a gift to give. The gift of a free woman. Only a free woman had such a gift to give. Only a free woman could yield.

Once she had come upon Vito in a conversation with a painter who had witnessed torture. She listened as Vito interrogated the refugee for the details—or the recipe—as if they were attending a hearing in which each particular is displayed in order that it might be examined before it is prohibited—one can not legislate against what one doesn't know, can one?—and then entered with this man into a minute analysis of his recollections wherein the torture was repeated in a thousand variations. The two men were having dinner together in a restaurant and Iris had been invited for dessert. Why not have another bottle of wine with the crème brûlée? One or the other, or both, were going to write a book. They fought for the check and gallantly offered the other the receipt—their credit card record would do for them—for their taxes. The book would be about survival. And what was survived. Afterwards he was preoccupied. Not (only) with nightmares but (also) with daydreams.

This was not unusual. She had had similar fantasies. Had wondered what she would do under different circumstance, how she would respond if. . . . How long would she be able to hold out, to refuse to give names, to keep her own counsel, to keep her bearings, how honorable she would be, how brave, how loyal. . . ? In the matter of pain, she hoped she'd last five minutes, at least, whether her endurance, brief as it would certainly be, was or was not accomplished through the humiliation of having learned how to eroticize her agony. Was that different at all from this game they had invented called "Walking the Edge" though Vito finally confessed in an unprecedented moment of weakness that he wasn't turned on by his own pain, by pain inflicted upon him, but being so much, himself, always, a man of peace, he was moved beyond gratitude when he saw her willing mouth contort, her eager body writhe, open, twist up to him.

It was not that she had been thinking of Rio merely as a lover but, yes, she wanted to create a world out of their bodies in the ways ideas develop from premises and universes sprout from words. She had always had the ability to know before her body was touched by another body how it would be when his life enveloped her. Lovers often believe that they will remake the world through their loving, that the earth will be fertile, that flowers will grow in their footsteps, that honey will pour from their mouths, that the gods will descend and celebrate in their bodies. . . . It is so ordinary an idea that who would think she would risk everything for such a promise and, as if adding emphasis to something she was saying . . . "You, understand, Rio, don't you . . . " would put her fingers gently on his arm and through that gesture establish for both of them the entitlement of eros and the efficacy of touch and the promise. But she wouldn't. Mustn't. Didn't.

She knew from the beginning that such a move was doomed. And it was not that they each had lovers. It was not even that they lived in separate countries. She had a life; he had a life. Responsibilities. Commitments. It was not even that they had come to the understanding that for each of them love must not be a tyranny that subsumed everything in its wake. It was not even because she understood that she was still closer to her birth than to her death and so was enjoined by life to imagine what might be and he was closer to his death than to his birth and so was required to recognize failure and limitation. His own. And her youth could not soothe such disappointment, bitterness, resignation.

But, following immediately upon the cadence of his words even in translation, then on the attraction of his voice and the subtlety of his mind, and the way she imagined his fingers moving on the trumpet and the way he wiped it dry using another fine brush and a soft cloth and wrapped it carefully in Chinese silk before he closed the blue velvet lined leather case, she knew that he would not speak English to her for very long because other languages had mothered him. She did not speak French and she did not speak Spanish well. Ultimately, he would be forced to speak to her in Spanish because everything he did was tender, precise and exacting and it was the language of his dreams and of his rage. But what, then, would she understand?

She foresaw the moment when he would lean over her, the heavy white linen sheets across her breasts, his face coming closer, his unkempt beard just grazing her shoulders. He was being drawn down by exactly what was drawing her up, that longing between them for something that neither sex nor tenderness could approach and he would begin speaking. It would take a moment for her to realize that she didn't, couldn't, understand. That he had had to fall into the language that he knew best—or rather that he would have to use those words which did not exist in any other language. This. *Este*. What he wanted to, needed to, tell her now—what made him a novelist, knowing this exactly, this, *este*, yes, and not that, *ese*, but this, exactly—but not only this, but what she might say in response and then what he might understand and then what she. . . .

Knowing as he did that language is a form for descending the stairs into unknown territory. A cave discovered accidentally, by pigs disappearing, let's say, into a hole in the ground, and the young boys who follow them find pictographs preserved for centuries because no light or moisture has entered since those wild singers and dancers departed, the coals of their fires still there in small mounds in the circles of the hardened ground. Everything preserved for exactly this moment, like a time bomb, like a message sent across the centuries and the boys know what the crowds of tourists who will gather at the same spot ever afterwards will never know, ultimately, that it was for them, only for them, that the pictographs were traced with carbon on stone. For those who can see and remember. And what they know, what occurred when they held a small torch close to the wall so they could trace the figures in the air with their fingers, they will never tell. They know that what they found and what this first sighting did to them, enacted upon them, is sacred and secret. Ever afterwards they will only pretend to be boys. A perfect disguise.

Spirits like the Sorcerer of *Trois Frères* were intended to dance through the centuries. Painted or etched into stone, ecstatic among the animals, they, not the caves, were the temples where the great presence was to reside through time. Living temples within temples. She knew how to visit such sites, how to slip away from the crowds, how to bend down in a niche, how to close her eyes, how to meet the eyes on the eyes of the wall, how to give herself (away) to it. She dreamed tigers and lions and deer, flight, rapture and prostration in order to give them all a home.

The earth was falling in upon these holy places. The brushstrokes of reverence and resurrection were fading into private ceremonies of dismemberment. The rhapsodic cries of the game were being distorted into terrible cacophony. Screams without poetry. The body distorted into flinch and spasmodic shudder. Mere food without sacrament. What you discover makes a man of you but what someone else will find who comes afterwards through following signposts or paying admission will not, except under unusual circumstances, alter one. The difference between the act and the subsequent observations.

There it was before her, she saw it all: it was the end. She would not understand. She would always be a foreigner in his arms. He was thinking of Lascaux or the caves in Spain while she was thinking of a cave she had recently visited in Minnesota with the same story of boys and pigs. What further proof was necessary of their incompatibility.

Years later, she realized they could/should have both been thinking of the swineherd, who, thousands of years before the American incident, had watched his pigs drawn down into the ravine that had opened up and closed as Hades pulled the Kore, the young girl down away from the light of day. A white horse, a manly figure with a black iron helmet covering his entire face, narrow slits for eyes, then a girl, white arms raised, white hands flailing, white dress billowing from the suddenness of their descent and then the pigs bleating, alarmed, then nothing. A thin crack in the earth as of sun and drought and even that disappearing within minutes. The young boy marked the location with a stone otherwise he also would have lost his place even if ever afterwards, he would marvel at this vision of the gods.

The young swineherd's name was Eubuleus, whatever it was they called him in Minnesota. While the distant and disinterested Hekate heard the terrified screams from her cave, he was the only witness of the abduction and without him the Kore's whereabouts would never have been discovered.

It would be OK for a year or two. The years it takes to excavate such a cave but then, afterwards as the light comes in and the slight acid of human breath, the effluvia from the skin . . . it ruins it all. There is no way to go down but to go down and stay there long enough to become one with the nature of the cave in the ways of the original singers and dancers. But Iris and Rio together didn't have the ways or the means, neither the innocence nor the knowledge, nor the time, nor the inclination for what would be inappropriate bravado. Would never have it. The war and the ones that preceded it had made sensible people of them. She would never ever be lovers with him in the ways she wanted to be lovers with him. Not the way she generally wanted to be lovers with someone, anyone, but the way she wanted to be lovers with *him*. Never.

From the beginning, she wanted to know how to open the door and pass across the threshold into worlds such as he inhabited from which issued such sounds of underground music and words that she had not ever imagined. She wanted to open the hidden door and climb down into the underground cave where the dancers, deer, bear, wolves, antelope peeled themselves off the walls and danced, their bodies blown round with the breath of music as she imagined might still be happening in the kivas of the Southwest where Kokopelli took the sacred wind stored in his humpback and blew life into the world with his flute. That she had always longed for and that she had always imagined. That she had not known existed. Had not known first hand. That she had not yet quite dared herself. That she had wanted to dare. That she had not known anyone (else) had ever dared. In words. On the page. That she had attempted but without being sure-footed, without agility. With dexterity but without confidence. Thinking she was mad. What a woman was supposed to think. About herself.

Breath. The curve of the horn rounding each note and shaping it so that it pierced her. If the breath could damage, erase what was on the wall, what did it do to the delicate tissue of another? A curator had confided in her that he used his own saliva to clean what was most delicate because it had a faint tincture of hydrochloric acid, (the exact nature of the compound being difficult to duplicate), and so, most gently, eroded what did not belong to the thing in itself. What, then, occurred between two beings who came close enough to breathe onto or into each other?

They would erase each other. He knew it. She knew it.

She caught Rio's eye and held it longer than he wanted to be held. She could see how weary he was. She had always thought that weary men wanted to gather the young ones around them, that they wanted to plunge into what was fresh so that their old skin would be renewed. Hades longing for the Kore because he had submitted to the Fates and so was condemned to rule the kingdom of the dead forever. An old man, old as immortality, longing for moisture. Longing. She was dragged down with the fragrant breath of poppies on her lips, hyacinths, narcissus and still he wanted her though she could not, Iris was certain, enter with Hades into a common language. And so Hades broke her. Open. Those red seeds the Kore was said to have eaten, those luminescences of vermilion and ivory, those dark and radiant stars, those hosts of time, were they not the very blood light of her own body that she [was said to have] devoured in order to be queen. Hail Persephone, Queen of the Underworld.

This is what Iris knew. She knew grace and perfume. She knew the dances of the field. She knew the dance of the hours, the daughters of Ocean, she knew the sweet abandon of the companionship of nymphs.

And she knew the plunge, the descent, the fall. Up to a point. And then she knew nothing. She was still a young woman caught in the momentum of her own scream. And so, ultimately, she did not have language for what appeared when one's feet touched the black sands or ebony pools of water that were at the depths of the deep. For this she had no language.

Because it was beyond language. Because it was a lie. There were no black sands glistening with quicksilver or fool's gold, there were no shimmering night sea depths, no clear pools of black water . . . there was what he, Rio, saw: compost, refuse, offal, the muck of decay, what shot out of the body when it was starved, beaten or murdered, the last exclamations before the final emptiness or silence.

But Rio wasn't Hades. Rio *was* Hermes. She had named him in her heart. And she wasn't the Kore, no matter how young he thought she was, nor was she Persephone, which he wouldn't have granted her either. Iris was Iris. Handmaiden. Servant. Water Gatherer. Temperate. Kind. Generous. Acquiescent. And like Hermes, agile. He was mercurial; she was radiant. We two, she noted, ironically, messengers of the Gods. But that Iris had been given the task of the rainbow bridge bringing the sweet nectar, the wine, the ambrosia to the feasting deities while his task was accompanying the dead to judgment, to the inescapable summing up . . . it had aged him.

But wasn't it also Iris' task to bring back a flask of water from Styx, the stinking river of hate by which the gods swore their oaths? And why then was she pretending she was a puella, so coy and innocent, hadn't she seen, hadn't she smelled hate?

Rio put down the empty glass, a few stubs of ice, an indulgence for the Americans, still tinkling there. Iris saw his shoulder hunch and she placed her hand on his right arm. "I will get more water," and made her way to the kitchen thinking she would be allowed in at least to fill the pitcher. "Let me, Hélène, you have been caring for us so well." The water was cool enough on its own; it came from their well. She returned quickly and filled all the glasses.

"In this century, there are still doors that can be opened, but one must, also, consider the realities. . . ." His voice trailed off as it does when one sees that the beloved has died anyway, and repeated it in Spanish, though Iris had already forgotten if they had been speaking English or French originally. English, surely. Not French. They had landed into Spanish.

Hélène was, Iris saw, skilled in Spanish. Hélène had learned the language for him. Had taken on that tedious necessity even though he had been born into French and so spoke it like a native, so that she could hold him fast, be his anchor or rappel and that meant that it was language not arms which held this man.

Or it meant, Iris began to suspect that in these times, it was the language that won or lost, through which one lived or died.

She was not good at languages. She did not have the ear of a trumpeter. She did not have the breath to hold the note. How the hell was she going to be a novelist?

She could read skin. She could read the palm of his hand. She could read the heart of someone she had never met who was standing with his back to her across the room. She could travel into someone's soul the way breath traveled down the length of a saxophone and could make music that way. She was a poet in her own tongue, but that was not sufficient. Rather it was the very intelligence of the poet that told her she would never—could never be lovers with him.

This essential inequality that existed between them. Male / female. Man / woman. More than these categories. She could see in the dark and he could see in his own dark. But he could not see what she could see.

No, he would always presume that she was essentially inscrutable and also that he understood her. He would presume that he understood her as well as any man understood the inexplicable; he would always presume that she did not understand. He was a man of language. It was not certain he understood silence the way she understood silence, or would ever understand the way she understood silence through silence. They would never know. They could never be certain. Her hand on the surface of his shirt or skin could be a deception according to his lights. It was utterly untenable.

Before, then, he even moved toward her, before she turned toward him, her mouth slightly open, her eyes wide, and everything in her poised, waiting, expectant, still, so still that anyone in the room would have been alerted by the stillness between them, before any of this occurred she said "No," to herself, "No, we will never be lovers."

There on the balcony, swirling through the traces of the smoke from his cigarettes, was the problem of civilities to be extended. Ultimately, the magician made everything understood. Master of the sleight of hand and tongue, he revealed what was hidden though she and Vito never agreed on whether the conversation had proceeded in French because Vito was so fluent in French and Hélène did not speak English or whether it proceeded in English because Iris did not speak French or whether it fell into Spanish more often because Vito and Iris could manage something there and it was the language of the country under siege. But when she reviewed that first meeting, playing it back as if it were a film, she heard only the tenor *cariñoso* of Spanish, its inflection *compasivo*, the affectionate drone of the language, the way the voice flowed over the words caressing them as if they were the person to whom the words were addressed, as opposed to the watery tides of French where the words were the waters themselves, or the more staccato and complex exactness of English, each unique, individual grain of sand.

Iris had an eye for pattern, its implications and meanings, and so she watched everything to see how things were done: whether this was a place where the shy guest was honored, whether it was the custom to genuflect to the language of women; or whether the rhythms were established by the patriarch, if there was one, or the oblivious vitality of the guys, or manifested from the elusive hermetic power, now you see it now you don't, that radiates from those protean sorcerers who sometimes seem androgynous or ephemeral but are simply elusive; or whether authority pretended to reside with the woman of the house, the one who was so carefully sifting thin needles of rosemary upon lamb chops, or was fetching carefully ironed peasant linens that had been woven and embroidered, and then hand laundered, just there in the house alongside the pond at the bottom of the hill and was tossing the tablecloth across the table with a commanding flourish after expertly brewing a dark espresso for all of them except for him, Rio, her lover, whom she plied with maté, his passion, hour after hour. Out of politeness, Hélène attempted some communication with Iris or Iris with her. They were, however, without language and Hélène, graciously, would not allow her guest to be separated for a single moment except for a brief foray to the kitchen, a white pitcher in hand, from the conversation for which she had traveled several days, across an entire country. Hélène would not think of allowing her to assist in the kitchen, no, certainly not, they each knew Iris hadn't come for that, and anyway, Hélène had her ways, preparing a meal; it was quite simple, wasn't it? and after all she was Parisian.

Iris noted the ways in which one language slid into another as if following or tracing history. His Spanish blended seamlessly into French, the Argentinean timbre of his *yo* almost indiscernible from the French *je*; they each carried a certain rasp or musk that was the exact and particular vibration of self. Iris leaned back into the cool night breeze to catch the melodies of the night birds and the meanings under the words or in the silences between the words a skill which as a woman and a writer, who if she is going to be any good at all first learns to listen and to hear, she had studiously developed.

Oh yes, there had been, she recalled, elaborate bilingual attention paid to each of the two women at the opening of each subject, but then the talk fell away from them without the two women finding each other in that lacuna as sometimes becomes the case. To struggle toward the possible companionship of women when they had no common language or known interest, would have been an error, leaving the men to gape uselessly as beauty floundered gracelessly. Although the talk had fallen away from Iris, it was not Hélène's responsibility to bridge that indignity as she had not been addressed in the initial inquiry. Indeed Iris had not known Hélène existed when she wrote, and Hélène was doing more than was required by attending the mysteries of the hearth on Rio's behalf as he had a toothache and it was all he could do to pick up the lamp chops on the way back from the dentist, light the coals, pinch a bit more rosemary onto the freshly slaughtered meat and grill them for his guests.

What Iris remembered was that she had stopped listening because she did not care for the kind of talk in which the very people whose fate was of great concern somehow became peripheral to the conversation in the passions and whirlwind of conflicts, conferences, plans and actions. And even as she was drifting in her own thoughts in her own language, she was also wondering when she would figure in some drama that Vito would produce and from which he would, as did so many of his colleagues, make a living. One got weary.

The woman in the cellar, wasn't she sick to death of all this analysis and the tensions between one way of working and another? In another moment, she would lose another tooth to history and its ways and means. And it wasn't that Iris knew any way to save her but that she couldn't in the moment, looking out over the Mediterranean, shivering even in the heavy sweater Rio had loaned her, believe that anything was coming of this talk, that it mattered now or ever, that it was anything but the way civilized people devised their intermittent meetings exactly so they would not matter too much, would not matter more than they could bear.

Iris wished she knew how to descend to the cellar. Something puzzled her: What is the difference between observation and bearing witness? She had hoped they would go down together because it was Hermes' duty to accompany others to the cold wind at the bottom of the stairs but since he wasn't willing—no, wasn't able in the moment—didn't descend there in public, didn't take guests there, didn't reveal his hand, had a toothache—she went on her own. Nor did she know how to invite Hélène to accompany her, how to enact the yet unmade, unreleased film: girls on the road, or sisters, separated at birth, coming together to right the wrong.

Their way. No way.

A tabby jumped onto to Iris' lap, arched her brindled back, autumn and black, dug her claws into Iris' willing thigh and meowed. Hélène bristled protectively and so Rio reached toward the creature to take her away, a gesture Hélène could not politely enact, but Iris wishing to make peace somewhere stroked the compass of its back, hoping to ease the yowl in its musculature. The cat stayed—whether it was Rio's or Hélène's never became known to Iris—and it eventually settled down enticed or appeased by the taste of cheese on Iris' fingers.

"Our mouser," Rio murmured and went on delineating the relationships between the political parties that had existed within the country before *el golpe* and the activities of the same parties, some members still inside while so many were outside the country these months later. Those outside, those who had quietly made it to exile, were trying as best as they could to follow the directions of those within but the prisons were filling and communication was becoming increasingly difficult, unreliable, sometimes impossible. The doors were being locked, the entrances and exits sealed.

As he spoke, Iris was reflecting, not on his body, but on his mind and how much more familiar it seemed to her than Vito's which she had never understood. They were wandering among the names and affiliations of so many people that she was reminded of the yellowing square greasy posts in the subway marked with the names of the stations so that the passengers speeding to a stop would know where they were and whether they should disembark here or go back into the dark tunnel to exit elsewhere. They went by in a blur, even those Iris knew. She had to pause and locate the last time she had seen them. . . . Z. seated forlornly among his own paintings as if he were at a stranger's garage sale, wondering if the cups of tea his wife, S. was bringing would be the last cups of tea—"Have more cookies. S. baked them especially for you. Don't ask . . . we found the ingredients. Real butter. Don't ask."—they would have with foreign guests before they would have to leave the country, if they could, and would become foreigners themselves. X. handing her a couple reels of film saying so casually, "Hey, dooooo me a favor, coookie. . . . I won't have any rooom in my suitcase when I return, I've been here soooo long—take them home with you, won't yooou sweetie.

"They're background shots for the documentary I want to make when I get back, ski slopes, sunsets, kids, things like that. Look at them when you get home. You'll see. Soooon." So casually and without any urgency, it seemed, that she believed him and took the film through customs and put it on a shelf in a cool room until *el golpe* when she had a hunch and looked at the film and just then X. returned. Safe. Immediately they found others and started making the film with the contraband footage that predicted and underscored the ways and means the military coup would be achieved.

A. walking away in the torrential rain that had caused the streets to flood up above his ankles, thinking we'll never see each other again, not ever, just as she was bravely calling "*nos vemos*" but A. didn't turn around. C. showing her poems and then shaking her head and gesturing with a match. She didn't burn them then but. . . . S. apparently waiting for someone—*or*—this had not occurred to Iris at the time—acting as a security officer for the various organizations that rented space in this building—seated on a single wood chair in the middle of an otherwise entirely empty cold lobby with a notebook on his lap and a pile of books at his feet while he and Iris chatted about American poetry, North and South. S. who would be in that chair in her mind forever as the space around the chair expanded and the foyer became colder and colder. S. . . . sitting in that chair . . . the chair in the empty lobby . . . becoming something else . . . the emptiness expanding . . . his books on the floor . . . out of his reach . . . a man thumbing through them . . . that American woman you were speaking to . . . who was she? . . . his feet bound to the legs of the chair . . . his hands bound behind him . . . a man tied to a chair in a vast empty room. A tape over his mouth. The putative gun in the pocket of his folded raincoat, was it for him or against him?

It wasn't how it happened to S. But it was how it happened to someone(s) S. knew, she knew and all the later joys that fell to S., after he left the country still couldn't redeem it. *The* poet, whom she'd never met except in dreams so real they made her tremble, was dead. And the Black Island was the Black Island, *negra, negra*. Is. was singing in a basement café alongside her brother An. who was still in a prison singing his mother's song, "*Gracias a la Vida*," in the desert in the moment they were speaking of him and V. was dead. "Sing," V. had been ordered. "Sing." And he sang as they cut off one finger after another. He never stopped singing. From *Over there* they could hear him singing still.

One night in Santiago, in 1972, before *el golpe,* Iris had risen from the small table littered with empty wine bottles, Chilean wine was a dollar a bottle American at the time, and throwing her down coat over her shoulder had walked out into the icy Santiago street in order to puzzle her way back to the hotel by herself—the music which would inevitably have been erased in the conversation between her and Vito— playing itself over and over in her mind, as she navigated by instinct or like a bee by scent and ran the urban maze of stone and brick buildings perfectly without hitch or interference. That year, there didn't seem to be anything to fear, or maybe it was that Americans had little to fear, even though she and Vito had, two nights previous, run from the police who were throwing tear gas canisters at demonstrators. Once again the innocence or inexperience of the American woman who didn't viscerally fear the police as much as she feared lone men stalking the night streets of a large city. She still acted as if her passport was engraved on her face even if the reasons this particular passport protected her so well preoccupied her, like a botfly burrowing into her scalp to lay its eggs, even if she hadn't any idea how to erase the privilege, external and interior, that despite her politics, settled about her like a French perfume. Earlier in the afternoon of the deluge, when an attack had been expected on the President and the government on the *Dieciocho*, the national holiday of liberation, she had stood before A.'s windows so that her face would safeguard him, while he eased himself in front of her, so that his motion would protect her as he lowered the blinds and, then, as if they were dancing a two-step, sidled her over to the L-shaped dining room that was protected from bullets but not bombs by the bookcases that held his own work, whose contents would, as A. watched on television from an embassy to which he would have to escape, be set on fire in the streets and other copies of his books dumped into the ocean near the American military vessels that had "just happened" to be on maneuvers in the area.

Iris didn't know any of this, which was to come the next year; there was still so much hope in the country, and people were talking to each other, using "*tú*" and discovering the dimensions, variations and possibilities of camaraderie it contained. A woman had motioned to Iris and Vito from her table in the crowded café, said, "There is room here, please join me, you look tired and cold." And later, as she was leaving, bowed her head just slightly as if honoring an invisible presence and admitted in a whisper, "You know, I never expected this, but since Allende, well, I am no longer lonely. Explain that!" The exact qualities of the future, the ways in which terror would slide into the interstices of the heart, the thousands of messages coming down from the sky, seemingly like snowflakes or angels but saying, "Turn in your neighbor," was not so much unimaginable as unimagined. What was concerning her then was not what was coming, she couldn't realistically predict that future that would become the present, she was not prepared for it, but what preoccupied her most nights, or rather, what made her generally fearful was that in her country her passport or citizenship did not protect her from those who regarded a woman without a man as stateless and so outside the international agreements, and so she was vigilant even if she didn't expect to run into such hooligans in such a city, in such a country that still at that early date exceeded and contradicted all her expectations. Right.

And as she had expected, there were no hassles as she made her way to the hotel that night before the hostilities began. She could still be comforted by the privacy allowed her by the passersby who nodded to her without engaging her in conversation and allowed her the dignity of knowing her way and her mind that cold night. Some months later no one she loved, no one, man or woman was safe on the streets or in their beds. The very men she had feared walking down the streets of her own country, well, they were over there in that other country, giving orders. That's how it was.

As Rio and Vito were talking, Iris edited her list of who had been killed and who was alive, who was free and who was in prison and whose soul and whose body, dead or alive, she still needed to pray for.

And so the talk continued in the way it did though all knew this talk didn't matter. Little could come of the fact that they had come so far to meet Rio and Hélène. And yet something that wouldn't have happened otherwise on behalf of the woman in the cellar or the singer in the penal colony would emerge. A certain necessary camaraderie was developing and maybe one would do something practical and supportive for the other, the right word, or review carefully placed, or a letter to the right person at the right time, and also they would each know there were two others involved somewhere and somehow in this *lucha,* and this would counteract the disabling nausea of the despair hours of early morning or the insomnia of the middle of the night.

So much for the conversations that were taking place. As for the conversations that were not taking place, Iris did not need to speak of these to Rio to know what they both knew, to acknowledge the primary assumptions between them. The way their haunted eyes met. Neither of them needed to make a declaration to the other. They needed no corroboration or discussion of the habits and amenities of civilization that one could no more breach than one could throw the chops, glasses, table and chairs into the sea in order for something new and useful to occur. And that it wasn't insensitivity or obliviousness that led them to speak this way, to let words ramble aimlessly but that they were in their own isolation chamber, locked and guarded, and were unable to do more than they were doing even while the woman in the cellar was both unable to speak and being tortured to speak. A vast wave of impatience and grief was welling up from the ground, a miasma which might emerge suddenly from an underground chamber, a gas composed of decomposing bones and terrors. A stink in the air.

Iris felt the damnation of her youth and its obscene hopefulness.

This is what she thought was true: If it would have been permissible for her to place her hand on Rio's forearm and look steadily into his troubled eyes, something other than the little of what could be planned on behalf of the silenced woman who was screaming at the very moment, would have come into being. Nothing as foolish as asserting that making love would make the crops grow or that it would heal the world or release the woman from pain. But something like this: In the silence of the touch, an alliance, then insight, then agreement, commitment, activities . . . magic. Who knew what yet. Anything was possible. If Rio had heard this, he would have laughed, he would have scoffed, he would have stormed out of the house in frustration, he would have tried to bite his tongue, tried not to say, "Don't be an idiot." He would have stroked her hair and blessed her for her youth and her enthusiasm and commended her to Vito's care, asked him to protect such a sweet, little one.

But when Vito engaged so passionately in political talk, she saw his mind working invisibly under the talk brainstorming how to save someone by imagining how he would, if it were required, save his own skin. Confronted by someone's adamant stare, his eyes skittered and withdrew into the kind of hazy dark light that surrounds certain vigilant mammals whose survival lies in the startle reflex. From empathy to action. He was giving his life to his work; it was a family tradition. His grandfather had done the same and his father. And through his work he had made alliances with those who are always in danger. And so, sometimes, he feared that he might also be in danger but it didn't last long. He was more concerned with creating safety for the others. So as he always found a way out of his predicament, he tried to do the same for the others, with the same brave presumptions that it was always possible. He was an American citizen with dual citizenship. Pain and great misfortune outraged him for himself and others. Inasmuch as his birth had, in his mother's view, saved his father's life and rescued them all from the poverty and squalor implicit in his adventurousness, Vito assumed he would live a charmed life and would never come to harm. His task, therefore, was to protect. He was not an aristocrat because of land or birth or title but because he believed that he was a man that the gods loved. And he cared for himself as if protecting their gift. Iris couldn't admit it then, but she was envious. Confronted by such confidence, she struck out.

"Talkie talkie talkie talkie talk. . . ." The song from her youth hit a scratch on the record in her mind and repeated itself endlessly. The woman who is quiet is rarely quiet inside herself. She is telling herself a story. She is telling herself the story she cannot speak and she is telling it again and again to understand how else it might be told. What had happened and what might have happened and what didn't happen. Iris was doing just that. Telling herself a story over and over again that had to do with the circumstances that had brought her here. There was one story coming to life when she first wrote to Rio, but another story replaced it when they entered his house, and another story it would take years to recognize being formed in the moment. This storytelling constituted the nature of a repair as, ultimately, the entire world that had been coming into being had unraveled.

This is how it had happened according to Iris. She had written to him. Why?

Because she had read about the tiger, that is had read "Bestiary" in that volume of J. M. Cohen's, *Latin American Writing Today* that had—she had told *that* story so many times in order to understand it, finally, herself—that had literally fallen off the shelf into her hand in Pickwick Bookstores on Hollywood Boulevard which was the first of the many bookstores in an increasingly corporate world to go. That fall had changed everything, her life had taken a turn that had taken her to Chile and then to Cuba and then to writing that letter which, she saw again, had taken her through another loop to this incomprehensible, but nevertheless, formative moment which she would marvel at ten and then again twenty years later, that is after Rio died. She didn't even recognize yet the mercurial Gemini that accompanied each of their sunny Virgos. She didn't know anything of what was coming. But she suspected something: That he might be her brother or her phantasmal lover or her *other*. Or more to the point, that there might be a solid resemblance between the writer and what he wrote and the man and the way he lived his life. She had a thing for integrity. It turned her on.

He had answered her letter with such alacrity, she thought of him as a sky diver, trapeze artist. As she and Vito had plans to attend a political conference in London. . . . Rio invited . . . her . . . her. . . , mind you, though, of course, she had had to say she was traveling with Vito; nevertheless, Rio had spoken only of/to her. Or, if that were not possible, he had written, jocularly, that since he was mostly in Paris he would jump over the channel with a hop and a skip and visit her. Hop! Skip! Jump! By these words, she knew him. A thin, pale blue sheet of paper, almost transparent but not porous, in an envelope of the same material on which he had handwritten the note in narrow and elegant letters with blue ink that spoke to her of the care he took with words and his kindness. Only, if she was to be in Europe only for a short time and during those weeks, he, alas, was going to be in the south of France. Summer. Writing. Yes, alas! But he had sent her a postcard when he arrived there, indicating the township but without directions.

> *You were behind already, sure, you can't*
> *keep up with things, with the days*
> *when you manage to get the letters answered*
> *and you reach out to pick up that book or record,*
> > *the telephone rings: at nine tonight.*
> > *friends arrived with news,*
> > *you've got to be there for sure, old man.*[4]

At this, his clear invitation, she had traveled across France to meet him. But as the intended meeting did not occur, the world that would have, could have, emerged from a conjunction of two souls, fizzled, flopped, was dead in the water from the moment Rio opened the door and Vito stepped forward and crossed the threshold, first putting out his hand and then introducing Iris. *Finis.*

Until that point, another world had been emerging. It had been eight at night when they finally came to the village which had no postmark of its own and Vito who was fluent in French went into the café for directions to the house of *El Mago* for he had given no street address either as there was probably no street address to be given. The waiter and then the entire chorus of men seated at round outdoor tables waved them on—"Straight, straight, straight and then left, sharp left—or else!" In unison they hid their tired faces in mock horror behind white linen napkins. If one didn't drown, it would be the fourth house on their right, facing the sea. And they didn't know any *mago* but if it was *el loco* they were seeking. . . . *Sacre cœur.*

They did almost drive straight into the pond. Because the moon was in the water rippling gold and silver, she wanted to drown. How did she know that the house of *El Mago* wasn't there among the rocks, transparent fish and water lilies? Hard left, they skittered across the soft earth and then were on the rough road of pebbles and so counting one, two, three, four and skidded to a stop. The house was dark. No one answered their knock. No car to be seen. No dogs barking.

She had written the letter and so she wrote the note. "When will *el tigre* be at home?" What had Hélène thought? She'd probably dismissed it with a shrug: another starry-eyed fan from America. Let it be, Iris. There was a big cat between them. The one that devoured what could not be swallowed otherwise. The cat was the place they were to meet. It was their destination. His tiger had installed itself in a domestic space, in a farmhouse in the French countryside. Her tiger had been imprisoned in a suburban neighborhood and had tried to make its escape. He and she had found their own ways to these great beasts, these regents of light and dark, these angelic ambassadors of the wild. They had stalked them. They had made their abstract and sinewy acquaintance. They had allied themselves with these predators who in a world turned upside down were so frequently hunted themselves. They had both observed what an entrapped animal must do. Because she knew tiger, she wanted to meet him face to face.

When Rio telephoned the next day, Vito came quickly to the phone as she been staring shyly at it without leaping to pick up the receiver. Knowing it was Rio, she had been allowing herself a momentary adjustment to an impending revolution in her life, trying to determine which language to bring forward, even if it was just to say hello, while Vito, presuming only that she was bashful, picked up the phone in dominant French and efficiency. So quickly did a world collapse. Disappeared without a trace. No traces in the world that subsumed what had been coming to be. Vito arranged their meeting introducing himself by saying how privileged he felt, how anxious he was to meet Rio, by speaking of his interests, the world they commonly inhabited, the classes he was teaching in political theory of the 20th century, how his father had read all of Rio's work, had introduced Vito to literature, the fundraising and organizing he had done for various common causes, their common associates and associations, his father's stateside connection with the Lincoln Brigade, the anthology, he, Vito was editing on film and revolution, the film festival that would accompany it, his book on radical films, the filmmakers and profiles of the subjects they studied, his hopes for all the projects, its revolutionary possibilities, (she even thought she heard him speak about *his* film, though he hadn't participated in its production though it had been assembled by X and Iris and others at her house, but she couldn't be certain because she wasn't certain in the language he was speaking) in this manner, she lamented, their meeting passed her by. Creation. Destruction. Such sleight of hand.

It is easy to step out of a conversation when it is summer and one is sitting on a balcony perched above terraced vineyards watching the sea. The conversation was, as far as she was concerned, to have been between him and her, and so the fact that it rambled on endlessly between him and Vito in whatever languages they spoke meant that he and she would have to find other means. Perhaps she was afraid she would have tired him with her earnest compassion and her unappeasable longing, but also Vito was definitely wearing her down with his lists and references and endless noble (now she was being snippy again) projects, complete with bibliographies and footnotes and his insatiable requests for information. Rio held his hand to his cheek as he had a toothache and shook his head sympathetically back and forth. Once she put her hand on Vito's arm—as she had prevented herself from doing with Rio—but in this moment to stop Vito from speaking so continuously. She had resorted to the way women perform such a deceit, reaching out to the beloved in irrepressible affection. Startled, he glanced at her, and she smiled so benignly, with such daring brilliance, turned on such a floodlight of approval, such radiant focus that he stuttered briefly, blinded and so staggered. She nodded. Approvingly. With infinitesimally small and most subtle gestures, she made him the object of such uninhibited admiration it stupefied him, left him speechless. Neither Hélène nor Rio could have missed her sudden luster. A long silence followed inevitably which was comfortable only for her. She exulted in it. She leaned back in one of the wicker chairs they had moved to after the meal that had preceded the sun set. The stars had come out. The sea that had been blue then had blazed orange and claret had disappeared inky black into the waters of the via negativa under small electric lights sparkling along the coast of the Mediterranean. She breathed deeply to drink in the effervescence of stars.

If you didn't know that a world had been destroyed through the raising and lowering of a telephone receiver, you would naturally think she was being bitchy. No surprise. After all, she and Vito had fought in Limoges as they were traveling toward Aix, then Saignon, and she had not forgiven Vito for not knowing that Lascaux was closed to tourists when he was the one who liked to make all the arrangements as if he were organizing a rally and also, again, he spoke French fluently and should know about such things. Because she had never been to France before, Vito had planned the entire trip except this detour to Aix and then Saignon which was her passion and which she had managed deftly by insisting that they stop in each post office along the way, as Aix or Saignon, one or both of those, was/were not on the map despite the postmark and so they had to follow the postal route backwards from collection point to collection point, until they found the point of origin, a tiny medieval village with cobblestone streets and a café where men drinking cognac and wine waved them on drunkenly down the steep incline to the small house where they had left a note for *El Mago*—for that is how he was officially known to herself. *El Mago* telephoned them first thing the next morning at their small hotel on the main street of a larger hamlet which had not been on the map either.

They were awake when he called because a market had opened beneath their balcony and sounds, colors, fruits, flowers, fish, bicycles, baskets, aromas, spices, francs poured out into the street like a flash flood at dawn. These human rivers that separated one world from another, night from morning, one could drown and disappear in such currents of *aubergines, gateaux, pain, fromages*. Vito had launched into a description of the tumult below and she could barely get his attention to insist he ask what they could bring—as it was there, the entire world, at their feet and they would like to bring an offering. Nothing, Rio, had insisted. They had it all. Even rosemary. It was fresh in the garden, it had just flowered. Huge clumps of it had taken over the sandy hill by their house that they regularly had to bolster by repairing the retaining wall which tended to buckle with damp earth and roots and Rio had taken to dreaming of exotic countries because the scent inhabited his sleep. Maybe he hadn't said this. She didn't know. She had begun imagining what Rio might have been saying to Vito from the dark cave of the other end of the telephone.

Vito was prattling on. Her intervention had accomplished nothing. In a moment, he would launch, she was sure, into his favorite spaghetti recipes and would offer to cook since Rio had had to make an emergency appointment with the dentist and he didn't want to impose upon Hélène, there was no reason that a woman should always have to cook when he could easily . . . and, (confidentially), with rather great skill . . . and. . . . This man, who had truly come along for the ride, had become a baroque device to disguise what was and was not occurring between them.

The other side of the underworld. Its underbelly. Dissolution. Disintegration. Anomie. Vito was deconstructing a text he had been reading. He had no faith in the narrator, he was saying. And why should you? Rio asked and began speculating on the dangers of faith and all those ramifications. It was all turning to dust, Iris was thinking and found herself rubbing her fingers against each other, feeling the grit roughen her prints. And why was it that Rio had seemed so much more substantial before they had met when his being had entirely occupied her imagination as compared to this moment when he, Vito and Hélène were there beside her as if they were real beings.

The words rippled out of the two men like the constancy of the tides far beneath them in the sea. "Cat got your tongue?" Iris taunted herself while her face, she knew, remained implacable.

"I never doubted," Iris ventured because if she didn't speak now she would be silent forever, that is not only for the length of the evening, but beyond that, would have no words for anyone, not for Rio nor for herself, nor for the book she was writing, "that the writer or narrator was trustworthy in the way he thought about the tiger and knew something of the necessity of the tiger's appearance in the French summer house."

"What do you think he knew?"

"Hunger."

"Really?"

"Well, yes, in the sense that the narrator is intrigued, I think, by the difference between will and necessity. He is, initially, dispassionate but then at the end he seems to recognize inevitability, and perhaps he smiles approvingly. The narrator that is. And then there is tiger. His hunger. He is hungry—not for food that would be simplistic—but to escape his situation and his action is his only possibility. He acts from necessity. His intelligence comes from that."

"From what?"

"From learning what it means to live well even when living is against one's own nature."

"I don't quite follow you."

"The house. It was against his nature to live there. But he acquiesced. Of course, the story doesn't concern itself with the fate, inclinations or nature of the tiger. Nevertheless, the writer is aware that just as the inhabitants are inconvenienced by the tiger, the tiger, himself, is recruited against his nature. The narrator knows this and I trust his knowledge."

"A metaphor."

"No. A tiger. The real thing. Not a metaphor."

"Well," he said, bemused, she could see, amused, "you understand."

"No. No metaphors here. Otherwise it would not have happened."

"What?"

"The collision of opportunities. His nature sanctioned by the deed that needed to be done."

"You speak like a woman who thinks the world can be set in order."

She dared the smile she had been withholding the entire night. And then she was following him, Rio or the tiger, the way any child follows the older child who knows the way. Not entirely behind, not hidden in his shadow, but also, at times out in front exploring while aware of the protective shadow of the taller one behind, who has only to shift his direction for the one in front to adjust to the change in light, like the black and orange stripes of the tiger, dark and light, night and day.

What she wanted was to walk with Rio toward the pond and to sit on the mossy rocks and to talk without words or touch about what was over there on the other side of the invisible doors that he opened and closed with such aplomb. But she could not pull him away to the cool breezes which hover among the hand cut stones of old farmhouses, the historically cold breath wrapping itself along the twisted tree trunks or the tumbling fences or the new corn. The moment when the temperature falls is not when dark comes. Maybe the young moon sets, or a night bird rises out of the damp leaves, or a pond rises in a mist from its day bed. Who knows what causes it. It is never at the same minute exactly. Only this is reliable; two actions in one: Coolness descends. Silence descends. As if one is a hand grasped by the other to assist in the descent.

Rio ultimately acknowledged that he had a toothache. He had been to the dentist who had treated him without, it seemed, providing instant relief. And Iris did not know if it was permitted to reach out and stroke the somewhat puffy cheek in order to soothe his pain; it was a skill she had but was not something she announced publicly. She could put her fingers on his skin and extract the pain. It would happen so quickly, everyone would assume the morphine had done it and would look at her transgression with polite disapproval.

In the cellar, at that moment, someone was slowly and methodically extracting a friend's teeth, one by one. Iris had not learned to heal across a timeline or a space barrier. When Iris looked at Rio she saw that he knew what was occurring. This was no naïve display of sympathy. The two events were unrelated by co-incident. Rio did not think he was sharing his friend's torture. He didn't claim to be suffering someone else's pain. Nevertheless the two events co-existed. Rio's tooth had been removed and he was suffering real and phantom pain that he had no desire to ease before he studied it soberly to learn its qualities. Iris was relieved not to understand any of the languages in which they were now discussing what was broadly referred to as politics, for it allowed her to settle steadily into the pain that flared out into the room as from an infection of lilies. No one has the power to ease pain who will not feel it in her own body.

So now she moved into the tight, hunched arch of the man bent over her friend, into his sinewy shoulder under a rumpled and sweaty infested shirt with dark rings stinking under the arms, into the bend of his arm, into the torque at his hip, into the tense crease of his knee, into the poised toe, into the urine splatter stains near his zipper, into the fat, groping dirty fingers which wrenched and yanked at a small ivory bone from a splayed open mouth of a young woman and the pain like a bolt of lightning leaped up and out in jagged pewter strokes. She had friends who had been struck by lightning and wired to electric sockets. Iris had also had such friends.

Rio flinched but she betrayed nothing of what she felt even if it was this that compelled her to observe, to experience and to remember. Exactly. Without language, without the necessity of translation. "I will get another bottle of wine from the cellar," Rio declared abruptly mid-sentence and stood up extricating himself from the conversation that he would not prevent from spiraling down into hopelessness. An uncomfortable silence followed upon him turning his back as he walked away. And by so doing opening an aperture to despair.

Iris was lying in bed, the heavy pressed white rough linens draped across her breasts and belly, while he awakened wearily, sat at the edge of the bed, pulled on his trousers, slipped the white collarless rough woven linen shirt over his head and stood up slowly, fearing that he might awaken or alarm her, walked out of the room, closing the bedroom door, so that she would not hear the final sound of the front door shutting behind him nor the motor of his Peugeot starting up in the chilly and gray cloud streaked dawn. Without looking back. Without knowing if they would see each other again. Rio knowing more than she would know. He would know something in all the languages he spoke that understood their fate. He would know the unlikelihood that any other meeting would occur between them.

And walked out of that door.

Iris was thinking that Rio's languages had prepared him for the vagaries and adamancies of fate. Rio's language knew tragedy. English, that is American English, had prepared her for nothing. While she had learned over the several years that they had been together that Vito's second hand English—his mother had, of course, raised him in Italian, the *bambino*, with its definitive old world intonation—prepared him for triumph and conquest. He wasn't Italian; he was a Roman.

And the door closed behind Rio. And she would never be able to open it herself.

There is always an unspoken arrangement when people meet as to who the principals are; a painter's decision regarding foreground and background, a novelist's decisions about protagonists and supporting characters are made in an instant. From then on, the work is irrevocably formed, becomes this or that because of the now inherent possibilities and limitations. Character is shaped by, *is* the dynamic of yes and no, potential and antipathy.

If an error is made and one character is inappropriately favored rather than another, takes focus when he shouldn't have, thinks it's his story when it's hers, let's say, one has to return to the beginning, must tear down the entire structure, dissolve all the words into the primeval chaos and begin again to form a world. No repair is possible. You can not decide in the middle of an emerging universe that you made a mistake about gravity, for example, and meticulously edit it out of creation while leaving everything else intact. The universe as you have known it will not cohere and if you want a universe, you have to start again. Sometimes, of course, after much action, interaction, reaction, it seems that a new character is being introduced who then begins to take focus. The narrator, for example. And you may assume that his/her presence is an afterthought.

But on rereading you will see that the narrator was always present even though sleights of hand had hidden him, had hidden her. It is not such an error that is preoccupying the writer. That night, Iris believed that she was lost in a narrative error. One story had been indicated by the earlier events and then something else, something untoward, she thought had occurred. In order to correct it, the universe would have to be reconstructed. Something alien had entered, like a broken gene, and contaminated the event and so a different world was developing. Frankly, she felt as if this something was unnatural, a mutant, but real, so real that her reality was being revised and the outcome . . . well, there was no way of knowing now, was there.

She would start again, if she could, but in order to do this well—how many chances do you think she would have?—she had to know exactly what had entered, and when, and where so that this error could be retracted.

• • •

Iris, give it up. There was no mistake then. The mistake is now. In the telling. You've told this before, you remember, and then you made a similar mistake. This narrative is not faithful to what happened. This is not how it was entirely. Time to distinguish what you felt from what occurred.

The grief that was so extreme when you left, and the entire week that followed as you and Vito traveled . . . you don't know yet, the depth of it, or the causes. But bless Vito, who spoke the language and made the bridge for you. Who was devoting his life to remedying a horrific situation and was often much more skilled at it than you were, given the nature of the world, the perpetrators, their victims and opponents. He knew how to play ball. You didn't know how and complained incessantly that it might be necessary. Vito, who loved you despite himself, and despite yourself, and who ignored the seductions that buzzed around both of you like flies over meat on a summer afternoon to heed his mother's and father's blessings for the two of you. And Rio. Who spent the late afternoon and night with you despite his extreme discomfort, pain, even, and who hadn't expected—or wanted—company because he was writing and his time was limited and everyone was always knocking on his door, and he didn't want to speak to anyone, not even to himself, because there were other voices to be set down, voices he hadn't even heard yet, didn't know yet, but was deeply obligated to nevertheless and above all else.

How is it possible to live in a present
buried ahead of time? There's nothing left
To do but pretend you can take it:
An hour by hour agenda, . . .
  Laura's arriving at noon,
   a hotel room for Ernesto,
    don't forget to see the ophthalmologist,
     we're out of detergent,
       the arriving refugees
       from Uruguay and Argentina

    . . .

         But you, from this side of your time,
         how do you live poet?[5]

• • •

Blessed Hélène had brought him to her small house far away from
everyone and everywhere so he could give his gift to the world, that gift
that could only come out of silence, and tried to warn him about
telephones and telephone numbers, postcards with his address on it,
(though she hadn't anticipated the consequences of post cards without
return addresses on them) all other types of communications, invitations,
responses. Then you show up and you weren't the first or the last to
assume you were a good cause and he should donate his time to you.
But wasn't it as important that Rio meet Vito who might assist in his
small, practiced ways as Vito, remember, had devoted his life to life,
that's why his mother named him Vito because she knew who he would
become if the syllables were right in the beginning.

So you had a fight. You and Vito fought. Who hasn't had a fight?
Sometimes he got tired of translating for you and wanted one language,
like Sanskrit or Esperanto between the two of you that would also work
for everyone else. But, most important, he loved you and it wasn't (only)
your body, but, especially, your mind and soul, and how often does that
happen in the world?

And you, you weren't merely a calf mooning. Why create a conflict,
here on the page, a literary conflict then, also between two women, that
wasn't there and doesn't add anything and continues the lies about

women—catty, petty, jealous, competitive—that does as much harm as all the other untruths that torture us. You recognized Hélène immediately when she came to the door and took your hand and pulled you inside to where Rio was resting overlooking the sea, his horn in his limp hand, unable to blow a single note because of the pain in his mouth, but needing to know if she could, knowing how far you'd come, what it meant to you to be there, what you had written to Rio and he to you and what the two of you were attempting, what something, difficult but essential, without language between you. And brought you a glass of water and a glass of wine, immediately, and a plate of cheese and paté and tried to waylay Vito so that you and Rio could have a little moment because she knew it wouldn't, couldn't last long. Chatted with Vito in French and Italian and even asked him about his sauces and the songs he liked and cheeses and what his book would be about. And all the time chopping vegetables so fine with a chef's knife that he couldn't help but be fascinated by the stroke so close to her long red fingernails coming down sharp, swack, swack on the wood chopping block.

Hélène knew what your heartbreak would be. She and Rio had themselves tried so much for so long and weren't stopping, for the woman in the cellar. . . . They lived with her . . . down there . . . heard her screams each day, each night as they walked down that long corridor, though try as they did, they couldn't find the passageway down.

Then Rio left the balcony and Iris walked down the narrow hallway enjoying the way the old wood was molded and shaped by the retreat of the earth, by the pressure of feet, by time, allowing herself to glance through the partially open door into the bedroom where a white silk robe was thrown gracefully across a mohair blanket—it had not been a casual gesture—and where his robe and his old Shetland wool sweater hung on hooks, where two brushes were aligned on a small table among a scatter of creams and perfume. Through the next door, she noted the books in the narrow bookcases of his library/study, and his notebook open on a small desk, a disorderly collection of phonograph records fanning across the floor. In the farmhouse where the tiger had sequestered itself, it was not possible to leave such doors ajar. To the contrary, one developed the survival strategy of opening a door and searching the room quickly before closing the door behind one and entering fully. No, one never left a door ajar for the beast might enter behind one, nor did one enter a room without searching for its inhabitant, who despite these careful ritual gestures could never be confined as it had the uncanny ability to appear in different empty places, that it had, it seemed, the run of the house as long as no one preceded it into an area. The human could invade the territory of the wild and then, of course, it would pounce, but the wild was prevented from opening the door into the sanctuary the human had already established for itself. Thus the essential gesture of their comings and goings was to discover the whereabouts of the tiger, not only on their own, but by trusting each other and also by attending the bulletins of the overseer, who was not, however, infallible, or the children or the last one to have seen the beast and so knew the location of the tiger who could be anywhere, by the stream on one occasion and at another time even in the music room or in the corridor, though this was not spoken of, between the bedroom and the bathroom.

Then she pushed open the door to the small bathroom, the original wood boards of the old farmhouse still unpainted or the paint entirely worn away by time, and was struck immediately by the thick white towels on a makeshift shelf in the small bathroom—icy white!—and the white hard milled soap and the erotic cluster of cosmetics and milky creams which indicated a French woman such as Iris would never be, and she saw again that she and he could never fuse their lives. Understanding this fully, she flushed the toilet and avoided using the bidet so he would know by the progression and absence of sounds what kind of woman she was and she wasn't, and that it was safe to come up from the cellar with another bottle of wine for this portion of his already disturbed life would not be further agitated. He felt the grief of this and she couldn't comfort him, nor he her. Wouldn't. It was like tempering metal—this heat and ice they would endure together or, rather, apart.

"We will do what we can." It was Vito's voice. Strangely quiet, deliberate, the voice of a man who was considering the impossible and agreeing to it. The bravado was gone from it. It was the voice of a sober man, full of gravity and concern. It was the voice of a man who meant what he was saying. She saw what was coming and was grateful for it but there was no object for her gratitude. They would do what they could. Rio had made her a gift. He had given her Vito. Not that he had given her to Vito, no, he had given Vito to her.

It was very dark on the deck. Despite the little lights she could see the stars and the Milky Way that owed its existence to any number of impetuous tricksters. When she'd spoken of Coyote, a friend responded with a Chinese legend that the Milky Way had been thrown into the sky in order to place a barrier between a weaver and shepherd. It had worked and the woman unable to reach her lover had returned to her work and to live out her life in the home of her sisters. A guild of maiden women weavers had its origin in this tale.

Anyway, they didn't know each other at all. Except for his books and her letter to which she had put as much attention as she had ever put into anything she had written. Except for the icy burn where she did not place her hand on his forearm. The emptiness where the impossible dwells. All the letters he did not write and she did not answer. The lost potential of sequences and combinations. Alphabets never, therefore, arranged or aligned, at least in that moment. Nevertheless . . .

. . . nevertheless. This is what wasn't said. Iris returned to where the other three were seated in the cool dark and as if Hélène had waited for her because she knew what she'd come for, Hélène stood up then and took that white embroidered tablecloth and unfurled it, flung it in the air over the table, over our heads, the soar of so many white birds in the air above us that we were silenced by the beauty of it, and we gasped that such beauty should exist in the world, could exist so quietly, and then vanish. Hélène silhouetted, all black, shadow, blue sky, sea, dark blue above, all black below, woman, sky, sea, and the wings, the wings of that great, those great white birds above us all.

The woman in the cellar died ten thousand deaths. They were not able to save her. Even if they had come together differently, they could not have saved her. Her grave? You must be kidding.

Later, perhaps it was after Rio himself had died, while Iris was driving her car down Pacific Coast Highway in Los Angeles, California, watching traffic, the road, and a V of pelicans making a come-back some years after the prohibition of DDT went into law, the light playing on the water, boys surfing, Iris turned on the radio and heard a woman say that the torturers pulled out all her teeth and then sewed her mouth closed leaving only the tiniest hole through which they sometimes allowed her to sip water or nutrients through a straw. The dull, brutal, insidious, intractable progression of the twentieth century.

Bring on the long, slow lament. Sound the horns that open the way. Give yourself over. Wail.

Not for a lost love, no such indulgence. But for a lost life. Lost lives.

"*Por fávor.*" Exasperated, "*Por fávor*, Hélène, bring me a maté."

"And an espresso. Please, for god's sake, Iris. Make it strong. Strong enough to swear by."

"Water, please. I'm so thirsty."

"Madam. We do not have room service in this prison."

PART II

ד

Every so often the words of the dead
fit the thoughts of the living . . .[6]
Julio Cortázar

What follows is the second story:

She was bereft after he died. They had had a brief correspondence when he was ill. Not wishing to impose upon him when he was vital but preoccupied, or more accurately, besieged, she could not neglect to contact him when he was ailing. Mutual friends also gave her news of his condition. And also from across the ocean and across the entire North American continent from east to west, she had been blasted by his grief when C. died. Iris began to understand the meaning of the words "an ill wind." Yes, an ill wind was blowing from the moment that C. became ill that by the time she died had become a malevolent storm, trees toppling and buildings falling. Not the right buildings, Iris thought. The few structures remaining upon which they could rely seemed to be tumbling every which way. Enough for her to fear that he would flee earth within a short period of time.

Increasingly, one's life per se didn't seem sufficient to justify living it. So she wanted his writing to be sufficient to sustain him and to insist that he remain among them, but she knew it was futile. He wasn't, after all, a young man overcoming writer's block or aspiring to success. He wasn't the equivalent of who Iris had been as a young woman, tremulous with hope and possibility, intoxicated by the possibilities of language. He had been writing his entire life. He had accomplished everything he had set out to do. What he couldn't fix, he couldn't fix. Or, it couldn't be fixed. That was certain.

Once more she was the naïf. As if writing, for him, hadn't become the ultimate Promethean woe. As if he hadn't died of the eagle devouring his liver for having dared. Wanting the writing to be sufficient was the same as wanting him to be sustained by torture. He no longer had time or heart to write as a way of escaping anguish. He couldn't write without meeting the world's urgency. Each day he awakened to the necessity of clearing a path through the rubble and brush of demands and atrocities so that he could find his own mind. Those early stories of the torque in the human psyche, those examinations of the peculiar and individual distortion had had to submit to fathoming the greater forces of violence, the countless ubiquitous faceless men with the submachine guns strafing the sky. He was born in 1914, for god's sake. He had lived, albeit from afar though under the unbearable weight of the despotic regimes of Latin America, all the fascists and Peronistas, through the terrible progression of the century from the battlefields of World War I, to the fire bombings of civilians, the Death Camps and then the Bomb. These ways had continued to filter down quickly into the daily life so that his continent was ultimately decimated by torture in the manner of the Inquisition. When he had assimilated this history, the way things are, he saw that Latin America, his land, was not going to be exempt. Cortez resurrected without warning. It was not only because Nazis took refuge in his territory, but that the pernicious global mindset of power and torture, North American, European, Asian, followed them the way smoke clings to a wool coat, into the remote regions they chose to escape their fate. They escaped, so many of them, but what they were, what they had been, what they had wrought, what they had inspired, what they had invented, what had become of those who battled with them, what dark clouds had swirled through Europe and Asia, came with them. A miasma, a contagion moved into this landscape too, and took hold as if the land had just been waiting for the proliferation of such death flowers.

In the years afterward, she examined the arc of his stories, noticing the ways in which he saw what he saw, his refusal to look away, his relentless adamant presence in the face of the eternity of disaster that characterized this time.

What was it that she had hoped would sustain him? Once, it had seemed that the woman in the cellar could have been sufficient, even in her silence, to speak for everyone and, somehow, one could bear her voice: Because one knew her? Because one loved her? Because one could devote oneself to her alone? Because such concern shaped one's ethical life? Because the singularity of her agony asserted the uniqueness of her suffering? Now the woman in the cellar was subsumed into a chorus of unremitting misery. Outrage overcome by hopelessness. The exceptional violation becoming the most ordinary, omnipresent torment.

Day and night, he was inundated by phone calls and telegrams insisting he attend one or another meeting or conference or "At least write something. *Por favor,*" in order to stave off the death squads that were springing up everywhere. "All we need is a letter from you . . . " He couldn't tell them that it was futile. He wouldn't.

> *You can see, all this is worth nothing . . . worth nothing . . . I've spent months making this shit, you write books, that woman denounces atrocities, we attend congresses and round tables to protest, we almost come to believe that things are changing, and then all you need is two minutes of reading to understand the truth again, to . . .*[7]

As long as he existed, they had hope no matter his state of mind.

But you, from this side of your time, how do you live, poet?[8]

He was pulled into it. Quicksand. Flash floods. He was like a man hiking a canyon in the desert, descending down, down alongside the sandstone cliffs to the sandy floor below. Above him, the sky, as it appears, is interminably blue. So many miles away that he can't see the clouds, it is raining. Whirling chimneys of black clouds with lightning in their bellies. A sudden summer downpour so concentrated it becomes a driving rain. It doesn't take long for the torrential waters to accumulate in the sandy dry river beds and funnel into the canyon and soon he is in the whirl of it, trunks of trees, boulders, red waters foaming toward the narrow place where he is walking. He is pulled into the swirling red waters without possibility of resistance.

The death squads got him without having to raise a hand against him or pull a trigger. What music do we play here? We are not yet at the funeral but we are getting close to it.

He died. In a brief exchange, the poet Claribel Alegría, who was still living in Nicaragua having, herself, had to escape El Salvador, had said he was doing well and then he died. End of an era, Iris thought. She was right, not realizing—how could she?—the implications of it. He died in France. Paris. Shit! *Merde!* His death was so far away. A fist punched into the paper wall of time. Ragged sheets flapping in the wind.

He was in the bardo between worlds. She didn't know what to call him. Sometimes she called him Rio. Sometimes she called him J. Sometimes she called him Julio, straight out, without fear or embarrassment. Each name represented a different relationship. Calling him Julio meant that she was going public with her grief and her love.

Having the right name for herself was difficult as well. She could pretend that she was still Iris. It was always a good idea to have an alias to fit all public occasions, particularly a pseudonym that allowed her to take a good look at who she had once been and who she had become under his invisible, distant but nevertheless, always present tutelage.

For a few days, she walked around in a stupor. Slept in her clothes. Didn't change them in the morning. Reread a few stories of his. Had a few improvised conversations with him wherein she spoke too much and too loud and he was absolutely still. Just what you would expect from a dead man. She couldn't even imagine what his response might be.

She hadn't seen Vito in seven years. They met for lunch and he had the same haunted expression in his eyes he had always had. His mother and father sent their regards and their regrets. There were no *bambinos*; they had relied on her hips. Iris was forty-four years old now and she wasn't relying on anything. She looked Vito in the eyes until he met her glance and held it. She saw that he liked living alone as much as she did.

The little French café that Vito and she had both liked so much had been replaced by chain stores—who cares which?—another stupid victory for corporate America. She and Vito fulminated about it as they would have in the past. Anger and outrage so much easier than grief. It made them feel close again. They found a little sushi restaurant that wasn't on a mall and didn't overwhelm them with rock music blasting. But sake didn't do it the way a *café au lait* would have. Sake had other associations; she needed to be with him in the lucid mind of the South of France as they had been when they had hope. When they, also, had gone to Rio for a dose of it. Vito began telling her about *El Mago's* visit to Cuba and Nicaragua. Vito had thought of inviting him to the United States to draw attention to. . . . There was an organization that would have sponsored. . . . They could have raised a great sum of money, he had thought, and get very good publicity, for, after all, he was *El Mago*. Now Vito was thinking about a memorial evening. Perhaps one in New York and one in Los Angeles. Maybe they could coordinate it with a similar event in Paris. Surely, their mutual friend A. would participate. What would Iris like to do? How would she like to participate?

She knew what she had to do. She locked the doors and took the telephone off the hook. She showered with water so hot it threatened to burn her hips, her ass, which were turning bright red. She put on a white blouse with a narrow mandarin collar and pearlized buttons that looked like a shirt he might have worn, if six sizes larger. Black suede pants. Knee high black leather boots with narrow three inch heels. Perfume. At first, she used Anaïs Anaïs because, after all, that writer had introduced Iris to Rio originally. But it wasn't her scent, too light and flowery though Anaïs had hated cut flowers and the perfume spoke of vases and arrangements; Iris washed it off and indulged Opium. Behind her ears and across her breasts and elsewhere. Better. She was dressing for his ghost. She was still acting the innocent one, unsure of how else to present herself in the world, oblivious to the possible consequences of invocation. She lit a candle placed it by the desk, found some sheets of thin airmail blue paper, got down to business, began to write by hand:

Dear Julio:

She typed up the letter so that she would have a copy. Then she folded the handwritten pages, sharpening the folds with the tips of her fingers, put them into an envelope, addressed it to him by name only, got in the car, drove to the post office and put it in the mailbox. It was midnight and she said a prayer to the moon as she mailed it. It would be a lie to say that she didn't expect an answer. Somehow she expected him to appear and she was scared out of her mind that he would. "Don't float in through the window. . . ." She spent a crazy week sleeping with the lights on and trying to get herself to forget him and the letter. "You blew it, Iris," she kept insisting to herself, reviewing the last ten years, berating herself for her shyness. They had exchanged books. There was so much that might have transpired between them.

Not long afterwards, *The Los Angeles Free Press* called regarding their annual Book Issue. Joan Didion's new book, *Democracy,* had just been published. Would she review it? Iris didn't know Didion's work well enough to feel qualified. But having been asked, she wanted to write something, to do anything to get her mind off him. "What other choices do I have?"

"Cortázar's *A Certain Lucas.*"

"Not possible," she said. "He's dead."

And then he wasn't.

The explanations meant nothing. The book had been published in Spain before he died. That was the logic of it. But the trickster was among them. *El Mago.* The newspaper even let her publish the letter alongside the review. In case he read the newspapers in addition to picking up his mail.

The book review: "Julio Cortázar Dead or Alive" and the text of "An Open Letter to Julio Cortázar" from *The Los Angeles Free Press* July 20–26, 1984:

BOOKS

A Certain Lucas by Julio Cortázar.
Translated by Gregory Rabassa (Alfred A. Knopf $12.95)

As I flipped through the pages of *A Certain Lucas*, I realized that I wasn't skimming the print so much as looking for Cortázar's signature, the personal dedication: "For you, Love, Julio." For who else but the great Cronopio [author, of course, of Cronopios and Famas] would take his leave from the dead to slip back and scratch his name on the frontispiece, or clandestinely insert a message near the book's spine as a sign that he had been right when claiming that death did not exist—although it was also clear from his last collection of stories, *We Love Glenda So Much*, that he was agonized, even broken by the human's race's attempt to invent death and the brutality appropriate to such an invention.

Argentine Latin American exile, honorary citizen [by virtue of hope and commitment] of the revolutionary governments of Cuba and Nicaragua, brother to those struggling against Pinochet in Chile, and, according to Carlos Fuentes, "the first figure of the so-called Latin American boom to go," Cortázar is also a fellow traveler in the metaphysical universe and that passport allowed him entry into dreams and marvels that contradicted all the premises of the schools of torture and the ambition of dictators, national guards and death squads. Cortázar is? Was? Shall I use the past or the present tense? Is he dead or isn't he? Would he believe the print on the jacket cover: "Julio Cortázar died in Paris in February, 1984?" I doubt it. Certainly not the man in the photograph on that same cover who points his finger at us knowingly through the broken wall of the other world.

That was no penned signature. So, I thought, I'll have a look closer for a clue as Julio was certainly going to include a message [he had quoted Sherlock Holmes to get those of

that he would automatically return after he finished writing it. I do believe in magic, but not this kind. Still, I hope he's right. I hope the book breaks his enchantment. And I wonder if the stories in *We Love Glenda So Much*, if "Graffiti" about the terror and camaraderie of protest, or "Press Clippings," about torture, official and domestic, or "Moebius Strip," about murder and forgiveness, were your attempts to break the spell. About magic—I don't know if my broken heart, my knowledge of *brujaría* (which you certainly understand) will bring you back. Yet, there is something unfinished between us and I don't think it is stubbornness or madness on my part that insists that this has still to be resolved. Oh, I don't mean psychologically. I mean something is out of balance in the universe and that it must be set right.

Fortunately, you were never a Californian nor a psychologist, so you will not tell me I must accept this pain. Tragedy rarely feels inappropriate; accident is somehow always comprehensible. This imbalance, this incompletion, has another nature. This is intuition, not protest. Also I do not understand my profound grief at this moment. The grief is perplexing

precisely because it seems so appropriate, that is, it verifies a relationship that, in fact, never happened—but, clearly did.

I am writing a novel about two women who are in love with dead men. Each woman fell in love after the man was dead. These women are not mad. Once during a retreat, I looked up from the Loren Eiseley book which was absorbing me and said to the patient waitress, "I've fallen in love with a dead man."

"That's what happens when you read," she answered sagely and then took my order.

One of my characters finally marries her dead lover. She carries no illusion that he will return to life; she marries him, his death. The other woman believes that she can conjure another man who's been dead for centuries. Each of the women writes to the dead man she's partnered with. You see, I have practiced writing to the dead.

I'm not mad, though I don't quite know yet how this letter will reach you. Ariel says you didn't believe in death and so I'm certain you'll return. As I recall, there was only one death you believed in. In the story, "The Man Who Was Mortal," a man witnesses the death of a young boy whom he has recognized as his own next incarnation. That wasn't your death was it? It wasn't that you saw your own double die and knew that you were the only mortal man in the universe? I looked for *Blow Up*, that collection of short stories and it has disappeared from my shelf. Are you covering up your traces?

How will you return? Please don't float in through the window. Don't come at night; that will be too melodramatic, and I will think I'm hallucinating instead of trusting your existence—so much for proclamations of faith.

But you must return. It's not finished between us. Nor between you and the universe. You know too much that no one else knows. And most important, you know that death doesn't exist. We need that knowledge to save us from the effects of our inventions.

From the beginning, we slid past each other like two people born in different universes, but from a common seed, who had met through the accidental folding of time but had been separated as time unfolded and could only run our hands along the opposite sides of the cosmic glass trying to touch. And the reality is that when you come back, you will not come here first. We were not even born to the same language. Yet, there is

a great pain in my heart as if the very closest one to me has died, as if the precariously balanced network has broken, as if the world has been irreparably punctured, as if there has been a blow-out in the universe. In Cuba, I saw a woman tear her hair and weep, Saturday-night mascara rutting her face, after Salvador Allende died in that terrible *golpe* when Chile went down. She had never even seen him in the flesh.

Maybe you'll come as a gift. Maybe you'll pass your story-telling stick to me. You came to know all the secrets and you told them in images that opened to those who were able to breathe them in. The secrets floated like pollen on the wind. They say Che, waiting for Fidel in the Sierras in your story, "Meeting," heard Mozart in the trees.

Why did you die, Julio? Was it the wound you caught from Carol (Dunbar) when she died of breast cancer in that invisible other war no one talks about? Was I right when I wrote to you about your "liver," that you were tired of being alive? Were the assaults on Argentina and Chile too much? Were Cuba and Nicaragua too threatened to keep you alive? Or had you not learned to bear the agony of countries when they are defeated by the politics of cancer? The disease most defeating is despair. Did you fall into despair? Did it all stop mattering? Everything?

Am I vulnerable to that despair? I think I may be and don't face it, like the woman who, finding a lump, turns onto her other side and goes to sleep burrowing her breast in the pillow, teaching her hands to remain at her side. Despair is the one I refuse. I believe my task is to be courageous. You don't say anything, Julio. I can't hear you or feel you. This is a terrible loss.

Don't leave us. If I fall into despair, I need your laughter, the wild games of your imagination, your *jeux*. I will need to hear Ariel reassure me, "You see, *querida*, he's here." Can't you hear Ariel saying that? The phrasing is perfect. I am trying to write this simply, so you can follow my English. I am trying to say this simply, so that I suffer no illusions, so that I don't entrance myself.

It's past midnight, Julio. The lupine are in bloom. I've waited for them all year. Last year, the rains came so fast that the mustard exploded in the fields and the small, purple lupine could not grow in that yellow shade. But this year, the poison gas is in the hands of men.

It seems to me there was a dance between us. When I first read *Blow Up*, I knew no one had told those secrets before. It was as if you were revealing the hidden script on the jaguar that Borges alludes to in "The Handwriting of God." At that time you were dancing forward in a cha-cha and I was following. Then when you wrote, "Press Clippings," it was as if you were following where I had been. As if we'd been speaking of these things through the ether. And when I read, "Moebius Strip," I felt a *frisson* and wondered if that's the story one writes before one dies?

What's the last story you wrote? Is there something still in manuscript that will explain everything to us? Or is there a story you thought of that one of us will have to pluck from the air and set it down? Who will it be?

I postponed writing to you when I returned from Nicaragua. Claribel Alegria assured me that you were better, that you were in Argentina for the Inauguration, and that there was no need to worry. I didn't want to write out of worry. I wanted to write out of joy. Still, worry often takes precedence over joy; it has an imperative to it.

I remember when I traveled across France, tracing you from post office to post office until I finally found the small medieval village where you lived and followed the gesticulations of the inn keeper, who cried, "*Le fou, le fou, l'écrivain*" and waved me down the steepest road I've ever seen almost into a pond before I swerved sharply and found your house. We talked for hours. You poured cold wine from the local vineyard. We ate lamb with rosemary. And, afterwards, I was dismayed because the beasts in us, the ones who write the secrets, had stayed in their dens, had not ventured out into the French Sunday afternoon. It was years and letters later until we finally met.

Now you and Anaïs Nin are both dead. Do you see each other? Do you listen to jazz together? Do you walk about Paris trading images in French and Spanish without worrying about fatigue or cold, drinking as much *café au lait* as you like because it won't keep you awake? Or are you content to be with Carol again? And what does she photograph now?

It was so dark in the ante-chamber of Clytemnestra's bee tomb in Mycenae, one had to strike a match to move a step. I stumbled against a man seated meditatively in a corner. Then, I sat down beside him: I had no light. Gradually, I discovered I could see. We were not both ghosts for we could see everything and those with light saw nothing.

It hasn't helped to write to you. It's been a shout into the dark universe. The stars don't answer. I feel very far from where I was conceived. Earth is a lonely place. How many of us are there in the network? Will new ones be born, or are we dying out? The other day, I wrote in my journal: "I'm a totalitarian nation-state run by an ideologue, a computer, a priesthood and the thought police. Within my borders, all the children have been killed." This also means there is no hope. I want to howl.

Is it possible that the essential task here is to find the others, as we found each other, and to go around with an invisible lantern asking, "Are you the one?" Your stories did that.

Today, when I saw the coral trees along San Vicente Boulevard, it was obvious they were women, great, hulking women, or lithe girls. They twist, groan and leap. When the spring comes, just before the leaves appear, thousands of coral-petaled birds break out of their gray branches. I think you would fall in love with them if you saw them. I think you would know that they dance in those moments that are invisible to our eyes.

I am going to sleep. It would help if you came in a dream. I am not afraid to dream you. When Anais died, Robert Cohen instructed me patiently until I learned to scream. But no one can teach me how to ease this grief. This is not mere loss. Your absence creates a spiritual asymmetry. This is a broken world. Come back to us, Julio, we need you here, and all the secrets we'll forget if you desert us.

PART III

ד

What is below is as that which is above,
and what is above is as that which is below
in order to perform the miracle of one thing only.
The Emerald Tablet

One life leads to another the way the stories flow. The young woman, they say, is always present in the old woman, is and isn't. Iris is disappearing. I■ is here in her stead. There are some resemblances and the phenomenon of sharing common memories. I■ has built her life on Iris' beginnings, but she has done other things with them. Still, there's a residue. What's the name of the world where I■ is living? Oh, yes, it is still *Here*, planet Earth, and he's still *Over there,* from her point of view. From his point of view, his world is *On this side.* And where they meet and when they meet, they constitute *Terra Incognita* between them. But after the letter she wrote to him after he died and his response, everything changed for her in ways she couldn't have imagined when he was simply Rio to her. He was Rio. No, he had been Rio but he was not quite, that is, no longer, Rio, was now someone else, as she had become someone else. Iris to I■ and Rio to J.. Leaner beings. The excess of self stripped away the way baby fat dissolves. They had become some other beings she had not imagined nor did she know if he had envisioned his present condition before he had crossed over. Crossed over, not as a euphemism for dying but as an actuality, had literally crossed over from *Here* to *Over there* and then to *On this side* (for this represents a change of mind that determines the nature of the place) and he has been transmuted in the process, reconstituted to accord with the laws of another universe. I■ had never had a conversation with him about metamorphosis before he died and this was one of the things she regretted so deeply. But then, she wouldn't have known what to ask. No matter how close they could have been, not even if they had been naked under the white sheets, with or without smoking the cigarette that followed lovemaking in his novels but not in hers, she didn't think he would have engaged in that discussion. True. It had not been the lovemaking that Iris had hungered for but the talk that follows the lovemaking. This is where eros resided for her vis-à-vis him. This is as truthful as I■ can be.

I▪ regrets that her writing is sometimes back in the sack again as if she were still a young woman. Writing about Iris resurrects Iris. That is how it is in a world where language is at the core of creation. The distortion is confusing to her for it misrepresents who she is as a writer and older woman, as well as who she was as a young woman, as Iris. Why then, this persistent reiteration?

Wasn't it always there, the last card for a woman to play if all else failed? Every woman in this culture needs such a backup. What I▪ hated in film, the requisite tit shot, cleavage, caress, lovemaking, upper cut, smoking gun, chase, and blow-up was lingering here in this work, the work of her maturity. It wasn't here because it had been lived and enacted there then, it was here because it had become an unavoidable universal trope, an alien implant. The same trope that had been alongside her—for emergencies—in her life since she had been a young woman. She hadn't known how to do it then without that prop in the wings. Do what? Be alongside him. Them. Writer among writers. Comrades. *Compañeros.* One of the brothers. Uh-oh, she's distracted by an ancient, long resolved longing. The trouble and the benefit of having positioned her desk before a window is that she cannot avoid the reflection of her face in the night glass and so she is always aware that she, I▪, is now almost as old as J. was when he died, that her hair is absolutely white, if still long and rather wild, and that she is not at all concerned with the ways and possibilities of his body, especially as he no longer has one.

She was not thinking of being lovers with him, she was thinking about speaking with him, about the possible conversations that had not occurred between them, about the circumstances that allow for such conversations, about the nature and way of intimacy, about where and how trust is learned between men and women and what is possible if they are not lovers and live several thousand miles away from each other and don't intimately speak the same language.

What is possible?

The word. The written word. And even that in translation. And now, she wonders, are they still living by translation since they are, again, in different worlds, even if there is no sign of the translator?

Even so, the word seems possible, and, so, perhaps, the world that is constituted by them.

All the books and letters she hadn't sent. But now, these are also in the past. He isn't *Here,* he's *Over there* and she is certainly older and there is some evidence that they are beginning to engage in an exchange, in some kind of transmission of mind. The kind of transference of vision that isn't very likely *Here* even if you are the student of *El Mago*. But elsewhere. . . . Fate, like a tick having waited, dormant twenty years, smells mammalian flesh, awakens, jumps, lands, burrows in, sucks blood.

If they have both arrived in *Terra Incognita,* it is by virtue of their desire to meet each other. I■ had been looking for a name for the place they are inhabiting together—if they are inhabiting a place together—and didn't know what to call it. The place where they meet, if they meet, if anything occurs other than her hope, fantasy or delusion. The third world. I■ had thought of calling it *We* but this leads to more confusions than seem aesthetic, accurate though the name is. So let's try *Terra Incognita*.

Let us try to describe this realm. Time doesn't exist in *Terra Incognita* in the ways we know it *Here*. The past, present and future are distinct from each other as they are *Here* but also they coexist and are co-extensive. This is what I■ imagines or thinks she perceives or is revealed to her somehow. I■'s presence is solid, as solid as it is here but J. is more of a firefly, flitting in, lighting up and then extinguishing himself.

You never know if you are going to hear from him, or see him, or not. Shall we say he's not material, but that doesn't mean he isn't real. After all, he seems to be able to wield the objects of the physical world with uncanny facility. He certainly answered Iris' call with a straight ball from left field. This is how I■ is thinking.

Once he made an appearance in the form of *A Certain Lucas*, her notion of the nature of reality changed entirely. Then it took ten, fifteen, more years for her to catch up to what she had come to know in that instant. Again, it's like the nature of the universe. There was an explosion and it takes fifteen years for the light to get to her. That's not quite accurate either. There was an explosion and a material object, the book, was instantly propelled into her hands, but then it took fifteen years for her to recognize it. The activity was instant because that is the way it works from *On this side,* but it took fifteen years for her to receive it because she was still *Here*. Now fifteen years later she is living *Here* and also, simultaneously, in *Terra Incognita.* Two worlds have coincided. A third world is constituted; its laws are entirely different. For the two of them, I■ and J., the laws of this strange universe, *Terra Incognita* are altering them profoundly. This is not science fiction. This is I■'s attempt to find language for a phenomenon that is entirely incomprehensible.

Here we are. It is more than ten years later for all of us who are *Here*. It is some time after 1994. Iris has disappeared as surely as if she had died. That young woman became someone else, became I■. I■ is married to a younger man, M. who believes in spirits. Perhaps we wouldn't be here without him. We would be *Here* but we wouldn't be here! Even though M. hasn't read J.'s work, he thinks he understands him. M. thinks he understands J. better now that J. is *Over there* than he would have when they were all *Here*.

That wasn't Vito's problem. Vito understood Rio then. He wouldn't understand now. "Well, that's Vito," is what Iris would have said, but then, Iris would not understand either. "That's Iris," is what I■ says. But J.? He is kinder. He knows what he knew and what he didn't know, couldn't know, what those who are *Here* are incapable of knowing. By their very nature, by the very nature of *Here*.

Back to the second story then.

I■ is the one who told the first story because she is the one who was reflecting on Iris. The first story was about Iris from I■'s point of view, but it was only about Iris. I■ didn't exist then, or at least we weren't aware of her existence, we were in the past before her awareness of the transformation had occurred. Then time passed and another story followed. First, it was a documentary. The evidence. Exhibit A. That part doesn't have a narrator, it just is. But then a story emanated from it. The second story. I■ is still telling this story, but reflecting on herself as much as on Iris. The second story is the consequence of the first story but it is I■'s story now. The second story begins with an intervention from J. and it alters Iris substantially, enough for I■ to appear.

The second story then. Who is telling it? I■ is telling it. She is telling it in present time, but you know how present time varies, sometimes you're present in the past and sometimes you're present in the future, and sometimes, here you are, now. She doesn't always know if she has the language or the imagination to render the liminal zone that she can enter occasionally and where she sometimes thinks she finds J. So she must rely—she would like to rely—on J. to assist her because of his momentary appearance, his ghostlike intervention in the matter of *A Certain Lucas*. This is an outrageous desire, but she can't stifle it.

Actually, the I in this second story is I■ writing about herself as if she were her own character, as in fiction or memoir, one is. She attempts to look at herself with the same scrutiny she brought to Iris. Sometimes, though, it seems as if someone else is writing, not I■ but another narrator. A third person or a text in third person. It is probably still I■ but with an overview and perspective on her way, perhaps, to becoming someone else. For example, who is writing this? I am. And who are you? I think I am I■ but in matters of identity one can never be sure, especially about oneself. Or I am simply I.

I■ begins to re-read his work. The rereading is different. She is putting herself in its tutelage. She wants to extract the internal vision and modus operandi that determined who he was, what drove him. She reads him word by word, studying each. Then sentence by sentence. And so on. She interrogates the prose the way she originally intended to interrogate his soul. She reads systematically, chronologically, watching the development of insight, concern and revelation. Watching what was given to him by fate. Trying to understand his destiny. But, she also reads randomly. When she does this, picks up a book at random, it often seems that something is happening between the lines. She is writing something and he speaks to it directly from the prose she has haphazardly opened to. As if his work had become an augury. As if she is truly being met by something mysterious and unknowable from *Over there*. Such events reinforce her hope that he will, somehow, assist her. She doesn't assume this is possible; she hopes.

> Since he not only writes but likes to go over to the other side and read what others write, Lucas is surprised sometimes at how difficult it turns out to be for him to understand some things . . . that it even makes a person mistrust, asking himself if there can't be an unconscious demagogy in that collaboration between sender, message, and receiver.[9]

Relying on J. has cosmological implications. Is it possible they might be in communication though *suddenly there's something like a dirty pane of glass between him* her *and what he's*/she's *reading*? Might she find the way through without having to indulge *the great flight of the . . . book against the nearest [brick] wall with a subsequent fall and a damp plop*[10]? She's older now. She's older than J. was when they met. Hard to know whether she is being led to wisdom or foolishness. I■ thinks she will finish the manuscript when she is seventy. She has four years. Then she will be as old as he was when he died.

The second story emerges from the event of *A Certain Lucas*. It doesn't materialize instantly like Athena being born from Zeus' brain, it comes to light and disappears, it begins and vanishes and appears again, year after year. I■ lives her life, a life which has nothing to do with J. She marries, she writes books, she continues as an activist. This means attending many meetings and organizing public events and speaking out.

> Time hasn't caught up with us,
> nor we with it,
> we're still behind because we're running too fast,
> the whole day isn't enough anymore
> to live for half an hour. [11]

It means holding council with the woman in the cellar and proceeding according to her welfare as much as possible.

> . . . the mundane recurrent nightmare
>   you're trying to get away from but the sticky
>   flypaper of duty stops you,
> the weight of the daily paper
> with the news from Santiago sea of blood, . . . [12]

But underneath this is an underground river that keeps flowing and that rises to the surface occasionally, the sweet bubbling up of a sweet spring, from which I■ occasionally drinks, and like all magic waters, it transforms her in that moment. She drinks from it and remembers and becomes fully I■ in that moment. It may not last long but it leaves its mark.

So I■'s life continues independent of J., but parallel to this life, another life dependent upon or interdependent with J. is constituting itself. That's the second story: the uncertain life of I■ and J., whether there is or could be a life of I■ and J. so that whether J. is or is not a part of the second story is also the subject of the second story.

• • •

So many years later, when J. was already dead and I■ was thinking about her own mortality,

> After the age of fifty we begin to die little by little in the deaths of others [13]

wondering, as J. must have done, how much time she had left and whether it would be sufficient to finish what she was currently working on, let alone what she had planned for the future, these thoughts appearing not so much after a bout of illness but of discomfort or disquiet in the body which spoke, as it ought, of the limitation of time, she realized that quite long ago, he had, with his death, opened the door for her and she had crossed the threshold to a world she would not have known so well without him and that this new work that was engaging her was as much a consequence of their meeting as it was a response to the times. Did we actually meet then, dear one? Is it possible we didn't miss each other as I thought? She thought about the Chinese curse: May you live in interesting times—in the times in which she/everyone was living, the time she shared with Rio and still shares with J.

Once they had been Iris and Rio. To think about it this way implied that something had come from their meeting on this side, *Here*. An Iris/ Rio kind of thing. London/Paris, hop! hop! hop! The Mediterranean, the South of France, the Italian Riviera, hop! hop!

Hop! hop! or Hip Hop was not what they had been involved in. No, what had happened between them is this: They had agreed without a word or even a handshake to listen, ceaselessly, to the voice of the woman in the cellar . Wherever Iris went, whatever she was doing, whatever preoccupied her—Vito, separation, despair, career, politics, activism, writing, dreams and nightmares—she knew, day or night, that Rio, also, just then, at that very moment, even in his sleep had been aware of the incessant tortured, deranged mutterings of the woman in the cellar. This is where Rio and Iris had been introduced and had become I▪ and J. even without what Iris considered a real meeting. The woman in the cellar , the object of their consciousness, became the conduit that existed between them, so that ultimately, like rhizomes under the earth, they were one unit, J. rising on one side of the world and I▪ on another. In this, J. was faithful. As she was. Fidelity, here, consisting of trusting the other's vigilance. They did this together until J. died. It was their dance for more than ten years. Unacknowledged, unrecognized, but rhythmic.

In this sense she no longer thought, despite what she had written to him and then printed in the newspaper, recriminations and requests passing from this world to the next, that they had fully missed each other. She was seeing that he had not been an adventure she would never have. This conclusion she came to even though Iris had written a somewhat accusatory letter to Rio some weeks after they met in the south of France, complaining that "the tiger was not at home, or, at least, didn't make an appearance when we were together. How do we meet in that place we had hoped to meet, that place between the worlds?" She was as outspoken and petulant, or brazen, (still a very young woman, forgivable as she was an American, for a woman of her years) in that letter as she would ever be and he, acknowledged that she was right and they agreed to try to remedy the situation through a correspondence. (She was also a very mature woman, even though she was an American, for a woman of her years, but she did not know which to lead with in this instance, and so she led with both, hence the inherent contradictions in their relationship or non-relationship.) The truth is that she was too shy to pursue it. Writing that letter where she felt she had bared her soul was as much as she could do and, always, she was concerned about his time and obligations:

> *You were behind already, sure, you can't*
> *keep up with things, with the days,*
> *when you manage to get the letters answered . . .*[14]

Her way of loving him, of really loving anyone, was her secret gift of giving them to themselves. Accordingly, they sank into an infrequent warm and polite exchange, an ongoing reserve, that would characterize their relationship while they were both *Here*.

But being sensible in her earlier reticence was being sensible then and now dead is dead. She continued, of course, without him. That is, persisted in who she was or had become. I▪ was the woman who listened to the woman in the cellar. But what about J.? Sometimes she thought she felt him pushing toward her from *Over there*, a mole digging, digging, digging under the earth, but without reaching her despite his persistence. In the beginning of his death, they never met each other even in the minute ways they had when he was alive. It wasn't the same person, it wasn't Rio, or who he had become before he died, but something, some one, an energy, a force without a face or a name, but familiar. Who he had become and who he could only become *Over there*. She had not understood, when she was still young in the ways one remains young before history takes its toll, that potential existed *Over there* as much as it exists here. Wasn't that one of J.'s obsessions as a writer and hadn't she sought him out just to understand it? J. was beyond and yet, somehow, though terminally elusive, also more vital and undistracted, she thought, having been freed by death from the urgencies of a private life. Perhaps one put time in *Here* in order to qualify for *Over there*. Or perhaps it was all an illusion and he was dead, dead, dead and they had missed each other and were continuing to do so and so on unto eternity. (Which meant she was a mad woman.) Nevertheless, she brews a maté in his honor.

• • •

Now, having found the walk I■ believed she would take for the rest of her life, and so feeling easy about what was coming and the probability of landmarks — the path that so gently rose up through the trees to the top of the holy mountain, Mt. Pinos, *ʔiwhɨnmuʔu,* where the Chumash say the worlds are in balance — she was startled by a corridor half way up the mountain marked by a guardian tree at the beginning and two sentinel trees at the end. It was her sense that these, the tall ponderosa pine and the two rare bristlecone firs that grow only in the Los Padres national forest where she had just settled, marked a door that opened and closed behind her as she entered the corridor and opened and closed again as she exited so that the territory beyond remained a pristine domain. These doors allowed entrance to the sacred meadow and beyond it the commanding twisted conifer atop an altar of stone, dominating the summit and glowing with a dark red amber fire as the sun set. It had taken awhile to recognize the corridor and what it opened to. Until that moment, the ponderosa, if she had noticed it in particular, was just a tree and what followed from it, was the landscape, pure and simple. And then, without being able to explain the mechanics of it, a presence, a code revealed, its individual nature in the other realm bleeding through, became apparent to her as the veils parted. It was a tree and it was a guardian. Both at the same time. She felt giddy and afraid. Behind or within or around the very real trees and the rough road that has been shaped by water and stones rushing down in the rains and the spring melt was another kind of geography altogether.

"You brought me here, my dear J.," she said as she entered. "This is your territory and since you're not among us, I guess it's my task to be the bridge." And then she shivered because the most commonplace word, "bridge" took on a different resonance on this sacred land of the Chumash. The Chumash people had come to the mainland from Santa Cruz Island by crossing the Rainbow Bridge. Those who weren't steady enough on their feet had fallen off the road of light into the sea to became the dolphin people. Now here she was making her home, planting herself, body and spirit on their holy mountain, their Sinai.

She wasn't much older than he had been when they met and she had the uneasy task of looking back at herself, trying not to be embarrassed by the puella she had been, her absolute inability then to see the consequences of innocence, its dangers and obtuseness. The way she had risked her relationship with Vito over a spat about language, her wild infatuation and self-righteousness about her own passions and desires that masked a coexistent timorousness, and so, more importantly, how she had threatened Rio's peace, the very little peace of mind he might have had. She was seeing herself through her own eyes, the eyes of an older woman, as he must have seen her then. Now her task was to be absolutely truthful. But to what? To how she had seen it then or to how she understood it now? She had also to see who she had become as the present Iris, that is I■, would know the story of her name and would not, as the mythic servant to Hera, violate the marriage bed which was always Hera's domain. Though she couldn't have gotten here, wherever here was, without the young Iris woman, bless her.

He wouldn't recognize her now, she thought, except that she understood that he had kept his eyes on her from the moment they had met and then, it seemed, equally after he died, so there were no surprises for him, though there were for her. One does not expect to be less familiar to oneself the longer one is living with oneself. One expects familiarity, but that isn't the way it goes. Quite the opposite. She was not the Iris she had been. She knew that he knew this.

Yes, there was something patently untrue in the first story as she had written it, trying to be faithful to the story as she had experienced it then or thought she had experienced it then. And thinking, as her friends and colleagues did, that self criticism was equal to candor and candor to truthfulness, it was essential not to ever let herself off the proverbial hook upon which even the great Inanna had once hung like a slab of meat. Increasingly though, she tried to distinguish between judgment and discernment. She had judged Vito; she had not discerned then who he was. She had never judged Rio, she had committed herself to discerning who he was. She had wanted to judge Hélène, it was only envy, but her better instincts had, ultimately, prevented her from doing so. She had and continued to judge herself though she didn't think she'd ever reached true discernment of her qualities though she thought she was coming to know the nature if not the entirety of her shortcomings, who she had been and who she had become. So now she was in a quandary that made it impossible to understand what had and what hadn't occurred when she and Rio had been alongside each other in the living world. If she wasn't honest the bridge, like the ladder in *Hopscotch,* wouldn't reach across between the worlds and he would not open the door. This impossible task to see things as they are, not to be truthful so much as to see the truth of them. Could anyone but *un mago* see that?

The problem lay in the fact that having been a younger woman and unmarried and therefore hungry, as American women are, though she tried to deny or escape this observation, and having lived her teenage years in the second half of the 20th century, and then being immersed in psychology, feminism and radical politics, Iris had not had any language but the language of eros—either the life and entitlement of the body, woman's and man's—Liberation! Liberation!—or the intoxication of connection and relationship after decades of detachment, distance and alienation—with which to describe what had driven her across France to meet *El Mago*. Perhaps another language had existed then, but she hadn't known it, and so she had spoken this inadequate language also to herself; it had become the language of her mind, the only language, the mono-language that accordingly isolated her within the labyrinth of its very limited meanings even when she intuited it was absolutely false to the situation. Yet it provided something, an antidote to the silence and meaninglessness that would have also subsumed her as the only other viable alternative then.

It had been a short time, not even a century, not even half a century, far less, that women had begun to imagine and live what a real life might be that was not diminished by gender and gender politics. They started out, inevitably, in the sexual arena, gender would necessarily lead one there and while it threatened some members of the patriarchy, it seemed to delight others, some of the very men that intrigued the "new" women, so to speak. And with or without women's lib, there was a hullabaloo about sexual liberation, and so the sack race was on to the sack. Which is to say, we can't blame Iris, she wasn't any sillier than anyone else, and she was offering her life to the concerns of the woman in the cellar and so we can forgive her her excitements and confusions.

Everyone she had known had indulged that language then, certain that the very buzzy, both scientific and scintillating, psycho-sexual, was at the core of things, the irresistible source of all discontents. It was not only eros, not even eros, that had driven her and she had known this but had been hog-tied before her real longing. She had needed a cover, and sex, even sex denied, was the best of disguises. To herself, she had thought of her quest in other terms but they seemed a bit too highfalutin to speak about. What she had told herself—even if she couldn't claim to be thinking this way publicly—was: He had gone through a door. He had gone through *the* door, many doors. She had wanted to go through that/those door(s). She had thought she needed a companion to assist her then, a man to guide her—what woman had been there before? And he was *El Mago*. Indubitably. She knew this, and she had wanted to explore *Over there;* she thought it was her birthright. She thought it was her fate. And so she had pursued him. As Psyche had finally pursued Eros once she saw, indeed, who he really was. Saw Eros was a god. The god.

Later, when she had other language because she was involved with other ideas, with ethics, for example, rather than her own Development, or Ambition or Identity, she was able to say she had gone to cross-examine him and scrutinize his life. Audacious and impudent!

It was a straight line between then and now except that there were these gates between the past and the present and, as with the corridor she had just traversed on the mountain, they marked the passageways between different worlds. And it wasn't as if, seeing where the path was leading her, she had done a 180° turn and regressed back to a blindly simple self or become someone else, as so many she knew had, but rather the opposite. She had rather cultivated the habit, like J., to leave the known world whenever the opportunity arose, choosing the interior landscape to explore—which was not, as she had been told, the landscape of self, but rather the landscape of no-self—while also trying to be faithful to the woman in the cellar whom she never forgot; they had become roommates so to speak and, appropriately, it had aged her.

Yes, there was also the woman in the cellar, no less present now though she was surely dead and her hair grayed and yellowed, having been unwashed for all this time, no bath, no food, no succor. There were more of these women than there had been before; the technology of torture had become a commodity, like sugar, computer chips or plutonium for which many paid a great deal of cold cash on the world market and then distributed it to too many countries and independent practitioners to count. No continent was free of it; it had become as commonplace and banal as oil or Coca-Cola and similarly pernicious as in its essence it was manufactured from the same elements, and profited from the same hungers and distributions. The economics and politics of torture and soda pop turned out to be exactly the same.

This woman in the cellar whom Iris had been faithfully keeping an eye on—watching her age without the advantages of aging, unwilling to forget her or let her drift into oblivion and so, ironically imposing upon the woman in the cellar the dubious gift of the long life, a limited edition of immortality—had become her consummate guide and conscience. Iris found a way of living by asking the woman in the cellar—who has no name and will be given no name here, except *Thewomaninthecellar*—whether what Iris had been doing or whether what I▪ (the older woman that Iris the younger woman had been) was doing was in *Thewomaninthecellar's* interest, or was of no consequence to her, or was against her. By this time there was more than one woman in the cellar and cellars everywhere and I▪ saw that her vigil had given her an understanding and perspective that couldn't have come to her otherwise. *Thewomaninthecellar* relied on Iris' and then I▪'s loyalty for without such attention the entire universe that *Thewomaninthecellar* still somehow stubbornly believed in—otherwise her sacrifice would have been merely stupid and deluded—would have disappeared. Without such faith, her fate would have been a foregone conclusion, would have imploded like a dark star and the woman, the knowledge of the woman, the world she had come out of, the world she believed in before her arrest, before all the arrests, all of it, the totality of kindness and concern would have vanished as absolutely as it was absent from the cell in which she was confined until her death. From the center of a dark hole, one can see the way force fields bend the universe toward the forces of annihilation, but the universe still exists and so there is hope, not necessarily for oneself but for eternity. This, then, is what Iris had offered the *Thewomaninthecellar*: she offered her eternity. When they met, Iris and Rio had taken up this task without realizing what they were committing to, and now that J. was dead, so Rio was dead too, they being almost one and the same. Rio had been the puer as Iris had been the puella. Then Rio had become an elder, not unlike I▪ now but afterwards he had continued on to become . . . what? . . an ancestor, a ghost, a spirit? . . Hélène was who-knew-where, Vito was continuing his work in the world, but as it was real politic that engaged him, his work was for the most part with men, so it was for I■ to continue. It was a work that no matter how gifted he was as a *Mago*, J. could not do independently from the other side. *The great magi, the shamans of our youth, successively go off.*[15] He could assist, he could inspire, he could remind, but ultimately it was a work for the living. It was *the* work of the living.

I■ did not let the strangeness of her wondering whether she would have enough time to write this piece, this book that somehow circled about J., nor what such a piece might be if it were, in fact to be the/her last piece, distract her from whatever fear she might have of dying. *I shall leave this hospital, I shall leave cured, that's for certain, but, for a sixth time, a little less alive.*[16] Yes. One day, it is certain, the symptom is going to be the symptom. And poof!

• • •

There had been another time just before Iris had discovered she was ill with cancer, shortly after she had met Rio, that she had started a manuscript with the words, "This is the book I would write if I were to die in a year"—awakening results from the advent of such words. Had she fallen asleep again and so similar words were appearing like some writing on the wall? That other time . . . yes . . . that other time, Rio had interposed himself into the novel/radio play that hadn't started out to include him but when it was done, yes, there Rio was.

> When I came home from France where I had visited Juan, the first news I heard was that Lucia had died. So Lucia is dead. If I were to write to Juan and say, "While I was away, Lucia died, you are responsible," he would think me quite mad. And to be frank, of all men, he is one of the least responsible.

They had been in the same room, they had watched the same sunset, they had mourned the same pains, but, according to Iris—and he had agreed, but she hadn't known whether he regretted it—they hadn't met, even after she had undertaken such a journey. When she returned, Lucia's sudden death was like the punctuation at the end of a long death sentence.

Lucia had died though she had made a pilgrimage to Mexico when there was no hope for a Jewish mother of two children who had lived a good life, the secular equivalent of piety, married to a respected engineer working for a war/antiwar think tank, imagining disasters, inventing the most efficient, cost-effective means to create them and then the ways to protect some portion of the population from them: education, preparedness, traffic control, evacuation, hospital supplies, rat poison, mass burial plans. Lucia found a small church she could reach on her knees from a mile away on packed dirt, broken glass and gravel. And still, when she climbed the stairs, on her now skinless knees and from an observer's point of view, ecstatic, entirely unaware of pain and scraped down the faded red velvet carpet runner the color of scabs and dry blood to the altar, she couldn't breathe any better than she had before and opened her mouth to wail for her life but the hemorrhage took her down. Her husband was at his office in the U.S. working on a facsimile of an atomic attack on a city of seven million when he received the call.

And why had Iris blamed Rio, of all people, except that she blamed everyone, men in particular—it was a time when blame seemed a necessary corollary to change—for this death of a woman, not like but also not unlike *Thewomaninthecellar*. That is, Lucia was silenced from the beginning and the men who were working on facsimiles of atomic attacks had put her there, or so Iris believed, even though the husband wept profusely at the funeral and shook his head incredulously, and would remain a broken hearted father of two children who would marry again, for their sakes, he insisted, and also so, in honor of Lucia, he could return to his important work and his social and political obligations. Iris blamed every man it was impossible to meet.

It had been so long since I▪ had looked at the script and even longer since she had read the original manuscript so that when she extracted it, dusty, worn, she was astonished, perplexed by what she found. What she had written and what was ultimately produced for radio was as raw and unfinished as what had transpired between them. And, for her, as compelling and so within minutes she was back in the drama of it, wrestling, as if she had never left it, with its issues and its concerns. Lucia! She hadn't thought of her in twenty years; that is the kind of immortality Lucia achieved in I▪'s manuscript.

> "We were both so civilized, Juan. Civilized, polite, well-mannered."
> "We were like two tigers who came together and didn't mate."
> "I don't mate behind bars," he hissed.
> "Against the bars. Against."

I■ didn't remember the actor who had played Juan, yet another name for the proliferating Rio. Nor did she remember who took her role. She did remember sitting in the recording booth for hours listening to the secret language of her passions spoken by others again and again, until they got it right.

> There was no precedent for a collaboration between a man and woman who did not intend to lust for each other. It was not in the body that I wanted to meet.
> And we both had friends who were dying and we both had friends who were in danger. And so we talked politics and gave it priority. If he had read my mind, he might have asked, "What do you want from me?"
> "I want nothing from you."
> "What then? Is my English bad? What do you want with me? Is that what I meant to ask?"
> "Yes," I would have answered. "That is the question: What do I want with you?"
> In the telling something is saved. In the telling. So it seems to me. It has to be.[17]

And why had she included him but that he was the biggest question mark around and every piece of work deserved a question at its core. Lucia had died and then others. None seemed to die naturally of personal causes or, as literature was once able to tell it, serenely, of old age, in their sleep. Iris hadn't died then. Writing the novel had saved her even though she hadn't known her life required saving. She finished the novel and discovered the illness, but by then she knew everything she needed to know about saving a life: Tell the truth and tell it all.

So many years later, I■ was back in the same stories that had never quite been told in such a way as to end them which is quite different from bringing them to a conclusion. Having opened the text she had written, she saw that life was not a progression as she had been taught, but a lotus, the parabola of each white petal returning her, yet again, to the central question that had formed itself through the agency of his presence. And what was the question—was it about life or was it about death?

If her life was being threatened again, why was it that J. was alongside her as Rio had been earlier though neither she nor he acknowledged it in what is called *this* life, *Here*. Had her life been nothing but a corridor turning back upon itself between one life-threatening illness and another with J. as psychopomp presiding over it? If this was the case, she would begin, only begin, mind you, to understand why that story of their meeting (or non-meeting depending on mood, the point of view, or the time of day) a small moment in a very rich life, a dinner after and before many other dinners, a flicker in time, had somehow remained central and definitive in her life. Who was this J. who had preoccupied her so?

If it was/wasn't necessarily her death which was the issue now, why had she chosen to try to write this piece? Was it the (last) piece one gets to write when one has come into the shadow of *Over there* and so has access to what one can't know otherwise, or was it just about time that she faced what one of her—one of what J. would call her "hydra heads"—knew. Time to come clean. Was it simply that she had finally come to a time of such confidence that she was determined to say what she had to say, not so much what she must say, but what she had been given and so had within her to say. Perhaps it was just too late and too embarrassing to be beating about the bush: She had been writing about the dead forever; she had had a periscope into the other world from the time she started writing even though she had always pretended otherwise: "I'm only kidding—it's only my over-excited imagination." You know that kind of apologia. One of those coy gestures that unsure women resort to even though it is definitively unattractive. I■ had been observing this distortion in the mirror for over thirty years.

Here's another possibility. She'd been seriously toying with this forever, that is for more than five years, and J. had gotten bored with her attempts and regressions and decided to step across, open the door from the other side to say, "Yes, it is true, there are living presences on the other side who can cross the border and I am one of them. And here I am."

There are thousands of ways to be a bridge. Walking through the corridor, I■ felt vertiginous with possibility. There was no difference, she began to understand, between passing through the corridor and being a corridor herself. One implied the other. When you go from end to end, everything that is there passes through you, and one is the green and blue waters of yesterday and tomorrow merging and flowing fast. It was beyond understanding. The ground was the ground, the trees were the trees and she was herself but also, simultaneously, there was no self. There was, she was, a body, arms, legs, blue jeans, denim shirt, hickory walking stick, old, tattered Tilli hat that had her name on it, and there was also a vast unexplored field of understanding, and more fear and gratitude than she had ever known. She felt herself in direct conversation, informed by, altered by, her thinking changed by, yes, this was certain, the windy, winding river of trees passing by—and everything else. In corridors, in the passage between a dark hole and a white hole, in what is called the liminal space, in the chrysalis between caterpillar and moth there is a state of non-integration, that is an arena where the absolute rigid boundaries of self and no-self do not exist. And so one is open to influences, one can be penetrated, entered, can be diminished or increased, edited and enhanced, so that the one who emerges at the end is and is not the same one that entered the passageway, whatever it is, from this tree to that tree or from Iris to I▪.

From behind anyone would simply have seen a woman whose curves were squaring and who was walking with very certain, determined steps up the mountain. A woman, from behind, who looked like she knew where she was going and why. But from within it was another matter altogether. The woman who was walking up the mountain was in flux as invisible presences becoming visible leaned toward her, entered her, protecting, undoing, and then, ultimately, propelling her life forward and around.

It was just as she thought this that she came upon a visitation of lupine, the flowers brilliant purple and white on their pert stems, and she stopped. She had not expected them in bloom at this time, at this altitude, at nine thousand feet, and because of their beauty in the dappled light, because she hadn't known why they carried the name of wolf, but once it was stated it was as if the wolf long hunted out of this area, or rather the shadow of wolf, the spirit of wolf, was there glancing with its golden intelligent eyes out of a den of leaves and petals and everything that had been hunted, hounded, driven out, extinguished came loping back with it into the living moment of pristine, amethyst light.

"Damn it, you're right, J.. Death does not exist. Imagine that!"

It is the greatest mystery that, as with creation, the events or energies of other worlds, coexistent and co-extensive, must take on the garments of manifestation in order to be known here and so are clothed in or are simultaneous with the quotidian. You can never know if a skin is just a skin, a fur pelt is just a fur pelt or if the brother wolf, an honorable if lesser being, is also an ambassador, a wolf angel, Wolf, the great spirit

Herself teaching the law of kinship and solitude, or Spirit, Itself, hunkered down into wolf form. A tree is always just a tree and yet it can be, is, something else entirely at the same time. Daphne knew this when she ran for sanctuary from the light to a tree form that would remain herself. The laurel. The highest praise and honor, recognized.

The *mago* learns from, is trained by, the very spirits who have manifested in bodies. The task is to learn to see so that what the eye rests upon becomes transparent, to see through the fur, the feather, the face. What the *mago* sees is the invisible and then he/she follows (in) its footsteps. Easier said than done.

Within minutes of passing through from here to there, I▪ picked a stalk with a tiny white flower atop it as if holding it in her hand would help her understand this and then her husband, M., who had started out after her and had just caught up, noted, because he was exquisitely tuned to reading such signs, that she had picked yarrow, the traditional divining stick used when consulting the I Ching. When she returned, she held a question in her mind as she put the yarrow on her desk and threw the coins letting them land alongside the stick so they could take on the emanations of the old ways.

What was the question?

When Gertrude Stein was dying, she was asked: "What is the answer, Gertrude?"

"What is the question?" she responded. And so Gertrude passed across. What then was the question?

What then is the question that I▪ asked?

She couldn't/wouldn't verbalize it. To do so would trivialize everything she had devoted herself to for her entire life. But, the question had much to do with J. even as I▪ and M. were hiking up the mountain alongside each other speculating on what the yarrow would say to the question in her mind. The question that I▪ would not reveal to M. she rather hoped that he would decipher from the answer that she received.

They reached the top of the mountain and scattered bird seed, as she liked to do everywhere. M. went off by himself, striving further up the trail to another summit while she remained contemplating the question. She sat down on a rock and had what she considered a heart to heart with J., asking advice, wanting answers. The wind whistled around her furiously. Her hands were white with cold by the time M. returned and they descended. When she returned home, she placed the yarrow stick on her desk and picked up the three Chinese coins that she used for divination. She threw them six times.

> The answering hexagram was 46 Ascending/Sacred Mountain *Sheng*.
> Ascending shows a procession up the sacred mountain . . . to . . . the ancestral temple where spirit tables of the royal ancestors were housed.
> Ascending describes your situation in terms of rising to a higher level and getting something done. The way to deal with it is to set a goal and work towards it step by step. Root yourself and push towards the heights. Climb the mountain and connect with the spirits.
>   *Nine at Second*
> The connection is established. Make the offering and climb the sacred mountain. Dedicate yourself to what you believe in and make the great sacrifice to the gathered ancestors. It is all there if you want it to be.

In the second hexagram, 15, the relating figure of Humbling, it said:
    The ideogram portrays spoken words and the sign for "unite."
    This second hexagram was the context through which one understood the first one.
    "It can represent future potential, overriding concerns, a warning, a goal, a desired outcome or a past situation that brought you to the present situation."[18]
The reading seemed to refer directly to I■'s writing project:
    "Keep your words simple. . . . Balance things carefully and correct any excess."

A clear imperative followed:
"The ideogram . . . suggests keeping words connected to the facts," which I■ interpreted as telling the truth no matter what. The hexagram itself was true to the mark but how true she would only know later when she would find herself wrestling with its sober directives:

> "Balance, adjust. . . . A lack is filled through activation of unconcious powers moving in underworld ways. . . . This 'humbling' cuts through the pride and complication of an over-developed ego. . . . The old character shows a man's face with an open mouth, suggesting words . . . QIAN shows words, YAN to

speak in such a way that speaker and listener come together . . . Think and speak of yourself in a modest way. Take the lower position. . . ."

Yes, only later would she know fully what these words really meant.

Space-time. She was in the corridor between here and there, the corridor that reconciled the past with the future. A corridor constructs itself from the unexpected events of the moment, from the carpentry of what is there for all to see and also what appears suddenly as out of nothingness, a particle appearing suddenly in a ring circling the nucleus and then as suddenly vanishing and appearing elsewhere. Each ring not so much a place as a dimension of time that has taken on a body. The events flit in and out like fireflies.

When M. and I■ were in Costa Rica, they stayed in the woods too long and night fell fast and hard leaving them in darkness as if they had been ambushed by a black woolen greatcoat thrown over their heads. Then, through the buttonholes, or ragged sleeves of the garment of night, they were able to follow the fireflies that did actually illuminate their path.

From this perspective, what I■ is just beginning to understand, from the eye of the electron microscope that is its own form of imagination, it is possible to see the rings as they coexist and the ways in which the **luminescent** guests flit from one dimension, world to another in the process of creation. But is that what is happening? Or is it that sometimes we see them and sometimes we don't: They've turned out their lights. Look, they've turned them on.

Or this: they move into another dimension without leaving the dimension they are in. J., here and there, at the same time is the way I would put it. But, for I■, J. isn't there with her yet, but the thought or memory of him, his (ghostly?) presence is becoming stronger the longer they are apart, the longer he is dead.

Is dead. Dead. Not really a noun, or an adverb or an adjective. Dead as a verb, a transition, an observation about there from here. Dead as in "a dead thing" has meaning to us over here as it fits with the limitation of our observations, but it is epistemologically in error. The point of all of this only to say that J. can't be dead a long time. He dies and though he is dead from this perspective, over here, "he" is something else entirely *Over there*. Is dead, equally contradictory. What we are seeking is something that more appropriately resembles "is living." Is something else, something fluid and changing, something that resembles a river or a life, but not like those on this side, but in the ways and vernacular of *Over there*. Like what? We can't say. Dead was once a verb but that doesn't help us. As a verb it meant deaden, to lose vitality, to become dead, to die. Dead stops dead at the border of *Over there*. Naturally the language being human-centric is by its nature blind to anything *Over there*. Our language doesn't permit us to speak of it and also we can't speak about what we don't know.

There is a door. When you open it and pass across the threshold you are in a domain where none of the laws of physics and, therefore, none of the laws of grammar apply.

Here is another possibility about which, again, we can only speculate. J. dies and is dead a long time, meaning that there is a process *Over there* that one enters after one dies and that process in the realm of eternity, [which is one of the characteristics, we believe but, of course, we can't know anything], of *Over there*, takes a long time. Thus it is possible that if I∎ finally encountered Julio after years of procrastination and hesitance, there is *someone* or some thing [rude] to encounter. [Again the language doesn't serve us.]

There is a spirit present to encounter.

Ah!

Here we are in the corridor. Trying to work with and bend the language so that it can describe or contain realities that have always been outside its domain. From the time they banned the witches— not the ones they imagined were witches and burned or drowned them with great ardor as in the time of the Inquisition or Salem, but the real witches, like the Witch of Endor who could, indeed, call up and converse with the dead—the language, following the lead of the culture, avoided the complexities of being and non-being that are engaging us now.

But, to begin again: Here we are in the corridor. And anything can happen here because we are outside the definitions and the boundaries and limitations of *this side*. And so it does. Anything happens. And happens so smoothly, so swiftly, without a ripple or a sound, that one doesn't realize at first what has occurred. A simple rote activity turns the world inside out.

Anything has happened. Here and now. Unnerved [a word that will repeat, seemingly endlessly itself in this text because the circumstances of undoing, by the nature of the experience we are trying to describe occur again and again with no diminution of affect] by it, I have no choice but to record the occurrence immediately in the text as follows :

Let us return to the lotus. It is not only time that resembles the lotus, but this manuscript which I am writing, moving forward, and then falling back to the very center of the flower and curving out again. The computer makes Julio's hypertext possible. We write and then move back into a little niche that was designed weeks ago. We may live here for several months or we make take a skateboard and scoot forward, back or to the side in an elegant move. Just as you experience it, dear reader, I am writing these words here on this page but having already written many of the words that you will find in the future. In this sense, the future or end of the book is already napping in the past.

While we are considering the way time flows back and forth, or the continuous present it forms, I■ was ruminating on what concerned her most at that moment in the I Ching reading: "The ideogram . . . suggests keeping words connected to the facts," which I■ interpreted as telling the truth no matter what.

So . . . approximately a page ago, I was using spell check for `<luminescent>` [see page 91] which—confession—I had misspelled and after making the correction it sped ahead to other suspect words, to approximately ten pages past this spot where we are presently ruminating together, to these lines: "We are involved in approaching a question of truth."

The text runs on as if J. has joined us in the discussion of the reading that we have been writing now. Lines from the future inserted into what seemed to come before and will appear again. In the future, it will be I■ speaking these lines but at this moment, which is past, future and present coexisting in the same corridor, it can only be J. speaking to us or rather it can only be J. who is inserting the words whomever he attributes them to:

<We are involved in approaching a question of truth.
"If you want truth. . . ."> [see page 106]
"If *I* want truth. . . . I'm not writing this. I would never dare. You're intervening. Death is not, apparently, what we̶—*I*—think it is. Death is revealing itself as a strange partnership with someone to whose existence I cannot testify. You can put words in my mouth. I accept that even I cannot testify that it is occurring. An

assumption, sometimes, and a hope at others. But I will not speak as if for you. I will not imagine the substance of your death.
"Death is, apparently, another opportunity . . . Death is another kind of life, both in time and outside of it . . ."

Surprising on two counts. First that we are taken here. Insistently. Now. And second, when we were speaking about truth the words suddenly appear underlined. And why is this? It is because the spell check dictionary has mysteriously switched to Spanish. Not any Spanish. Spanish [Argentina]. Every word then incomprehensible to it and begging for correction. Spanish. [Argentina] Go figure.

In the old days, such a moment would be punctuated by a clap of thunder or lightning striking the ground, sulfur burning the nostrils. No such event has occurred. The rainstorm that began this morning continues but the wind doesn't even pick up as I continue at the computer. I can't stop. Something is occurring that demands that I yield to the event [Humbling advises "yielding, taking the lower position, being compliant and reverent"] wherever it takes us because simultaneous with J.'s outburst is another change in the computer that has just proceeded from "luminescent" to "question," which, it suggests, we change to *questión* a consequence, again, of the dictionary switching *lenguajes* languages to Spanish [Argentina.]

Hello, Julio, welcome trickster. The dictionary has set itself to Spanish [Argentina] and refuses to return to English and then it does. This puzzle with its underlining that indicates that we have left one world for another, one language for another, we leave to the reader to investigate and while assuming that J. has joined us, we continue. (The underlines come and go, I do what is needed to change the default language back to English [U.S.] but it slides out again and Spanish [Argentina] slides in and then out again.)

I▪ and J. They seem to be at it with one another. I▪ is intrigued but doesn't know what to make of it. She's intrigued by the synchronicities and strange events that are occurring—the computer dictionary converting to Spanish [Argentina] without her ability to convert it back to English until she leaves that particular section. She has set the default language to English [U.S.] again and again, but to no avail. She has removed French as a secondary default language, one that she can reference at will, (Spanish [Argentina] was never of this category,) but this has made no difference. All of this occurring almost twenty years since Iris received *A Certain Lucas*. I■ reviews what has led to this trying to understand a phenomenon that has some precedence in her imagination, but has no precedence in her life—yet, here it is.

. . .

Ten years after I■ received J.'s gift of his posthumously published translation of *A Certain Lucas* through the unlikely agency of a newspaper who had paid her no attention otherwise, (or since) I■ had an audacious idea. An idea so audacious, absurd and outrageous that she tried to hide it from herself first by forgetting it and when that failed, by attempting, instead, to write a story about it, about someone (else) who had such an audacious idea and acted on it. It was a simple plot line: A woman writer is attempting to write her next book in collaboration with a dead writer.

Through the simple device of writing "she" instead of "I," of giving the action to a character whom I■ intended to call Raizel, of writing as if it had indeed happened in a fictional universe instead of the plot centering upon the question of whether it could happen/was happening. What I■ intended was to avoid the consequences of such a prohibited event while keeping the lark of it.

Why Raizel? Because the name had the sound of angels and I■ thought she needed a little angelic assistance to pull it off. Over the years she had found that a character often followed her name into life. Names having certain histories and associations and resonances became imperatives and an entire narrative might develop around one name that could not possibly develop around another. Nothing more required than the name. And then . . . well, what was imagined did or didn't occur, and if it did it wasn't in any form that I■ as writer imagined.

The story lines weren't quite clear to I■ and she was absolutely determined not to do any personal research or experimentation in order to see where the story might go. She set out as she often had, certainly without an outline—she left those to journalists who had to be faithful to what had happened—and proceeded by intuition, letting the inner dynamic of the story take over. Stories and characters have their own life, given a little protoplasm to start with, they embody themselves quite quickly, and extend in a far different direction than the writer imagined initially. Some writers, like doctors of old, test the medicine first before prescribing it, or write only what they know from experience rather than what they might imagine, but I■ was certainly not proceeding in this direction in this case.

Everything about this plot was tricky, but perhaps the most difficult was rendering a character who truly had the capacity to invoke the dead. Though she had decided who this fictional narrator might be, from what point of view this event would be described, she followed, rather than led, the story in her mind from day to day. At first she conceived of an omniscient narrator, as cynical and skeptical as I■ thought her readership would be. Then the first narrator underwent a sex change operation, as it were, under the skilled hand of a psychic surgeon and emerged a woman narrator as omniscient as before but less cynical and less skeptical, a woman who identified with the protagonist's purpose, with her vision of what was possible in the universe despite society's reluctance to believe in the possibility of or condone such a collaboration, particularly when it was a woman (writer) who was entrusted with the credible task of raising the dead.

This was a complete change of point of view. I■ now imagined a fiction entirely within the minority rather than the majority perspective. A minority that accepted that possibility, indeed the reality, of the dead cooperating in such a way—and with a woman. It was not hard for I■ to make this adjustment, she naturally identified with the underdog but even though she had never had any difficulty imagining a woman revolutionary, it had never occurred to her that a woman might carry great spiritual presence. It wasn't that she didn't think they could, she had never thought about it. A respected and charismatic spiritual teacher who was a woman was not plausible in her tradition that, to her knowledge and experience, had never endorsed women as mystics, great teachers, prophets or adepts. She had lived with this lacuna her entire life. The vision of a woman carrying such spiritual presence and agency was so impossible, implausible in her tradition, it could not be imagined without the entire tradition deconstructing. Vanishing. Without a trace. The triumph of anti-matter. It could not even be imagined.

Here I■ was wrestling with the very nature of language. How words deceive us. Because we can say it, we think it, anything, can exist. The mind that speaks a certainty is unwilling to accept impossibility. It rebels. It roars in protest. Yes, this act of imagination that I■ was daring had been outside the realm of possibility for her entire life. A lacuna is not a space that can be filled by something. It is a space into which nothing can enter. Never. It is not a space. It is not like form and emptiness. It is a space which is a nothing. It is not a zero. It is naught.

I▪ could not, through an act of will, see what she had never seen before. If such a vision is to come to be it comes upon one. That is what happened to I▪. It came upon her and it undid her. It undid her in the way it would have undone her tradition. It smashed all of her assumptions, all her truths, all the laws of her being to smithereens. Just the way the actual appearance of a dead writer in the middle of her text, of Raizel's text would have done.

I▪ always assumed that breakdown was a result of limitation; she had not ever imagined that she would be broken down by possibility. Surprise!

As it happens, there was one woman mentioned in the sacred books of her tradition who was identified with such extraordinary spiritual powers that were always reserved to men. But she was no model. First of all, she had no name. Second of all, she was a pariah. And thirdly, the wondrousness of the deed was subsumed in the story it served and so she had a mention but no acclaim, and even most of those familiar with the Old and New Testaments were not particularly aware of her at all. She was certainly not a model for Raizel, nor, really, a precedent.

At the outset of the original story, there had been a campaign against all the witches in the kingdom. But then the king needed a witch. And this one was found and promised asylum if she raised one of the prophets, Samuel, who had recently died. She acquiesced. The prophet appeared. The king asked his fate. The prophet predicted his death. It occurred within twenty-four hours. End of story.

If one believes the testaments, the woman had indeed existed and had done what no one had ever imagined a woman could do. When she emerged from anonymity, like Lazarus recalled against his will to his own mortality, she was understandably nameless. And after she served the king by practicing her sacred art one more time, accomplishing the miraculous on his behalf, she remained nameless and without praise.

This task that was given to the woman was not one she sought out. After she accomplished it, she was despised. But she couldn't refuse the king who had wanted her dead. Either way, all ways, she suffered. It was a lousy deal any way you looked it, this task of calling up and speaking to/for the dead.

She is known as the Witch of Endor. For a time, I■ thought of her as Woe, but the name did not serve the woman any better than her title and place of origin. Whatever name I■ imagined failed and so the woman remained without a name even in I■'s imagination.

I■'s protagonist, Raizel was a woman not unlike I■ except that once Raizel had the idea of collaborating on a literary work with a dead writer she was enchanted by it. Any writer knows that when a character gets an idea it is difficult and often impossible to rid him/her of it. Raizel was insistent. Insistent on the idea and insistent on her life which were ultimately the same. For she was the one who was carrying this idea. Without this idea, Raizel didn't exist. This meant that I■ could not shake the idea either and so was doomed as she had been so often in the past to yield to inspiration, much as she tried, and hopeless as she felt, to accomplish it with the panache and authority she knew it required. Much like those hapless ones whom spirit mounts.

I■'s fear that she could not pull this off did not at first seem to be so great a problem for I■ as it could be for her character, Raizel. If Raizel failed at conjuring and so failed at the alliance, if Raizel's story, the one Raizel was attempting to write, would go belly-up, that was that for her, pfft, kaput. However, it was still a good story, in its own right, for I■, since it was the nature and inevitability and tragedy of failure that interested I■ and not hocus pocus—*hoc es corpus meum*—after all.

This is how I■ rationalized her situation. But no matter how earnestly I■ alleged that this was, therefore, only Raizel's dilemma, it turned out to be I■'s dilemma as well. If the (fictional) collaboration was to have any credibility, the dead writer had to appear in the text alongside the living writer otherwise, the entire project would appear as a manipulation at best or a farce as worst.

Try as she might, I■ couldn't imagine writing the book *as if* this were occurring. Even if it was a fictional world that she was conjuring. She had never had any interest in fantasy literature. Whom then would she, herself, invisible but present behind the narrator, invoke on behalf of Raizel? And would that writer come forth? Raizel, aware of the precariousness of her existence, did not volunteer a writing partner. Her life was so much in I■'s hands she wasn't going to blow it with the wrong choice.

Dante had chosen Virgil, someone more skilled or at the least more experienced than he. He had had to choose someone who was beyond him and then he had to negotiate the exchange so that Virgil would agree to lead him into the labyrinth. The choice became more than a selection, it was, inevitably, an invocation. Dante was a fine writer, but still we don't suppose he invented Virgil. Surely he would not be so presumptuous with the writer he admired above all others. We have to assume that Virgil did, indeed, join him in the inferno and accompany him on the way down. In other words, there needed to be a true confluence between one world and the other, the waters of each had to meet as the mystic texts tell us they, under certain circumstances, are likely to do.

There was someone that I▪ could imagine invoking. Someone who had himself imagined proximity with the other side. But why would he enter into such a profound and intimate act with Raizel who was as yet unformed except for her obsession? I▪ couldn't move past this question. It had, she secretly admitted to herself, only been a ruse to distance herself from what seemed to be occurring in her mind. And so I▪ gave up the fictional project. *Finis.*

But maybe not. She was left . . . agitated. The fiction left her but the idea didn't leave her. Raizel died a quiet death but the archetype that had inhabited Raizel didn't leave the premises. It hovered in the air without a place to land. Disembodied. I▪ pretended to be disinterested in it. Certainly, she wasn't going to. . . . She was definitely not going to . . . not going to. Definitely not.

• • •

Raizel was kaput. But she had only been a cover for an obsession that was coming undressed. If Raizel's success had depended, ultimately, on the success of the narrator and if I▪, copping to it or not, was the narrator who was ultimately responsible for coming up with the goods, well, then why not try it. No time for blushing in the corner, no time for looking down at her shoes coyly, no time or space to play the innocent. Not the innocent again, not again, please! I▪ was intrigued, she was challenged, she was, she admitted, old enough to attempt it. If she failed, who would know? And what did she have to do with the rest of her life?

Well, as we will see, she tried many times and, as anyone would have predicted, failed. Her failure didn't mean that J. didn't exist, though he might not, though it was likely he didn't; it simply meant that she was incapable. Incapable distressed her. Some friends, M. included, thought, without knowing the exact content of her ambition, that if there were those who might be capable, she could well be among them. She was in that stage of her life when being overly modest was more cloying than genuine. At some point, she realized that she had to know something of who she was so that she could fulfill her responsibilities. Hanging back with her knees clenched and her toes pointed at each other was hardly an endearing posture at this age. The times were difficult, the political situation had never been worse, one had to do what one could. It was not a time to be concerned with what she wanted to do or what would bring her peace and serenity. Peace and serenity in such a time?

Such a dilemma was inherent to what I■ considered second stage feminism. Carol Christ had once written an essay insisting that women could not be advised, as in Buddhism, to give up their egos if they didn't have egos to begin with. Now first stage feminism was gaining a self. Well, you know how much time that takes and some people never accomplish it, or never think that they have accomplished it and so spend their lives involved with the question of self, of me, that sometimes becomes the familiar if dissonant aria, "me me me." That, I■ hoped, was beyond her. Without indulging inflation or being self-preoccupied, it was time to do what was called for, what needed to be done. And if she had the gifts, she had to apply herself. Imagine if J. had spent his time wondering if he was good enough to do what he was called to do.

As Jorge Amado says:

> Antes que todo, quien quiera escribir sobre Julio Cortázar para marcar las extensas fronteras de su actuante presencia debe resaltar la importancia pura y simple del escritor. Sin no fuese él el escritor que es, límpido y profundo, cuya elevada calidad literaria amigos y en enemigos, correligionarios y adversarios, progresistas o conservadores, ciudadanos de ésta o aquella parte, cada uno con su verdad y su deuda, pero todos de acuerdo reconocen y afirman.[19]

At a certain time, one is required to step forward and do what one can.

And Antonio Skármeta

> Cuando Allende fue elegido presidente y aun no había asumido el gobierno, Cortázar no esperó una invitación oficial para hacerse presente en Chile a compartir el júbilo del pueblo.[20]

Or Margaret Randall

En febrero me tocó llamarte para plantearte la ida a Bismuna… diecinueve norteamericanos—de los que son "amigos de la humanidad" vendrían en una Vigilia por la Paz. ¿Estarías tú dispuesto a estar con ellos, un día . . . o dos? . . . Me gustaría ir como uno más de ellos . . . y por todo el tiempo que dure la vigilia." Y así fue.[21]

One does it. One steps forward. One follows one's imaginings. With J. it is/was unavoidable, one follows his lead and finds oneself without the usual impediments in the world of the imagination, or one hopes for this, because he calls one to it. And so, of course, one writes to Cortázar as if he is alive . . . grammar not withstanding, his liveliness, even from *Over there* cannot be denied. So on the occasion of his death, he is addressed as follows, as one of the living, by Margaret Randall:

Julio, aún antes de que el que me pidiera la conspiración de estas líneas, terminara de explicarme el contexto yo comencé a hablarte en silencio.[22]

And again by Juan Gelman:

querido julio:
*   te escribo una carta porque no puedo hablar de vos sino con vos.[23]*

And by Eduardo Galeano:

Julio es una larga cuerda con cara de luna. La luna tiene ojos de stupor y melancolía. Así lo voy viendo en la penumbra del entre-sueño, mientras desato las pestañas. Así lo voy viendo y lo voy escuchando, porque Julio está sentando junto a la cama donde despierto y suavemente me cuenta los sueños que yo acabo de soñar y que ya no recuerdo o creo que no recuerdo.[24]

And finally by Claribel Alegría and Darwin J. Flakoll:

Otras imágenes de Julio: . . . empañado por la visión de Julio errando por la playa, solitario una vez más, iluminado por los rayos del sol poniente.
Esa fue nuestra última impresión del colosal Cortázar, pero no será la definitiva. Nos ha jurado, que regresará a Managua a fines de este año.[25]

Yes, I▪ agrees, she cannot write about J. without speaking with J. There is the dilemma and the possibility. In the whirl of admiration around J.'s imagination, and the way he awakened it in those it touched, his unique form of *shaktipat*, I∎ was, herself, encouraged, as if his presence illuminated a real part of herself that was otherwise entirely hidden, his light making visible the secret ink.

• • •

We have come to a crossroads. It seems like an impasse but we must call it a crossroads. It is not clear how to continue.

This is the dilemma. A sentence needs to be written and it unclear how it is to be stated. We are up against the issue of pronouns and whatever is decided will, as in the case of character and protagonist, determine everything. As an entire universe will arise predicated on the pronoun, this decision regarding pronouns is critical. It is not a matter of style or form. It cannot be made arbitrarily. It is not a fiction. The writer doesn't create a world so much as the writer perceives what is already there, albeit invisible, and searches for the exact words to render what has been revealed to her . . . uh . . . to him . . . to. . . .

Here are the possibilities:

We know exactly how much time passed between J.'s death and their first contact after his death. He died in February, 1984 . . . and then I∎ wrote him a letter a few days later . . . and then the newspaper called and then. . . .

But between that date and the event which is coalescing right before your eyes, the time is unclear. Was he in touch with her all that time? Or did he enter her life or she enter his death only in 1994 when we find these words in her journal.

> Dear J.:
> . . .
>   There is always a dead man in my novels. I don't mean I write novels about people who have died . . . oh yes, I have done that . . . but there are dead men who actively participate in the contemporary situation. For example, there are two dead men in the car that Dina Z and Sybil are driving from the airport in Tel Aviv to Jerusalem. Jeremiah Abazadik is recently dead but Shechem has been dead for centuries. It is 1981. . . .

Having written to him once and gotten a response, she seemed to be trying her luck again. It doesn't seem like anything came of it. But somehow after the debacle with Raizel, I■ tried her own hand at something and, as was her wont, picked up a book of J.'s and, immediately after writing the above, came across this paragraph that she had certainly forgotten.

> What was riding alongside the driver that night was a dead man,"
> I told him . . . Can you see yourself in a car with a dead man leaning
> against you, speeding along at seventy miles an hour through the
> solitude of the pampas? Five or six hours in which so many things could
> happen, because a corpse isn't the rigid entity people think it is. . . .[26]

"We have come to a crossroads." What is meant by *we*? Or whom do we mean by *we*? Or whom do I mean by *we*?

The first *we* seems to refer to the community formed by writer and reader. A writer creates a world and the narrator and reader participate in it and thereby experience a common fate. After all, the narrator is speaking to the reader. The narrator may be pretending to speak to herself or himself but ultimately the narrator is speaking to the reader even if the reader is not yet born. To the reader and so with the reader and so "we."

I■ began to research J.'s work again.

> Little he cares about the individual situation of the readers . . .
> that's why it isn't necessary to give ground in either the coming or the
> going: between him and the others there will be a bridge as long as
> what is written is born of a seed and not a graft.[27]

Here is another difficulty: What does "We have come to a crossroads," mean if I am not writing this to or for a reader? This we is not necessarily only the we of writer and reader. Who are really at the crossroads and did they arrive there by traveling together or do they come upon each other there?

What if I am writing this for you, to you, my dear J.? To pretend otherwise is to create a device, a literary artifice and once that occurs we are in the domain of the lie.

If I am trying to write this to you, for you. No, if I am attempting to write this with you. If this *is* what the entire effort of these pages is about.

Exit Raizel, enter I■ in the wink of an eye.

If I/ I■/we are successful, then, perhaps, there will be pages for others to read in the future. If the pages appear in the world, then whomever is reading the pages has been invited by you, by me, by I■ to read them. It is not that I am trying to shut the reader out, but, rather, that I am trying to bring you, us, in first without really knowing if such things are possible in the universe.

OK, this being established, we can go on: When/if the reader picks up this [hypothetical] book, then a relationship—even if the narrator is dead, has died—is established. Time as we know it is replaced by a field of space-time which integrates past and future. A novel accomplishes the astrophysicists' dream, it manifests the unification of time and space, then, now and then, as well as allowing for other reconciliations including reader and writer, writer and narrator, self and other, I and you and you and I■.
Let's try again and keep the reader out of it.

Certainly one can always write, "It is not difficult to calculate how much time passed . . . " or even more simply "He died on . . . and she wrote him a letter on . . . and then. . . ."
Or, "Nothing is known of what did or didn't transpire between them from the date of the review and 1994 when an entry first appeared in her journal." Then again, we (the we is once again ambiguous) find reference to him in her journal again in 1996 but nothing extensive until the summer of 1999.

We knew we would come to this crossroads. This we, clearly, is not the community of reader and narrator because the reader had no idea we would come to this crossroads and the reader has, as all travelers have, the right to stop here, the right not to continue on the road, the right to turn back. No, this is another *we* altogether. This *we* is the *we* of the narrator.

[The reader may wish to skip these minute distinctions.]

Now, *we* could write *I* here. *We* could write, "I knew we would come to this crossroads." I or I■ could write, I knew we would come to this crossroads. Or, she knew they would come . . . or he knew they would come . . . Or, I knew I would come to this crossroads. Or, I knew I■ would come to this crossroads. Or, I■ knew I would come to this crossroads. This dilemma is not a writerly one; it is not that the author is having difficulties establishing a credible narrator. It is another problem altogether.

[Dear Reader: start again here.]

If I write *I* without involving *us* in the dilemma then the stratagem, I—We—as author, think that I/We would be entering into a deception. But it would not be a literary deception which is common enough and often entertaining; it would be an ontological deception. You see, I do not believe that I can say that I am writing this book no more than I can write: "*I* know exactly how much time passed. . . ." Every time I attempt the first person pronoun as if the narrator, no, the writer were an independent and autonomous "I," I feel the reluctance and vertigo which any author recognizes as she/he find themselves setting down words that are incorrect, inappropriate, misleading—that are lies and that hint, also, of plagiarism or theft, which Hermes, god of lies and thieves would certainly understand. But Hermes, being the god of truth, would certainly punish as well.

I attempted to write, "I know exactly how much time elapsed . . . " but I couldn't do it. Even when I put those words on the page in order to present the possibilities, I felt uncomfortable. I am extremely uncomfortable having typed the words in this paragraph. The lie of the I. Philosophically, the I is a lie.

When I■ finally relented and began this, I■ didn't know, what J. probably always knew, that there is something fundamentally unreal, non-existent about the I because it is loyal, more than anything, to its own specious existence.

I was looking for some words from you to settle my mind or my stomach on this issue and so I glanced through Manual for Manuel and in the first pages came across this: "*To discover that the I is an illusion. . . .*"[28]

The I is an illusion. The I is a lie. Still, it doesn't disappear. Found out, exposed, it doesn't disappear. It may, in fact, proliferate. Years later, you were still wrestling with this dilemma:

Now that he's growing old he realizes that it's not easy to kill it.
It's easy being a hydra but killing it isn't, because if it's really
necessary to kill the hydra by cutting off its several heads . . . at least
one has to be left, because the hydra is Lucas himself and what he'd
like to do is get out of the hydra but stay in Lucas, to pass from the
poly- to the monocephalic.[29]

If this is truly an impasse, this fiction is dead in the water. But if it is a crossroads presided over by the venerable psychopomp Hermes or the more awesome magician Tehuti [Thoth to J.C.] also known as Hermes Trismegistus, patron saint of *Hopscotch*, then we are being given the opportunity to travel between the worlds. Not, you understand, only from one world to another, but also between the worlds, in the space between which is formed, like an ecotone from both worlds, in the liminal area which cannot distinguish past from future nor life from death because it, by its nature, is formed from, partakes of them all, and is far more than the sum of its parts. The corridor. The bindu point of the imagination that each and all of the possible narrators of this book are always insisting is a real world and where they all reside together in raucous felicity. The quintessential incredible, inconceivable, unimaginable, incontrovertible *we*.

So who are [who is] this *we* who pass[es] into the area in-between or inhabits it or creates it out of its own flesh? A passageway that is neither limbo nor purgatory, but is the place in-between, enriched by becoming, being, the third tone, both at one with those who have merged into each other and so entirely different, a third or utterly different note that forms when two or more tones collide. Life based upon the simplicity of the two becoming one in another form and another body altogether. And why not this note, sent out from or on the breath, meeting another note sent in a similar manner, and the two yielding to each other in awe of the invisible third that appears without warning and hovers above them, an angel, we might say? And why not then, this collaboration, after waiting so many years?

So, then, attempting integrity in a time when integrity is entirely meaningless to the culture, we have come to a decision. We will not dissemble. <We are involved in approaching a question of truth.> [see page 93]

(Uh-oh. Here we are in the place of truth we spoke of earlier, a place that seems to be ruled by Spanish [Argentina] no matter what I do to try to correct it. A region of the text that is ruled over by a deity to whom, it is clear, I [as the person at the computer] must yield.)

"If you want truth. . . ."

If *I* want truth. . . . I'm not writing this. I would never dare. You're intervening. Death is not, apparently, what ~~we~~—*I* think it is. Death is revealing itself as a strange partnership with someone to whose existence I cannot testify. You can put words in my mouth. I accept that even I cannot testify that it is occurring. An assumption, sometimes, and a hope at others. But I will not speak as if for you. I will not imagine the substance of your death.

"Death is, apparently, another opportunity . . . Death is another kind of life, both in time and outside of it . . ."

"But you have—had—to find a willing vehicle. Someone to yield. And you have been successful, *mi querido.*"

• • •

Querido:

What is being asked of me here? You are not a device. But after all these years, I want to learn how to be with you in who you are. How to be with you in the pure way you come to me. How to be with you in your death.

Another threshold to be stepped over. Another door to be opened. As long as I was acting as if this is a novel—(one looks for the exact literary device)—we were not in communication. As long as I was trying to write a novel with you, as we were attempting a novel together and also thinking I was writing this damned thing myself, the activity was murky.

You may have the desire to write a book with someone living; if so, you must have a hundred different possibilities for partners and I'm only one of them, still, I'm trying to step up to the plate. You can be straightforward about your desire; you know more than I do about the value of such an act. My task is to meet you however I can. And in the way of spirits, you are certainly not monogamous for you come to those who call while those of us who call you forth must be ready to be completely devoted to you. I accept these conditions.

When one calls out to the other side, as we do, as we must these days, there is never definitive evidence that we have been heard or answered. And yet there are signs. These signs are called stories. They become stories because extraneous, unlikely, and yet most ordinary events strike, like lightning, and set another narrative aflame or leave a scar upon bark that we can read, or we find that our bodies bear the traces of the pathway of light returning to earth. The yarrow sticks, or books appearing through the mail without warning. Your first love letter from the other side was a book about Lucas. And this is mine/ours. And so we proceed.

Do you have anything to say?

This is not a novel.

It's not a novel?

It's a fiction.

• • •

She was sitting under the trees, above her a *lucas*, a clearing, an eye. She, at first, was not thinking about the *lucas* but struck by the presence of the emptiness. It was not a burned out clearing, not formed by human effort, but a natural *lucas* designed by the trees themselves that had planted themselves in a circle. Above their green pinnacles, the deep blue sky was so clear she might believe for a moment that the twentieth century never existed. Sitting there, quite content, I■ began her habitual search for words. I■ believed she couldn't see without words and yet, truthfully, the search for them obstructed her sight.

But for whom were these words? She was sensible, she did advise herself sternly that it didn't matter whom the words were for. And the fact that she couldn't rely on memory to retain the experience became another kind of distraction. Where indeed were her glasses, papers, pen?

Recorded words certainly weren't for J. because the dead don't need to read over one's shoulder. Anyway J. was the quintessential urban man who, despite the tortures of the century that he had known intimately, still believed in the human world or, perhaps better said, didn't see any alternative. Behind him was both urbanity and barbarism and before him the same. He had been sustained by imagination, hadn't he, the wild beauty of the word, the tiny gestures of urban life, the baguette, the bottle of wine, cheese, maté, whiskey and jazz, camaraderie within the everpresent loneliness and failure. His equivalent of what I■ called a "journey" had been to explore the wilds of the highway system, challenging himself to cede to its labyrinth and see what happened when he and C. got lost in its loops and coils. They were certainly different from each other. Bless C.. She had been J.'s redemption. When she died, J. took the short cut to *Over there* to catch up with her. I▪ couldn't imagine him in the woods. Or deliberately silent for days or weeks at a time. A vacation, maybe, but could you live here, J.?

In these times of a disheveled and touristy return to Nature, I join ranks more than ever with: (a) Max Jacob who in reply to an invitation to spend a weekend in the country, said, somewhere between stupefaction and terror: "The country? That place where chickens run around raw?"[30]

I▪ as character is outside in her *lucas*, but the writer, I, is inside watching the stellar jays speeding about the bird feeder accompanied by John Coltrane on sax. Tenor and soprano. "Giant Steps" and "My Favorite Things" again and again. Jay comes screeching to a halt. Squawking. *Skwaak.* Up a third. I haven't heard this call before and I've been listening to them for years. It's almost—almost—like that other call that *swuauk swuauk* from the one I call Satchmo, the B jay whose crest is thin and scruffy, the old man who visits every a.m.. This jay is listening to J.C. and is responding within his own range. He scatters seeds from the feeder for birds like the thrashers who prefer to, and quails who must, peck seeds from the ground. *Skwaak. Skwaak. Skwaak.* ¾ time.

• • •

Several jays, the sun bleaching their wings, streaked across the eye leaving a blue trail. The white whirl of the woodpecker's wings. A code. The task, which must not be thought of as a task, was to use the eye that had opened up above her to see something beyond and to speak. To the language of trees she was to attempt the speech of silence. It was still a long time, not even a breeze in her mind. When she looked for herself she was, mercifully, gone.

She had found a passageway hole to go through . . . to. . . . A hole out of here and its cacophonies and certainties, its interminable self-centered human chatter. . . .

We know exactly how much time passed between J.'s death and *our* first contact afterwards.

Death stands there in the background, but don't be afraid.[31]

She was startled. The words appeared as if emerging from a litmus stone, a faint sound becoming coherent, a pattern emerging.

This, she realized was what she had come to believe was the confirmation of a conversation between them. The words he had written in the past emerging as the proof or the bridge to this present and so their future. She didn't understand the logic of it, but she held on to it fiercely as one does to any scrap or rag through which the bereaved can constitute the beloved. His words, his own essential signature, his DNA.

• • •

This morning's words, *From the other side,*[32] encourage me especially as so many of the questions I am wrestling with you already wrestled with. Every sentence requires me to ask the question should I write "I" or "she" or "we"? In the manner that you began "Blow-up":

> *It'll never be known how this has to be told, in the first person or in the second, using the third person plural or continually inventing modes that will serve for nothing. If one might say: I will see the moon rose, or: we hurt me at the back of my eyes, and especially: you the blond woman was the clouds that race before my our his our yours their faces. What the hell.*[33]

Let's get on with it.

We know exactly how much time passed between his death and her contact with him and we will speak of it as we see fit. He died in February 1984 and . . .

• • •

Twenty-five years after their first meeting in 1974, after the long while in which they unsuccessfully attempted durable connections, J. and I▪ were beginning again. This time I▪ made the first advance. In 1984, despite the evidence, she hadn't really trusted it or him and certainly not herself.

In 1984, though he was already dead, or because of it, he sent the book to her. I■ then read *A Certain Lucas* and did homage to the gift in public but without having the tools, that is the understanding, to comprehend what had indeed occurred, let alone what had occurred between them. To be in conversation with the dead can be taken as an exotic event and so awed, as she was by it, and honored, she was also startled and confused, dazzled, certainly, and, finally, embarrassed by what she had said in public, wanting to be taken seriously (not wanting to be seen as a madwoman, her constant refrain) and yet shy of fully speculating on the implications of what had occurred between them, she described what had occurred but without interpretation—letting the reader decide, trusting the reader to . . . etc. etc.

I wonder whether someday I will ever make it felt that the true character and the only one that interests me is the reader to the degree in which something of what I write ought to contribute to his mutation, displacement, alienation, transportation.[34]

That is, she let the writing about it distract her from what might be its meaning and implications. That is, she didn't allow herself to be fully altered, as would have been appropriate, by so startling and inconceivable, yet real, event.

Another ten years. In such a period of time, Odysseus had fought in Troy and had spent another ten years coming home. It was 1994. And she hadn't stopped thinking about him. She had J.'s photograph which she had entitled, MAN EMERGING THROUGH A WALL, his kind of lucane window, mounted on the cork board in her bedroom along with her family, her friends, the entire kinship network.

So as to shorten the introductions, the one I told you thinks of something like this, suppose that everyone is sitting more or less in the same file of theater seats facing something which could be, if you wish a brick wall;[35]

She came upon these words at 2:33 p.m. on Tuesday, August 01, 2000 long after she'd arranged and then removed the family and kin photos, including the image of J. emerging through a wall and after she'd begun the project of writing with a dead writer which she had asserted she would never undertake. Anyway, it was forbidden.

There is a prohibition against raising the dead and though she didn't give a fig for the Judeo-Christian construction of the universe, she was still inhibited by those prohibitions and their enforcements as they have been inscribed on her soul, which she had always considered colonized by the system. But that didn't mean the recognition of this liberated her.

An elemental horror of trafficking with the dead afflicts the living. She felt a shudder when Cortázar approached the esoteric in his books—the dead aren't quite trustworthy; they don't play by the rules. They are dangerous. The Navajo also experience that primal disquiet and won't enter a house where someone has died because the *chinde* is trapped within the walls. A Navajo will do his best to die outside so the hogan can be preserved—otherwise it has to be torn down.

Some of the failure of her manuscript over the years certainly had to do with her visceral fear that she was violating the most primordial taboo. Once you started trafficking with the dead, you didn't know where you would end up, but it couldn't be good.

There are several things, J., which are disconcerting here. I have spent several years coming to this writing, seeing it as the final development of what I have been doing as a writer, a final and exhilarating freedom, the ability, in the end, to put down words that reflect the reality that I have always seen, its vital nature, so many protons and neutrons banging into each other, creating an effulgence of worlds upon worlds, only to open a book and discover you were exactly here so many years ago and I didn't know it. Am I a marionette through whom, you, the dead one, are speaking? Or is this what I have being hoping for and fearing, desiring and invoking—that you are speaking alongside me on the page in ways more subtle and pervasive than I ever imagined? And, as it should be, I cannot tell the difference between my inclination and intent and yours.

There is no doubt that the things taking place here cannot possibly take place in such a strange way . . . [36]

• • •

A long, violent earthquake releasing the strong odor of sulfur from down under came rolling through just before dawn January 18th, 1994. Several bookcases, including the one where J.'s books were shelved, horizontally so there would be enough room for them all, and a mirrored armoire fell over just missing the bed where I■ and M. had been sleeping. The hill behind their house sheared along the tension and slipped ominously toward the house. Walls cracked, dishes fell off the open shelves, all the Limoges porcelain broke; each piece her mother had so painstakingly purchased by saving up for it for years and also returning all of Iris' wedding gifts for cash so the mother could buy, at a substantial saving directly from the importer, service for twelve but with eighteen dinner plates, eighteen white, moth-delicate porcelain, translucent dinner plates, and twelve salad plates, soup plates, hors d'oeuvre plates, dessert plates and bowls, cups and saucers, demitasse cups and saucers, ashtrays, and also every conceivable serving dish, bowl, tureen, carafe, ewer, jug, platter. This was her poor mother's fantasy of a life she would never have. Nor would Iris. Because Iris never wanted it, although she had briefly attempted to act the part of the dutiful daughter, accommodating her mother's dream by giving dinner parties for the first years of her first marriage, a marriage which soon failed, porcelain dinner plates or no, and the ritual then failed too, long before Iris had met Vito. Long before she had a cup of coffee in the town of Limoges itself, following a most painful fight with Vito in the Limoges tiled bathroom of their small hotel. Green squares with yellow flowers composed the floor, walls and ceiling so that they were trapped within their anger as if wound without chance of escape within the center of a bouquet of chrysanthemums. The acquisition of, but not the shattering of, the porcelain occurring long before she actually met the man coming through the wall.

A year after she had picked up the inches of broken china, broken crockery, glasses, clear and cobalt blue mixed with spilled olive oil, vinegar, soy sauce, salsa and wine, she had the cracks in the walls and the foundation repaired, the house painted, and the wall of photographs removed because M., whom she had since married, could no longer bear making love under the smiles and benevolent gaze of all their relations and ancestors. Sometimes she wondered whose eye in particular unnerved M. so much. For herself, she had not been uncomfortable under the gaze of the living or the dead, but then she had not been unnerved by folding her naked body into M.'s under the crucifix in the guest quarters at the convent at Dachau, the last station of their pilgrimage to the Death Camps, but despite what they had endured, he had shivered with the shame of it. Still the dilemma of how one honors the dead— through invoking the gods of life with all their wet and sticky effulgence or through reverting to the deep and respectful abstinence of soul—had determined not only the way they passed that night but all the nights of the rest of their lives.

Back to their bedroom. All photos now out of sight, out of mind, but not quite. Still present those ancestors, and perhaps this is what we mean when we say a house is haunted.

Finally, even though she had hidden the MAN EMERGING THROUGH A WALL behind other walls, the power that was inherent in the image seeped through all her devices even that sophisticated tool of inertia and inaction called "not deserving," "this is irrational," or "you must be kidding." Secretly, she began something, after all, she had done it once before with notable success:

June 26, 1994
Dear J.:

Beginning and end of letter. Other times, a few banal sallies and what she couldn't convince herself were his retorts. But he did say this:

"Do nothing else but try to cross this barrier between the living and the dead."

Not on the page as she was writing, but as if a voice was speaking to her emphatically in the middle of the night that no one else could hear. The counterpart of the "letters" she had been sending to him through her mind. Eight years later, she tried to reread all his work to see where he had written those words, forgetting that it had been a psychic message from him to her.

Other missives followed that I▪ wanted/hoped to identify as his, claiming she would not have thought of them herself or that she didn't recognize the language. However, they were not at all what she expected he would have said or written when he was alive especially as most of these communications from the dead or allusions to other worlds were more like visions from hell or experiences of enormous loss or danger than generous assurances. Still someone/something was placing alien thoughts in her mind. Reverting to psychology, she interpreted the images as communications from her unconscious, fears and terrors, undigested experiences, projections, not a spirit and not a ghost. Nevertheless, she proceeded doggedly, determined to develop whatever skill was needed to make this work. She was a beginner again, as unsure and tentative as she had been when she had been Iris.

Words came randomly. She wrote them down dutifully.
I■: ". . . ."
J.: ". . . ."
Etc. But they were hers most likely, she admitted. They didn't sound like him. No matter how she tried to bypass herself, the words reflected the way she thought. Her two cents imposed, most definitely. Abstract. Preachy. There. He definitely would have razzed her about her bombast. He didn't let anyone off the hook in *Hopscotch* even if he was kinder to La Maga and Talita than he was to Oliviera, and did/didn't they deserve it? He would have encouraged her to be as unkind to herself as possible if she ever wanted to be a serious writer. The only reason to allow self-indulgence in a book is if you are willing and able to make a mockery of it.

She called it writing and she pretended to be recording his thoughts but actually, it was not that he spoke to her but that, since Raizel's demise, since there were no intermediaries or obstacles to negotiate, she thought of him all the time and found him everywhere, as commonplace as dead leaves at her feet and as persistent as birdsong. Fortunately, no one read her journal where she recorded what she thought he was saying, attributing to him almost everything that came into her mind that she didn't understand and holding him responsible for a lot of rubbish that was truly hers.

I■ began to put her journal away at night, closed down the computer, initiated the use of a password even though M. was, as she liked to tease, computer-impaired and wouldn't have known how to get into her text. It was as great a change as locking the doors of her house might have been. She cordoned off a territory that no one else could enter and called J. into it. Though she had sometimes read raw pages of various texts to friends in the past, no one read this journal, no one living that is and as for the dead, who knew what they heard or saw or read. Why, the wind that had just come up might well be the invisible fingers of a ghost ruffling the pages to see what was going on her mind.

. . .

Early on she had begun to think of him as a bird. And so when a bird surprised her she was as likely to attribute the apparition to J. as to bird nature. Once again, she was encouraged by auguries with which she persisted even when she saw that she might justly be accused of making a mountain out of a little mound of horse shit. Approaching the I Ching again, this time asking for an image that would reveal something of his nature to her and it replied politely:

62 Small Traverses
A flying bird brings the sound when leaving. Let the little bird tell you, your place is below.
It . . . presents the image of the Flying Bird, the words that will cross the river of life and death.
It is concerned with making actions and the words of omen coincide through very scrupulous attention, a ritual in which every detail counts and every step is carefully measured.

She began, as she was instructed, to observe the small because that eased her. The instructions regarding the river of life and death, these unnerved her. All reassurance that there might be a connection between her and J., though she wanted nothing but that, further undid the little equilibrium she had regarding the nature of her life.

The blue jay stared at me from the balustrade, as if I, this woman in the house, might be a thief or an interloper and I thought of J. so immediately it was if I had been pecked. Then, it came, it seemed whenever I began writing. A flash of sky against the living green or the heart stopping streak of this bird soaring and descending. J. in his bird form, blue, small, insistent, curious, verbal and observant.

[Spell check, you probably have noticed, is slipping in and out of Spanish [Argentina] again. So much underlined, loud as the shrieks of these blue jays.]

The CD player has started turning itself on each day at noon. John Coltrane sliding into the room. She turned it off the first time, afraid, really to approach it, but doing so finally, mid solo. "Sorry, J.C." she whispered. Afraid, he'd come and haunt her from the other side. But, it did no good. Next day, he started up again and played through to the end of the CD and turned himself off. And then the next day. She's used to it. But not calmed by the music.

Here was I up to her nipples in music which she'd never had an ear for before. When she had met Rio, though he had never played for her, Iris had learned the way of music. The way the language of it slips into the body, then spirit enters and alters the temple it inhabits. When J. had begun slipping in, it was music that entered her and afterwards she began writing about music, about musicians, for years she pursued this without ever thinking that it had been J. all along jazzing her.

In Cortázar's "The Pursuer," Johnny Carter couldn't find the words, or the music, though everyone insisted he was a genius, insisted that he had found *it*. Too early he died of his own life, of dreadful visions and failure of the human coursing through his veins along with heroin, exploitation and other desperations. Johnny had played a horn. The way a god might play one. Johnny could see across to the other side even if he didn't have the words that could have saved him, because there are no words to do it. He knew what no one will admit: there is no saving. J.C. couldn't save his own life, how was he going to save us?

She put on a CD. "Ornithology." Black, black, black bird.

Johnny Carter saw the other side, saw *Over there* and when he came back he knew he was in hell, without access to *Over there*; he knew this and it killed him. His very own hell. Hell is always our very own. There was no *Terra Incognita* for him, no way to bring the vision back and live it, no territory, no language, no future. And so J. wrote J.C.'s epitaph, as an epigraph at the beginning of J.C's story:

"Be thou faithful unto death,"
Apocalypse 2:10

And then it says in the same small letters:

In memoriam Ch.P .

OK we have a dedication too:

In memoriam J. C.

I wanted to collaborate with Cortázar ... I▪ wanted to collaborate with J.. Want to. . . . Want.

Watch out for what you wish for.

• • •

You can begin anywhere and everywhere the story is different. Still it turns around a central fact, a certain coincidence upon which afterwards you discover you've built your life. He died. She hadn't known him really but then he died and she couldn't bear it. Something more than the writer he was died. Something in her died. Some forever unrealizable possibility. She began to think about him. She began to think she had a right to some part of his life. The clinical assessment that a shrink would make was clear. She began to write to him, pretending to write to a dead man, but writing really to a dead man she pretended was alive. And then it happened. She asked for a visitation and it occurred. I▪ received a book from a local newspaper to review. *A Certain Lucas.* It was his book. This was no accident. She/I▪ built her life around this incident.

That is the core of the story. We tell it again and again. It is the center and the story spins out from it. Returns to it, goes out again, back and forth, in all directions. I▪ returns to it again and again and I do also. Because it is an unprecedented event. Because acknowledging the event changes the nature of the universe. The nature of the universe changes or one's understanding of the nature of the universe changes. Now one is in *Terra Incognita* and discovers it is a real place.

From here it can go anywhere, spin out from the hub of the wheel or the terrible mouths of the hydra. It is an explosion of stars, a universe forming where every point is the crossroads at its center. Accordingly, this became the center of her life, in the mind or hope of a dead man. She cut his picture out of a book cover. The man is gazing at her through a wall. The wall is death. It is made of stone. She knows that wall. Once she came upon such a wall when she was visiting the countryside. There was a break in the wall and she went to look through it. She was face to face with a goat who left the herd to nibble at her hair. Eshu the old goat was looking right at her.

In Africa, they point to a wall and say, "When Eshu appears there will be a door in that wall." Or they say, "Eshu is the door in the wall."

I▪ moved to the small bathroom adjacent to the room where she was writing, and looked at herself in the mirror pressing her face almost become. Or hoped she was. Hoped she could pull it off. Hoped for the impossible. Hopes. *Esperanzas.*

> "They [the esperanzas] are always trying to see that the famas dance hopeful . . . The esperanzas called out the other esperanzas and the cronopios formed a circle around to see what would happen."[38]

• • •

I do not know how this is to be written. I■ did not know how it was to be written. My instinct is always to reach toward the letter. I■'s instinct was always, to . . . I■ was also, by nature, a epistolary writer. It is because a book is such a intimate creation, she had to address it to someone, even if J. is—was—you are—dead.

When you died, prematurely, as far as I was concerned, before we had accomplished what had been intended for us, I wrote to you immediately, certain, yes, that you would receive my missive. And by the evidence you did. And responded quickly. Quicksilver, my dear Hermes, Monsieur Psychopomp.

But if in this case, the manuscript is addressed to you, J., *querido,* it raises other literary qua metaphysical issues. Forgive me, I am reiterating what has already been said. You do the same thing so I follow your lead as if I could stop myself from obsessing. You see it is impossible to speak of this only one time as if it were not a mania, the constant and ur question upon which the entire nature of the universe—not only her/my own private universe, imagination and life—but the universe itself—stars, comets, galaxies, black holes, quasars, planets, gods, elephants, urination, defecation, ferns, history, evolution, persons, passions, wisdom, understanding—upon which the entire universe rests.

What is (really) possible in relation to the dead? And to what purpose? What does the *Thewomaninthecellar* whose mouth was sealed by external force in response to her refusal think of all of this? Does she imagine that assistance from elsewhere is possible? Has there been any evidence? Ultimately, will you be able, J. C. to speak for her in ways that will matter?

I■ wondered if a text developed by a woman who thinks she is writing with a dead man can ever be anything but a text developed by a woman who thinks she is writing with a dead man. This was one of the places she lost confidence and gained bravado by reassuring herself that there might not be any recognizable difference between a text written *to* a dead man, and a text written *as if* with a dead man or, because we don't know anything ever, a text actually written *with* the dead man, or a text attempted at the insistence of the dead man who also tells her/me nothing or . . . everything.

We are caught now between the device and the art.

Different universes operate according to different laws, yet sometimes the laws intersect and can be translated one into the other; one can travel across these trajectories and when this occurs the worlds are united. Such crossroads are recognized as the site of the divine and are given names—Hermes for example, Tehuti, Eshu-Elegba, Hekate. These are the gods of the crossroads. That is these gods *are* the crossroads.

You don't know what any of this means until you know what it means. Then you are in the crossroads, realities running through you like kundalini making you shiver and tremble, like the god on the cross crucified, or Odin on the world tree, having become the intersection between the worlds, and as you hang there struggling to bear the pain and the ecstasy, you find the incomprehensible words that you wrestled with for years and understand. The words do not easily reveal the meaning but when one has been initiated by circumstances then one knows where one is because the old words you didn't understand confirm it and illuminate the path that others have walked before. Or so you think, because you've written such words yourself before thinking you understood; but you didn't. And may not now. Although you know more than you did then. [Maybe.]

In the photo I love, dear J., you are peeking through a wall. I stuck my head through a similar wall and came face to face with a goat. Pan, I wager. In the old days they recognized that pure white goat as none other than J.C. in his musky form reeking of holy sacrifice, but then they turned him into the devil, poor dear. And what does the Old Goat think of all of it? Do the two of you meet and play chess, *Over there*, where you are now? Not down there, but *Over there,* where the entire universe shimmers.

"This ceaseless riff on our persistent and endless relationship, Julio," she whispered, smiling as she heard the accompanying long melancholy demand of the horn, the music of her soul, tortured and free simultaneously, a lament and a celebration, a narrative, a novel in sound proceeding to an ending neither the musician nor she could imagine in the moment. And behind her the old superstitions as reported in the OED—riff: "out of riffes in the earth, burning flames arose" or that "the bodies of witches may pierce through a chinke or riffe of a wall"— the rapids or ruffles or ripples or shuffles such as they were attempting now, it seemed to her.

• • •

M. had poured three glasses of wine. A French red with a fine label; he must have made a special trip to a liquor store with a wine cellar. He was paying the kind of attention he only rarely extended even to special guests. One for her, one for him, and one for . . . "the old goat," M. said.

"Have the two of you reconciled?" she asked remembering a conversation in which M. had announced that he didn't want to engage in a triangle even if the third party was only a ghost. She hadn't taken him seriously then, he had a tendency to characterize her work as "the other man," as she, in turn, often lamented "the other woman."

"He comes to me also," M. said, raising his glass to tap hers, "Salut," and then tapped J.'s glass as well. How much did M. know, she wondered and how did he know it? And what did he mean that J. came to him also?

Suddenly, she had to think about fidelity. She had been with M. for many years, but her past was seeping into her present. Fidelity, but to whom? To the man she had married or to the man who had known her first—but not ever in a biblical manner—and had initiated her? Or was it J.'s fidelity that concerned her, or M.'s?

Her heart broke for the trouble that could be brewing between the living man and the dead man who resembled each other not at all and in some instances exactly, for the trouble that could be brewing among the three of them.

"Listen," M. insisted, "I'll tell you what he was thinking; I know how a Latin American man thinks. It's a world you couldn't have a clue about but I can hear him whispering in my ear.

"I wager when you sent him that book of yours, he went into a tailspin. If he hadn't been undone by you until then, he certainly was then. What were you thinking? That he would read it as a neutral text? Don't you think he saw it as a come-on?"

She'd forgotten about the book she had sent him, so taken was she by the book, . . . *Lucas*, he had sent her. It wasn't the first book he had sent her but it was the one that had changed the world. But it was the first book she had sent J. that M. was referring to.

"It was my first published book, of course, I . . . ."

"Of course, you . . . but, remember dear that playing innocent is its own game and every man, especially a Latin American man knows that one. . . ."

"But, M., I was living in another country, I was living with Vito, I wanted. . . ."

"Yes, that's the point, you wanted and he knew it."

M. took the book from the bookshelf and all he had to do to make his point was read the subtitle on the rouge cover aloud in that musical style of longing and awe he had developed from reciting T. S. Eliot as he drove around the city in his car: *Skin: Shadows/Silence: A Love Letter in the Form of a Novel*, he crowed because he was certain he had her cornered. He came to where she was on the blue couch looking, as she liked to do, at the trees and the blue jays weaving ribbons of blue feathered light through the pine needles and he enacted the title as if they were playing charades: "*Skin*," he whispered rubbing her upper arms and then passing his hands into her blouse and massaging her breasts. "*Shadows*," he murmured, bending over her and lowering his hands past the elastic band into her turquoise silk trousers and then, "*Silence*," he gently placed one hand still scented with last nights sex, his fluids and hers in an elixir, over her mouth. Then he slapped his thigh with the thin book whose soft paper cover resembled European editions. He dropped the book to the floor and she picked it up and opened it at random surprised that it was his copy and that he had underlined it:

> The conversation of the body. The vocabulary of the body . . . A book of gestures. A book of shadows. The man who is bending over me is cutting off the light and his outline is imprinted upon my mouth.
> . . . No. Get off my back. . . . do you really believe that I wanted to accept those shadows that fell upon me like hot irons, carvings, linoleum knives. As if I wanted to be nothing but the plate or the piece of wood or the finely surfaced rice paper on which someone else's design could be left.

"It was my first book," she repeated. "It was the first sounds from a woman who had always been silent."

It had not been about sex. And she'd never wanted to have a child with him. She wasn't pretending about this. Maybe this telling of the story was all J.'s idea, perhaps it intrigued him to write about a young woman seeking him out in the south of France, dragging her lover to what would have to be an awkward meeting in which Vito could only come out the loser, and then her telling and retelling the story as if it were scripture and held the secret of the universe. I▪ had finally come to think of herself as an independent woman writing a fiction about herself when maybe she had been J.'s character all along. He was her fiction or she was his or both. Vertigo.

M. surmised that I▪ was naked again in this new prose, naked as she had ever been, and he wanted to know the reason for it. And yes, I▪ held nothing back because it was foolish to hold anything back from the dead who see through the clothes and through the body and its pretenses, and I▪ had the hope of meeting the dead on their own terms.

M. and I▪ had been reading the Nation. There an essayist noted that, for the most part, those who objected to violence in television were old, women, or intellectuals and I▪ found herself in all three categories. Is nakedness becoming to an older woman? Iris never thought she would be old, never even considered what it might be to be older. She tried to imagine eternity in order to make a commitment to J., whoever he is/was or would become, none of which, dear J., we will learn from this text.

"How can J. be coming to you, M. if he is a figment of my imagination?"

"That's not the way I read it. You're taking dictation. I know it because he is whispering in my ear."

"And what is he saying?"

M. had that grin on his face that appeared when he wasn't in this world and wasn't anywhere else I▪ had ever been. A grin without location, whose intention, therefore, can't be known. "What does he say to you?"

"He says, you never knew anything about men."

"Really?"

"He says, you still can't tell what belongs to you and what is his. He says, you would have been a great piece of ass in bed but he likes the way you're naked in your prose."

"Am I making a fool of myself, M., thinking I can write a book where someone speaks to the dead?"

"Not to me. I'm intrigued. Anyway, he's a great conversationalist, I wonder that you haven't finished the book twice over. If I were writing it, I would have a thousand pages by now."

"Well, maybe he speaks so loquaciously to you because you were such good friends in your lifetime. Compared to you, I must certainly look like a fool of myself in letting it be known that I presume we had a relationship, though we met only a few times, and exchanged only a few letters and. . . ."

"Careful, I■, you are so upset you've repeated fool twice in the last 15 seconds." I■ tried to swat him, but he leaped out of the way while grabbing two wine glasses, his and J.'s, in a graceful aerial maneuver.

I■ was having an attack of jealousy. *Está celosa.* She figured J. would understand. She didn't know if he had been prone to it himself, but the women around him must have been. There had been plenty of them. For herself, obviously, she didn't mind sharing him now with anyone or everyone, anyone, that is, except for M. She didn't usually think in terms of property rights or territory, but in the area of the creative, she insisted, "What is mine is mine."

She was glum, her lower lip was probably sticking out in a pout, and she had returned to the interminable letter she was writing to J., a letter outside the text, but its constant accompaniment.

. . . you were never out of my heart or consciousness even when I wouldn't impose upon you for more than what we managed. You had your own life and I knew, instinctively, how besieged you were and wouldn't demand more of you. And then, despite my youth, for I was not yet forty when we met each other, the kind of youth which bites into the apple that is both forbidden and out of reach, I. . . .

Here I■ faltered . . . because it would be so easy to write: I■ or I loved you . . . but that is not what it was. Iris wondered, yes, if she could love you. Or if you could love her. Of course, she wondered that. It was before she/he/they/you had had cancer and love would become something else. The love that coexists with mortality is quite different from the love predicated upon eternity.

They stayed at the pool a long time falling into a mutual and comforting silence. M. had said enough to confuse her but also enough to inspire her. In a few days, M. would be traveling and she/he/they would see how essential he might be to this text, whether or not he is a/the trance medium or whether you/J. will choose other ways to insert yourself, bodily, into this collaboration.

It's not a trope but a reality that called to I■ to be no more than scribe or to set down what has been set before her eyes to observe. She had over the years, without knowing what she was doing, developed a fine eye for the truth of how things are. And this work then, which appeared to be part fiction and part memoir was for I■ the meticulous labor of fabricating a unique little universe from the most exact(ing) observations.

On the way home, M., who is devoted to Eshu-Elegba, was improvising on what it means to mediate between the worlds. Eshu speaks all the languages of all the gods who can't, as it happens, speak to each other. When there needs to be a conversation, Eshu is there, is the inbetween. The door in what would otherwise be a wall.

I was trying, still, to keep this writing between us, *entre-nous*, while so grateful for a marriage so sweet and agreeable in its commonality of mind. Actually, I was pondering a phone call I had received from our brother, A., who thinks of you every day. How did it happen we were speaking about you this time? Q. his younger son, was at university doing an independent study on synchronicity. And his mother thought he should speak with I and get a reading list. A. had recommended *Hopscotch* and Q. was deep into it.

And I said, "I've just read it for the third time, the magic number, getting it, I think, this time and being in it or having it in me and both of these, it seems."

And that's how we got there, or here, that is to you. Was the novel a critique of those who lived in the other world and ignored this one? as A. suggested. (We'll let him critique these paragraphs because we don't want to misquote him and, anyway, as he is one of the brothers, he must have a chance to put in his three cents. It's only right, this field in which we're playing cannot remain a duet if it's the world and we're all in it.) I said I thought the book was about the difference between theorizing about the other world and living in relationship to it. Ultimately, I wrote to Q.:

. . . Synchronicity: I was lecturing at a conference in Washington D.C. and speaking about Tehuti aka Thoth aka Hermes Trismegistus aka Hermes—that is spirits or principles that mediate between and connect the worlds . . . like Hekate, Eshu-Elegba, and other gods of the crossroads. [In the book I am writing at the moment Julio Cortázar takes that role.] It was at the moment when I was describing the passage through the Duat [underworld] where, according to Egyptian mysticism, one's heart after one's death is weighed against a feather. Tehuti sits at that scale and observes the balance . . . at that moment, exactly at that moment, a feather floated down from . . . from where? . . . and landed on the head of a woman. . . .

What does this mean?

Well, first of all it's a good story. Such stories are precious, exactly because they are complex and esoteric and lead us where we might not go otherwise.

But, you say, it was winter, people were wearing down jackets, so it obviously was coincidental.

This explains nothing.

Third of all, this incident doesn't mean anything in itself, but the story opens up a path. Then one tries to discern the nature of the path revealed and decides whether to follow that path and in what manner.

It is very important when studying such things not to get literal minded or fundamentalist . . . if you know what I mean.

And then, because he's reading *Hopscotch*, I continued:

Synchronicity: I was actively thinking about synchronicity, about Thoth/Hermes Trismegistus/ Tehuti because of what I'm writing which is sort of in a funny way about Julio. Then, A., your dad, calls regarding this. What *am* I to think? Isn't this synchronicity? So, attached, you'll find Chapter 2 in which I duplicate a review and article I wrote in 1984 when Julio died and when something very synchronistic occurred.

A. thinks that Julio thought that looking toward the other worlds was a dead end. And I think that Julio had begun to realize that the other worlds are coexistent with ours and one seeps into the other and that's how synchronicity comes to be. One doesn't leave this world to live in the other, but it takes an adept to walk in all the worlds at once—to mediate between them—to hold, as the physicists would say, all the dimensions, at once. Oliviera couldn't because he was lost in his own mind and wasn't able to yield, as any adept or conscious person must ultimately do, to the other realities or see anyone else's reality, here or elsewhere. In other words, when one is in the realm of Hermes one becomes hermetic and multi-minded by yielding (This, J., is where I got a little bombastic and you can skip this part.) ~~up one's ego, by erasing oneself in favor of the god. Ego, then, is a kind of blindness. When it dissolves then we can see so much more including the others around us.~~

That's the kind of thing, Q., we get to understand, if we're lucky, when we're . . . who knows how old. Sometimes the gods are generous and break us down early, smash us, and sometimes it takes decades. But we wait, anxiously, for the blow. The question is: Who does Oliviera become after he breaks his head? Well, I think he becomes Julio, the one who . . .

So what do you make of it? And who are you? Have you dissolved yet into Thoth . . . himself . . . and, I ask my recurring question:

Is this all your doing? Whether it is or not, I still feel the need to tell you about it. What else is there to talk about when all this is going on?

There it was. M. was talking about Eshu without knowing that I was relating everything he was saying to the conversation I had just had with A. and the e-mail she had written to Q., watching one world being superimposed upon another and the second or the third space they created also being superimposed upon another world and so on. . . . How thick it gets like walking under water and then when you add the dead . . . It **is** all going on at once.

• • •

As the gods of the crossroads do not distinguish between literature and life, it's not only that something happens and the writer pounces on it immediately, making material from everything she/he sees so that no one is safe from her/his appetite for experience, but the movement is in all directions at once, what is written affects the living and the dead as much as the living and the dead plop themselves down in the living room of the novel and put their feet up on the furniture. This has happened to me many times and it's not the first time you, J., have been implicated though when it happened the first time, I didn't realize that you were sticking your *cuchlefel* in the soup even though Iris was fresh from being with you— or not being with you as I▪ was thinking then—Iris having returned to London after her adventure or misadventure in Saignon.

Iris and Vito had just been to see Rio and had returned to London, for which Vito had a fondness because it was nothing like his childhood, and he felt the gray rain tempered who he was, which was often too much even for himself. He was a big man in the manner of Brooklyn or, more so, Rome, and equally expansive in his Aries nature so full of crimson, magenta and other fires, that he required more than a normal amount of rain.

He craved London despite its wild and irrepressible summer gardens which he pitted himself against, as with a sporting competition, a lush field of emerald golden against golden, scarlet against scarlet, cerulean against cerulean and so indigo in combat with indigo until London won and it finally rained ceaselessly and he could wrap himself in his gray London Fog trenchcoat and be gratefully extinguished. He was by his nature a warrior and had found some ways to be compatible with peace by fighting for it. Here they were in London. It was not her choice. But here they were and if it hadn't been for London, she would never have met Rio and her future would not be emerging, as it is, from the unthinkable, shaped by it, its progeny.

At that moment in 1974, A. entered the room and the rain and cold of London intensified until it was the rain and cold of the last moment they had seen each other in Santiago. It was the *Dieciocho* 1972. Everyone had been alerted to expect an attempt on Allende's life and a military coup. The rain was torrential. A. had driven Iris and Vito just so close to the house of the painter they were going to visit. But no further. They did not ask where he was going nor why he couldn't take them further. One didn't ask any questions at that time even if one was in the middle of a street in the middle of a torrential rainstorm. They got out of the car in the middle of the street because if he had driven over to the curb, the water would have undone his brakes and maybe even the engine. So they stepped out into it. And A. came out also. And stood there.

"*Nos vemos,*" Iris said. "No, not ever," he answered.

Even if it had been sunny that afternoon in London, it wouldn't have been because exile is exile and so one is always outside what is real for everyone else; the sun is shining but one's feet are wet and the rheumy fevers are dripping in one's bones. It had been warm in Saignon and warm on the Italian Riviera, warm in Vito's ancestral house, but it was cold here and lonelier than she had ever remembered with a forlornness that entered the door with the stamping of shoes on the bath towel laid down by the threshold and the shaking of a black umbrella, water beading down it onto a small puddle on the old scarred wood floor that would not dry by the time A., big, nervous animal that he is, alert, restless, apprehensive, would pick it up again. He couldn't stay anywhere for a long time but had to be somewhere that was nowhere for him but an appointment or a meeting or a false hope or a hideous and unbearable accounting.

Rain, as if nothing had happened since the three of them had last seen each other three years earlier except that everything had happened. A world had been blown up, an invasion of the Presidential Palace orchestrated by Iris' and I■'s, my own government, Allende shot and killed—they called it *el golpe*—A. hiding out, and then agreeing to take refuge in an embassy, and then secretly transported to a waiting plane and then waiting for his wife and child and then living in too many houses and countries to count. . . .

I■ was able to tell A. about Rio; it was sometimes her fate to be a go-between, a psychopomp in training; they had just been with Rio; she knew how Rio was while Vito knew what he had said—this was their most useful division of labor—his prodigious memory and attention to detail and her intuitive sense, her reading of what was between the words she did or did not fully understand because of the languages they spoke or didn't speak together. She could feel something for which she had no words but which had to do with being in-between the two brothers, being both a bridge and an obstacle and, so perhaps, a sister to them, but maybe not even that then. She wasn't certain the way she became certain of it later, that is, *now*, after J had died, knowing without question that she had become a sister over the years the way a rainbow darkens into certainty against black clouds.

Iris was finishing another novel, which she was calling *Scars On the Body Politic*, in part about Chile, which she had begun in the fall of 1972, not the one she would soon send to Rio, an act which years later would alarm—and maybe arouse—M., but something else, something that was also between dream and waking, between yes and no, between did and didn't, between hope and despair. She did not know how to end it when it was raining outside and they were seemingly all awash in flooded streets even if it appeared they were sitting in a large cold living room where Vito and she also slept and wrote and spoke. A. and Vito had been reiterating much of what had been discussed with Rio and Hélène and now they were planning some actions and writing notices about them while Iris found herself taking down the words in-between which became the coda of the book. Neither of the two men knew what she was doing and each would have shrunk from being involved in such a manner if they had known—both writers, both so careful and deliberate about the words that were associated with them, the words that had their name attached to them, that were attributed to them, especially in such a time of spies and dictators, in this horrific era that should rightly have been named The Era of *Thewomaninthecellar,* but she was letting their light pass through her and they were, inadvertently, dictating the conclusion. And so a piece of work that had been conceived in Santiago came to an end. But whether there was a covenant of a rainbow in the sky or not, Iris could not know.

· · ·

Coda:

The revolution has a heart,
Ariel Dorfman

And so it is ending. The red book closes, the manuscript comes to some conclusion or not. Nevertheless one arbitrarily decides on a beginning and an ending. And nevertheless life continues to seep out of the pages and refuses to be contained within them. The pages are damp. With sweat? With tears? We do not know.

What is the last moment then before the parted sea sweeps together again? What is the last scene? What token, what sliver of bone do we incorporate within us so that we can walk away altered, with a scar on us, saying, here, here is the place we were touched, here is the place we were entered, here is the spot which can never be whole again?

Listen, this is the last moment. And as I write this, as she is sitting there writing, repeating, reaffirming, he is sitting beside her at her right arm. They talk and then there is silence. Sometimes he breaks in on the silence and sometimes she is the one to rupture it. They are like waves, one folding in upon the other, receding back into the same pool so that we cannot tell which waters belong to which rhythms. They separate, break over each other and merge. Separate, retreat, break, braid, merge. Separate, retreat, break, braid, merge. Separate. . . .

And so it is. And it is appropriate to say nothing more, except one does not have absolute control, sometimes reality steps in and alters the direction. Sometimes a bird flies against the window, and then one must stop and take it in and heal its wounds. So listen, this must be told in a whisper. The slightest rustle may betray the delicate moment. Lower your head so we may whisper in your ear.

She is writing. He is sitting next to her. But you do not know who he is. He is there, the one you know. Yes. But someone else is beside him. Yes . . . ahh . . . her friend from Chile. Reality is distorted into a thousand pieces of glass, diamonds, jewels. Each piece more perfect than the last. Each brilliant. He is alive. He is breathing. Even at this moment, he is smiling, wiping his glasses, returning to his work. Breathing. Oh, he is stirred, broken, uprooted. But he is alive. Here. How do we come together? I cannot tell you anything but that he is next to me. I cannot tell you his name. I cannot reveal where we are, who he is, where we are going, what room we are in, how long we have been here. All that cannot be known. He is short. Or tall. Dark. Bearded. Blonde. Shaven. You cannot know anything of these details which preoccupy novelists and filmmakers—these distractions. They are conditions which change and which define no one, tell us nothing. If I were to describe his heart, the muscles, the arteries, the vena cava, then you would know everything: it is exactly like yours.

He is working as I am. The two men are working together. A new work emerges from their fingers which is like a child—sometimes it looks like one of them and sometimes I think it looks like the other. And the words stand there bold, independent, even arrogant, and they distance themselves from these parents. The words stand alone. And they look up asking: "Have we done this?" Proud.

Ah, they are well taught, she thinks. Their voices merge, blend together and when they talk at the same time, one thinking aloud perhaps while the other reads the text, she is pleased to listen to this murmur, this lulling of voices, which reminds her of the sweet reassuring drone of women's voices, a harmony, a coming together. Work and love. She thinks, "speak to me," and they speak to her, they interrupt her writing. One of the asks her a question: "What do you think?" And she stops. The fingers pause in a word. When she returns to the typewriter, she does not know what the word was but another word has suggested itself because of this interruption. Something in his smile perhaps. Or in their joy of being together. Alive. Yes. Outside the wind has come up and the leaves thump and blow, the pattern of the tree against the sky different at every moment, it is the same tree, but it is never the same. I know it was not changed over night yet were the outlines traced we would have to conclude there is a great difference. How else could it be from this marriage of tree and wind? The phantom lovers who caress us, alter us, how we adore them.

As she writes this she is smiling. Why not? He is alive. They are together. . . . They interrupt, they say, "Iris . . . " and she realizes she is not afraid that they will speak to her because she wants nothing else but she is also afraid they will say something that will break the tension.

And the words. Oh the words, the sounds, their voices are white, swift, sleek, powerful. They break into her. Puncture her. She is permeated.

"Can't we say. . . ?" one of them asks.

Can't we say, yes yes yes, we can say, here now, because we are washing these words, restoring them, taking them one by one, bathing them in this blood, in this new womb, and the egg is punctured, is broken into and yet it doesn't break—imagine—the yolk, yellow, mobile, is invaded by their sharp bodies, these words, these men and it does not put a defense, it does not create a shell, it does not say, "Enough."

Oh, but you say, I have heard this before. I know about her and how she is entered, how she spreads her legs and how one crawls in and then another—one forces his way, one is invited, one is submitted to, one is seduced, one and another and another and another who disappears.

But that is not it.

She is no more invaded than they are—they enter her and she, she enters them.

Just at the moment when she is smiling, just at that very second when her love for them spills over into her fingers moving on the keyboard, she hears him say, "There is bitterness in us. Those are our people. Dying."

They were chatting, laughing, writing and suddenly without warning, this bitterness enters without announcement as if the wind had exploded in the tree top or the rose had been ruthlessly torn from its thorns, the blackberries, the currants all pummeled into a red pulp, the bottle broken and the wine running into the street. What did he hear? she wonders, what did he hear even without hearing it, what voice was he responding to? She is attentive and alert although he no longer seems to be listening for anything but she assumes responsibility on the chance that he is subliminally aware of danger, the faintest smell of invasion clearly perceived by him. His very tension is her warning. She listens to every nuance of sound, every creak in the house, every minute variation in body heat. She is protective of them as once he protected her with every instinct in his body. What does she hear?

A breath behind the wood. The rub of cloth between the legs. A finger fumbling in the pocket. A hand sliding down wood and metal. The shadows of sounds. But they are sufficient, she is not such a fool that she requires a bare footstep or a fist against the

Even insanity. Clinical insanity. Still different than anything she had ever known and not what a young woman could possibly imagine.

She had heard a voice in her head. It had said, "Stop writing the book a young woman would write." She heard it and immediately pressed the delete button on a lot of ideas, plots and characters and stories she'd thought it essential and chic to tell. It was not only about writing about an older woman, it was writing what an older woman wanted or needed to write. And the older woman wanted to collaborate with an older man. With an old man. With an ancient man. With a man who was beyond age and time. Because he knew so much she didn't know and she wasn't competing with him anymore or longing for his gifts and his privilege and she wasn't shimmying or shaking her shoulders, she wasn't lifting her eyebrow, she wasn't pursing her lips, running her cat tongue over them, she wasn't smiling and seducing, she wasn't playing the innocent or the vamp in thong panties, giving him the come-on, none of that. And she wasn't dowdy either nor defeated; she was magnetized by forces that were beyond her and she wanted to know as much as she could know about the unknowable before she died, when knowing it all would become part of the territory.

• • •

I understand something now about character and narrator, about them and myself. Here it is. What is happening in the moment is happening and so it is happening to me, happening to me while I am talking to you. You and I in the present moment. That's when I say I. But what happened to someone, even if it were only a moment ago, it happened to her, the one, inevitably I'm reflecting on, trying to remember, interpret, understand, shape. It happened to I■, not to me. The past does that. There is no way we can speak of it accurately. It is always a reflection, seen from a perspective, I becoming I■ and so a composition.

And in this case, I■ may also be composed from our joint vision, emerging not only from me but also from you, so certainly a character. Iris on the other hand is not your invention. She's mine. I try to see her clearly in the way she could not, did not, see herself clearly when she was herself in those moments when you met each other. Iris and Rio. Confabulations.

This is the progression then: Iris and Rio and Hélène and Vito. Then I■ and J.. M. enters somewhere but we're not sure where in the progression. Then I and ?. We don't know the last step because we don't know who will or won't appear.

Jay comes to a flying stop on the porch rail. Cocks head. Lowers it. Drops head further. Cock and drop. Cock and drop. Jay is listening to Steve Davis on bass. He/she can't hear it quite. I turn up the volume. Head cocks. Drops. Stares into window. Takes note. When Davis finishes, Jay flies away without a stop at the feeding tray.

Let's do it again. The cast of characters. This woman you once knew—all too briefly—when she's writing in the first person and when she is writing to you, she is I. She sometimes calls you by your name, Julio. No reason to create a fiction here. She is writing to *you*. She is not writing a novel. This is her life, her life's work, what everything in her life has led to. Nothing else matters to her. Anything that would impede the direct communication would totally undercut what she is attempting. It is the most important thing she is doing. It is the most important thing she can imagine doing. Everything in her life has brought her to this moment. Who is saying this now? I am. I am speaking about myself. Present tense. This moment. Present moment.
New bird sounds. A long demented repetitive cackle coming from the pines by the stream. Pharaoh Sanders warming up. Woodpecker, steady and rhythmic. Oboes of mourning doves and band-tailed pigeons.

If I am successful. If this is not madness. If this is not delusion. Then there will be another narrator's voice. It will speak of I■ and J.. It will be a blend. Two horns. A duet. Soprano and tenor sometimes. Sax and drums. A bit of piano. J. C. accompanied by Elvin Jones just out of jail. Miles. Trumpet. The trumpet opening the way. The long blast of the Tibetan horn clearing the way in the bardo. Drums call the spirits and then the trumpets clear the path.
Belongo. New Orleans. A funeral. The horn clears the way to unite the corpse with the spirits. That crossroads.
In the background, the bass. Keeping the beat. The low tones. The past. The original rhythm. The bloodbeat. Dam dam dam dam. Iris and Rio become one. Two aliases because they are fully invented through retrospect and reflexivity.

• • •

This is how I got the courage to begin this morning, Tuesday, July 25, 2000. I went to the oracle deck that M. made and took it in my hands and said, aloud, so I wouldn't be fooling myself: "May the one who is guiding this work appear." I did this last summer and your face appeared, Julio. I wanted more than anything for your face to appear but I didn't believe it would come up again. Chance is chance.

I shuffled the deck the way I do with loose fingers waiting for a card to jump out. And then, I don't know why, I turned the top card over knowing it was not you, Julio. And it wasn't. I don't know what it was. I didn't even look at it. And then, there was a card sticking out from the deck, and I turned it.

Welcome, Julio Cortázar.

This morning, Julio, skimming through the pages of *A Certain Lucas*. That first letter that you sent to me from the other side. I find my notes, fragments, on the back cover:

> "Whatever is possible is in the imagination or rather whatever is in the imagination is possible.
> "Every review, article, begins w such love, the writer, incl this me, feeling the need to say they knew him, trying, in fact, to touch Julio even through the print & thru death."

I browse through the pages unsystematically, beginning at the back and then, inexplicably, skimming to the front and proceeding and then, at the end, I'm back to the end, almost and find the 4 x 6 onion skin in your hand, 3/15/83.

What do you want to know first? What you said or where I found the letter?

This is what you said:

> *Your message made me feel better. I found it the day I came back from Nicaragua where I had spent a month and a half helping the 'nicas' in my way . . . Now, back in Paris, I feel so lonely without Carol that a word from a friend is more than welcome. Thank, you, I also remember that meeting in Los Angeles, we were so happy there and then. I'll send you a new book, my way to feel nearer you.*
>
> *Love,*

I won't try to duplicate your signature here . . . except this long, cursive ⟩ is close.

Where did I find the letter written on paper so thin I didn't know it was there until I actually turned the page to it:

Steady Steady, Six Already

> *After the age of fifty, we begin to die little by little in the deaths of others. The great magi, the shamans of our youth, successively go off . . . Then—everyone has his beloved ghosts, his major interced- ers—the day arrives when the first of them horribly bursts out in the newspaper and radio scene. Maybe we'll take some time to realize that our death has begun on that day too; I knew it the night someone indifferently alluded to a television news item that said Jean Cocteau had just died in Milly-la-Fôret and a piece of me fell dead too onto the tablecloth . . .*
>
> *The rest have followed along, always in the same way, radio or newspaper, Louis Armstrong, Pablo Picasso, Igor Stravinsky, Duke Ellington, and last night, while I was coughing in a hospital in Havana, last night in a friend's voice that brought the rumor from the outside world to my bed, Charles Chaplin.*[39]

You know, Julio, where I was when Charlie Chaplin died. I was walking on the beach:

> In the beginning we walk on the California beach and you say it is your ocean like the one in Chile, a little wild and gray and powerful. And you say you'll take me there when the Junta's dead . . .
> Still your son begins to draw on the dark sand. And he draws a picture of Charlie Chaplin and we laugh at the turned out feet and the round eyes and he draws a big bubble which says, *"Je suis Charlie Chaplin,"* This is a few hours before we hear that Chaplin has died but we don't know he's dead, we're just walking along the beach meeting a friend who said he'd find you and your son's drawing a man with round eyes. . . .

Of course, you know this, Julio. It's from the poem I wrote for A., "Naming Us By Our Eyes," that you and C. published somewhere in

Spain . . . I never saw the book but I remember my surprise and delight when C. asked for it after A. sent it to you. Soon after that, C. died and then . . . you.

The pieces we lose when someone dies, do they fly off to be with the dead? Is the part of me I lost when you died keeping you company somewhere? Is it easier then for each of us to die because so much of us is already on the other side and as you once said to/of me, "*so friendly.*"

So she had had a partner from *Over there* for fifteen years and she hadn't known it. She had prayed, implored, beseeched—whined—for such an alliance and it had been there all the time but she hadn't noticed. Didn't think she deserved it. Didn't think a woman. . . . This woman. . . . An American woman. A Jewish American woman from Brooklyn. . . . Such a history had made everything unlikely in her eyes. A certain confidence which determines the realization of a text was lacking.

Her friend, the poet, P., had been speaking of John Berger's last novel, *King*, just a few days before, saying "He will never write a bad novel because now he has the 'confidence.'"

She didn't have the confidence yet about this work she was attempting. Another friend, MK, who she thought of as one of her brothers, as P. was also a brother, had critiqued the last piece she had written by saying it faltered because she didn't have the "confidence" and so it had holes in it—not like lace—not the divine emptiness, which hand spun fibers had embellished, but awkward holes like those that tore the embroidered Indian cloth when she tried, some mornings ago, to remove the wax that had spilled onto the line of flowers and entangled itself with the delicate colored threads and had, unintentionally, removed wax, threads, cloth, flowers, all of it. Or like the spider web in the corner of the porch that she came upon this morning, which she assumed was spun by the spider she had transported from its niche in the shower to the deck—it had gone very unwillingly, had resisted the glass she had tried to push under its body without injuring any of its delicate legs—so haphazard, irregular and unraveled was the web, the way it is said spiders spin whose flies have been laced with LSD. She didn't know where she could find confidence and so she passed the essay to someone who had edited her work before. And she said, I need confidence, the way someone else may ask for a pound of ground turkey—free range at the least and, hopefully, organic too. Sara Blackburn was confident. Inevitably.

Having known J. herself, and his work, as well as anyone had known it, him, having been his editor, Sara knew confidence when she met it eye to eye . . . or could elicit it. And then, the poet, Paul Blackburn, Sara's ex, who I■ was reading now had translated *Blow-Up and Other Stories, Cronopios and Famas* and so. . . . And this also inspired confidence. But I had never given this manuscript to Sara before Sara died, or to anyone else. She didn't have the confidence.

But also she didn't know what P. meant about confidence. Because there is the confidence that occurs when one confides something in another, and that was happening between them, it seemed to I■ that J. was confiding in her, or that he had confidence in her, for why else would he appear? And then there was the kind of confidence A. was thinking about when he wrote *Confidenz.* And that was another matter altogether except that it was informed by the kinds of experiences *Thewomaninthecellar* was suffering. There were so many brothers, and, what was so difficult for I■ was knowing if she was or ever could be part of this circle of brothers. She hadn't ever asked anyone to translate the letter that J. had written to her on *el 21 de julio de 1976*—exactly 23 years ago today. Today. In which he had said, *". . . sé que estoy muy cerca de ti en el plano de la sensibilidad y de muchas otras cosas que nos acercan a lo esencial."*

She was lost. She was distracted and so she tried to get hold of herself and return to the matter at hand which was not about voluntary contact but about invasion. M. knew about this but he didn't call it invasion, he called it trance possession. M. believed in the ancestors. He spoke with them regularly. He didn't think he was raising the dead or violating the social order or undermining the universe or committing the great sin that would bring the world to an end. The dead were just the ancestors whose work it was, he insisted, to speak to him or others. They dictated. What was the big deal if they helped out someone who—here he was humble—could use a lot of help? The challenge was to not stagger too much like a drunk, under their weight when they mounted him.

Even when she saw that she herself was speaking what she would never have known to say, or accomplishing what she did not have the means to accomplish, or healing, even when she saw *that* occurring, she could not imagine this . . . J. present like a Buddha or a Cheshire cat or a ghost, grinning.

She was barely used to the idea that J. had become a spirit who was haunting her when she also saw that she wasn't being given an exclusive.

Spirits landed where they landed and one fell to one's knees, not necessarily gracefully, the way M. had fallen into the swimming pool in the dark when he had been following the black Labrador, Dr. Bones, who had stopped to drink. M. had sunk to the bottom and finding himself underwater had sat there, cross-legged, to see what was being asked of him now that he was down under. That's the kind of man I▪ had married when actually she was trying to become this kind of woman herself.

Later, M. looked at her straight in the eye as they were walking down the mountain and announced that Julio, not J. mind you, but Julio, himself, the one and only Cronopio, the great senex, Tehuti himself, was trance possessing him and M. was now the oracle—a holy middle-man, as deeply to be trusted as the visionary and demented Pythonesses of Delphi or the Sybil of Cumae who had sat on three-legged stools over the holy smoke pronouncing terrible words, hallucinations and prophecies tumbling out of her mouth, pell-mell, one holy letter after another—so I▪ could damn well take dictation from him. Is this, she wondered, what marriage is or has come to and she looked at her body in the mirror to see the holes through which anyone who wanted to was entering her or sucking out what she had thought belonged to her. Community property. Without any discussion, they were on the way to becoming a genuine triangle, something she had avoided her entire life. Praise the gods!

She yielded to this too as soon as she was aware this triangle had no eros to it and she honored J.'s need and right and authority to offer himself as a eucharist to whomever and how many he chose. And even in this submission, she understood that she was being educated and the chaff of her being—property, exclusivity, territory — was being winnowed away.

She had not fully realized that J. had always been the hierophant, the psychopomp, because she had not believed, after all these years, that she had had the right to find herself initiated by such a one. He belonged to others. To the world. To the worldly. And the secret code they had shared, speaking and not speaking, daring and not daring, was fully and then not fully honored in all the worlds he had inhabited while he was alive, for he had, wily craftsman that he had been, written as if everything were an outrageous fiction, a sleight of hand, a derring-do of imagination and not the investigation of and reportage from the real worlds within and without the very jurisdiction that most people asserted to be the only reality. And anyway, this Señor Coyote sometimes wrote about *Terra*

Incognita as if it were hell, the thinning of the veil between the worlds only making it even more possible for evil or danger to slide around even into the present from elsewhere, so that time no longer protected one, as if the future had ever been safe from the machinations of the past and wasn't the repository and culmination of what had gone before. Actually, it was the thinning of the veil, whatever the consequences, that intrigued J. while the distinction between the realms was what sustained I▪. It was exactly because I▪ saw that no paradise was implicit here, no direction toward paradise was extending from here, that she looked to *Over there* for hope. To him, now.

She hadn't ever thought she was living in paradise though she sometimes wished it was purgatory so there might be an end to the way things were and were increasingly becoming, but she did think there were realms that were . . . were outside such categories . . . she believed in . . . beneficence, perhaps, somewhere, and she believed in . . . beauty. And beauty was not neutral or amoral, of this she was certain; if one could be certain about anything. She was more inclined to be certain of this than J. had been. J. would have guffawed at such conviction. Other convictions, he did not laugh at. He had been a man of deep conviction, that is, principles. And he had given his life to them and now, it seemed, also his death.

And so what had started in their lifetimes was continuing. From his end, it seemed to be as simple as that. Body, no body. She had claimed not to be interested in his body anyway. But for her, it was a whirlwind such as M. and I▪ been shaken by the night before when they had put Django Rheinhardt on the boom box and in a moment they were in the swing of it, only M. had no clothes on while she was wearing only a white batiste nightdress, slightly shirred under a square of lace down her shoulders and across her breasts, the stitching by her heart slightly undone and never mended because such tears, such signs of unraveling excited M., and whatever had been implied when she had danced, so, as a young woman, was happening now between them even though M. was complaining of the vertigo of landing in the dance hall of the dead listening to ancestor music grinding dem bones into a white potion, a rhythm she knew and M. didn't and so she didn't remind him that it hadn't been her idea, but his, but not his exclusively, as it must have been J. pulling them both back into the vortex he had himself written about as past, Earl Hines and Hawkins, Bix and Bird, them guys pulling

J. toward them, he pulling her, as C.P and J.C. were now pulling her, a veritable landslide of figures falling into that music which had no boundaries or decorum and undid the psyche with its terrifying intelligence, they were all going down down and yet at the same time the future loomed and demanded that they go forward, for without that thrust and advance one's life was a fizzle.

All of this so clear, so clear and still I▪ wondered about J. and his intentions.

When I▪ wasn't playing games, being coy, when she admitted her age and acted accordingly, she knew about men and women and what is and what isn't possible and when a friendship existed or a man was reaching out. Let's see if it will stand her in good stead. Will she recognize his call finally because he's not going to play cat and mouse and she is going to have to reach out, put a hand out, down, and catch his as he comes up from nowhere, sulfurous and grinning. As a way of avoiding reality, she had been thinking that she could arrange this, it, him from her end. When, if it is to be at all possible, the energy has to come from his end. Up. From that cave in the earth. The way the myth tells it: Teeth were thrown into the earth and men stood up. An army from the white ivory of hope and despair. The best she can do is sow the original tooth. Wait. And meet whatever comes.

So this: The trembling of her/his white hands, her white dress/his white garment like so many wings beating softly, moths against the black flanks of the horse fleeing the light for the dark caverns, the fluorescent sheen of the helmeted figure who grasped her/him in his radiant arms is ultimately reversed when her/his time of emergence has arrived and she/he ascends within a geyser of blinding light, not only the sun coming forth by day, but the resplendent moon on its lunar barque coming forth by night. A procession then as the earth yawns opens for her/his cortege of spirit animals as if born from an explosion of pomegranates, ruby fireworks of hot magma and cataracts of speeding particles of volcanic light.

Yo Julio!

None of this to be witnessed with the naked eye. One must be as cautious with this incandescent dark as with an eclipse of the sun and so must use mirrors and smoky glass and must hide oneself within a cleft in the rocks as the spirit passes by.

How do we know that he didn't direct her hand from the beginning because he dreamed, as the dead are enjoined to dream, of worlds coming to be born as all worlds are from the humus he had become, from the rich, dark soil, from a tangle of roots and the smolder of decay. How do we know that he didn't come up in that explosion of smoke and magma to enter, even as she had enjoined him not to, through the glass window to sit by her bed and pass the words as through a hypnotic trance into her sleeping brain one by one so that when she awakened she didn't remember her dream, but nevertheless, felt inspired.

How do we know that he didn't call her down to him in the ways that people have, over the centuries, been called down, earth suddenly giving way so that pigs plummet downward squealing and the young swineherds traipse after them hoping for a great adventure or young boys trip upon an entrance that earthquake or flood or drought have suddenly revealed. An accident, we say, because we cannot recognize the call and think we are the ones designing the quest and so believe it is by our own free will that we find ourselves "wriggling like snakes, arms pressed close to our sides, pressing forward like snakes. The passage, in places, hardly a foot high so that one's face is right on the earth and one feels as if one is creeping through a coffin. And so, yard by yard, one struggles on, some forty-odd yards in all. Groaning. Heart pounding. Will this thing never end? Then, suddenly, we are through, and everybody breathes. It is like a redemption."[40]

• • •

She looked back over his work and saw that they had indeed been speaking in the same idiom for years but she had not had the courage that he had had and so had stifled what came to her while he disguised it in the form and language of fiction so that everyone thought it was his imagination. That it was a game. Another of his disguises. *Un jeu.* And as with any esoteric teaching, only those who were to be educated by it were, and the others, deeply enthralled by the presence of wild beauty and untrammeled intelligence were more than grateful and would not or could not, take on more. The door between their world and his world was shut so tight they didn't see any evidence of it the way a secret panel in a wall must remain secret and betray no sign of its existence. Until Eshu. . . .

And so she was both encouraged and annihilated when she desperately turned to the Holy Letters and asked the question such Letters could not answer which roughly and inelegantly translate: Help! How shall I proceed? What shall I do? What is going on . . . so on and so forth. And shuffled the cards as she had come to do with her eyes closed until a card flew out of the deck in a high arc and fell back on to the desk where she was writing and it was

ד

Dalet. The door. When she had done this, this manuscript was long started and the name, *DOORS* well established. What she felt was a mild *temblor* as from a far distant earthquake or a wind coming up suddenly just as one has spoken something surprising and passes over one, the barest embodiment of spirit that causes one to pause, no more than a breeze or shudder in its weight, but everything in its import.

> *"One of these nights I'm going to tell you about over there."*
> *Oliviera said. "I don't want to, but its probably the only way we can*
> *get to kill the dog, to use that image."*[41]

I■ awakened in the middle of the night, Akasha who always slept against the side of her bed making a den/pack out of the box spring, alert, her ears pointed upward, was listening to her name, Iris, whispered in a windy voice, but when she opened her eyes from the dream of Anubis there was no one in the room. M. was in the living room writing and though he often whispered his words aloud, he had not said her name, he had not recited the lines he had been writing, he was still grappling with exactness and had not yet begun working with resonance. Only after seeing how absorbed M. was in his work did it occur to her that it was J. calling her to what was becoming a sacred text, in that it was not entirely her own as she was consistently being reminded. She would never herself write in such an idiom and was not used to finding the hermetic so deeply embedded in the densities and vernaculars of everyday life. It was just a whisper as of someone wanting to awaken someone else. And so she turned on the light, got out of bed, pissed, returned and sat up, picking up *Hopscotch,* opened it at random as it was 3 a.m. and started reading: *"All of us, Talita, you and I■, we form a triangle that is exceedingly trismegistic."*[42]

In *Hopscotch*, Oliviera had come back into the lives of Traveler and Talita uninvited and his presence or rather his presence even when he was absent, overwhelmed, informed and disordered their lives, much like the dybbuk she was living with. I■ understood that J. would not be so disconcerting a force if he were embodied. M. would not have so much difficulty imagining how he would treat the guest, what wine he would offer him, how he and I■ might escape for a little private *tête-à-tête* or even groin to groin while J. was in the room stretched out full length on the couch demanding maté. I■ knew that M. was uneasy about traveling and leaving her in J.'s hands, phantom or real, and though she saw that his fear was as much literary as imaginative, she was taken by the trismegistic triangle, that is by the dynamic that crossed dimensions between *Here* and *Over there*. Basically, M. couldn't figure out how to close the door that had been inadvertently opened. Once J. was in the house even the door to their bedroom seemed permanently ajar, a breeze blowing through that was not the vanilla scented breath of pine but a colder wind that certainly carried the aroma, or taint, of elsewhere. When such a door opens, two different worlds coexist side by side and the door itself becomes the universe of the two of them, inspiring a continuous and befuddling interchange that occurs as the particles of *Here* dance around and partner with the particles of *Over there* in a dizzying do-si-do.

Now that J. was a presence looming large in his own absence, it seemed M. and I■ were both becoming his characters. Once, in the ways they were living out a fiction that had been written by the great shaper some thirty or more years previous and another in the ways *El Mago* was shaping their lives at the moment just as he had shaped his characters or his characters had shaped the others they had encountered on the page. Magic indeed. I■ had never expected to be the object of it. She was honored. And perplexed. And wary. Meanwhile, M. was sitting in a full lotus position, calmly meditating with a deranged smile on his face, obviously out of his mind and enjoying the journey.

It occurred to I■ that after one's death, one might be called to incarnate, to become one's characters and thus enact oneself among the living. That death was the door through which one honored the creation of oneself forwards and backwards in the act of writing and so J. was

Hail Thoth, architect of truth, give me words of power that I may intuit the symbols of dreams and command my own becoming. I stand before the masters who witnessed the working of magic. . . . Isis who worked the charm and Hathor who interpreted the stars . . . they are goddesses of beauty and of wonder and of revelation. I too am a wo/man who dreams. I, too, believe in miracles and I work my spells well to achieve them. I wait to come forth by day in Sept, city of shredding the veil.

Hail Thoth, architect of truth, give me words of power that when I speak the life of a wo/man I may give her/his story meaning. I stand before the masters who know the histories of the dead, who decide which tales to hear again, who judge the books of lives as either full or empty, who are themselves authors of truth . . . And when the story is written and the end is good and the soul of a wo/man is perfected, with a shout they lift her/him into heaven. I, too, am a wo/man longing for perfection. I wait to shine forth I, Manu, the place of the setting sun.

Querido, if I weren't ignorant there would be no story. If I had known then what you meant when you wrote, ". . . she calls him Manu," I would not be wanting to be with you here in *Terra Incognita*. I would have protected myself.

Hail Thoth, architect of truth, give me words of power that I may tell the truth of my own becoming. I stand before the masters who witness the judgment of souls . . .

Querido, I am standing before you in the judgment hall and the feather is being weighed against my heart.

. . . I stand before the masters who witness the judgment of souls, who sniff out the misdeeds, the imperfections, the lies and half-truths we tell ourselves in the dark.

Hail Thoth, architect of truth, give me words of power that I may complete my story and begin life anew.

Hail Thoth, architect of truth, give me words of power that I may create myself from my dreams of becoming.

Hail Thoth, architect of truth, give me words of power that the heart of my story may beat strong enough for a wo/man to rise up and walk in it.

> *Awakening Osiris; The Egyptian Book of the Dead,*
> translated by Normandi Ellis.

(Perhaps you have noticed that Spanish [Argentina] which plagued this chapter of the manuscript for several years and then, mysteriously disappeared, has returned exclusively for the prayer to Tehuti from *The Egyptian Book of the Dead*.)

Welcome Tehuti, Hail Thoth, Architect of Truth, Oh Great Emerald-Feathered Lapis-Hearted Ibis Bird of Light, Oh Most Honorable Dog-faced Baboon, Who Creates the World through Words.

Clearly we are all putty in Your hands Tehuti, Thoth, Hermes Trismegistus, Thrice Great One.

• • •

Now I know that something has begun. We are in terrorland. The jays listening to J.C. "My Favorite Things," are silent before it. A humming bird is perched, unmoving, on a branch. The wind is paying mind. I've written about this before: They say the river that separates the living from the dead ceases running on the Sabbath so that one can cross from one realm to another. It is Tuesday but it is a Sabbath nevertheless because the separate worlds are gathering themselves into a we.

The light in the trees. Utter stillness. The skull of a steer on the post silver in the shadow. Holy letters in the spaces between the needles. Bless you, Julio, in whatever ways the dead receive the hope of the living. Bless you.

Oops! The sun is descending behind the mountain. Ra is entering the Duat. And I can't see the keyboard anymore. I am ending this chapter in the dark.

PART IV
THE KING'S WITCH

ד

Even the smallest of you is capable of raising the dead[45]
Oral Torah

Animals and morning birds stirred as the wind picked up its yellow body, unwinding its concentric folds and sweeping away the patterns that had been written on the sand the night before, so that anyone who had fallen asleep when the wind had fallen like a rock skittering down the incline of the sandstone cliff, rolling a little at the base and then settling into eternity, would have missed the secret writing that is at once creation and augury. The woman could sometimes read these signs. She went out to see whether this morning she could decipher the sand, the chance scatter of pebbles, the random configuration of ravens, a broken twig that had fallen upon another twig, the passages of clouds. When they were transparent, chance was turning its other face, intent, to her.

Just as she didn't know whether an external hand had traced those exquisite ridges so like the salty sea astonished by gale and tide, or whether the phantom hand was still within the sharp peaks and smooth hollows, as she also never knew when she stirred the morning pot whether she was an instrument of the invisible power that had tormented her into a holy alliance, on occasion inhabiting her so completely there seemed to be no difference between it and her, or whether it had already left her and she would remain bereft, circling around her own empty chambers where something other than herself had held dominion. But what she did know was that it moved in her according to its will while she could never of her own volition or desire approach even the furthest flung curling edge of its presence. The circles she drew each day in the morning meal, stirring the cereal, accompanied by prayers, were praise cycles that invited the first form of the Holy One onto the grain and so became a sacrament for her kin who were well nourished without knowing the cause. She rarely spoke about what she did. She was not by any means certain of any efficacy in her motions and was more astonished when there was evidence of it than she was disappointed when the morning meal or the prayers she uttered on someone's behalf were no more than what they were, a tasty and nutritious porridge, or cries of anguish, her beseechment no more effective than anyone else's utterance of hope or desperation. To be confident of her power or to speak of her attempts at ritual interventions would destroy everything; whatever vitality was in the gesture vanished immediately when presumed or exposed.

She had been taken as a child but had, herself, revealed nothing of the abduction to anyone. Nevertheless, it became increasingly obvious to those around her that she was one of those fortunate (or unfortunate) chosen ones to whom they could come with their pain, their illnesses and requests. She didn't, couldn't, wouldn't refuse them whatever they asked because she was intrinsically kindhearted, or to be exact, innately broken-hearted, and because her condition rendered her increasingly responsive to suffering and its healing. Ultimately, she had devoted her life to this as if without thinking about it, without making a choice. Someone or something had asked and she had acquiesced, but without conviction and without hope. She had been ravished so gradually since childhood that only when vertical lines began to appear alongside her mouth like the blue copper lines etching the sky onto the cliff behind her dwelling through the continuous flow of water from above did she begin to see that the process of not knowing was followed by the surprise of knowing dissolving immediately into not knowing what she would know later, so that as she got older she realized how consistent and unalterable the not knowing was, and yet how deeply she had been taken into a vision and how skilled she had become in walking according to it. But also she did not speak of what she saw or did or understood or hoped for or feared because such vision was ineffable, and, also, it was forbidden to speak about such things. Twice forbidden. By God and by the king.

She was afraid of God and she was afraid of the king. These were two different fears entirely though they could seem the same, as each issued death penalties for speaking these mysteries. The great teachers said one must keep silent or one would be struck down. They said one must not speak about the unknowable as if it could be known. There weren't many who had been chosen to carry the sacred in the manner of this woman, but those who had yielded to the demand were careful not to speak of it and they brought forth whatever gifts they may have been given with reluctance, assuring whomever came to them that they had no intrinsic gifts but were merely the vessels, cracked at that, through which something beyond them and unknowable sometimes spoke or acted. Whether the voice would come or not had nothing to do with her. She had no will in the matter. She was simply there if it pleased the voice or vision that used her as its temporary dwelling place.

It was no lie that she and others like her often didn't remember what they had said when the voice, in whatever form it had taken in that moment, spoke. They awakened out of a trance or a deep sleep, perplexed and sometimes so ravaged by the holy intruder it seemed as if spirit and self could not coexist in one body and, accordingly, the human presence had been forced into exile. As if they had been plundered and so fatigued as to be beyond curiosity, relying on the audience to tell them what had been spoken through them. This did not mean, either, that they themselves weren't affected by the presence in their body, the voice in their mouth, even if they didn't consciously remember. Whether they were marionettes, altered by the nature, sequence and repetition of the gestures they were pulled into, or whether they were like hand puppets bearing the internal imprint of the fingers and palm that bent them now this way, now that, when they were chosen in this way, they were no longer only themselves, or rather what they would have been if they had been forever untouched. They were shaped, marked, altered. But who they became and where and to what they were being called, that was always an enigma. About what they saw or heard when the invisible, if only for the briefest lightning flash, became manifest, it was forbidden—that is, it was impossible—to speak. This death that the great teachers warned was inevitable if they spoke what could not be spoken was not a punishment, it was not imposed; it occurred in the ways that apples fall from trees. To speak of the ineffable was to trivialize or distort it. This was axiomatic, despite one's best intentions to render the awful, the terrible or the splendor. It became something else than what it was and, accordingly, one lost the connection with the essential. "Between illusion and truth, there are seven hells and seven heavens," she used to say, but nothing more. It was the way she understood the injunction against graven images. Even though, or because, people had created them, they were taken for the thing-in-itself. What had frightened her as a child was her ability to look through rather than at. No, what had frightened her as a child was her inability to look at and her propensity to look through; she never saw what others saw and they did not see what she saw either, although they tried.

Even as a little girl, she had been pursued so that she would explain how she knew that a child was on the way or that someone would die or whether a dream augured well for the community or whether the dreamer was cursed from the actuality of carrying monstrous imagery. But she always remained silent about the source of her knowing. The source and the way of knowing were the same and she couldn't reveal them.

When she was five years old she dreamed a fight between two men in a field of stones. The younger man had tried to restrain himself from returning the blows of the older man, but when the older man insisted that the young man give up the small portion of grain he had harvested in a nearby field he had cleared painstakingly by hand because of some imagined affront to the older one, some specious impudence, the young man picked up one of the stones and gesticulated with it, wildly tracing wide circles in the air quickly turning dark from the whirl of it, a sight more frightening than if he had actually hit the old man on his temple. From this the young girl surmised her young uncle and his companions were coming home early, and when she told this to her mother, the woman didn't even stop to wipe her hands on her skirt but clenched her fingers around the young girl's upper arm and dragged her to the stream, dunking her in the water holding her under so that she sputtered and spit, her mother hoped, all prophecies from her mind. When her uncle did indeed return, her mother would not talk to the girl for a week thinking that the girl had been the cause of this misfortune.

"He was a mean and selfish man," the uncle said about the landowner. "He wanted it all from the beginning. That was his plan, to have us do the work and then dismiss us just before the harvest was fully completed. It doesn't matter, a storm came just as soon as we left and he hadn't brought the grain inside. His crop is ruined. Ours would have been too had we stayed. We did bring something home because we had suspected his cruelty and selfishness and so we hid our portion away bit by bit during the nights. It was in a small cave not far from the road but well outside his fields.

"Let the girl teach us to dream," the uncle said but the mother would have as soon hit him with a stone which was just as well for the girl did not know how the dreams came to her.

"Why would you be punished for teaching us?" her neighbors asked. The girl bit her full lips which if they were fruits would have burst with juice and honey. This is what she had witnessed: Cut off from the source, people died. They languished, they lost their souls, they became lost themselves, meaning fell away. It was not a punishment, it is how things

with these large, staring, bovine eyes, with these broad calves, with this broad mouth that uttered words he would not have understood, with this voice that sang the vowels at dawn in a soprano and in an alto at nightfall, as she had been taught, as she had been taught to raise and lower the register of light, this woman who uttered these incantations that he feared; not this woman, he did not know her. Their equality derived from this discrepancy. He had had to cast a wide dream net to catch her but when he did, he didn't know who or what was in his hands. He was ignorant in his examination, she could have been anyone and he would not have known the difference; he did not know he had found her, he may not have even known he had found someone, he was so dense with fear and ordinary, regal, inexpungable self-importance. He wanted something and she was the means to it. She was an instrument. A tool. Nothing more. A convenience. A mere means. Nothing in herself. But he didn't understand what this meant. He thought she was his means. His convenience. His tool. His mechanism. An apparatus of his will.

He condemned her. He banished her. He sent war parties against her. Then long after the king had banished her, he searched for her. It was not the scouts he sent to be certain she was gone, that was not the pursuit that worried her, it was his own relentless searching, long after he had been assured that she and her kind were gone, that there was no trace of her, that she would not, could not return, that the land had been cleansed of her, that it was immaculate, his kingdom. Long after that, he set out each night, hungry and lusty for her, wanting her and hating her and searching her out and entering into her and probing her and never stopping to know that he had found her, that she existed, that she was someone, that having found her meant she had eluded him and his decrees. Yes, he had found her and so his triumph was his failure but he didn't know it. He didn't know when he had her in his hands while she knew instantly who he was the very moment his rough hand, the hand of a warrior, perfumed and oiled but not gentled, not kindly, not asking permission, entered her dream.

"Why doesn't your God protect. . . ?"
"Shh," she placed her fingers over the mouth that had sweetened hers so many times so he would not violate the sacred.
"But, if He were . . . ."

"We're here, aren't we," she said. "Where we've always been. So don't . . ." And placed her hand between her husband's thighs where it was warmer than any other place.

"I'll protect you," her husband said again in his sleep because he loved her and he wanted this.

She snorted or she wept. Because she loved him and she knew his body and how the seeds he carried had taken root in her and that the children who were asleep over there in the corner where the tent she had been forced into so they could vanish—wife, husband, children, flocks, herds, possessions, vanish—touched the sand, liking, as children do, small places that remember the angle where her upper arm had pressed them against her breast as they had nursed, and where the smell of the animals lingered and mingled with their own animal smells, all milky cheese and pungent like the goats and sheep and cattle and camels, when they put their small fists in the animal joints, between the forelegs and the belly, or where the shanks rubbed against the groin, where they could get lost in the sway of moisture, oils and odors, small places, familiar, distinct, secret, their own.

• • •

The flaps of the heavy tent woven of sheep's wool are closed from the inside where the king is sleeping, or, more honestly, is pretending to sleep, convincing himself that his prone position indicates confidence and his confidence is based on reality.

This is what I see. The king is alone, half reclining against the rugs and pillows, holding something in his hand, observing it, weighing it, as one weighs an artifact that is calling one to task. A spear, for example, which has been used to bring down a goose or an eagle. The dead bird in one hand, perhaps, and the spear in the other. In this age, it was a spear or an arrow or a slingshot, but in another time, this time, it would be a gun and there would be no difference except in the number of geese or eagles the gun could easily kill and how quickly. But perhaps the dead bird has already been put into the sack or has been handed to whomever will pluck its feathers and prepare a meal or create a trophy from what was once a life. The gun is still here. In the hand. As one cannot interrogate the gun without interrogating one's own life, what is the question that is being asked as the man feels the weight of the gun, examines its design, tosses it up and down slightly in his palm. This king is not interrogating a gun. It is long before anyone has thought of a gun. If the idea of gun had occurred, he would have one and the gun, the spear, the object he is interrogating would be side by side.

The king is holding his member in his hand as if it were an object, feeling its weight and the lack of it. Tossing it up and feeling it land on his palm does not excite him, it does not claim its past life no more than the bird can be restored to life through the king's regret. The king is wondering about the nature of the object in his hand which is not an object either, neither living nor dead, neither independent nor dependent, neither him nor of him nor separate from him nor not him. His hidden scepter. The source of all power. And feels the weight of it. Examines the naked purple darkness of the blind reptilian head whose hood had been cut away when he was an infant. An original tempering. A covenant, his father had told him when he came of age, between him and his God and his people and their God, between him and his people therefore. He has studied all the covenants, the series of agreements his people negotiated or accepted that he was supposedly the guardian of. Pacts or deals? Which were they? And this one, where the infant was flayed, so to speak, what kind of promissory note was it that had been negotiated before he had the will to concede or to make the sacrifice?

He has heard stories that the Egyptians believe that at their deaths their hearts will be weighed just like this against a feather. If he fails the test, he will be exiled to the realm of Apep the adversary, the serpent of the dark, then thrown to Ammit, the Devourer, to be consumed in the fire of her mouth. He does not know the language of the Egyptians anymore, that is, he does not know it well, and he has been taught that it is a language that holds untruths at its core, but he believes that there is a realm with an adversary, and he is afraid that when he dies he will be thrown there because his heart has become a stone. She does not believe this, but it is not because she does not know suffering. She distinguishes two kinds of suffering, that which is not understood but is mitigated by understanding, and that which comes from the State and has no reason. That is, the suffering that comes from the State does not have a nature, it is not a creature or a wind, it is a crude thing, it is made with a thoughtless and heartless hand and so it is without beauty.

Around him all the forces of darkness are gathering. Or these are the words he has mouthed in order to gather his armies and the loyalty of his people. It had been his greatest challenge to find exactly the right words to rally others around him. This is not how he had imagined his role but what he learned once he had stepped into it. He had imagined . . . he didn't know what he had imagined . . . it was all gone now, his hopes, dreams and fantasies and what remained of it all was the necessity to find the words which would lead him forward as if he and his people were one body—not even a column of ants walking or a swarm of bees led by a queen—but one body, one war horse, the legendary centaur who had no rider and he was the head.

There are many legends of kings who were first boys in the field among the herds or learning the ways of the wild. He was one of those living in his father's house according to the ways of what runs and what flies. We understand when we hear these stories, that the beings of the wild are the great teachers and so we feel dread as the king leaves his teachers for the whispers that are heard in those walls that have been erected to create a great inside against the great outside. He was a young boy of the fields far away from the place where the people would build a palace for a king that would embolden them. But he was a young boy who had not learned to distinguish his dreams from his desires. At the very same moment that he had felt a desire surge inside of him he had heard a clamor from outside himself, "We want a king." The two calls—the first from within and the second from without— were so very simultaneous that he could not interpret them but as a sign and he allowed his desire to grow to meet the call. He did not know why the people wanted a king, how a desire to be ruled was experienced within someone. He had never felt it. He had only felt the desire to run, to gallop, to leap the stone walls and all restraints, to follow his own will. Now that he was coming to appreciate the need for exactness in language, he paused in his ruminations. To follow his own will. To follow. There was a will and he was to follow it. Whose will was it? Had his will not been his own? Had he indeed followed and is this what the people had wanted? Had they wanted someone who would yield to their will as if it were his own and follow it, carrying them with him because they didn't have the wherewithal to follow it themselves. Had they not wanted to follow *him,* had they not wanted the wild ride, and if not, why had they chosen the best horseman in the region as their king?

The horses whinnied in the distance. It was a sound that comforted him. He had taken to noting what he had been thinking when the horses

PART V
RIFF

ד

On top of everything, I don't buy your God," murmured Johnny. "Don't come on to me that way, I won't put up with it. If it's really him on the other side of the door, fuck it. There's no use getting past that door if it's him on the other side opening it." Kick the goddamn thing in, right? Break the mother down with your fist, come all over the door, piss all day long against the door. Right? That time in New York I think I opened the door with my music, until I had to stop and then the sonofabitch closed it in my face only because I hadn't prayed to him ever, because I'm never going to pray to him, because I don't wanna know nothing about that goddamned uniformed doorman, that opener of doors in exchange for a goddamned tip, that . . ." Poor Johnny, then he complains that you can't put these things in a book. Three o'clock in the morning, Jesus Christ.[46]

The Pursuer

You pretend you're not playing with fire inviting someone, a ghost, to come in. You say you're always talking to the dead and then you say, because it's Yom Kippur, the day that honors the dead, the day one is or is not written into the book of life, the day of atonement, even the atonement for speaking with the dead, that you're finally going to talk with him:

"Hello, Julio, how are you down there? Do you like your quarters? So, you'd like to write a book together. No problem. Come over any time. You don't even have to knock this time. I'm not afraid of you anymore as I used to be when I was afraid you'd come in through the window of my one story house, which you could do with your long legs easily enough, though you could have come in through any door; I didn't/don't lock the doors."

Then you're walking up the mountain again, full of rhapsody because it's just a wee bit cold and the man coming down the hill on his bicycle, white beard, shorts, is smiling benevolently and you've done your mantra, TRUST, and he says, "getting cold, isn't it," and you smile, "Yes," thinking it's perfect, everything is perfect, you're climbing the mountain, you're not afraid, TRUST, it will come out OK, because today is the holy of holies and God is good, don't you know, just like everything worked out for the best during the middle passage and the holocaust and the atom bomb dropped on Hiroshima and Nagasaki and depleted uranium replacing the sands in the Middle East, and just like that private moment that Wong introduced Oliviera to when some ones were torturing that man in China, and slowly, so slowly, cut off his genitals, or the perfect example of extraordinary memory and unexpected compassion among the thirsty, raging decimated refugee herds of elephants coming upon their own, dead, gray ashen dead, do you know how very gray an elephant gets when he's dead, or how very, very ashen the bull becomes when he falls down with bullets or spears in him from a helicopter or a van or men on foot and crushes his own viscera with his own weight and then lies there while they hack away at his tusks until his kin come upon him with the tusks gone, gouged out, red holes as large as the entrance to hell on his face, or *Thewomaninthecellar* who could be anywhere and who is anywhere and everywhere and who you are not supposed to forget, get it? Not supposed to forget. But still you're thinking, TRUST and, in fact, you are trusting, and it is right to do so, you stop to write down something on the folded piece of paper you carry in the front pocket of the shirt you always wear now just in case, with the pen clipped on to the flap, some immortal words or perceptions you're afraid you're going to forget and then you laugh at yourself that you think writing this down is more important than . . . than what? Than the sunset at the right moment whether or not you make that appointment and you're late for it—you know it's supposed to be 6:55, and it's almost that, it's 6:30, and you've got a good ¾'s of a mile to go up, get it, up, but no, you've got that new age mantra in your head, "Everything is as it's supposed to be," like the child soldiers in Sierra Leone or the very young people dying of cancer, some even before their lives, their own lives have really started, thank you for the new environment we've been given that is like the moment millions of years ago when the world switched from carbon to oxygen and now it is going back again, if you can't eat bread, eat cake, you can't breathe air, live without, or the old growth trees that are being cut down, no, everything is exactly right, the right people in the right place shooting the wolves reinstated in Yellowstone and Arizona, and the nine befuddled adolescent condors outside your window that are roosting on someone's porch and shitting all over it and being chased away with loud claps and garden hoses because they didn't learn to read maps well enough, though the Fish and Wildlife bulletin says they're intelligent, and didn't listen to the instructions to stay within the narrow vicinity of the tiny little preserve that's cut out for them up there on top of the mountain, on top, get it? They're supposed to live up there where God comes sometimes while people have the entire lower realm, and the guy who shot up the Baptist Church or the guy who shot up the Jewish Community Center summer camp, or the kids in the schools that took the guns and shot up their buddies who didn't like their trench coats, "Everything is just like it's supposed to be," TRUST.

No more crucifixions, you mutter to yourself or g-d, strange isn't it that you can't remember, ever, how to spell that word and have to rely on spell check; no more crucifixions, so you're not going to be hurt climbing the mountain alone, alone in the woods, as the sun is going down, going toward God. Right. And you're thinking, it's Yom Kippur, the holy of the holy, and you want a glimpse of God and you've been praying all day, so you deserve it. These prayers will protect you like they've protected people through the ages. Right! And then you get the idea that J. whom you're going to contact, that J. needs you. You've been thinking this all summer. J. needs you because he still wants to write as if he weren't goddamned sick of it by the time he died, as if he hadn't done it all, to perfection, yes, p-e-r-f-e-c-t-i-o-n, as well as anyone ever had.

And then you get this idea as you're walking up the mountain, having finished making your silly little notes on the folded papers you will paste so carefully into your journal, and you walk blithely along, thinking it's OK if you don't get to the top for sunset because everything is going to be OK, hunky-dory, and you're marveling that you're 63 and you're alone in the forest and not afraid, not of bears or mountain lions, actually you're not, and you wished you had remembered to put a note in your wallet that says, "if a mountain lion or another wild animals causes my death, do not hunt it down, I was in its territory and was its proper food," but men, men are another issue and you are afraid of them for good reason, you think, but still your step is so springy even though you're at 8,500 feet and climbing, climbing, how did you get so agile not doing exercises, not doing yoga, not working the steps or whatever sports equipment is the definite rage now, kick boxing, and suddenly as you're trying to recognize where you are, there's the tree that . . . and there is the corridor, isn't it . . . and there are the two . . . and the fallen . . . and you come upon a sign that you don't remember being here where you are or are supposed to be, having been walking another five, ten minutes up at such a—brisk, lively, youthful, bouncy—choose whichever adjective you want, you used them all feeling so satisfied—pace, and you walk a little slower and more cautiously and then you realize you were walking so fast, so nimble, so sprightly, because you are walking back down— can't tell down from up—TRUST—yeah sure—and are down to the beginning of the hike, there's the goddamned gate across the road where you started out saying, ROAD CLOSED TO CARS.

And what were you thinking, dear one, as you were bouncing along? Well, you were thinking that you had made a mistake. That you had been so excited when you were a young woman that you'd come across someone who thought the way you did even if he was far, far ahead of you and you'd never catch up, and now, of course, you'll never catch the sunset, you were late to begin with, it was going to happen at 6:55, that's what it said on your computer, Yom Kippur, the holy of holy, begins on September 19, 1999 at 6:55 p.m. and you had to stop to make some notes for the goddamned book that you claim is only for you, or for you and J., or for God, g-d, god help us, and so you couldn't keep your appointment with g-d up at the mountain, couldn't make the effort or the sacrifice, couldn't resist going to the store to buy a lighter, couldn't resist putting the letter into the mail—it'll only take a second—and then, then, you turned around, you were so infatuated with yourself and what you were writing, thinking, you turned around and went back to the beginning. Well, at least, you didn't indulge the thought that He sent you back. And so you start out again, trudging this time and admitting that up is harder than down, and that your ticker was having a time with it and that you shouldn't push it and try to trot or gallop because it isn't certain your heart can take it—and anyway, admit it, you didn't have the strength or breath—and people die, even you dear, could die despite your mantra TRUST, don't push it.

All the time you were coming down the mountain when you thought you were heading toward the heights you were thinking about J.'s darkness. How you hadn't noticed that A. is right, that Julio didn't trust the other side, that he had always known that what was on the other side was going to get you the way it did in each of his stories: the axolotl ate you; the woman who had been beaten again and again and was waiting for you in the middle of the bridge, freezing cold, she entered you and took your life and left you there; the man, you finally found the story A. had told you about, the man on the motorcycle who was besieged by strange thoughts he didn't understand. Desperate to fuck the woman he had fallen in love with, he didn't know he was inhabited by the man who had raped her and who had been offed by her friends; he wasn't himself anymore, he had become the murdered man rapist back to do the deed again, the dybbuk had found someone who was likely to give himself up to this, was happy to find a chick to love, and wouldn't notice, he was so empty himself when someone moved in and so and so, on and on, and so on. The dead aren't benevolent, they aren't the ancestors, *Over there* isn't paradise, and anyone who plays with the trickster gods better know that life isn't a bowl of cherries and Tehuti isn't a little singing ibis bird.

And so now you're climbing up the mountain and you're trying not to dwell on it because you're thinking about so many things, and trying not to care about missing the sunset and you're thinking that you'll go to the top anyway, because you started out and you have to finish, because that is the way one does it without hoping for a certain outcome like a sunset or a pot of gold or healing or longevity or enlightenment, or being noticed by the great beings of light, certainly not that, that's not why you climb the mountain or sit on the zafu or keep silent as you have been trying to do for two weeks and haven't managed it for one day, not one day and even today, the holy of holies, when the phone rang at 7:45 and then again at 8 a.m., you thought about answering it when you had said, no, no, no, today of all days, I will not answer, not even if it is . . . or . . . or. . . . But at least you didn't answer it. At least you turned off the monitoring device. At least you went upstairs and turned off the ringer. Opened the drawer, read the instructions on turning off the phone that you've kept with the hammers, screwdrivers and other tools, sneaked some fresh, organic sugar peas, or cheese and crackers, wondered that you can't remember how to turn a lousy phone off when you've done it so many times, wonder that you've interrupted this to do it, go now. . . . Nuts. Nuts will keep you going on this day when you're supposed to be fasting and not writing, certainly not writing.

What you know is that you're certainly a little nuts even if you've talked to someone every day, being mostly silent has made you a little crazy. Crazy enough. Crazy enough to think that J. had gotten it wrong and you have it right. That he'd never made it across to the other side where it was . . . wasn't. . . . And you have an idea that you'll write the story of climbing the mountain twice. Once will be the way you'll tell it . . . the way you're certain it will happen because you TRUST and it will have a happy ending and once the way he would tell it, the way you will try to faithfully imagine how he would tell it. About a woman who does it all right, sits on the zafu, talks to the dead, does all the rituals right, keeps silence, or doesn't, but her heart is in the right place, and she's praying her heart out, and she prays the right prayers or doesn't, but she is sincere, she is so sincere, sooo sincere, and she goes up the mountain, and she meets the man on the bicycle and they great each other cheerfully, cheerfully, imagine such a word in these times, like Isaac Babel who believed in merriment, can you imagine such a man who believed in merriment— merriment!—after he was arrested, someone asked the arresting officers, "Did he try to make a joke?"

"He tried."[47]

She meets the man on the bicycle and he greets her warmly, perhaps a touch too warmly, seems like he wants to talk, but she has to get to the top before the sun sets, we don't know why, it is just essential, and if she doesn't, then . . . danger . . . like walking down a city street—don't step on the cracks—so she rushes ahead, doesn't look back, doesn't see him put down his bicycle, doesn't see him begin to walk about the mountain, big grin on his face as he ogles her ass. . . .

It took years to find out when Babel died and whether it was true or not that he was dead because the authorities kept trying to cover his death up even after he was rehabilitated. Rehabilitated is a lovely word that means they created a false case against you, tortured you until you admitted it was all true exactly as they had invented it, or told you it had been as they were torturing you, and you began to believe their story was the right story because they were trying to save you and save your family as they really didn't want to torture your wife and child before your eyes until you admitted it was all true, but what choice did they have as you were lying and didn't care about anything else or anyone else but cared about your lies . . . that you didn't when you did etc. . . . those men whom you had not been able to believe, you had not been able to believe would ever indulge in torture, other things yes, starving whole populations, maneuvering things so thousands, millions probably, died of manipulated famines, sending innocent people to work camps in Siberia, preventing them from having any livelihood whatsoever, except what they could scrape together secretly through the good offices of the tiniest handful of people who had enough courage to feed and protect those they love and respect but only because there were no computers then, and so the relentless tracking of movements and activities that would have prevented all kind and compassionate and brave interventions, was not yet possible. But, if there had been, well, we can't even begin to imagine how inconceivably terrible it would have been then, destroying literature, intelligence, culture, compassion, all rational thinking for the sake of some fantasy of a revolution that ultimately has only to do with personal power and state control. In the meantime, all the best of them were sometimes worn down into thinking maybe it was for the best in ways the poor intellectual couldn't possibly understand. Babel, Mandelstam, all of them, inevitably lost their balance, distrusted their own perceptions. After all, everyone around them was either testifying to the rightness of it or was dead, had been shot, and usually both—and you know there had to be a reason they took them away, didn't there?

Why not ask *Thewomaninthecellar*, she will explain it you. But not torture, they wouldn't/couldn't torture—not torture—none of them could believe in, imagine the rumors they had heard about torture. So at the end of the entire terrible history they introduced the word "rehabilitation" which means that they admit there was no case against you, or against your husband, wife, son, daughter, lover, because you're dead already, and they let your wife, husband, son, daughter, mother, father, lover or someone else, ultimately, probably no one you ever knew, a stranger, a kind stranger this time, glimpse the letters that you wrote while in prison, the ones that say how sorry you were for what you said about others, (not the ones that say you're sorry for the things you did, not the false testimony you signed about who you were (not) and what you did(n't), no one ever gets to see those.) These, someone gets to see, or someone secretly reveals the letters Isaac Babel wrote at the end, and this case it is Vitali Shentalinsky, deputy chairman of the commission created in 1988, forty-four years after your death, by the literary community for "the Artistic Legacy of Suppressed Writers," who discovers among many other files, "Case #419, Babel, I. E, where he said that he was sorry that he signed false testimony, that it wasn't true, that he never . . . and neither did the people he said did . . , the ones he loved, they didn't either . . , no one did . . , he didn't . . , they didn't. . . , you didn't; it was all a bunch of lies you just couldn't stand the pain when they tortured . . , couldn't. . ."

In retrospect, as A. N. Pirozhkora points out, knowing about torture doesn't help anyone because Babel once had a conversation with Yagoda, then head of the secret police and asked:

"How should someone act if he falls into your men's paws?"

"Deny everything," Yagoda advised. "If one denies everything, we are powerless."

But as A. N. Pirozhkora writes, "Those words go with Babel into prison, but the advice failed him."[48]

> *My primary obligation as I see it is to remove this terrible stain from my conscience. . . . The thought that my testimonies not only do not serve the matter of clarifying the truth but are leading the investigations to mistaken conjectures torments me unceaselessly . . . I ascribed anti-Soviet acts and tendencies to the writer. . . . All of this is untrue and has no basis whatsoever. I knew these people to be honest and staunch Soviet citizens. The slander was called forth by my faintheartedness during the interrogation.*

And at the trial he said,

"I slandered myself and others under duress."

These are, according to the translator, Anne Frydman, your last words at your trial and the last words we have of yours. [49]

It wasn't anyone's fault, ask *Thewomaninthecellar,* no one can stand that much pain and the torturers know this. The very ones you couldn't imagine could ever torture, they know exactly how much pain to inflict, in what combination of physical and mental duress; they don't have to apply more, not as much as would kill you but just enough to make you sign against someone you love and who trusts you. At the end, they tell your wife, husband, mother, father, children, cousins, lawyers, anyone who might still be alive, if anyone is, that they have killed the someone who created the false story and documents, who got all the necessary testimony from others upon the basis of which you were tried and shot, or that whoever did such a terrible deed has, nicely, kindly, thank you very much, committed suicide. Now your work which they confiscated when they arrested you, or which they found when they came back to search the apartment they sealed, or the miserable tiny room without furniture you were sharing with how many others for the second or fifth time, and which, now, they can't find, burned probably, your journals and your handwritten manuscripts, the single copy of the short stories you were working on, the ones you begged them to let you work on while you were in prison, this work, it can finally be published. The union of writers which means those who survived what you didn't/couldn't/wouldn't survive even though you did your best by publicly taking a vow of silence, can now publish an honorary volume and have a gala evening reading in your honor with people coming and testifying what a great guy or gal you were but when the volume is ready for the press, they ask so very politely, *sotto voce,* ". . . that story, maybe you leave that one out, save it for another time when. . . ." That is what rehabilitation means.

This is what Nadezdha Mandelstam says about Babel . . . Nadezdha, whose own Osip Mandelstam, the poet, the one she calls M., the poet like there had never been a poet, as they say Babel was the short story writer like there had never been a short story writer, she says this of Babel . . . and this of Mandelstam. . . . Well, you'd better read it yourself.

You'd better read her *Hope Against Hope,* or Antonina Pirozhkova, who was Babel's second wife, what she says about Babel and how it was, you'd better read *At His Side* or you will remain innocent and innocence is dangerous, believe me, innocence is dangerous; it is lethal.

But, I didn't tell you what Nadezhda Yakovlevna Mandelstam says about Babel in *Hope Against Hope*, which I just brought down to the computer so I can copy her words exactly only to notice that something has spilled on the white letters on the black background on the black, lilac and gray book cover, and what has spilled, I don't know what, borsht perhaps, has filled in the H and the o and the p, g, a, i and it looks like blood, that is what it looks like. Blood. I could wash it off and I won't.

Page 6, the very beginning, four pages into a text of three hundred and ninety-five pages, so you will know at the outset what it was like, when she is addressing the questions of a daughter of an important *Chekist,* a member of the *Cheka,* the secret police, who had "told his daughter never to admit that she had done anything wrong, and always to say, 'no.'" This man with a cat, who "could never forgive the people he interrogated for admitting everything they were accused of. 'Why did they do it?' The daughter asked, echoing her father."

And Nadezdha Yakovlevna Mandelstam says, "Whenever I hear such tales I think of the tiny hole in the skull of Isaac Babel, a cautious, clever man with a high forehead, who probably never once in his life held a pistol in his hands."

And toward the end of he book, before Mandelstam is arrested for the second time, Nadezdha Yakovlevna writes, "That winter I began shouting in my sleep at night. It was an awful, inhuman cry, as if an animal or bird were having its neck wrung. . . . I still frighten people with this terrible cry at night. That same year, much to the alarm of my friends, the palms of my hands started turning bright red at moments of stress—and still do. But M. was as calm and collected as ever, and went on joking to the end."[50]

Even later, she writes, ". . . I was considered particularly lucky because I got a letter—the only one—from M. and thus learned where he was.

> *"I was given five years. . . . My health is very bad, I'm extremely exhausted and thin, almost unrecognizable, but I don't know whether there's any sense in sending clothes, food and money. . . .*
> *"My darling Nadia—are you alive, my dear?. . ."*

"I immediately sent a package to him there, but it was returned to me and I was told that the addressee was dead."[51]

So much for jokes and merriment.

There was a time when you used to black out or blank out when reading such testimony, too much dark, or too much light brought to the dark, and so missed something, and after that read without understanding, skimming more and more and so, and so, until you were startled awake by your torpor and forced yourself to retrace your steps, to go back to the beginning and start again, so slowly now, so very slowly reading word for word, and pausing between lines so you can see the hand that reaches up to pull another tooth from the mouth of Thewomaninthecellar, you can see it so well that you can feel what it is doing to the woman . . . and so you learn, better than meditation, to be present and not look away.

After you had learned this you were so happy that you had found someone who wrote about *Over there*, because you needed hope and if this world is hell, then isn't *Over there* paradise? You didn't get it that he felt, thought, knew, saw that *Over there* was dangerous, too, and came to get you like a man in a green chair reading a story about a murderer coming up the stairs with a knife to attack a man reading in a green chair. . . .

So you were going to write two versions of one story of a woman going up the mountain at the end of the twentieth century, the last Yom Kippur of this millennium, and quickly moving toward the millennium itself—that black hole—and having faith, TRUST, despite everything, despite Inquisitions. . . . Your own ordeal too, the one you, I■, went through, you aren't an innocent, not entirely. You don't want to make a big deal of it, as it wasn't as if they killed you, imprisoned you or tortured you, though a man had stood up during a talk you were giving—it was some years before you meet Rio and so you knew something of what he knew first hand—and pointed his finger—there were several hundred people in the room—and said in a loud if very shaky voice: "That woman should be burned at the stake." It wasn't as if she (Iris) wasn't followed by the police for years and it wasn't as if they hadn't created false testimony against you/her and it wasn't as if they hadn't poisoned Iris's neighbors against her and it wasn't as if the equivalent of the *Cheka* hadn't deprived her of a livelihood for several years. No, I■ isn't an innocent. It isn't as if she is saying it can't happen here. Despite everything, though, despite Inquisitions and the Holocaust and the Bomb her country—not the enemy country, but her country—had dropped, she still has hope or faith or trust and believes it is her task to TRUST even if it kills her. But, trust isn't what is going to kill her. Something else. Having trust is the test. In what? Trust in the existence of . . . that is on the other side of . . . and when you go through the corridor . . . there is a door and on the other side . . . is . . . and maybe you see it only for an instant . . . and it is sufficient even if afterwards you die of people. Even if whatever is on the other side couldn't/wouldn't/doesn't interfere. Never. But it is there and that is what you TRUST.

She (I■) believes, demons or no demons, that what is on the other side of that . . . door . . . is . . . she wouldn't even use the words benevolent or not benevolent . . . out of that category . . . it just . . . well . . . it just . . . is. And that is sufficient, she thinks.

She had been thinking that he would write the story another way . . . who knows what happened to her at the top of that mountain . . . death, disappointment, emptiness, banality. The man she met who smiled at her so benevolently, how was she to know that he was the one, not her, who was in touch with the spirits, waiting for such an opportunity, praying and meditating, patient as a tick, his desire for love, for fusion, for connection, for submergence, to be lost in the deep green leafy forest of another human being, his Daphne, at last, and having had an inkling that his wish would be granted on this day, this holy of holies, he would find her, the one with whom he would be in alignment with the deity and determine, according to his most sacred intuition whether or not she should be written into the Book of Life. Who knows? She realized, as soon as she had this remarkable plan, that she couldn't write it for J. or pretend he was dictating a text. She isn't half as good as he was and much as she thought they were, somehow, in cahoots, it wasn't a literal collaboration if it was a collaboration at all—if anything, an influence that was effective and affective, but more than that she couldn't assume or assert, and so she couldn't write it nor try to take dictation and then say, "J. wrote it. You know like Yeat's wife taking dictation, from the invisibles, *A Vision*, they called it with Yeats claiming it was his—she was only the channel, the instrument, inanimate as instruments are for the entry—naturally he put his name on it, because if it were angels dictating from *Over there* it was definitely for his sake that they were doing it because, after all, who was his wife and who knew her and what kind of rep did she have?

So I▪ thought, she would write a few sentences, they would most obviously be the same sentences as in her version, so she would have to go first, though that wasn't an ideal plan, except that it made her look like the buffoon she was becoming and why not, as she was under Tehuti's tutelage, with his blood cousins Hermes, Eshu-Elegba, both tricksters. Because the only way to get you where you need and want to go, you must be deceived, misled, hoodwinked, because otherwise you won't go. Where these spirits want you to go is not the swept path where the brambles have been trimmed into formal shrubbery, in shapes, g-d help us, oblong bushes escaping containment at regular intervals, and occasionally burgeoning into deer or griffins or harpies and then smoothing out again into the staid, green rectangular walls that so carefully demarcate the safe space and its secure possibilities. Being devoted to the trickster did turn one into a kind of clown, albeit sometimes a holy fool, but she had no illusions, thank g-d about the holy part, and so it would be transparently what it was, writing his view of the story, it would be a literary device, an artifice, the kind she'd been complaining about and trying to rid herself of, but pointing out its existence and inevitability also, in the book, and so the mechanism would be blatant and obvious, but being unable to avoid it, she would continue it until it was necessary to turn the page—she would work it out with the book designer—and then she would write: "Read 'Moebius Strip,'" let's say, or another of his stories, no illusions now, she would leave it to the reader—call this an interactive text if you want—to intuit how J. would have seen I▪, this foolish woman tripping up the mountain, and what he would have imagined transpired, or couldn't possibly transpire, from such a beginning.

And so, yes, you're thinking all of this and then you manage—some years on the zafu have to amount to something—to put this and everything out of your mind because you've discovered that you're talking a mile a minute inside your mind, first to no one in particular about the book you're trying not to think about, and then, less likely, to J., and then to g-d, or that is what it sounds like, and you realize that meditation is about silence and there's no chance for anyone or anything, ancestor, angel, deity, to get a word in edgewise because you're going at it, what you think, what you see, how grateful you are, TRUST, how you're doing it, yattita, yattita, it's all you, you, you pretending you're climbing to the Mountain because of—yack, yack yack, TRUST.

Sssssshh.

Then you get there, almost to the summit, though you've missed the sunset, and you're really tired and your heart is going bang, bang, bang, and you find yourself praying, Dear G-d, help me get there if I'm to get there, it's beyond me to do it on my own. And just then, yes, though the road has been dark the way it is after the sun is scheduled to go down, you are struck directly in the eye with a point of light from the sun which hasn't set, and then the road turns and it's dusky again and when you look up again as you're going along you see sunlight, amber, sweet running honey amber hanging in the very tops of the tallest trees, their pine needles forming great golden nets and between a green lattice, the half-moon is shining down on you. This helps. You've got a second wind and you try to go faster, but you can't, and so you don't, but you hope, don't hope, it's not about hope, it's only about . . . it's not about anything, just don't hope, just be quiet, damnit.

You don't speed up and you don't slow down and you walk at what is a possible pace, heart pumping but not breaking, and there is the dome of the last great hill rising to the left and the dirt road continuing to the right, rising slightly, until you have to climb the steep rise trying not to step on the broken pale mat of alpine moss pinks, you call aphrodites, and you come to the very edge, the summit from where you can see the desert stretching out pale yellow, as if a giant had pressed it flat and smooth with his feet, almost nine thousand feet below, and the little town you live in is down below in the green nook of other lower ridges, and there to the left, to the west, there is the brilliant red sinking disk of the sun. 7:03 p.m.. If you didn't remember that Huxley, with all his faith in *Over there* got blinded looking at the glory of it, you wouldn't have looked away but you do, and J. and his darkness be damned, you can't refrain from saying, "Thank you," and "Thank you" again. Trying to find some respectful silence with which to meet this moment, you get down on your knees, yes, you do, let J. write a satire, let him find the terror or ridiculousness of the moment, whatever he wants, J. is the trickster, but you're looking at the sun, and it's dangerous, the light is, and you know it, so you bow down for a thousand different reasons, you bow down, full prostration.

When you're up on your knees again, a slight bird-like cock of your head and you notice a tree to your left, you only have to move a millimeter and it covers the sun and saves your sight. When you look again, the tree resembles the Burning Bush. You could describe it, but let's be respectful here. The sun is setting. 7:05. The tree *is* the Burning Bush.

Now, it is 7:09. Now the tree is just a tree. And that's that.

PART VI

ד

Little by little, his senses grow disembodied, and he is hoisted and turned over on the black plains; he no longer sees nor hears, nor smells nor touches, he is gone, departed, let loose standing straight as a tree encompassing plurality in one single enormous pain, which is chaos resolving itself, the shattered crystal fusing in an orderly pattern, the primeval night in American time. [52]

Julio Cortázar, *The Winners*

M. came in like a delayed storm. One weather front meeting another before it could be decided which would pass and which would hover and then clothes, candles, books, birdseed, everything tumbling out of his arms as we moved toward each other. "It could have been a month," I said.

"I can tell that," he said, "just by looking at you."

"Or three months."

"You can take three months if you wish. I'll bring you food."

I could see it. His car pulling up to the driveway. The secret honk. He would take my note carefully pinned to the door: Please honey, bring hand cream, kefir, twenty 3-day votive candles green or blue—no images, and certainly no Virgins on them please, birdseed, fish, rice crackers, cartridges for the printer, 2 HD High Density disks for the A drive, a novel, please honey, a good novel, or two, I'm reading ten books a week, and a new Tony Hillerman novel, write to him, tell him I'm desperate, Nadine Gordimer, Toni Morrison, Ondaatje, Berger, Garcia Marquez, something. A. He must have written something new. Look through the mail again, surely he sent a manuscript. Look through the bookcases, make sure I didn't leave anything of Julio's behind. I don't know what. Yes of course, I checked the last book. Go on the web. Who knows? Miracles happen, particularly around Julio.

He got out of the car stamping and blowing on his hands, placing the bags of groceries, "paper no plastic, yes I know the weather is bad, but that is how she insists it be done, no plastic," and the lifeline of supplies that he had brought with him and was putting on the porch out of the way of the snowstorm that had won and was dumping itself everywhere.

Then the tentative knock. Could he come in for a moment? An hour. An overnight. "It's snowing for God's sake. I have to wait for the snowplow."

"It comes in the morning."

OK. He won't talk. He won't ask me to talk. What is there to say? Each week, less and less.

That is the future. This is the present.

"How many novels did you write?"

"I have a few thimblesful of words."

M. is intrigued. I don't say anything. Snowbound, we relinquish our walk and make a fire before which we tell the stories of the last weeks apart.

I tell M. a dream. Three snakes were coiled about each other on a telephone wire. One drops down to the ground, ten feet long and follows me to my office, insisting itself into the room as I reach for the drum to . . . I don't know what . . . to accompany it wherever it wants to go.

"Tehuti." This is the first word that M. says. "I can see that Tehuti was with you," he says.

I would not have thought of Tehuti. But M. remembers that Tehuti sometimes carries the caduceus, is the god of medicine, of astronomy, of writing.

And then he speaks about Tehuti, the holder of the secret knowledge, the one who mediates between the worlds, who inscribes creation in the Akashic records, the one who gives the words of power, the healer. I begin to reel at the extent of my forgetting and the way I cannot wrap my mind about this neter. All the more reason to pay attention. But there is another kind of attention that can be paid. The kind that occurs when the mind abdicates its hegemony and gives over to what it cannot understand.

Who is Tehuti? I am wondering. Who is this god that is between Julio and myself? Who is this god that I forget to honor, whose rites I do not know, whose domain is so vast I can't encompass it, healer, trickster by association, more hermetic than mercurial, who appears like the coyote appeared, striding down past the chair where I usually sit to watch the flickers and the lazuli buntings, taking in the territory, wondering if it was the right real estate for him.

"Julio was with you, was he?" M. muses. It is different this time, the way he asks. He accepts it. He understands. "He is a powerful spirit, that one," M. says and begins speaking as he is used to do, telling me what I wrote, what it means, how I spent the time, what I am thinking, what is coming. I have been waiting for this, waiting to tease him, waiting to challenge his assumptions of who I am and what has transpired and what I am to do about it. But, also, I have been waiting for him to come so that all the pieces can be put together, so that I can know more than this sentence and then that sentence, this bird and this silence and this moonrise and this intimation and that whisper and that wind down my back. So that through his seemingly, rambling observations, a self I didn't know though the parts cohered, might make itself known.

But something has altered and M. is different too. M. is speaking of all of this but without inserting himself within it. He is aware of what occurred between us, reading my face or movement, or seeing through the mirror of time so that everything that was is as plain as everything that is, however it is that psychics or mediums or clairvoyants, clairaudients perceive what is entirely invisible to everyone else. He is at the theater. We are the actors. The script was written by the invisibles. By witnessing the play, it becomes real, it lives, as memory does, in an arena we can both enter, agree upon, and respond to together. We are together in this. I can reenter the theatre now that M. verifies its reality. We are together as members of the sacred audience. How is this possible? M. is suddenly not jealous. And so he doesn't need to be part of that drama that passed and, needless to say, neither of us knows what is coming. And for myself, I do not need to keep him away. This is no longer a private drama between Julio and myself. How can it be, if Julio is a spirit? No one has any rights to spirits. Spirits aren't monogamous. Isn't that the point? They aren't monogamous and there isn't only one. Plurality all around.

Write a second book, I instructed I■. *Living with the Spirits: A Household Etiquette*.

How we fight over the gods:

There is only one and everyone must recognize that one. Or? Or we'll kill you. Or the other approach: this god is ours and you can't have this god. We are the chosen ones, the true bloods. This is our way, our Book, law, ritual, fire, pipe. It is the true way and you can't come in and partake as if it was given to you. It will never belong to you even if you go through the seven fire hoops of conversion.

"I was maddened when he first moved in," M. says soberly. Then the memory of the madness comes over him like a spell and I can see that he is fingering it like a coat of many colors or a cloak of invisibility, something that will alter him if he throws it about his shoulders. His eyes are beginning to glow but with the cloak only in his hands, he is safe to observe it, putting it on, even to test its fabric, will change him again on a cellular level. He had been, as he put it, out of his mind because he had known when he first encountered J.'s presence in his home that J. was a real spirit and so to be reckoned with. A spirit had moved in, as spirits do, without asking permission. One moment one is living alone and the next moment one is tripping over a shoestring or finding that one is speaking about the most private feelings or ideas to an audience. M. and I∎, lovers for so long, were no longer audience only for each other. Now there was a third. The private was public as the inner life became inhabited by someone, something else, both alien and intimate. And she wasn't treating Julio as if he were a spirit, but rather she was tongue in cheek about it, cat got my tongue, Cheshire cat at that—a woman having an affair and admitting nothing.

As soon as he entered the house, M. recognized that I∎ understood fully that J. was a spirit and she was no longer cavalier about it. "Coy" was the word he had used to himself as he watched what he sometimes thought was a spiritual flirtation replacing the erotic one, a flirtation he had considered substantially more naïve. "My wife is spending all her hours in someone else's mind." His words.

Or someone had taken over hers. She began to know the other mind better than her own. She offered herself to him so that he might mold her as he saw fit. She offered no resistance. She opened to him as well as she could. It was what she called her creative practice. Not a muse; she wasn't willing to call him a muse. The opposite. Someone back from the dead. Someone she had invited to return. Unpredictable. Insistent. Potent. More than that, in his way, omnipotent. The way a woman can yield, a back bend, legs spread for balance, palms flat on the floor, heart like a flower, the center exposed. But earlier, without admitting he was a spirit. Calling the man back from the dead and not admitting he was a spirit.

There were two birds seated on a branch of the tree in front of her window. Both facing away from her. Both absolutely still. Looking out into the green belt. What were they observing? She had not seen birds settle this way before. Jay moves but only changes branches. They are still watching something. Several minutes have passed. She is still now too. Several more minutes have passed. That time she was always remembering in Costa Rica, when they had stayed too long in the rain forest and had made their way in the dark, their path illuminated only by fireflies, they had emerged at the entrance to the birds who were absolutely still, watching that light of the sunset that had been invisible in the jungle. She begins watching the clock. She has watched these birds for years. She has never seen them pause so in the afternoon. Immobile. Observant. She will not move; she is afraid her shadow will disturb them. Pygmy nuthatch flies through. No affect. Wind comes up. They are still. The phone rings. The female grosbeak flies to the feeder. The jay scratches, looks for mites under his feathers, flies away. Ten minutes or more has passed. How still the world can be before what we cannot see.

But I■ was different now. The person who had spent the last week with J. was a woman through and through, sobered and focused. I■ had clearly been to hell and back in the last day, had descended to the river Styx and brought back the dark waters. A gift had been given to her and she was determined to do what was necessary to receive it.

"He came across," M. whispers. "And you said, yes. I can see it on your face and the way you move through the house. You are light again. Almost a girl again in your movements and a woman in your soul."

And so M. knows. He knows and soon I■ will know something at least.

"How fortunate," M. is speaking as if he was with us, "that you have recognized him, that you are offering him a welcome, a place, have made him an altar where he can be. It will be a good thing for the world that he has a platform from which he can teach us something, can sustain us."

M. is dead serious. Jealousy gone. We're a household of three. *Fait accompli*. A *ménage à trois* of a different order. I look around. The pale blue, almost lilac, throw covers the torn upholstery, but will the spirit see through the disguise? I have had to stop drinking wine for a while and I don't have a decent bottle of red to offer J. Buy a bottle of red and drop it off before you leave—the snowplow will clear the road well enough for you to go to the market, come back and then leave.

Everything turns around and tips. North pole slips the few feet that turn the world upside down. Rivers rush elsewhere, oceans slip over the land, mountains are buried under green sea water, pine needles like seaweed in the cresting waves, the fluorescent fish of the deep take their first breath of oxygen straight up.

Aho, Julio. How do I proceed? You don't like autobiography, you say, you don't like the occult. What is it you mean by this? The constant and unquenchable I, I, I? The confession of family secrets and the descriptions of sexual prowess and exotic escapades? And the occult? The assumption that "everything is for the best," that each bird is a messenger, that one has been given special powers that one can use flamboyantly so that tables climb the stairs and cold winds blow open the door and hurricane through the house?

You are so quiet, J.

The strange seeps through your books. Tigers are in the house. The little teeth under the wristwatch bite. Real teeth or just the bloody time eating away at us? These ghosts that appear to me from your books, they bite.

Spirits or not, death will come. *Thewomaninthecellar* depends upon us. The guns move against those we love. If the spirits exist, then we bow down and say, "Welcome. Thank you for coming."

The words rise up in my throat, the invocation that I know from the sacred rites. I whisper the secret words to myself and turn to M. who, as is his custom, pours three glasses of wine.

PART VII

ד

We are in the beginning of a third story. A story so tiny, so imperceptible, we might not even recognize it as a story. Nevertheless, it is a little world, as all stories are, discrete and coherent within itself, and it has taken the infinite time it takes to get from one world to another to reach it as its affinities are with elsewhere.

And who tells this story? Well to begin with, I suppose I is the one telling the third story. And who is I? I is the one who is exploring I■. The one, presumably, with an overview. The part of her that has become reflexive and reflective. I suppose you can call I the narrator. Omniscient? No one is omniscient. I is the one who is trying to understand something instead of running away from it. I is still I■, as I■ is still Iris, but carrying another perspective. Omniscient in the way of narrators who have developed a broad perspective, but who still must be careful not to pretend to omnipotence. The narrator is constrained by the laws of reality and reality is a far larger territory than humans imagine when they define it and so constrain it.

These are the kinds of considerations I■ learned, in part, from J.. Certainly, his existence confirmed the possibility for her of a writer walking his, uh. . . , her talk. And certainly he was a model for the young Iris who wanted to learn how to craft language so that it conforms to reality. Conforms to reality instead of limiting reality. Conforms to another reality whose laws one doesn't know. This instance. Even if I knows more than I■ what can I, or anyone who is not of that world, possibly know about *Over there?*

Who is I? This is not the time to ask such a question. Such a question can't be answered. Sometimes, there are questions that should not be asked.

Let's proceed. Here begins the glimmer of third story. The one that, increasingly, is located in *Terra Incognita* and so by the time it is rounded off it may be too far away from us to be visible to our naked eyes. The one where nothing is familiar to or certain for I▪ and where I▪ sometimes sees things that can have no words accompanying them yet. A world that needs to be named in order to cohere *Here* though naming is not necessary in its intrinsic realm. I▪ reflects on the two earlier stories and the third world they form in time. Why is this so important to her? Because in the telling there may be a path to what might be called . . . uh oh . . . J. would surely cackle if I▪, or I, wrote "truth" yet again. She means how things are. How things really are.

I▪ didn't realize fully, hadn't acknowledged, where she had learned so much of what she knew. It wasn't that she had learned it directly from J., but that she had been called to him and his work, originally, by sensing that he knew something of this world that she hoped existed. And then, encouraged by who he was or seemed to be, she had gone on to learn about it the way one must, through the ether. A literary critic may trace influences from J.'s work to this work of hers, but really what will be found are called co-arising phenomena.

Sweet Iris, she didn't know better, so she asked for his talking stick. That was not what she really wanted; she would have found it worn, shaped to another hand, the wrong size. She liked to wear M's worn, time-muted flannel shirts, but only as night shirts. When she went to sleep, they were a means of wrapping herself within his embrace, or his dreams, but during the day, she didn't even hang them in her own closet.

What J. ultimately offered her was the assurance that the other side existed and could be known. And if he could find it, then, she hoped, she could as well, but, she insisted it be in the day time, in the very bright light of day. She was a loner and did things on her own; she only needed to know there was a way. But, if it happened, correspondingly, that he was shaping her, hands on, by the way his words or thoughts impacted her, she would risk it all for the ability to move along the way.

Iris and Rio met because Iris was a young writer, not because she was a young woman. They met because Iris needed to know the difference between reality and fantasy. If Rio lived a life in accord with his fantastic prose then he was living a real life. If he lived a life distinctly different from the visions he was offering to the world, then everything was fantasy, i.e. fraud.

That's the truth of it, is it? So, Iris really came to *interrogate* Rio. You, I▪, used the term advisedly earlier, knowing from your long acquaintance with *Thewomaninthecellar* what such a term might mean.

I had no idea of the nature of the seduction you were contemplating.

Iris had no seduction in mind.

No, it seems, she was set on something more pitiless.

It takes a long time for the future to change the past even though the past is always impacting the future, the future being only potential until it isn't. It is going to take a long time for I▪ to reflect on interrogation and its implications. Oh innocence, how it persists. At least I▪ recognizes that this description might be apt, Iris will never understand why a seduction could be small potatoes compared to an interrogation of soul. But I▪ is old and experienced enough to sense horror looming in the area of self-scrutiny. But that is as far as she has gotten at the moment.

The insight begins to work its way into her consciousness, but she has to leave it in the background because there is still something she must say in order to be free and so she continues as if nothing disconcerting was said.

Despite what has just transpired, when I▪ reflects on Iris, on whom she had once been, "smart and sexy wins the race" are the words that persist in her head though she has done everything to expunge them.

Let's not go through this again, you've whipped this horse to death.

One last time, there is something to be said that wasn't said before.

I can't imagine what it is.

I can.

Well, let's try, but also know I have something to say about it.

Do you want to say it now?

I'll wait. I like the last word. But, after you run through this, it will be time to get on to the real audacity.

I▪ cocked her head, as birds do, when they are alerted, but there was nothing there. Then I▪ continued as she had originally intended.

In retrospect, she wasn't clear within herself whether the thought that Iris had been a flirt had come out of the scorn an older woman might have for her younger and most foolish self, or whether the Iris she had been had truly once lived by icy seduction. When I▪ reflected on that part of her past, she felt a certain revulsion; it had an insidious quality she hadn't recognized before. Unscrupulous, she determined, and, if that were not bad enough, ineffective. It clearly hadn't worked with Vito unless it was the formula *he* had been living by. What Iris had learned from Vito was the extremity of desire, the way she could extend herself so far toward the other that ultimately she disappeared herself entirely. The old pull taffy game.

Try as she might I▪ couldn't pull herself out of Iris' fixations: watch as she falls into the pit and vanishes.

There were other ways of disappearing. Vito loved to talk and by default, she had learned to listen and this served her as a writer better than any other approach. Even writing was a form of listening; the words formed within her by means she never understood while her task was to listen to them and set them down. A chance conversation, the aroma of a half-heard phrase lingering with the cigarette smoke as a couple passed in the street, sweat and irritation, perfume and languor, an argument in a restaurant enmeshed in the odor of meat frying and blue cheese, a dispute in the bank and the affront of cleaning fluids and the terse smell of money, the ways good-byes were said with or without lipstick or after-shave, the earnest entreaties of a child, sticky fingers, grape juice and chewing gum, such fragments that had served as auguries in ancient Greece were the elements she focused upon in order to create a fiction. She never thought of herself as the originator but rather the crafty one who stalked forsaken phrases in the night streets. She couldn't be talking or lost in her own thoughts and hope to catch them—they came fast as rats emptying out of the dusk between the government buildings in Bogotá on their way to Chile where she would meet A. and everything would begin—she and Vito astonished by the rodents' casual audacity—or the sulfuric flare of lightning before the rain came—you never got a second chance. She was still as a cat. Waiting. She didn't particularly care for cats, house cats, that is, but J. liked cats, and so the phrase.

She had called it their division of labor: Vito talked and she listened. That's how she got silent initially. But look, she is still giving Vito the focus. An old habit. Vito has been out of the picture for more than 20 years. Ultimately, he was not responsible for her descent into silence and what became of her, even if Iris had never known what was expected or hoped for from a woman. What I mean here is that Vito can't take the credit for Iris gaining the basic tool she needs as a writer.

At first, Iris had assumed they would have children, but she didn't know if the idea occurred to her when they first met or when she met his mother. It never happened. Her own mother had, according to Iris, "shot her wad" with the Limoges and was allowed no additional expectations. Her father was *Over there* but neither Iris nor I■ had ever made a phone call to him and she didn't know if he would have wanted her to have progeny or not; he had left the task of influencing his daughter in the domestic arena to his wife. For himself, he had wanted what a son was supposed to be to a father, and so when he had an opinion about Iris it was that she would be independent of it. Iris might have stated, at some time, that children would have been too noisy but we don't think she ever thought about it consciously. Ultimately, children became an idea that no longer occurred to her. She was, increasingly, moving toward the dead not the living. Over time, she would admit that she preferred their company. Their gravity. What they had discarded, relinquished and what they knew.

Frankly, silence quickly ceased to be a reaction to unfulfilling love affairs, but became original to her again. The paraphernalia of personality began to fall away the further Vito *et al* receded to the background. She was able to recover a way of being from the vast ocean of a real self that was habitually colonized in the time and culture we are discussing. Slowly, over the years, she made inroads—if one can make inroads into the sea—dove deep, learned to breathe under water, lived as if among the great silent creatures of the basso profundo, learning their songs. It wasn't that she was lost in her own thoughts, she had to eliminate them as well; anyone's chatter, his or hers, would obscure what was coming toward her that she was designated to receive, alter, and send out again in another form.

What might have been entirely random, of no consequence, might become in a work of fiction, the very core, the center, the inauguration of vast worlds. But it might come like the faintest breeze or a ripple in the tide, and if you missed it, it was gone. A single phrase in a jazz composition that later became someone else's opus—but you had to be fast.

Like that dinner in the south of France when Iris had first met Rio. An evening that could be judged in the course of a lifetime as quite unspectacular, unremarkable, entirely forgettable, commonplace in certain crowds, but that she was in Europe and traveling enhances the ordinary moments. Instead, it became a core story, the kind from which the direction of her entire life developed, an origins story, in fact: ultimately, I is who she is because of that story.

Critics had mistakenly labeled her writing as ephemeral but that was only because they couldn't put their finger on that quality that defined it, her concern for the vanishing, for the eerily hermetic. As if she were standing still, outside of time, watching it ripple by. As if she were trying to capture the nature of wind or letting it capture her. Of appearances and disappearances. That is what she was looking for . . . a few words, murmurings, a hint of before and then what might be, but no more than an intimation, the faintest trace of possibility and then something manifesting from it, absolutely certain and adamant, but for a moment, and then that vanishing too.

Her friend's art show: A gallery on La Cienega had agreed to paint the walls, ceiling and floors shark white, so sharp and highly lit it cut into you, set you on edge, blinded you. The artist, Celia Glazer, had aligned many flats of strawberries on several dozen highly polished reflecting trays set on white tables. That was the show. The strawberries. When you entered, it was forbidden to speak and no music either. No hors d'oeuvres, no wine. You walked among the berries as if, in the ways of the old great courts of Europe, a select audience was invited into the royal chambers to observe the dying. Well, the strawberries *were* dying. We are all dying, Iris reminded whoever would listen, herself included. It was the essential information without which no text, in her mind, had substance.

The curators suggested that visitors return in a day or two, and then again, and then again. The photographer came three times a day, as the gallery opened, in the middle of the afternoon, and then at closing time. Black and white, and then color film which when developed showed, at first, only white and metal and the changing shapes of red and then, progressively, the alteration of form and the smudge of the subtle sequence of the colors of decay. First the perfume and then the odor and then the blue, slightly hairy stink of the rotting fruit. It penetrated the gallery's walls. Ultimately, they had to have a funeral, but it was private. The curators thought Celia was missing an essential photo opportunity, but she insisted on a small gathering, the family, so to speak, and no media. Artist, curators, a few friends (Iris included) solemnly buried the remains in the atrium between the reddest roses and the white star jasmine. They dug up the grass, laid in the mash of what had once been plump and upright berries and covered it with new grass sod. In a few hours, no one could have known that the land had been disturbed. And the show was over.

After she left Vito, Iris realized that solitariness could become solitude, and then I▪ was there. Now I▪ was trying to identify the moment of her own birth. It was easy to know when Rio became J. Death did it. What was the exact moment when the maiden, Iris, in the privacy of her own reflections on herself, actually became a woman, and what qualities differentiated one from the other? Leaving Vito hadn't done it, though it might have, nor did encountering J., though that might have as well, if she could have encountered him, as opposed to Rio, when she was still Iris.

I■ reflecting on Iris is the plot. Also I reflecting on I■. I observing them all. Seeing oneself as an other, with the same willingness to condemn and praise. I■ couldn't become herself until she knew this incontrovertibly. Vito is irrelevant to the story but the woman's habit of reflecting on her own experience through the lens of her relationship with a man is persistent enough to be pernicious and so the woman rarely has the opportunity to meditate on the true nature of desire. Imagine desire independent of the object of desire. Imagine desire independent of any object. Imagine desire. Independent desire. Desire itself. Ahh!

Age, she realized, was bestowing an unexpected privilege. She was able to examine her behavior without indulging paroxysms of shame. Was it, she reflected, because she was carrying more of the masculine, a beneficial, in this case, hormonal shift that, to compensate for the chin hairs she diligently searched out and removed each day, let her identify with what *is* rather than being crucified by what should be, or rather, what she should be. The men she had known seemed comfortable with *is,* accepted *is,* loved *is* and often as not, justified or accorded their behavior with *is*. *Is* was a great god, they argued. Yes, *is* was/is the god of the moment. Or, at the least, a savior. This is it. How it is.

Maybe, she thought, only she wasn't sure she could see *is* plainly. Sometimes, she thought *is* was conflated with other forces—which ones?—the ones we are talking about—desire, wanting, those ones that serve us. Yes, *is* was god but who could recognize it?

Well, still, that's how it is.

But anyway, she was, as people of her age tend to do, ruminating on her life and saw now what she had been entirely blind to for all the years previous, that she had continuously desired to be connected to J., had longed for him, his presence, his way of being in the word, [sic, that is how it appears on the page and she isn't going to edit it out as it may be prescient. Simply, then, write it also another way] his way of being in the word and the world. His death had only enhanced this longing instead of diminishing it. Not the longing for how it might have been between them then, but an increased passion to be connected with him now. Death had made him only the more alluring. Only the more compelling.

And then she said in her most Iris thought-form, "You understand, don't you, it is not sex I'm longing for," as if she hadn't asserted this continuously for one reason or another during the almost 30 years she'd known him.

Now that I seems to be lilting toward his "presence," she sees the necessity of understanding. Desire, it appears, is not something she has outgrown though it has acquired yet another face; she no longer confuses it with the erotic, nor would anyone observing her, nor would he, any longer, she hopes.

She has, she acknowledges, finally disentangled desire from eros. That is she has disentangled desire from Eros. If the Greek gods, or Egyptian neters, or other deities are conscious configurations of energy, vast and differentiated intelligences that carry certain particular aspects of reality, so that together their various colors form the rainbow, form the One, are the One, are the myriad faces of the One, and if desire is not Eros then who, what is desire? Or if desire in an older woman is not an affiliation with Eros what is it then? In carrying desire, with whom or what is she allied?

The question is as disturbing to her as the possibility of his appearance. Everything that occurs within his vicinity confirms a reality she cannot really encompass but toward which she has been ineluctably drawn.

There is evidence, you know. What is occurring cannot be denied.

She refuses to speculate on the source of the last two sentences. Which of her selves or who or what has spoken this? The best way to avoid the conundrum she is in is to return to an earlier, less developed way of thinking, to return, as she often does to avoid new anxieties, to an old and familiar anxiety, to return to her old obsessions as if she hadn't just stepped away from them.

Hold on then, we are going backwards: If he thinks, (she is pretending to consider what might be occurring between them), that it was still desire that called him back into the world, then everything is diminished. Even as she thinks this, she knows he is laughing at her. Does she think she is so powerful that her desire can revive the dead? She is glad for his laughter; it punctures her solemn remorse for the present. Even before she was able to ruminate on the ways in which she failed to change the very ways she persistently misunderstands—the very ways that were never really eros to begin with—he steps in to refine his angle on the ongoing cosmic joke. He who wasn't much troubled by the many faces of desire but rather intent on recognizing its nature, its *is-ness*. She goes on as if he isn't there or as if his appearance isn't a world-shattering occurrence.

Where are they? You want to be located. Of course, we don't blame you. We want something solid under ourselves also as we approach disorientation with the speed of a spaceship heading for Mercury, the little planet blinding with its quicksilver light.

· · ·

We are on an airplane. That is, she is on an airplane. She is returning from a visit with old friends she hasn't seen since she was a young woman and also meetings with colleagues to discuss the ways of healing from torture. She prefers to say torture rather than trauma, the current catch-all for everyone's unbearable pain and experience, personal or political and thinks the event itself requires focus not only the after-effect. She knows something of what is required to allow the tortured to tell the story again and again in detail as excruciating as the event but different if someone is truly listening, so that each electric shock to the genitals, each blow to the delicate fingers of the hand, is spoken, communicated and released. She wonders how many therapists working with the torture victim have inappropriately recused themselves from investigating torture itself as if such a concern would distract them from focusing on the ongoing work of trying to integrate the individual into the oblivious and unmindful present. *Thewomaninthecellar* had asked I to be sure to distinguish one pain from another though it may be that the same methods for healing apply to all.

She has said No to the movie. She has said No to the headset and the canned music. She has said No to the newspapers and conventional magazines. So she can yield to the inner dialogue that is finally possible.

He's left her with a muddle. She knows he couldn't take it anymore, no more than if they had arrested and tortured him. They did, ultimately, break him down even if they never, literally, had their hands on him. But, it's gotten worse since he was *Here* and she needs him, they all need him, need what only he knows that is useful to such a time, this hell. Torture so widespread the individual voices are lost in the din and one wonders what the point is anymore even from the point of view of the torturer, since it's all become so loud and commonplace, the useless pain of it, like trailers for the movies. And for her, the unbearable cacophony of human voices mixing with the screams of animals tortured on a daily basis, vast fields and forests and bloody rivers of the uprooted, herded, exiled, captured, imprisoned, tortured and screaming out. "They've upped the ante," she whispers to him hoping the dead can bear more than the living, and wondering how the acceleration is affecting her, wondering where she is numb or oblivious or simply unable to care.

So of course she wants him. What other voice could possibly make a difference in such a din? Let's raise the dead, she thinks and buries the thought in a small paragraph so as not to startle anyone. If the dead could speak, then maybe the word might have some possibility of alleviating the insufferable condition of *Thewomaninthecellar*.

The text that I▪ is engaged in summons her to look back in order to see where she is going as she doesn't have time now for false starts and misdirections. It is not that there is a path, right there, in front of her to uncover, but rather that there is a specific trajectory, of many possible trajectories that can be postulated, that is exactly the right one to follow into the future. Julio, *Thewomaninthecellar*, trauma, the dead, this kind of desire that has overtaken an older woman, they all seem to be connected, and she is looking for the fine line they formed, what in her life accorded with these and what was finished and could be left behind, and what was no longer interesting, and what she must, now, pursue. Vito, and the timeline that emanates from him, are to be discarded. A distraction, attractive as Vito may be as an older man, whose shining black hair has turned to ripples of gleaming tungsten and is still something to grip. Bye-bye, Vito.

Now, she needs to find the coordinates behind her and move with those even if she thinks there is a brick wall in front of her; it is a brick wall she will have to climb over, break down or pass through. And she is not going to do this if she is hung up about desire.

Magnetism. Not desire. Magnetism.

She knows about magnetism and the old magus, hermeticism, old Hermes, Hermes Trismegistus, Thoth, Tehuti, uh-oh. . . . Certain assumptions made by physicists proved not to be true: such magnetism, for example, does not decrease over distance but to the contrary increases.

"But," she says, continuing to condemn and excuse herself, simultaneously, for what we hope is the last time, "I wanted you to step across the line. I *wanted* this."

Perhaps hours passed between that statement and this question or, perhaps, just minutes, but, inevitably, just enough time for her to scrutinize her soul. "Do the dead *want*, J.? Do they have preferences?"

What might have been his rebuke seemed to come back immediately and she gives the thought a male inflection with a Spanish accent slightly modulated by French: Why do you think I'm here? Do you assume you're a force of nature? Or an anti-force? Do you think your desire runs the world? What does that imply about the dead?

Two tendencies in the history of literature: the one who is determined to raise the dead—like the Rabbi of Prague who creates a golem to save the city and the sorcerers who traffic in evil deeds for their own gain. The second, the *dybbuk* or ghost who insists on haunting the living and is assumed to be undeveloped or unfinished in his dying, so is unable to, cannot entirely cross over without gaining the necessary satisfaction, without assistance from the human realm.

Which story is she, are they, in?

The golem was not one of the dead.

Certainly, she knows this, but still there is a resonance she can't explain.

And the Rabbi didn't do it for power or money but to protect his people.

"You mean there is no resemblance at all between the activity of the Rabbi and the activities of sorcerers?"

They all come to a terrible end.

"Because?"

Because that is how it is with the forbidden that violates the natural order.

"And so for us?"

We will see, won't we?

"But, being dead, you won't suffer."

Do you think you know the circumstances of the dead?

"I know that I don't want *you* to suffer."

You mean that *you* don't want me to suffer. Yes, that is what always motivates the actions of good people, but it doesn't seem to matter what we want, even though we began by discussing desire.

"I am afraid that I have called you here through my wanting and that it is another face of the same wanting that led me to you in the first place and that. . . ."

I don't see any signs that you are suffering from necrophilia, he seemed to chuckle.

So, she considered, if the dead chuckle, does this mean they can feel desire? And where is desire located when it is not in the body?

She could participate in this, she could go off into abstraction, she could cogitate about the changes in his nature since he had died, she could wonder about the nature of his being now, and forget what was so important to her because she was living. The kinds of thoughts that occur when one's feet aren't on the ground. Had she, thinking she was acting ethically, if against the prohibitions of tradition, acted unethically? Had she violated the cosmic order, and had she done this out of the oldest, least conscious motivation, out of desire?

Tarot card: the devil. A chain around the throats of the two lovers. The chain sits low on their chests; they can easily remove it. But they don't. Desire.

They want to be connected and this (wanting? desire? inclination?) is called the devil.

She has to get up from her seat at the computer and make herself a cup of maté in order to busy herself around the kitchen and neutralize the tension around what has to be written. When she was thinking all of this she had been on an airplane, but she hadn't written it on the airplane. Hence the kitchen. She is beginning to see something that she hadn't seen before. Something about "interrogation."

• • •

"Let me tell it, J. as you might have seen it:

"Iris not only lamented that the two of you hadn't met, she accused you of not meeting her, she assaulted you with her disappointment. She assumed that she was entitled to such a meeting. She assumed that her desire for it was pure and imagined that someone like you would recognize its virtue, yes virtue, and would respond accordingly. If anything, Iris thought she was virtuous, even more virtuous by not wishing carnal contact with you, but an exchange of mind. What could be more lofty? She was righteous in her pursuit.

"She assumed that your failure to meet was your failure to see her worthiness, or your masculine or intellectual detachment, your preoccupation with worldly things, your obsessive focus upon your work, your fear of 'trouble.' Actually, she thought none of these, but that your failure to meet was your knowing, what she also knew, that nothing was possible between the two of you.

"But I can see now that the reason the two of you didn't meet was because you deliberately hid your intensity. Older and more seasoned, you knew that your first responsibility was to protect your art. She wanted an intimacy for which there was no ground between you. Her desire was vulgar; it existed outside of any relationship or connection between the two of you. Her desire was unable to consider the value of your work before its (desire's) own requirements were met. The value of your work, not honored in its own right in this instance, was being manipulated to support the possibility of her own work. Kill the king. The king is dead. Long live the queen."

In telling the story this way, I◼ felt a unique freedom as if she had been separated from her own point of view and fully absorbed into another way of seeing. It was exhilarating and she pursued her own past with all the passion of a triumph and vendetta.

"She didn't stop after your clothes had become transparent under her gaze and dissolved in the chemical bath of her inspection but continued, through the skin, flayed you without announcing her intent or procedure, and then went through to the bone, reduced you to a skeleton not unlike the meticulous work that Wong had brought to your attention, a record of torture folded in your wallet. She didn't stop. She pressed on. It wasn't violent or forceful, the touch of her scrutiny. More than determined, it was inexorable.

"If you couldn't tell that she wasn't suffering from romantic thrall intensified by literature, political drama, all that high exoticism, nor the mundane heat of an overexcited woman wanting an affair or a mate, or a maté, you would have turned your back on her in a moment. But she told a good story and she insisted you believe it: She had been in a bookstore and the book which had fallen into her hands, "literally," she asserted, had revealed the precise and exquisite patterning of the world as it was in its shimmering reality, a world she claimed to have been instructed to enter, and she wanted you to guide and accompany her. She had that much presumption. "Bestiary," was in the book, of course. Also she must have seemed incapable of resisting or modifying this examination of the one she wanted to guide her as if she was, without having volunteered, one or all of the forty-two assessors who participate in the scrutiny of the soul in the Duat.

"Each assessor is related to a particular territory and also a particular crime to emphasize the qualities that each geography protects and what occurs when these are ignored or violated. The assessor from the far north is concerned with the cruelty that arises out of bitterness, extreme isolation and overweening self-reliance while the assessor from the equatorial region is responsible for the wretched crimes of thirst and other betrayals. Each geography had its own laws to contain desperation and these laws translate into customs and behaviors, and woe to those who violate these and set up their own (human) laws in opposition to these. That's how closely she examined you, looking at you directly and continuously and wouldn't, despite Vito's presence and Hélène's, lower her gray eyes flickering with yellow, green, blue, amethyst, brown, black, silver, when you raised yours. And not the slightest nod of acknowledgement. Verifying everything you said as you were forced to approach the assessors as one does to engage in the negative confession: I did not murder. I did not hate. I did not lie. I did not betray. I did not co-opt. I did not exploit. I did not steal. I did not disdain. I did not dishonor. I did not profane. I did not fabricate. I did not dissemble. I did not look away.

"Yes, if she had been seducing you, she certainly had not devised an amicable approach. She could have modified her compulsion. Really, it was rude. A modest dinner. A summer night. Strangers who had virtually invited themselves to your summer residence where you went to escape all visitors and she had, by her own admission tracked you down from post office to post office because you hadn't, deliberately, given them an address or a summer phone or directions. And there she sat asking the kind of questions that only the gods had the right to ask.

"And when she wasn't tracking you, she made the most outrageous conversation in whatever language suited her whether she could speak it fluently or not. She had the annoying habit of asking questions about the people the three of you were discussing though it was hardly pertinent to reveal their personal and family lives, manners and habits. There was the moment when you and Vito were speaking about L. who was just then, as an exile, dominating the literary scene with his brilliance and political acumen but Iris interjected, 'He's a womanizer and his wife, who is quite gifted if conveniently mousy, types his manuscripts for him and stays at home most nights. He doesn't think of anyone but himself and his "great art" and he makes mileage out of his "situation." I don't give a fig for his work,' she concluded almost in a whisper that was searing in its disdain, and then like a waiter entering into the mystery of the linen flower, she returned to her maddening narrow folding and unfolding of the napkin from the dinner table. She could well have been an avatar of Madame Defarge. And you must have noticed after being with her a short time, that she had the habit, an internal nervous tic really, of counting the number of 'I's in anyone's speech, your own as well.

"It didn't matter to her how you responded, whether you thought about her when she left, or what turmoil had entered your sanctuary with the letter she had sent upon her return to the States: 'We never met. I came to meet the tiger and we never met.' She continued relentlessly yielding to whatever was driving her, without compunction taking you down alongside her if it came to that.

"And what had she wanted from the tiger anyway? To be devoured by it in the library as had happened to the uncle, but without being misled as he had been, walking into the room deliberately knowing the tiger was there. She was betting, didn't you think, on your appetite, supposing you would be hungry for her as if you didn't have more than enough in your life to digest."

There, she had done it. Iris had become her own character and so she was free of the past, its confusions, self-assurance and endless repetitions.

In I■'s imagination, J. sighed, relieved, finally, of the needs of the young woman. She thought of the many older men she had known who had hungered for the touch of a young woman as if it might restore them to something they had once been, their elixir of life, their monkey gland treatment, and concluded that Iris, companionably might have hungered for the senex to whom she could make an offering.

I■ writes but really she is speaking to him with the camaraderie that can only come between two people who have lived a long time and have, at the least, age and many foibles in common: "I can see now, after all these years, something of who you are or may have been and what it took to become that. Iris wanted to see it immediately. She wanted to see the source and path of your genius. She wanted you to reveal that. To reveal *that*. What kind of wanting is that?

"How naïve to assume that privacy has to do with the body and not with the mind. She hid nothing, she wanted to hide nothing, she assumed nakedness is a virtue under all circumstances . . . the American girl, again . . . and she wanted you to reveal your mind. Audacious. Perhaps even insolent."

An illness had overtaken the wolf, Akasha, and her behavior had changed and, as if to care for herself under such circumstances, she retreated into her wolf nature. I■ had not understood until this moment why Akasha, feeling fragile, and consequently vulnerable, had insisted, after so many years of being otherwise content, in searching out a small knoll and then concealing herself in its bushes to relieve herself. Hunkering down, she looked warily about herself and it still took a long time for her to feel sufficiently safe to let go. Every being has a right to hide. I■ had been startled by this idea in a time when privacy was less and less protected. She hadn't seen any relationship between her youthful espousal of openness and the way surveillance had become commonplace. "Every creature has a right to hide." She had been pondering this without applying the dictum to herself. Before anyone entered a room in the "Bestiary" it was necessary to look and see if the tiger was within. Perhaps, the tiger, likewise, checked to see if any human was in the room before he entered, not because he was hungry, but because he was trying to take cover. *El Mago* had hidden from her. Well, of course, he had. Magic only took place in the dark. Didn't she know that?

There it was, Iris' wanting alongside her own wanting and Rio and J. had been the object of these great forces of the psyche that had, like the winds that form the universe, shaped Iris and I■ as they impinged, with who knows what consequences, on *El Mago* himself, no magic able to insulate him entirely from all such demands.

Who are you?
What aliases do you go by?
What other personae have you adopted?
Where do your ideas come from?
What laws do you obey?
What laws do you deny?
Who are your associates?
What do you believe?

What are you thinking about?
What do you dream?
What influences you?
What motivates you?
What are your work habits?
What hours do you keep?
Where do you walk?
Where do you travel and why?
What do you think about?
What do you read?
What do you write in your journal?
What plans do you have?
What is your life's purpose?
What do you support?
What do you deny?
Who/what do you recognize as a higher authority?

And again:

Who are you?
What aliases do you go by?
What other personas have you adopted?
Where do your ideas come from?
What laws do you obey?
What laws do you deny?
Who are your associates?
What do you believe?
What are you thinking about?
What do you dream. . . ?

And again . . . and again and again.

Yes, certainly, she had wanted the answers to such questions. She didn't know how to get at what she needed to get at without such questions. She stopped to enter heartbreak as it called to her. It was a mild acid that had some residual sweetness—no harm was ever intended on either of the women's parts—but still, like a wine that has turned to vinegar, it ate away what it lingered upon. How well she knew the dark.

How she had violated the dark without knowing it, without knowing she was impetuously interfering with what she loved.

She sat still thinking about his books, fingering his . . .

At this moment, a blue jay, an old one, I think, so scraggly were its head feathers, perched on the non-existent rim outside the window, exactly before her eyes and looked at I■ so intently through the glass, she had to take off her glasses, and look back, and so they remained for a long time, he trying to maintain his balance without a ledge for support— a long time—too long for it to be anyone but J. in his bird form—and at this moment . . .

. . . fingering his well worn, dog-eared books, feeling the great love and admiration for a spirit who had manifested so grandly in his human form and given the world, herself included, these great gifts.

"I am sorry, J.," she said most deliberately aloud as she typed the words into the manuscript, so that he would know then, no matter the years it had taken her to know it, that she was, indeed, filled with remorse, though without knowing how to make amends to a man who was no longer living and to a spirit whose ways she did not know.

Then there was Iris who also deserved her apologies and had been left behind in her youthfulness trying to carry a measure of world pain that was too much for anyone, let alone a slight and solitary woman who was overburdened with an overwhelming measure of hope, and its companion, accountability. She owed Iris an apology too. The last thing that served Iris was a stern conscience shaking a rebuking finger with a yellowing striated misshapen nail in her face as if there had been another way to become who she had to become.

J. didn't answer but Iris did. The Iris woman rose up from the deep and the dark where she had been and spoke. I■ could feel herself dissolving before this presence who spoke now in another voice, mellowed perhaps over the years and from whom she could not, would not now, disassociate herself.

"From the beginning, there was no one that I could have asked about the nature of reality. If Rio were living it, then it was true. Or there was a good chance. But if Rio wasn't, if *he* wasn't. . . . It wasn't as if hunting Rio down was a calculated gesture. It wasn't as if I made a list of Latin American writers to see whom I could get closest to. There was only that story and I had to track Rio down. This is the truth of it.

That single story, "Bestiary," had been sufficient. I thought I could construct with a certain accuracy, some of the configurations of such a mind who would write such a story, and I wanted to see if he existed. Did such a mind exist? Simple as that. Was it the work of a confabulist, the pyrotechnics of disembodied imagination and mind, mind, mind run amuck or did it emerge out of the entire life and breath of a human being? Was the story real?

"I had read many stories. I didn't run off and try to find Asturias, Garcia Marquez, Vargas Llosa, the blind Borges, Juan Rulfo or Carlos Fuentes. No. I read their work. My own work changed. A world opened up that offered possibility because it looked like the inside of my mind. But I didn't track them down. I didn't become a stalker.

"It was rather that they advised me to contact you. 'Oh you must meet him . . . ' one said and then another and then another. I didn't think I deserved it, hadn't earned the right to . . . but it is clear that once the idea was planted, a determination grew in me to meet it. I wrote and asked, 'Might I?' and you wrote back and said, 'Come.'"

I once thought of appealing to Neruda. After all, there are legions of dead that one can call out to.

And what happened?

I couldn't. There wasn't the same intimacy. Or rather, I didn't feel that we belonged to each other. Or, he didn't say, "Come."

You said, "Come."

"There is one more thing I have to say, Rio, though we have sworn not to speak of it any more, but, having indulged me so much over the years, please do allow this last explanation. I was not dissembling when I told myself that I didn't want to have a tryst with you, certainly didn't want to live with you, or enter into any domestic arrangement. It was past the time in history when a woman married what she was not permitted to have herself in order to get as close to it as she could and so served it, often devotedly, but never partaking for herself. The servant to the spirits is different indeed from the servant to the man. It would have been hell to live alongside the Colossus, for that is also, secretly, what many that know you call you, when what drove me so incessantly was the question of whether a woman might find whatever the path might be to whomever she might turn out to be herself and whether anyone who really knew about walking alone in the night might show her something of the way. Lucho, of the uncontrollable hands, was so eager to try to help Dina [sic], of the uncontrollable hands, though, when stymied, his fingers did find their way to the 'Throat of the Black Kitten;' I thought you might also be willing, if you could, to lend a hand."

• • •

It was like a piece of music, the way a theme was introduced and developed, and the way the instruments blended into a common melody so that for notes at a time she couldn't tell how many breaths were blowing all together. Yes, he had invited her, "Come," and in the sweetness of that call that might have also been a request, they had entered into the domain that allows one to ask the question of the other and not be impertinent, but rather the querent reveals her own vulnerability in the face of the question and there they are the two of them with their hearts on the scale before the terrible feather that determines their fate.

In the dusky light, where I■ could still make out J.'s features in the photograph that was often so daunting, but now seemed to have softened, as if he were conceding the connection that had existed between them, yes, from the beginning and their first contact. In the naturalness of the conversation and the seeming fact of an exchange, I■ dared to consider that they were passing over a barrier so easily, as if a wave was lifting them over a great rock that low tide would certainly reveal, and that she was speaking to him the way she might speak to M. or to a beloved, to a brother. Something had become implicit between them. And, though she had anticipated that vertigo would accompany this moment, actually all that she felt was the swell as she/they were lifted over and then the sweet sinking onto the smooth surface of the sea, however deep it was beneath them, on the other side.

This is what I■ had longed for, what Iris had longed for, and now here it was, not poof! as in the movies or comics—though it was that sudden— but rather like a sigh, simply that—Aah!—and the body settling down into the old chair that would continue to hold it in *Terra Incognita* even if one traveled all the way to *On this side*. And truth to tell after so many, many years, it just appeared out of thin air, the ways the old stories describe such happenings. A visitation.

It had not occurred to Iris, nor to I■ before, except in the matter of *A Certain Lucas* bounding through the airwaves toward her, but this was different and so much less dramatic and more real. She knew she wasn't talking or writing to herself. It would be heresy to think so.

I am no longer myself, she said to herself. I no longer feel like myself. I don't know who I am anymore. It was the mystery of vast space and not knowing where to locate herself there. There was no location. Wherever she thought she might be, vanished. She no longer even wanted to ask the questions, "Who are you?" or even "Who am I?" because she knew there were no answers to such questions and history would not inform her. A strange and blessed kind of amnesia settled about her and she rested in it and closed the computer and went out into the woods and watched the jays and the night fall, and the moon rise and move to the mid-heaven, and when she came back to the house she was as silent and as satisfied as when she had gone out as if something permanent had occurred and it was true, she was no longer the woman she had been. She realized then she had known this for some while but she hadn't understood and so it hadn't been acknowledged, and so it hadn't been, and now it was.

It had something to do with no longer being I■. It had to do with that strange transition first from Iris to I■ and now to I that had allowed this small dialogue with J. that seemed to have made all the difference. Something had fallen away, and because of it, another face of wanting, of desire had been stripped away; it was like losing 2 pounds, entirely indiscernible.

• • •

The moment she had had intimations of such a shift? It was a totally ordinary morning. Nothing unusual had occurred the night before and there was nothing she was anticipating but when she awakened from yet another dream about Thewomaninthecellar she understood that she would never stop trying to relieve that suffering and yet I■ now knew with certainty that there was nothing, ultimately, she could do. And that was that.

What does it mean to finally become an I? Maybe it means defeat. Then you give it all up. You start working from another premise, from one that cannot be named "victory" or "success." What then? Necessity.

And once you're with Necessity, you're with Fate and Destiny, that trajectory she was trying to find in the underbrush, by looking backwards instead of ahead. Iris had known that it was her task, being a girl, being a maiden, being a Kore, a no one, to manufacture a self, and if all she had was determination and bravado, she would use those and they would suffice. That was the necessary activity of a younger woman. But those elements and ambition didn't serve I■ and certainly didn't serve I. I had to be excavated from all of that and remain pristine in the way that the essential sacred image lying dormant in the rough stone can be revealed only when all excess has been carved away. I■ had been heading toward something beyond the self-created I. Actually, she had just understood that while a self created I■ was conceivable, a self-created I was a contradiction in terms. Further, I■ and the dead couldn't really coexist in the same universes they currently inhabited. They either had to go elsewhere, as to *Terra Incognita,* or they had to use some inter-world version of the mails or the internet, so that a neutral object could pass from one world to the other without being entirely undone and then, only, if possible, reconstituted. The universes they each inhabited were governed by different laws and his world couldn't tolerate an I■ because it was, by its nature, substantial, and his universe of the dead, would, by its nature, deconstruct it in an instant.

In order to be with whatever might be *Over there*, or for J. to be *Here,* or *On this side,* the essential obstacle between the living and the dead had to be sacrificed. That is, however long it lasted, this I (I■) achieved it (not something to be achieved but something gained, so to speak, in the loosening) and then she gave it up. It was as simple and as quick as taking in a last breath and then

. . . . out.

This was the necessary preamble to participating in the gathering of the dead. Not the raising of the dead, not that missionary zeal, but rather the final separation from the hegemony of secular mind, the humble sacrifice of the delusions of self, its pride and its ambitions, the joyful sacrifice of everything that asserts the triumph of a particular species of the human, so that one can take one's quiet nonspace among the ancestors who are gathering at such a time. How the spirits break us down by puncturing our assumptions about ourselves and the reality that we believe we create and shape. Here she is, that Iris person with all her naïve hypotheses created from hope, desire, passions and hormones, finally become I■ and thinking she knows something, smiling benevolently on Iris and the struggle to become something, when she also must offer herself to the compost heap so that someone else, more no-one than someone, can emerge, free of what we can call, as a short hand, western mind: western mind and all its chatter and stupidities, its dogged misinformation about the nature of the universe and its role in it, its belief that it is shaping It and that there is nothing beyond this or greater than it(self). Assuming this, until the dead come like a sandstorm pitting the skin, eroding the flesh, nicking even the finest white ivory bones until nothing remains but the willing knowledge that the dead can rise and speak through us, that the nature of the universe, with or without our help and cooperation, with or without our agreement or understanding, permits, even necessitates, our capitulation to them.

(Another full prostration is required here so I■ is flat down on the floor, arms outstretched where she notices a remnant of self left, there, at the end of her breath, and she attempts to release it, breathing out still further, but, also, the attempt itself negates it. "This is as far as I can go toward you," she confesses and for a fleeting instant feels what might be an O at the end of her breath.)

History, reason, rational mind, science, invention, experimentation, thumb screws, bombs, rockets, missiles, all of these are wooden matches in the ultimate windstorm, that whirlwind that wraps itself around the voice that speaks in no human language, in no language at all. I■ was being brought closer and closer to the still small voice from which all manifests. One breakdown after another including the continuous failures of the manuscript that I■ was trying to write. And then this—when she had given up, when she had accepted her own inability to manifest anything, when she was humbled fully, a voice no louder than the barely audible twittering of the wren in the oak began to make itself known—its song amplified in the undeniable wind and its semaphores—called to her on the way up to her hermitage where she intended, for the last time, to approach the intractable manuscript, and she stopped and got out of the car.

Summertime. She had a week before she had to go east and she intended to hole up in her cabin in the mountains and have at that stubborn book again. She was returning to the Holy Mountain and she was going to try again to make contact with him, that is, to write a book with him. This is the last time, she swore. She'd been at it for ten years, and it was almost twenty since he had contacted her special delivery. Driving the curves first faster and then slower than was good for anyone, she pulled over to the shoulder because something was agitating her. That little bird voice. She needed to write down the inchoate thoughts that were pecking at her. First she just tried to write something down, but nothing came. Then, disturbed by what she saw, she stepped to the bushes to remove a plastic bag tethered there and, immediately, he began to speak, authentically, *his* voice.

She understood for the first time what she was doing and that she had acquiesced to a strange influence, or perhaps even influences that could be from *Over there*. She had no desire to create a cosmology to explain the mystery or what was necessary to acquiesce to it, but if she were being interrogated by her *paredros* she would have to confess to two contradictory possibilities: the ancestors were coming and the dead gathering on the one hand, and on the other, she was harvesting the fruits of the solitary creative life now that she had disappeared sufficiently to finally to be of service.

• • •

Remember, she was on an airplane. We were trying to locate her on that Wednesday, 2003 Planet Earth, *Terra Incognita*. An unnamable, unidentifiable territory. She's reading one of his books she hasn't read before. *62: A Model Kit.* She has saved it for this moment that precedes her return to the Holy Mountain and some time to be with him, their rendezvous, their yearly *luna de miel*, but this time she was determined to give herself to the book, not the one she is about to read, but their book, the way one gives oneself, fully, without anything held back, without any restraint or hesitation, no matter what M. thinks or fears, give herself to a lover, a real lover, one who has finally appeared, the angel, the emissary, the one. He had appeared, as he would, waving a flag, albeit a plastic one, and she, recognizing him and the white flag, had snatched it knowing it was time to surrender, and so had said, "I do" or "I will" as the case may be and then he revealed what the two of them had been up to together. Finally understanding the undertaking after so long, she also understands how long it had been that they had been at it—ten years!— and she all the time, coy, pretending it wasn't happening, as if he wasn't, as if, as had happened to her when she was a child, after laying out the New York Times across her lap as they sat next to each on the subway, the only two in the car, both having gotten on at Gravesend Bay, also pretending to be strangers—as if he wasn't slipping his hand under her skirt and moving up her thigh with his second finger lifting the elastic of her panties so his third finger could edge its way, and she, reading the news and following the arrows of the current war, where the armies were and where they were going, and how soon they would knock the hell out of the enemy and with what artillery, and she was acting as if he hadn't intended to find her secret place. And here we have it again, the pernicious recurrence of erotic, even pornographic imagery, to convey the opening of the door into the concealed chambers. Is it because we who have lost the knowledge of the hidden caves with their tiny labyrinthine passageways that open *Over there*, are failing to seek the hidden wisdom that we fear even more than the *c* word we substitute with malice and with hope?

He explained it all to her, explained the book, its direction and her role in it after she claimed that flag and yielded to the spirit he had become; it had been waiting for her. It was hers. "I do." Then she understood what it took, and how long—ten years—to relinquish all resistance, all fears, all wild imaginings and give in to this one to whom she had been drawn, shall we say, pledged, from the beginning. Not that she was entitled, but that she had been given.

And so though it looked like continuing, she was starting again.

There it was. And the time available. And then the return flight from east to west with nothing to accomplish. And so the book that she had never yet read. She opened *62 . . .* with some expectation—after ten years of starting and stopping, starting again, getting nowhere—his words already enlivening and confirming the moment—

The first page, not unlike the "Table of Instructions" in *Hopscotch* refers the reader to:

" . . . the final paragraph of Chapter 62 of *Hopscotch* which explains the title of this book, and perhaps those intentions will be fulfilled in the course of it."

She reads this and goes on. But then after a few pages is stopped in her tracks and goes back, extracts *Hopscotch* from her voluminous purse and reads

> . . . life is trying to change its key in and through and by them,
> that a barely conceivable attempt is born in man as one other day
> there were being born the reason-key, the feeling-key, the pragmatism-
> key. That with each successive defeat there is an approach towards the
> final mutation, and that man only is in that he searches to be, plans to

be, thumbing through words and modes of behavior and joy sprinkled with blood and other rhetorical pieces like this one.

that this might initiate a conversation with him; it had happened before.

"Each successive defeat"—it was almost absolution. Was that a smile on his photograph, just a glimpse of it, the appearances and vanishing she liked so much, hints and intimations, only the faintest smear of hallucination, enough to make her consider the possibility that each failed attempt had had a purpose beyond the demonstration of her loyalty—and, yes, she had written other books in that time, but without deserting this project of theirs entirely—and now defeat had become the most desired goal. As in the Tower card in the Tarot, "all fall down," all the structures of self, all opinions and habits had to go; the demise of the old order, the collapse of defenses and obstruction were essential processes so that the two of them might actually start their two-step together.

She returns to *62:*. . . . She rereads the first few pages. Then goes back to the beginning, *Hopscotch* open on her lap as well, consulting the two as if concordances to explain what is occurring right now, this minute, between them.

62 is the crossroads between *A Model Kit* and *Hopscotch* and also the hexagram she's been working with, the one about the Flying Bird that must refer to him because it speaks of "the words that will cross the river of life and death," and that advises her, as if she doesn't know where she is: "This time of transition is a journey through liminal space where rules dissolve and borders are crossed."

In *62* of *Hopscotch*, he'd gone on a bit of a harangue about the way science was thinking about the mind and its chemical essence. And that had taken him from randomness to intent, though it wasn't necessarily human intention that dominated entirely. *62* . . . followed the random and the haphazard, also will and willfulness, those elements from which *life is trying to change its key in and through and by them.*

Once life tries anything, she thought, we've got . . . meaning. Meaning wasn't quite the word that fit both of their intentions, so she avoided his cringe but didn't stop and look for the right one because they had fallen onto another crossroads, and they were involved in the equivalent of a three-dimensional hopscotch or a life-sized game of Go, and so "meaning" be damned.

He'd run into the theories of HH of the U of Göteborg, Sweden, speaking at S.F., USA, (2 mos, according to J. C., before he wrote Chapter 62 of *Hopscotch*.) on *"the chemical theory of thought."*[54] What followed was a long footnote in the novel that we may as well excerpt here in another footnote.[55]

I■ was reminded of Francis Crick's astonishing hypothesis: "You, your joys and your sorrows, your memories and your ambitions, your sense of personal identity and free will, are in fact no more than the behavior of a vast assembly of nerve cells and their associated molecules. As Lewis Carroll's Alice might have phrased it: 'You are nothing but a pack of neurons.'"[56]

A new way of understanding the Emerald Tablet: "As above so below." Big bang in the sky and big bang in the mind. It's elementary, dear J., all there is, apparently is one set of chemicals continuously imposing upon another.

The point being, as J. doesn't have any chemicals anymore, how can this be happening?

She's on an airplane reading *62* . . . and once again, it is as if she's fallen into their common mind. They allege that it's all chemistry; she actually moans and catches herself as the passenger next to her in the window seat looks over concerned, despite these occurrences between us that postulate the non-chemical appearance of a conscious reality, DNA-less and RNA-less. Despite this moment so subtle, quiet. . . . (Yes, she is convinced that for some nanosecond he is smiling at her from his photograph, and that his unwavering stare oscillates, that his eyes change position, wax and wane in intensity, acknowledge this moment.) I awakens from another of her rants. No need to impose it on him. He certainly knows it and with more elegance, frankly.

• • •

Monday, July 21, 2003 on a flight from Newark (6:35 a.m.) to Chicago to Los Angeles (10:58 a.m.), after which I and M. nearly missed each other as they wandered aimlessly and without intersecting between the three different ATA terminals, mostly on foot, I dragging a small valise on wheels, her purse packed with pills, books, wallet, writing materials, socks, etc. too heavy for her, and a plastic bag from Macy's containing various and sundry items including but not limited to shoes, and M. both (i.e. that he was) driving from terminal to terminal, and then (he was) parking and catching a bus, or walking or slouching toward . . . and not that I was driving as well, as she had just landed and had no wheels except for those two on her suitcase. . . . She'd gotten past Chapter 62 of *Hopscotch* and was in the first pages of *62. . .*, realizing that the text in its content was matching her activity of reading and they were both involved in parallel associations and resonances. Not that they shared any associations, but that they shared the process of associating and both were cogitating on its mystery, its improbability and consequences. He seemed also to have heard the long mournful arpeggio that announced the coming and the going of the sacred vehicle of coexistence. Life would have its way. Call it what you will, chance or accident, the great mystery of universal mind ceaselessly combining absurd and incongruous events into mergers that revealed implausible unities and unassailable meanings.

What is the nature of the universe in which such things happen? I ponders, riveted to *62. . .*, even as she is watching for M. who is circumrotating the Moebius strip of arrivals and departures at LAX. Despite checking her suitcase, purse, shoe bag, once, twice, three times to re-establish the precarious balance that immediately falls apart, she is not overly distressed by the long wait, knowing that she is returning to her sanctuary and a brief writing period, insufficient to the task at hand but sufficient to begin the process of calling her *paredros* back into the human world of letters.

Synchronicity, a word Julio would never use with such affection, is daily vernacular for I▪, being at the very core of what is occurring between them, what *is* occurring between them, what has been occurring since the very moment he sent the book from *On this side*, an event far more notable and incontrovertible than the occasion of a certain Juan's circumlocution in *62 . . .* regarding the synchronistic event of a book and a meal. What would Julio have made of this event that obsesses her? I wonders. This event in which he is, seemingly, an actor, part and parcel of the synchronicity.

And with this, I glances across the desk, through the golden flame in the candle that was once carved with the shapes of elephants, to the pixeled, if only mildly pixelated, face of Julio, Julio whose eyes meet hers (again) as if he is alive and I feels that sometimes familiar frisson that must be the impulse Julio described in that paragraph in *Hopscotch* that seemed to have led to *62 . . .* and so to this moment, sliding so rapidly from one neuron to another until it has reached all those neurons it fits[57]—the proverbial key in the proverbial lock—that gets icy cold from the speed with which those designated neurons rapidly construct the required protein that results in a note, G, (or *sol*) on the trumpet, or in joy and satisfaction, got some or ain't got no, or that undeniable validation of his presence, an otherworldly shiver of recognition and delight.

I wouldn't have written this, (I notes). But, I would have noted the coincidence that J. was talking directly to her for the entire journey from Newark to L.A., as she turned the aging pages of *62 . . .* poking her with his bony finger, one life to another, obsessing about a moment in a restaurant and a coincident moment with a book.

To tell it briefly, in *62 . . .* Juan had bought a book he didn't really want and then entered a restaurant he didn't want to enter, just in time to be seated, the victim of circumstances—life announcing its hegemony over his will—rather uncomfortably, behind a man he could observe in a mirror who had just ordered a steak by the same name of the author of the unwanted book—Chateaubriand—or a "bloody castle" as he called it, for starters.

This is *my* topic, I noted, and settled into the pages, turning them ever so slowly as I■ was reading the Avon version, now yellowed and brittle, circa, *mas o menos*, 1973. Thirty years ago, we note, just before we met.

Juan is heading back to a café or a zone or a configuration of concerns and passions, an interception of billiard balls or a conjunction of minds, an arena of interconnections, a story composed of stories, or he is headed toward an aimless series of hits and misses, while I is heading toward her own café of the mind, her personal awareness of a zone of interrelatedness called *Terra Incognita*, her, or their, "Play Ball," or Hide and Seek, with the intriguing refrain "Ready or not, here I come. Anyone around the base is it!"

I thinks she's going to score this time, she's going to reach out and touch him, eyes closed or eyes opened, she's going to play tag and win. What is at stake is mindlessness vs. mindfulness, the pointless vs. the pointed, randomness vs. precision, (not randomness of activity as the activity in the brain is very precise, if pointless) chance, vs. focus, and, yes, the entirely arbitrary vs. the consequential, significant, meaningful, vs. what carries great weight and circumstances. What is at stake is the way the world is seen and so established and so manifested, and so is.

Let's put it this way: Are you willing to say, "The hell with *Thewomaninthecellar;* her 'pain' is only impulses hitting neurons and making proteins_" (How the hell are you going to punctuate the previous sentence—with a "period" or with a "question mark"?) Or are you willing to say you don't care how the pain gets registered in the brain, we are in the domain of a real woman, suffering the unbearable, that we, though we think ourselves innocent, are implicated in, because of what we did or didn't do, and it is our responsibility to get her out? Let's put it this way, I run knee or no I run knee, what is at stake is death vs. life and it will take a dead man to prove the liveliness of it all.

• • •

I▪ turns the pages. She and M. have found each other. She is back home. She is reading again. Waiting for M. she read the first 25 pages over and over again. Then she started over this evening and she doesn't know if she is reading or dreaming. If this is a night dream or a living dream. She doesn't know any longer what a dream is, but that it is more than she ever imagined. And then, wondering how it happened that she is in this dream, she is, yes, actually, in this dream, this is a dream, she turns the page that she dog-eared as she got off the plane long before she saw M. loping toward her, like a bedraggled Russian wolfhound, and finds herself in J.'s dreamscape—"*I enter my city at night, I go down to my city/where they wait for me or elude me, where I have to flee . . .*"[58]—dreaming his dream where what meets is unmet, where lost objects and lost souls intermingle and become each other, the non-crossing of crossroads, the place of misadventure and misalignment, of misbehaving and miscalculation, misconceptions and misconstruing, misfortunes and misfits, misgivings, night cemetery of a lifetime of near misses and misses "*and you, from time to time, are in the [airport] too, but your [plane] is a different [plane] your Dog is a different Dog, we'll never meet my love. . . .*" It's all so upside down because they are meeting right there, now, thirty or more years later, meeting exactly in the unmeeting. And here comes M. Syzygy.

Or to find, having, herself, just thought of dreams and their misinterpretations, in just such a landscape where she was stumbling in her language and he striding forward in his, to find that he was lost in dreams the way she has been for decades but always thinking this was not and would not ever be his territory in the way that it was hers.

Concerned that the dreamscape was not as much his territory as hers, she has kept dreams from him only to find that, in fact, he was living there all the time. A happy covey of confusions here.

And there's more. It's all coming alive. His reality moving like the fog that comes in over the hills turning chaparral into a delicate Japanese landscape, or Tuscany or the South of France, into her reality. And, if time isn't from here to there which it can't be, you see, then she/hers is moving into his. Is this the chemical soup HH was postulating?

It is a bit of a soup. It is not just that they are meeting in the dream but that something is occurring that is making her hackles rise. She wasn't more than four pages into his book before she saw that his characters had moved into her book—her book?—well, at least, she thought the first part that I▪ wrote was her book, that is, she thought that I▪ had written it. Here we are. She postulated it. *Terra Incognita* and it turns out to be true. She postulated *Terra Incognita*? Did she? You can see what it has meant, what it means, to her to find that they are in *Terra Incognita*, that it exists. That she is wandering where past and future cohabit. Oh my, she really is wandering in such a landscape and it is, also, as it happens, as she had just discovered between the plane and the sidewalk, it is also occupied by a character she thought belonged only to her book.

It turns out that he has his own Hélène and did he sneak her in when I▪ wasn't looking because she was thinking then that she was autonomous. The Hélène that Iris met that afternoon in the south of France, who wasn't named Hélène anymore than Rio was named Rio or Iris was named Iris, *mais non,* was not hers exclusively. Her Hélène was his, of course, except in name. But in the way of writers, I▪ also thought she had invented her when she named her, as she was, until this moment, entirely ignorant of his Hélène, that is, not the Hélène of their meeting but a Hélène from *62. . .* , another Hélène who has to be accounted for. An independent and sovereign Hélène. Life and literature being what they are, this Hélène of Julio's will inevitably attach herself to whom I▪ thinks is her Hélène. Julio's Hélène bleeding into I▪'s later story, so that I▪'s text is no longer her text alone as Julio's—or, in this case, Juan's but not only Juan's—associations assumptions, experiences, are, without prior agreement, fundamentally altering the text that I▪ wrote, even though it is well before there was even a thought of co-writing—or, at least we can say, well before I▪ thought of it, and (take a breath we are almost at the end of the sentence that must be done without stopping) and this most singular Hélène is, in retrospect, imposing, at this very moment, an entirely different perspective on what occurred when Iris and Rio first met. I▪ was entirely ignorant of Hélène's existence (as per *62 . . .*) and will not know, herself, who Hélène, her, [sic] own character, actually is, until she finishes reading Julio's text and learns the entire history that will willy-nilly be revealed. A recovery not unlike that which occasionally accompanies the amnesia of trauma but is here emblematic of another kind of forgetting altogether. Hélène, as in *62. . . ,* meeting Hélène in *Doors* and what crossbreeding is occurring there?

The lightning stroke, Tehuti, blazing through the worlds, welding the past to the future in celebration of the ceaseless present. (We won't interrupt this narrative to tell you that these lines above were written minutes before I was roused from her chair to stand in speechless wonder, the sky suddenly dark, followed by lightning and so more thunder, the rain shattering down and the lightning blazing through the dusk.)

Hélène. If Iris had known how difficult it had been for Juan and Hélène to come together, that it had come to be only after a long series of failures and mishaps, betrayals and misadventures, that Juan had longed for her, the one it seemed impossible he might ever attain, would she have not have tempered her longing and flagrant pursuit, that first meeting? And had Juan known that he would be living in the south of France with Hélène in the summer of 1974 what would have happened with *62 . . .* and would it have been written at all?

• • •

He has come. It is obvious. Welcome *El Mago*. Whoops, too soon. He has not made an appearance but the territory in which they might someday meet is revealing itself, she thinks. *Terra Incognita*. And she, I▪, is beginning to think that they have always been connected, that their meeting in France was the momentary shortening of a cord that had tied one to the other from the time before time. A time that began before she was born and continued after his death.

I pauses before the text, bemused. It is strange, this way of writing, of constructing a sentence, of thinking that is not her way at all, nothing like anything she has ever written, not really a style she would have pursued, not natural to her, not what she would think of writing for those who have, in the past, read what she has written. It is strange, this way of writing, of constructing a sentence, this way of thinking that is not his way either, nothing really like anything he has ever written, probably not really a style he likes, not natural to him, not what he would think of writing for those who have, in the past, read what he has written and yet there is something to the hybrid that is appearing that reminds her of him (though we don't know what he thinks) as she reads the words on the page as they appear from the quick working of her fingers. Hybrid. She, who is more scribe now than inventor, likes the word, is glad he offers it to her. Hybrid, reminding her of the Hydra heads but being the next stage in their development. The Hydra heads that were hewed to a single body but each independent of each other and so, inevitably, at war, but this hybrid, neither here nor there, but here *and* there, a way of being, AC/DC simultaneously, the impossible and yet emerging evidence of an inconceivable collaboration, the improbable cross between two distinct species originally the offspring of a tame sow and a wild boar, or possibly a hinny issuing from a she-ass and a stallion, but in this case the yet unborn progeny of a living woman and dead man, so no mongrel offspring of two different breeds, though it is not for her to judge whether this text is such a whelp or cur of low degree.

Astonishment. His low key, her extravagant astonishment, her amazement, his trumpet, her saxophone, in the face of what cannot be explained within the vernacular of the rational mind or by the abstruse speculations of researchers on government scholarships who want to discover the physical basis of life and thought so that they might invent it better. The astonishment before the unexpected, inexplicable parallels between them. The astonishment before the incredible and implausible intersections. . . .

And she finds herself, wandering again in circles, in Uroboris, in eights and infinities.

What she didn't notice until this moment. What she hadn't seen was the way he divided up his book, *Hopscotch*:

From the Other Side
From This Side
From Diverse Sides

The way she has seen it:

Here
On this side or *Over there* (depending on the perspective)
Terra Incognita

The first possibility: She saw this, registered it, filed it away and wrote accordingly without remembering it was his way.

The second possibility: She saw this, registered it, filed it away so that she could go back and alter her text to accord with his.

Try again:
She's always been on the same wavelength as he, but it's her book.
or
He is dictating the book.

Try again:

Try Л.[59]
?
Make it bold.
Л
Oh!
Л

Bingo!

The deeper she gets, the longer she is at it, the less she understands. Correspondences arise . . . Who wouldn't think she is plagiarizing or working out an elaborate, if foolish plan, making a literary game out of pretending to forget or not noticing when, who wouldn't assume, she has either known it all along or is scavenging through his text, carefully copying and denying, copying and denying? Who wouldn't think it?
Л

About **Л**. She had come upon **Л** when she had found herself searching for a symbol that might represent the two of them. She had not expected to come upon **Л**; it had all been a surprise to her. She had been musing about this text and then it was as if she had been taken over and directed to search by some external force, as if she was "*in the center of something* *that came from somewhere*" and helpless before it. Searching aimlessly through the symbol file on her computer, rebuking the inner compulsion, that nothing would, could show up that would, with a single stroke, represent a partnership between the two of them, she had certainly not expected to find herself in the Cyrillic alphabet, and was inordinately shaken by the discovery of **Л**; it had seemed so foreign, she had to attribute the discovery to his insistence coming at her like a tornado from *Over there.*

Pause. She has finished reading *62. . . .* She has been looking through it again to the dog-eared pages and sees, what she had not seen before. You understand, dear reader, that while you are compelled—unless you are reading the alternate version of *Hopscotch*—to read in sequence, that no book is written absolutely in sequence, that we go forward and then we go back, and that now, with the invention of the computer, this back and forth motion is more common than uncommon, and so after something is written, we return to it, insert an idea, change a phrase, edit, amend, elaborate, expand, that each writing is an endless agitation and re-investigation of the original moment, an endless present, again, literally uniting the past and the future.

And so, I▪ returned to this moment in time and space just above of the **Л** and paused there on the computer while feeling, for no reason she could identify, the need to go upstairs to the deck where she had left *62* . . . after she had finished reading it this afternoon (some weeks after opening it on the airplane) and she began to wander through the pages in a desultory manner, beginning at the beginning and then looking at dog-eared pages and then coming back to the beginning to . . .

The Russian alphabet. Yes, she hadn't known until this moment how much he had, in fact, had to do with it.

When she had come across **Л**, she had had to track down a Russian speaker to see what **Л** meant and how it might or might not represent them. But now, sauntering again through the book, she is even more agitated, unnerved by what is occurring, by what is on his page that relates to what is on her page—in this case he says in the very beginning, on the 7th page of the novel to be exact: "*The fat diner had unfolded Frances-Soir, and the full page headlines suggested the false Russian alphabet of mirrors.*"[60]

Each time such an event occurs, she thinks she is reconciled to it, that the next time it will occur, she will not be frightened by it, certainly not surprised by the synchronicity which is nothing less than his tapping her on the shoulder, or climbing in the window, despite her request that he not startle her, from the other side.

She hadn't needed, then to go through the dictionary of symbols on her computer. She could have, if she were more adept, followed his direct communication and looked into the mirror of his book directly to find his patently clear instructions regarding the Cyrillic alphabet and. . . . This ЛI they have become. This two. This ЛI.

Don't forget what the line says exactly: *the **false** Russian alphabet of mirrors* and whatever that implies about ЛI.

Who *are* you, Julio Cortázar?

Part VIII

ד

The hardest thing is to surround it, to fix its limit where it fades into the penumbra along its edge. To choose it from among the others, to separate it from the light that all shadows secretly, dangerously, breathe.[61]

Julio Cortàzar, *To Dress a Shadow*

The doorbell rang in the middle of the night. At first, being alone, I was afraid to answer the door but then, as the wolf wasn't alarmed, I opened it. The dark was filled with stars and Mars, almost at perigee, the closest it would be to planet Earth in 60,000 years, loomed red in the eastern sky. I went outside and sat in the *lucas* looking up into the night, watching the inexplicable as the clouds came in and created another *lucas* around Mars and then the surrounding belly of the newly gathered clouds turned red. Premonitions and portents of war and disorder as Mars approaches, but that is not the story the sky is telling. The sky is speaking of the beauty that can be observed through the pinhole that extends from one reality to another. Excitement is rising in me like a planet and traveling across the elliptic of my heart. Or let me put it this way: something is rising in me that wants to meet the circumstances of the sky in the way, some say, the circumstances of the sky affect the movements of our hearts.

I have been waiting to tell you a strange, most fearful and yet, oddly beautiful dream. A dream of war in the location of great beauty and isn't that what I am observing now as the clouds gather and disperse, take on the cloak of red fire and relinquish it to the starry night and the great constellations through which the ruddy planet spins a most bellicose or tranquil orbit so close to our lives.

Certainly, the doorbell hadn't rung, but something awakened me and called me outside to this strange wonder of red and silver, that is, in its way, the kind of alarm that asks the soul to be still and wait for understanding even when we doubt that it will ever come.

Mars has wandered into the western sky that is hidden from me now and so I make my way into the house, relishing the silence that is descending as Mars rises, and knowing that I have to make my way here, to this form that we have found or that I think we have found, that I imagine we have found through which I speak to you where you are *Over there*.

It seems as if the house is colder than the night when I▪ settles down at her desk but it is only that she is so cold because she cannot escape Julio's gaze. She is looking at a photograph of him. It is not the one where he looks off into the distance, *Here* but looking *Over there*. It is not the one where he is looking through a wall that has been broken open to create a *lucas* into another world. It is the one where he is here and looking straight at her, but you know that he is not here and his gaze which is adamant, firm, unbending, resolute, persistent . . . which is mesmerizing, which is insistent, which is full of gravity and determination . . . is the gaze of an adept or a sorcerer, the gaze of a magician of the highest sort, a gaze which gives no latitude, allows no play, is determined to cross from there to here in order to engage in a true act of theurgy, the one she strives for and fears.

Maybe the veil is thin, thin enough, my dear J., she whispers to the keys of her computer, so that I can tell you this dream that haunts me so that we can carry it, the two of us, for it is too harsh for me to carry alone. How much tenderness she feels for this man she once knew who has accompanied her for so many years.

I have lived with this dream for almost ten years in which time it has become a searing presence, a memory that I cannot escape or abandon. In some country where I have never had permanent residence, these events happened or are continuously happening, and refuse to be forgotten. To forget them would be a profound betrayal, similar to forgetting my worst misdeeds. These are my dreams. They want me to be responsible for them and to them. They have, like you, become presences, sometimes companions of a sort, sometimes jailers. I am relieved when I see them because I am shamefully grateful for the familiar company, yet I also know that I am in their hands. There is nothing I can do to alter them or to affect what happens between them and me. As there was nothing I could do in the dream but watch my activities unfold, an actor encased in a role predetermined by an unknown but exacting scriptwriter who cannot or will not affect the action but who must bear witness to it. And what would I change, in the moment of bewildering circumstances suddenly and pitilessly imposed upon me and upon everyone else who is similarly condemned to participate in them? What action might I be certain of, which action's outcome can I guarantee? But to forget these dreams would be to affront the continuous present in which the nightmares rightly repeat themselves and repeat themselves incessantly for purposes we cannot yet know. In the meantime, *Thewomaninthecellar* and our dreadful nights.

I had taken a ferry to an island. For all I knew, I was the only passenger on the ferry. It was an old ferry. I had had some coins. Enough to pay the ferryman. The island had risen out of the sea, blue green waters were rushing down its harmonious marble contours, rivulets of turquoise and emerald were cleansing the tiny curvilinear streets, charging through ivory crevices, until it was there, crystalline in the sunshine. Maybe that is how it appears, when we hope we're coming to Paradise even when we're not.

There was a ferry. And an island. And I got off the ferry. Then I was with friends, a man and a woman, who were not you, J., and not Thewomaninthecellar, but might have been at some point in these incomprehensible lives of ours when we were all together.

The three of us, a poet and a woman young enough to wear shorts in a foreign country, and I are going house to house on this island that rises out of the sea like a breast. I don't know this in the beginning, but I know it afterwards when I am looking back, grief-stricken at the island and I see the breast rising out of the small chest of land surrounded by water, an island that no one had mapped before. We have just disembarked from the ferry and are rushing door to door, making our cyclical way up the curved slopes of this island, white island, blue, blue sea, sunlight as I have only seen in Greece. Brilliant. There is a threat of a war, of invasion, of insurrection. It is our responsibility to tell the people that an invasion is imminent and we do not know if the enemy is from elsewhere or whether this is the culmination of an internal uprising, brother turning against brother. But there, to my right, to the east, outside my vision, invisible and not necessarily real, is the shadow of another smaller island that is a launching place for the attack. We have come here for the purpose of telling the inhabitants that they must prepare. We are not of this place but, somehow, once we land here we know what is coming.

We are winding our way up the helix of narrow streets, with oyster white houses, blue doors and blue shutters, doors, windows opening wide into that blue that only exists near the Aegean, as even if you buy the paint on the isles of Poros or Santorini and bring it elsewhere to paint the window panes of your white house with it, it will not be the same color as it was since this blue depends, as all blue does, entirely on the quality of the light that streams from a sky, clarion blue, so blue it is pure bird song as the isle rises from the sea like Aphrodite herself.

And now we go down. Speaking, entreating, attempting to organize whomever we meet to resist. It is tiresome, going from house to house, trying to explain, not speaking the language. What will be the outcome? How can they resist? How can they defend themselves? This goes on for a long time, or for an instant, it is impossible to gauge how much time has passed.

The poet disappears into a blue oval that becomes a dark entryway. My woman friend, who is nameless, follows. Even now, I am cautious about the naming of names, even dream names in dream states; we must practice the essential etiquette of survival. The two dash in and out as if they know the women of the houses, as if they are old friends, as if they are residents, as if they belong here, as if they are protecting what they love.

Then everything changes. The light disappears. The environment becomes sinister. Those strangers or brothers, most likely, on that other island, how well armed they are.

I step into the utter darkness of one of the brilliant white houses where a congregation of elderly citizens are hiding. It is hard to know if the rooms are truly dark or whether it is fear that is darkening the house. My friends have disappeared, perhaps they are continuing their labor but, as if in their place, here are my dead father and mother.

I go into a room where the women are sequestered. They look up at me, anxiously, pleading. I look around the room and then I call a particular old woman out. I do this. And then another. And then another. I have been given criteria, but what they are is vague. How can there be criteria? I am going into that room and calling women out and those whom I am choosing have a chance to survive. All those whom I don't choose, all those who remain in the room, all of them, and they all know it, all the rest are certainly going to die. As I look around the room I am searching out whatever liveliness, whatever kindness or generosity remains in them. I am forced to trust my intuition. I turn to my mother who has been waiting, agitated and terrified outside the door: "Is there anyone I should have chosen that I overlooked?" She knows this community far better than I do. These are her peers. She knows. Whom am I to choose? She must choose, I decide; she knows who these people are. She must choose. I stare into her eyes but she doesn't see me. She is in the state of shock of one who has found herself, unexpectedly, before a firing squad. She must go back in and choose. She does this without protesting but in the next moment, when it is far too late, I understand that we have committed a crime. The women know my mother and they know what she has agreed to. They know that the ones she chooses will live and all the others that she does not choose, though she lived alongside them, worked alongside them, they will die. They know also that she will live. I have asked my mother to make such a choice. A few will live. If we do not choose, no one will live. I/we try to choose those who have life force in them. A spark. Something that will survive, that will have a future. My mother has collapsed from grief and shame and the life force goes out of her. And now, whom will I choose?

But it is time now to choose the men. My father, bowed with resignation, accompanies me into the room where the men are gathered. He knows the soulful ones, the ones of light. I attempt to choose those who can carry what they must carry with heart. I decide. Or he informs me. Then I go back in the room—or he does—and too many are chosen—six or seven men walk out of that other room instead of three or four . . . because . . . because that is just how it happens. I pray that we can save everyone we have called out, that we can get away with saving so many. The light they carry, this must be preserved. This is what I am choosing. And my father.

How long do we have until our survival will be certain? I ask my father to look at his watch. He tells me the time, but I need the date. It is December, 1944. It is December 25th, 1944. We are still in the war; I do not know when we will come to the end of it.

There is a scuffle outside, the door opens and a ray of light like a sword unsheathed at high noon cuts into the blackness. I step toward it and once again, I am with the poet and my woman friend as if I had never been in that dark house, as if my parents had never existed. When we entered the houses earlier, the doors were open but now the doors are closed. We must enter the dark surreptitiously to find the guns and break them down. We say it is so the invaders will not be able to use these weapons, but it means that these people will not be able to defend themselves. Then I know something that I do not want to know. We are doing harm. My companions, my kin, my beloveds. How easy it is to get swept up against one's nature. It's dizzying. We are on the down curve now, heading back toward the transport ship which is waiting to take us, everyone, that is all tourists and visitors to safety. It is the ship that brought us to the island. We have lost our multi-colored totes and tapestry carpet bags long ago, the ones with silver edged blue flowers gleaming in a tangle of silken vines. Mine was so heavy, I could barely carry it up the white alabaster stairs that went from the sea to the houses and past the houses to the summit and then down again.

We are at the maw of the ship, from which the long intestines of cars have exited so that the people who are waiting most gaily can enter. I am stepping up to enter when the poet, behind me, raises his foot in the manner of station conductors pushing people onto crowded subways or an SS officer insisting an old woman into a cattle car, and places his shoe squarely against my ass and shoves me in as the wide door slides shut like teeth biting, slides down and shuts.

The ship has become a crowded refugee boat but without the passengers knowing the nature of our departure. I go upstairs looking for the level where we were before as the ship begins to sail out of the harbor. Standing at the rail, looking back, without luggage, without a sweater or shawl against the coming night and the sea winds, I see the setting sun illuminating the red nipple of the summit of the breast of the island.

Only now do I realize I am alone. My friends have stayed behind. They have chosen the war; they will kill and be killed, while I will survive. War is war.

The boat pulls away into the twilight. Stars appear revealing how far away everything is. The departure of the ferry has gone unnoticed and no alarm has been sounded. My friends, the ones who are dearest to me, have made a choice, one they knew I couldn't/wouldn't make. I am safe and who wants such a fate?

A voice speaks from wherever it is that such voices originate: Invasion is not something one protects oneself against.

Perhaps I have not understood anything. My friends were breaking up the guns and I was afraid of such a radical choice. I thought I was acting on behalf of peace but perhaps I was simply being defensive, and we know that fear and defensiveness take us directly to war. Invasion is not something one can protect oneself against. Who was invaded, my beloved J.? Was it/is it you or me or both? I say the words over and over again trying to understand the incomprehensible: Invasion is not something one protects oneself against.

The voice continues, speaking so quietly and without fanfare but nonetheless disturbing everything I understand as it has for almost twenty years:

We choose whom we save.

What does that mean? It means that we can extend ourselves to help save someone only so far, only so many times. Only so much effort or focus or concern is available despite the openness of the heart. And so we choose those we save. We have to be willing to choose. No one can save everyone. But each of us can save someone. We choose, then, whom we save. Whom do you choose, my dear I▪?

The island quickly disappears as if it never existed. The boat is laden with women who imagine they are still on vacation. Food is being served, canapés, hors d'oeuvres, *meses* including *taramasalata*, Kalamata olives, dolmas, feta, Greek bread, American sandwiches. They fill their plates with so much more than they can eat, looking around anxiously for wine and then for coffee. The women drink so much champagne they forget themselves. I▪ stands alone on the deck, the wind blowing her hair black as night. She cannot see the island any more. The stars appear and the evening star, but whether it is Venus or Mars I do not want to say.

There are legends, aren't there, of islands of bone or coral that rise out of the sea and then as mysteriously disappear, as if an assault had been made on paradise and it drowned.

Behind us is the war. My friends are there. I am on the boat. No good will come from this.

The name of the island is Shaddai and the island looks like a reclining breast with an altar at the very tip where the nipple might be and the blue and green waters of the rivers of woe, lamentation, fire, oblivion and hate are flowing down to the sea as it rises.

This is how Iris dreamed it, and then this is how it remained after I▪ continued to dream it and this is how it remains now that it is mine and I continue to dream it. We thought we had been brought to hell and this is where we had been brought. Certainly, we couldn't stay. It is not a place for the living to remain. Still, we have seen it, Shaddai, the breast of God, milk and honey and the wars that are made against it.

Why, J., would I call you back to hell when you have escaped it? A spirit is just a flash. A little light. Fireflies. Fleeting here, but steady there wherever *Over there* is. These dreams did not come to a young woman. They came to us just after you died and just before your emergence.

Part IX
Return

ד

Many will come in my name.
Matthew 24:5

He had anticipated his return with dread despite the predictable fanfare. He had never known what would engage him enough to consider returning, but he knew himself and the places where he was susceptible to supplication. This time it was a voice, full of inadmissible longing. A woman fighting with herself, calling him and then afraid of calling him, refusing to call him, but, nevertheless, doing so ceaselessly. Who she was did not change the conditions of return; she would not make it easier or more difficult. She was clearly a messenger, another form of the strange angel that surprised everyone *On this side* when it appeared to them, recognizing the call through all disguises. Annunciation in that place they called *Here* was the manifestation of Holy Conscription *On this side*. So it wasn't I*, in particular, that aroused him. Or maybe it was. She seemed to be rewriting his story from her own imagination, staying with a very few basic facts and improvising upon them. He wasn't sure she would get it right, the others hadn't. Actually, he knew that no one could get it right; there was no right to it and never would be except in its infinite and continuing variations. However, what he liked about her variation was that she didn't claim to be telling any truth about him but seemed more attracted to the lark of it. Also, she seemed to be asking for his opinion and input but without ever claiming that he had responded and so she was not privileging anything that appeared on the page as the truth, though, in truth, she did over-use that concept as if it could or did exist somewhere, as if she could, herself, aspire to it. She would have to get over truth if he was to join her in any kind of collaboration, or he would have to burst her bubble. He thought she was up for that—this is what was intriguing to him. She also gave him a lot of room to be so many versions of himself and gave herself a lot of room for being wrong and contradictory, despite her own truth fetish. If she had her way, he might return or actively influence those who were interested in him like she was, but on the condition that each one would, by sacred agreement, write something entirely different from the other, equally if similarly, cogent, convincing and authoritative. Similarly they would agree not to argue about their perceptions but would see that they would all be exactly right, distinct and parallel like the different colors of the rainbow she seemed to like so much.

Attractive as her offer was, her enticements, her seductions, her fervent prayers, he could not overcome his great reluctance to return. He wondered if he could return to her circle without his presence becoming widely known. Her invitation did refer to the assumption that he would return. Reinforcing that hallucination certainly needed to be avoided at all costs. One very ambitious CEO or PR man and everything would get out of hand.

However, there were possibilities in her proposals, because there were built-in safeguards. She could write whatever she wanted; no one would believe her regarding his return. She could have her book and he would be safe; very few, if any, would notice. He suspected she might be interested in entering into such a bargain—it isn't as if she expected attention or wanted him to create it for her. The ones who would read her book, if any, would consider its literary qualities and would assume it was a Fiction as she forthrightly called her work. So he would be protected from the consequences of a publicly accredited reappearance. Those, who were really clamoring for a big public scene with trumpets and clarion calls (really bad theater, he thought) that would redeem them just by its occurrence, would never hear about, let alone read, her work. Thus, she had everything going for her: she was a woman; her desire was personal and it had nothing, thank G-d, to do with her "salvation." He was beginning to think, he could grant her this little boon without committing himself to anything that would endanger him, the planet or the future again. She was likely not to upset the apple cart that he had inadvertently upset a long time ago by failing to restrain his friends' impulses to attach his story to an older and rather bloody story that had begun with apples. OK, lady, he thought, go for it. It can be our own little tête-à-tête.

He felt an immediate lightness. After all she had been pestering him for a long time and her constant beseeching had distracted him from attending the larger questions it had raised, which now, because of a conjunction of historic circumstances and some spurious predictions, were pressing and unavoidable.

But, speaking of return, she had raised the real issues that he had to consider. He took a breath, if breathing is what spirits do, and began to ponder the great mystery that was before him.

He was gravely apprehensive that his entire story would be relived exactly as it had occurred the first time. Isn't that the way it always happened? One was born to a place, lived out one's story in that place, went away for a long time, long enough for everything to change, and then one came back and everyone expected, no, insisted, it be the same. This is not what he meant when he had attempted some preliminary sketches of what he had called the prodigal son. He hadn't had a chance to do some real editing, but certainly he hadn't intended the returning young man to become the exact simulacrum of a father's self-serving distortion of the ideal son. But that is another story, one, hopefully, he could work on if he came back. It was clear to him that if he returned, he would take another shot at being a storyteller. Literature had advanced since he had been around; there were many readers and fascinating ways of duplicating texts, even instantly and all this intrigued him. People could read his story without having to endure a sermon about it.

OK, this could be his trade-off. When he came back, he would set certain conditions, some of which would simply pleasure him, and being a writer, frankly, is what he longed for. He wasn't going to let others tell his story again and he, certainly, was not going to allow himself to be vested with kingly authority, spiritual or otherwise; he had had enough trouble with power to last him 2000 lifetimes.

Another condition of his return would be extending his story into old age. He wasn't sure if it would be a man's story or a woman's story, but he was determined to see if he could tell, and so live, at least certain parts of it elegantly. He was beginning to understand how a story created a life and a life created a story and he wanted the pure dance between them. Now that was worth returning for. He felt a surge of joyous vertigo and possibility.

But back to his story or what was alleged to be his story. He had to consider what had happened to it, its falsifications and distortions so that it wouldn't happen again. To the extent his story was his story, it was his because he had been born at a certain time in a certain place to certain people to whom he would always belong. Now his parents and ancestors were disdained and persecuted and had recently been the object of horrific murders that had almost destroyed them all and so shattered their souls that they were beginning to wreak similar violence on others.

His alleged followers had wanted him to be recognized by the elders when any sensible person knew that it was for the children to honor the fathers and the mothers. He would have to be certain that his parents and ancestors were honored; he had been too young himself to secure this into the future even though his life as he had lived it, as opposed to what was said about him, honored the substance of his beginnings. His wise qualities weren't merely ascribable to rebelliousness, but to roots and tradition.

He also believed that what made a good story, and a good life, was the precise way it posited myriad variations on a theme, so many possibilities. This story that he had lived and its conclusions couldn't occur again because the historic and cultural circumstances were entirely different now. They had been entirely different five minutes after he had been born. Who he was then would never again be possible. Any astrologer knew this and based his or her insights on just such essential knowledge. But now there were sightings of him everywhere as if he, as they thought or imagined him based on the specious history they had created through codifying his story, could possibly appear out of elsewhere and still be himself. He was, after all, who he was exactly because of his particularity and the ways it expressed universal qualities. However as he read the text that purported to speak of him, he found himself lost in clichés and caricatures that lacked verisimilitude. He thought a fine literary mind could show that the writers had failed to demonstrate the development and complexity of his character and its relationship to time and place.

People assumed, however, that his story, or, rather his first life, for each life was only and especially a story, was the only story, the right and true story even if the one who had lived it knew it hadn't been a great story. Now with hindsight, and the addition of the literary mind, he thought he should simply start again as if he had never been. Then they wouldn't know that he had returned because they wouldn't recognize him as they couldn't/wouldn't detach the story from the person. To them his original story was a good story because it was his. He was who he was; how could it be otherwise? His story. Good story. The same.

He, himself, thought entirely differently. In his heart, soul and understanding, there was absolutely no reason to relive or reverence the original story. To the contrary, he thought it would be a violent and pernicious act to revive the story and give it credence. Increasingly, the story was diabolically contradicting the essence of who he remembered himself to be.

In order to change the story and, particularly, its end, he would have to change the beginning. This was getting interesting. If he changed the beginning, the moment of origin, in kind, intent and place, another end would follow inevitably and he would have an entirely new life. He was, he admitted sheepishly to himself, also involved in the first story and couldn't yet, specifically, imagine his origins and biography entirely distinct from the original story and the doctrines that proceeded from it. What if he didn't recognize himself? The possibility of being so free enlivened him enough to consider returning. Except that it wouldn't be he that was returning, not the he everyone recognized and hoped would return in order to save them. That was another delusion—the thought that anyone could save those who couldn't save themselves, or that anyone could save others when he couldn't save himself or his teachings.

Oh, it wasn't so much that he hadn't been able to save his life, though that had been bad enough, but he hadn't been able to save himself from the distortions of those who purported to love him. His murderers were what they were, but his friends had inveigled him into a story that she—that I■ person, the one who had been badgering him, liked to say— "had no future." His advocates persisted with the story as it had been given to them, accepted the end of it, praised it endlessly. They even took to wearing the instrument of his great torture and failure around their necks so that anyone who came on them unawares would necessarily assume they were of the tribe of torturers that had installed itself and proliferated so dramatically, one of those weed species that takes over by overwhelming everything in its path. Then they pretended to draw lessons from it, but, truly, what lessons could one draw? They had, he noted, valorized his death so profoundly that they had gone on to develop a literature that could barely imagine itself without violence or murder. This is what his life had come to.

From year to year the story had changed, as stories must, in the mouths of storytellers, but no one had had the moral fiber to enter deeply into the possible variations in order to get closer to the lost truth, the truth that had disappeared at the very moment that the final event had occurred.

There had been a death. A premature death according to everyone who loved him. Look, just come back, they said. We'll do it again. We'll do it differently. You can't do it differently if you're still holding on to the old story. Give up the story, he said, and I'll come back. I guarantee it. If you give up the story, I'll return. It will be our dance. But they couldn't hear him.

It was no use. They said they heard him but they acted as if they hadn't or as if they didn't understand. Here and there anonymous writers had confabulated things he had said, or might have said, or interpreted what he had said, or predicted what he would say, uniquely enough to be engaging as long as no one version became the story. These stories sometimes had merit and he sometimes recognized himself in them, even though they spoke to a maturity he hadn't been old enough to attain in his lifetime. But, the combination of his character, and the character of these writers, shed a sweet and benevolent shade on the torturous fires of inquisition that the other stories too often inspired.

What disturbed him, whether these stories pleased him or, more often, violently displeased him, was that these visions or fantasies became part of a text that was considered as sacred as his life. In a world such as the one to which he was to return, this was considered a great publishing success and so had priority over what anyone considered genuine. Would he have to change his values and learn to think in such terms if he returned?

The ones who told his stories, especially those who claimed to tell them exactly, weren't the kind of writers or storytellers he was or aspired to. He could never understand why this story, that had become canon, fascinated people so.

It was a story written and interpreted after his death by different writers, some of whom were stylists, but some of whom weren't. All of them distorted the original tale, some left out essential details while some versions were lost entirely. He liked to think the lost stories, at least, had been the good ones. In any case, these versions weren't his stories; they were *their* stories and so were completely deprived of his eye and craft for meaning and vision. Further, they lacked the modicum of satire, humor and self-reflection that every good tale requires. There was also the additional problem of canon leading repetitively to cannon fodder, a transition that mystified and wounded him.

And then, of course, the redactors had left out the influence, perceptions and activity of the girls and either hadn't given them a book to write or had, as likely, buried the ones the girls came up with, for surely the girls understood things differently from the boys, and it was just that difference, *viva la . . .* that was sorely missing. *Las Magas*, by their nature, challenged the male coven that had made his story so dangerously *precious* and not one of the girls would have been so benighted as to title a book about his death, "Good Tidings." It isn't how girls think. And then, there was Mary, that brilliant, devoted and passionate wench whom he would never have considered maudlin as she was the one he obviously favored. Her favors had sustained him so profoundly in his life but his cohorts had put out bowdlerized versions when they must have known one can't possibly write a decent tale without the bite of the dynamic and dizzying interchange of male and female or lovers at the least. He had known that much even though, or because, he was just a boy so necessarily carrying boy wisdom when he departed. Their attitudes dismayed him and reflected badly upon him. He was also unnerved by the way these texts disparaged the means of renewal and creation. One of the girls, if not several, should have had a chance to write her own vision of how it had been and so how it was . . . how it is, how things are.

He had been thirty-three. A boy. This was the first mistake. To end the story at this moment when like any *puer* he could hardly see beyond his own ego and imaginings, his inevitable fascination with himself. To allow it to end without imagining the eye that age would give him. He should have been far more than twice his age when his story concluded. Odin hanging on the world tree plucked out his own eye in return for wisdom. He was there long enough to learn to see and then he got off the tree. Remorse. Ordeal. Descent. There's no point in going through an ordeal that ends in death before the true and beautiful fruits of initiation can be plucked. No one benefits from it, not even or especially oneself. In the Odin story, people got the runes after his ordeal. Not dogma, but the means of insight one could wrestle with, spending a lifetime trying to understand.

If you asked him now how he would have liked to be remembered, it would be as a storyteller and not as a *puer* who didn't get a chance to become a *senex*. That's another reason why he, had he had the opportunity, would certainly have changed the ending and written an opus that detailed the development of a mind that had potential and would come to a good end. If only he had had the opportunity to write his memoir, either directly or through the multiple fictions that streamed through his mind, each one a particular, and hopefully even peculiar version of multifaceted creation that he loved so much. Responding with a critical eye and a literary ear, he was dismayed by the internal inflation of the story and the way this justified the suppression of all other stories when the best nights of his life were spent sitting around a fire with other raconteurs intoxicated with the heady wine of one sacred romance or sacred creation story after another.

He had imagined all kinds of stories coexisting: men's and women's stories, and best of all the stories of those who had made it to old age and whose peaceful deaths had been a vital offering to their communities. Then, of course, there were there were the stories of the elements, the animals and the fabulous, the gods and demigods, all those mysteries. What happened to those? His story, well it wasn't his, he didn't write it and, it wasn't about him, not really, not who he had been, this specious tale had replaced them all. It made a dull world. Dying again and again. They loved the dying part. They loved it best.

No, it wasn't his story anymore, never was. Sometimes he thought it was a curse. Sometimes he wanted to shout to whoever would listen: Please write another ending. There's going to continue to be a whole lot of blood on everyone's hands if you keep living it out pretending it's my will.

But the storytellers argued that the ending couldn't be flawed because their missionary success, albeit often violently imposed, proved that the story was a fitting vehicle for the divine. The story was so popular from generation to generation and from place to place that it had become the very nature of the world. They couldn't wait to live it out again. Only this time, everyone who believed the story would fly up the way he had. [He wondered where that would leave him.] Each of them would have a private space missile and launching pad that was the early 21st century equivalent of an American President's campaign promise of two chickens in every pot and a car in every garage.

He'd better come back, they insisted. It would be glorious. He would see.

At this moment, he felt the vulnerability that is native to the human species. Inevitably, on his return, they would impose his story no matter what his wishes and they would arrange it so someone would go after him as they had before, and he would be what they called "crucified" in one way or another, which was another way of speaking of being double-crossed, and they would say, "We told you so." It wasn't as if they hadn't spent centuries perfecting the art of crucifixion, practicing on anyone and everyone they could find. They had made a real success of the killing business.

Why were they so committed to this passion play? There were hundreds of theatre pieces that were just as intriguing and dramatic.

Also he didn't know why they were waiting for him now. Someone's imagining in the past had gotten to the literal minded and they were setting the table. This time it wasn't a last meal they were offering, but something like a last war. There were many things he couldn't fathom about the way they thought, giving a great war in his honor was one of them.

This meant that that before anything occurred, before his heralded return, before he was able to reveal himself, to make his naked and transparent presence known, he would be forced, in solitude, to reflect on his own innocence and the harm that it, his story, had inflicted whether or not he had written it, whether or not it was his story. Somehow, he was responsible for it; this was his terrible fate. Perhaps it was that he had not originally thought to see how his story would be used against him and everyone else. He had not considered the evil (a word he distrusted, even despised, but was forced to recognize in these instances) consequences and implications for humans and, by default, for all the beings of creation when he had begun to develop and communicate certain parts of his life that had become, inadvertently, a well known narrative. Well, what writer can imagine how his work will be understood and what influence it will have twenty years after it is published or after his death, let alone two hundred years or two thousand? But if he had been a writer, he would have, at least, considered these issues as a writer must to have a coherent and convincing text.

He wanted a second chance. You can't see the implications clearly when you're living it, but if you spend twenty, thirty years or fifty years trying to develop and refine the story, you have a chance of getting a damned good yarn in the world that can do a lot of good without being *the* tale and *the* good.

So now he was back to the original dilemma. He didn't write his story. Others wrote it. He was innocent, but still it had been a disaster. Uh-oh, he saw, one of the pitfalls. He wasn't innocent. No one was and this is the essential point—no one is innocent and no blame. In fact, the assertion, assumption or desire for innocence was bad news from beginning to end. Innocence isn't good or bad, it just isn't. And not being innocent isn't good or bad either, it just is.

Well, what if he came back and there were no stories. Fat chance. OK. He would choose the opposite. Many stories. The writer again.

Writers were never innocent and they knew heartbreak. Heartbreak was a good beginning. Heartbreak and remorse.

He would first try to understand himself and then make himself understood and then would try to understand others; there would be that give and take, ultimately both enlightening and endarkening. He was old enough to reflect on the consequences of his own behavior and his own complicity in a scenario that he might have directed otherwise, but didn't. He would learn everything he needed to know now about human and divine grief from ruminating on the consequences of his first life.

At the borderland of his return, the writer would suffer the first story again, but this time in the ways the living had suffered it for centuries because of him. He was not to blame, but also he was to blame. He didn't want to be exempted from their suffering which was why he had come in the first place, but now he had an obligation to redeem them from the suffering that was, inadvertently inflicted upon them, by the nature of his original experience. Perhaps he could write a few tales that would undermine or replace the first story without entrenching themselves as some sort of gospel. The bottom line was that the people had their own suffering; it was more than sufficient for the wisdom they needed to live. Every life had its moments of misery but these coexisted with the beauty and delight that is inherent to life and the natural order. This ordinary misery—he would like to know something of it—it could be a good and endless source of story telling and imagination—without distorting it or adding to it.

It does not really matter how he came here or how he came to a certain development. The details of his rebirth and development would need to be kept secret because the public nature of his first life had caused such harm. His incorporation into human life was originally intended to reveal something of the nature and character of the divine, but it had boomeranged and become a lethal weapon against all those who had a different, but equally true, and often more realistic relationship, with divinity. He didn't remember now why he had also assumed that the divine was commensurate with extraordinary suffering. Had he had a broader view, the story might have turned out differently. Oh, if only all the living and the dead could be alongside him in this excruciating activity of soul searching. Uh . . . careful . . .

here was the danger. He couldn't blame others. He had to take full responsibility himself.

He had to do this without anyone knowing that he had returned. Otherwise, he was in danger of being caught in the old story. If he were to return, it really had to be a private affair, for his own purposes. His return had to be accomplished without imposing pain on virtually all living creatures.

But here was another intriguing dilemma: he wanted to support anyone's sincere belief in the reality of the divine. He would give it some thought. Maybe, he just had to leave things alone so that the sacred that had disappeared with his demise could seep back in—this time through pine cones, wolf cubs and blue jays. Yes, probably all of those and more so. A little bit of jazz to liven up those tedious and self-righteous hymns.

Well, if he could be sure of this then he could return and live quietly while the holy continued to insert itself again in all life. The sacred had coexisted with the world since the beginning. It had thrived. But, he noted bitterly, it had been undermined after his appearance and the distortions that had followed. If there were even a kernel of truth in this, and it seemed there was, he would have to be very careful. Very careful, indeed.

So he came back. This is what the writer thinks. Second coming. He was standing here, now, and looking without looking away. He had to see how and why their natures had been turned inside out by the story that had been enacted, supposedly, to redeem them and those to whom they ministered. He began to look for the evil that had been done. But then he saw himself courting trouble and stopped himself before it was too late. He couldn't choose to look for another who might be responsible for this evil, couldn't attribute the horrific consequences to an imagined Satan or devil, or to a specious original sin that tainted all of creation. That had been a big mistake. The myth of the great hero battling the great villain had led, in addition to other troubles, to such simplistic literature—good guys vs. the bad guys—you couldn't even call it literature anymore, especially as they rarely got it right about who was who. In the cowboys and Indians story, he certainly knew whom he identified with, and given a choice, which he would insist on, which path he would follow. The woman hadn't associated him with the Red path but give her a little slack and she might. He wouldn't mind trying it out.

He was getting distracted. There were certain ideas and principles he had to refine. His return had to be as invisible and consistent as his presence had been for centuries. Remember he was thinking of coming back as a writer, that hadn't left his mind for a moment. There could not be a single story that could encompass it. That single story was certainly one of the tragedies. Forget triumph and trumpets. If the truth were told, it would take a thousand, thousand scenarios to encompass it.

And why should he take the same shape he had taken before? So many shapes were possible. He had already taken so many shapes himself. He wanted to know everything. There was no shape he hadn't entered and no shape that he had not continued to embody. So there it was. He was everywhere as he had always been from the beginning of creation with a thousand names as appropriate and proper and with a thousand, thousand arms.

As for the story they were waiting for, something had to be offered to them, but, this time, something different from his own. His story as he was coming to understand it was being revealed to him now for his own purposes, for his own enlightenment. Still, he wanted to offer them something, if surreptitiously, as they wanted a story and were ready to fabricate one and would kill for it if nothing else appeared.

Yes, he wanted to be a writer. But, he got it that one writer could also create havoc. So if it turned out that there were a lot of really good writers and he could secretly be just one among many of them, then, at the least, he could have a really good time. But if he wanted to be a really good writer, he would have to give up his preaching spirits. Moralizing ruined a narrative. If he could keep his opinions to himself and describe how things are, he might get good enough to kibitz a little, indiscernibly influencing plot or character for others. He could become an imperceptible muse. Maybe nothing would get better, nothing would improve; his own story as it had been told and distorted, maybe it wouldn't disappear as he hoped, but, hey, he would have the joy of what the writers he eavesdropped upon spoke about: creation. Imagine what it would be to learn something of that. Creation, itself, didn't do harm as long as it remained as varied and complex and surprising as this little planet required for its own existence. And then he realized that the other planets with life on them hadn't been exposed to his story and were doing very well without it. Many stories was clearly one of the answers.

If, on his return, he gave his newly lived story over to other writers to improvise, to invent the thousand, thousand variations again and again, putting their funny and peculiar names on the tellings, everyone would realize the necessity to seek out many stories to reflect upon and take to heart. If this were possible, he would begin to see how to separate a life from a story so that he could live like anyone else. Why did he need to be special? He could live wherever he was called within the restraints of the shape of that life. He would enter wherever he was called to enter whatever life he could. But he would never announce himself and certainly would not assume that this particular incarnation out of myriad incarnations was the one and only true way. Despite or because of the many stories, they would probably think that he had not returned yet. Some were saying the story of his return was a fabrication, anyway. Maybe these truth tellers would be heard.

Would his acolytes make their damned war anyway? Maybe not. Maybe they would not make the war without him. Maybe they would think about getting old and wise. Maybe they would not sacrifice their sons and daughters. Maybe they would not think that was such a good idea. Maybe they would get lucky and catch a glimpse of him in unexpected places. Maybe there would be sightings in trees, or among ptarmigans, in ironic stories, or in the faces of very aged women who practiced the old ways that went back long before he had even been an idea in the mind of a narrator. Maybe he would be forgotten. Maybe this particular story that was so dangerous, that had caused so much harm, more harm than any other story in the history of the world, would pass out of existence, so that his essence in all the ways it could be known might be revealed.

Yes, he thought it might a good idea to try coming back anonymously as one of those legendary fabulists, great raconteurs, mythmakers, one of those outrageous humorists, satirists and clowns, inventors of tall tales and wild imaginings that he had heard about but hadn't had a chance to read as much as he would like. He ruminated upon coming back this time as someone multi-lingual and exceptionally tall who, had, what they called, a way with women. One of those coyote, trickster figures who knew how to do and undo everything that might otherwise get out of hand. Yes, he would try his skill at jokes, *jeux* and spiels, at *famas, esperanzas* and *cronopios*, not entirely but sufficiently irreverent to puncture dogma with such deft strokes that he would, himself, be enchanted with the pop.

PART X
CONFESSION

ד

In the Egyptian tradition the deceased is really judging himself and the Assessors are the projections of his own heart—it is the truthfulness of the individual himself that tips the scales of Maat, and nothing else.

The Book of Doors

Julio comes in the door and settles down, his long legs stretched out the length of the couch that is still too short for this colossus, and so he moves the coffee table, arranges himself on the carpet but not before signaling toward the CD player. He's on the floor and so I is on the floor. They agree on "Kind of Blue" and here comes eternity, a wind stirring up the transitory and the dust in the room.

M. stands at the door bemused. Is he waiting to be introduced or is he going to vanish into another world and so avoid the consequences of witnessing their coexistence? A line she attributes to T.S. Eliot enters her mind and, perhaps, also his: "Human beings cannot bear very much reality." The music is the ether that carries the moment; as they say, a milestone, and here is Davis on trumpet, and when Coltrane picks up the tenor sax, who's to say but that J.C. is among us.

"I'll leave you alone, M. says, kissing her on the forehead and closing the window as he exits the room as it's a cold wind that's blowing in. He returns in a moment with two gourds, each topped with silver and two *bombillas*, a gift he had just given her. The steam from the *maté* curls into the room, she sucks in the tea from the metal straw and then he is gone, and she thinks it would have been a good thing if he had been with her then, the four of them, Hélène, M., Rio and herself, in that dark time when they had hoped to find a little light among themselves. But then, she probably wouldn't be here, now, with Julio. Longing has brought her here. So, it was good, after all, what they didn't manage then, because of what is possible now. Bless M. she thinks, because he wasn't there then and because he is here now, in the next room, as he might have been in the kitchen then with Hélène, allowing Iris, finally to say what she needed to say to Rio, having traveled such a distance hoping for that possibility.

So easy. She wonders why she waited so long. Julio is here. The maté is steaming. All she has to do, apparently, is write the words and the event occurs. How easy magic is—one small step from concept to manifestation. Why didn't she accomplish it sooner? It would have saved her all the abysmal efforts around the manuscript. But then there would not have been a text. Has she kept him waiting so long while trying to write a book when a simple abracadabra would have sufficed? One week, when she'd had a particularly hard time with the book, M. had purchased a lucite wand with a moving liquid center of green and blue stars intermingling. "It's for my wife," he explained to the toy store owner, not certain why the recipient needed to be named, but as if to reassure the proprietor that it would be used by an adult who was trained in matters of the occult and would not abuse its potency or purposes. Had she thought of raising it and describing a series of figure-eights, the book itself might have progressed differently in swirls of words.

"Julio comes in the door and settles down, his long legs stretched out the length of the couch which is still too short for this colossus, and so he moves the coffee table and arranges himself on the carpet. . . ." Spoken. Written. Recorded. Sealed in the Akashic records; sacred memory assuring existence.

Only the room is empty. Empty of presence. She is there alone in a space that appears to have been ransacked. No couch. No coffee table. No chair. No CD player. No Miles Davis on trumpet. No J.C. on sax. A room so devoid of itself that its dimensions collapse until nowhere is the only local address, and between her and the void is the brick wall she had anticipated, but this time there is no man coming through. No man. No one. Certainly nobody. No body.

We are at the end of the book, Julio. A conclusion has to be reached. To continue as if this isn't the end is to deny the sacred order that has brought us to this moment. I have nothing to say. Oh, there is so much I could write about, but it would be a distraction and an indulgence. A book moves ineluctably to its conclusion. Nothing the writer does should deflect it from its inevitable realization. I offer the opening paragraph as evidence. Here we are at the moment. As I like to put it—the moment of truth. And I am speechless before it.

I wanted evidence that you exist and the only indisputable evidence she/I can imagine is the written word. But, I cannot attribute anything to you. It violates who you are as a writer to insist that you have participated in the writing of this book. You are a trickster and it has been a romp.

A long silence ensues.
She waits for him to rebuke her.
He is silent.

The play between them, the hypothetical give and take of story and language, the games, the hide and seek, the catch me if you can, the trysts and rendezvous, ruses, flirtations, seductions, exploitation, sleights of hand, ploys and pranks, conjectures and speculations, all have come to an end. The end. There is no where to go. She has hit the veritable brick wall. A brick wall. On one side are the living and on the other side are the dead. And here they are. Only they're not. Or he's not. Or, rather, we don't know about him, can't know, but she knows something of herself and it isn't what she expected. This isn't Iris beating down the door or I▪ flat on the ground, humbled in gratitude. After so much effort and rumination over so many years, not without success and its exhilaration, not without almost completing a substantial manuscript, she ends up here, abjectly alone and up against the intractable presence:

The future divides itself up, Machiavellian:
the farthest thing away has one name, death
and the other, the here and now, dumptruck.[62]

She is quite certain the entire manuscript has to be thrown away. After all her efforts, it is dead in the water. It has no future. She can't end the book in the only way that it must end. She won't merely postulate his appearance. And she won't lie.

She turns to the place Julio would be sitting if he were there. Listen, she says, this is the way it was. Imagine the scenario: You are a well-known writer with a reputation for writing about the occult. The dead move through your work like a thread in a needle or a scatter of yarrow sticks waiting to announce an augury. A young thing with literary aspirations comes to cross-examine you about the veracity of your assertions, about the validity of your inventions, about the authenticity of your visions. The young thing travels quite far to get to you and is not shy at all about admitting her intentions. The young thing wants to know if you are playing around, just fooling around when you write, or the young thing wants to be your lover. Let's say the young thing wants to be a writer but if you can't help her with that, then she'll settle for being your lover, but she lets you know its only for a roll in the hay, as Americans put it, and only if her prose fails. Sour grapes. Young and imaginative, this one has some notions about spirits, but doesn't know how to go about them without a little help from a bridge the young thing imagines you to be. Here's a ladder. Can you meet this one halfway across the great gorge?

All these words. She's stalling. She wants time.

If I let you in, J., and objects start flying around the room. . . .
Sassy is as sassy does.
Sorry, that was demeaning; you're not a poltergeist.
She's *Here*, Planet Earth, what do you expect?

She continues. "It's not that you weren't willing. It's not that you weren't able. It's not that I didn't believe you *could* come." This is the moment of reckoning and even she knows it, and so she pauses and deliberates and proceeds slowly, testing each word before she says it. She wants to be speaking the truth. She wants to be speaking the truth more than she wants the book to end, that is, succeed. Perhaps, she also believes that the book will succeed if she speaks the truth, but this idea isn't quite an ace in the hole, rather a dim hope she can't indulge now. Now she is after the truth and, this time, she has to come up with it herself. Not *her* truth. That's the current lingo. Thirty years ago, everyone was following *their* erotic urges and then *their* bliss and now *their* truth; she wants nothing so indulgent and deceptive. *The* truth. She wants to see what it means to speak the truth. No matter what the cost. The truth.

Everything written here was designed for this moment. Not the moment of their meeting at last, but this moment, the final and ultimate Duat, the plunge and tumble into the dark waters, the gathering of the spirits apprised and anticipating the holy of holies, when I finally confesses to the 42 Assessors of time and place, confesses. . . . And who is to hear this confession but the one who listens to the confessions of the heart and weighs it against a feather. Blue feather from the tail of a jay wafting down through the pine needles, one of the multitudinous, weightless wings of sky. Tehuti, himself, tall enough to bridge the expanse between all the worlds, stands, as always, into eternity, ready to hear the heart speak. It is time to confess the heartworm of deceit.

"It is, Julio, that I always knew that, ultimately, I would be afraid to open the door and so, ultimately, I would betray you."

This is a true statement. She knows it because it smarts as if she has been smacked across the face.

Almost twenty years writing about the possibility of collaboration, scrutinizing and testing each sign, being exact, refusing to indulge hope, honoring skepticism, and then, almost against her will, capitulating, accepting, yielding, conceding, surrendering finally to the overwhelming evidence of the presence of his presence and now, here, at the end, she is teetering, vacillating, dizzy. She is confronted by—or she constructs—a great ravine between what is stated, written, recorded and what is true. Everything she has written stands in contradiction to this moment, and still she cannot simply say what she wishes to say. She can only say what she must say.

She's talking to herself, saying what she would say to him if he were in the room, the words go round and round, repeat themselves, she obsesses, the proverbial broken record, like those disks she saw spread out across his bedroom in France, his bedroom, *and* Hélène's bedroom, she reminds herself, their bedroom, the records like a fan of tarot cards, each one telling a story, each piece of music, a pictogram of their life, their single life.

A woman had an idea of writing a book with a dead writer. Where did she get such an idea? Does she think she made it up? Wow! Great imagination, she has. So she starts writing a book about a woman writing a book with a dead writer. Wow! Imagine that! But this time, she doesn't say, as she would have before: Did I make it all up, Julio? Did I, Julio? Julio? Julio? J u l i o?

She doesn't indulge this. Because it doesn't matter if she speaks to Julio or doesn't speak to Julio, if Julio answers or Julio doesn't answer, if logic demonstrates that he has been speaking to her, writing to her, through her, or not. The evidence is in the text. If she read it over, she would be convinced. So it is not a matter of Julio denying her anything.

It is that she is afraid at this critical moment to cease equivocating and open the door wide. Her reluctance, her hesitation thus renders him irrelevant to this moment. It is as if she has offed him. Dead.

And yet she knows there isn't anything to the book except the question of their collaboration. There aren't any marriages or murders, any life threatening illnesses, divorces, adulterous affairs, assassinations, intrigues. No plot. Just the daily, grueling terror of trying to imagine how such a thing might occur. And when she finally imagines it, wraps her stubborn, fearful mind around it, then she closes the trap. Snap. Shut. And so it doesn't matter if he comes across or doesn't come across; she won't let him in. What is she thinking? It couldn't be anything as banal, could it, as "It's *my* book."

The locked door is the answer itself. Why would she lock the door? Because someone might come through. Who might come through? A dead writer? Well, that's the plot, isn't it? She's just a woman trying to work with a plot that intrigues her. There's the edge. The edge she knew she would have to face. Raizel faced it and failed and now she is up against it.

In the face of her own *j'accuse* she responds, I refuse.

If I open the door, I'll know you exist.
If I open the door, I'll know you exist.
If I open the door, I will know you exist.

The words are doing what words are supposed to do. Creating a world. In the beginning was the Word and. . . .

She has committed the essential act of defiance. She has denied what she believes. She has locked the door against it. She has denied . . . She has denied the very spirit she approached when he was merely a man, a giant of a man, but still a man, to find out if the spirit world is real, and since that meeting almost thirty years ago, *siempre en un contacto de eternidad precaria.*[63]

"Who said that?"

It's absurd to conflate spirits and words when most of the ghosts she knows speak in eloquent silence.

"Of course," he says in his own elegant and hermetic way, both opaque and transparent at the same time.

Of course, he wasn't going to write a book with her. Let's distinguish, please, between a literary imagination . . . and . . . the facts. Of course, he wasn't writing a book with her . . .

. . . but that doesn't mean he isn't real.

She hadn't wanted to write with him when he was alive, why should she try now that he was dead? She wanted to make him real the way he was when he was alive—lanky, thin, tender, unruly, oneiric, kind. She wanted him to long for maté and Chivas Regal. She wanted him to be alongside her, her *paredros*. But that isn't the way of magic. The way of magic is to make things real.

This isn't Iris. This isn't Raizel. This isn't I■. This isn't I. This isn't a character, or a narrator or a protagonist. This isn't a novel or a tall tale or a fiction. This is the moment. This is the moment of truth.

Confess before the 42 Assessors. Allow your heart to be weighed against a feather:

Confess:

I wrote about you, J. as a spirit but I wasn't prepared to believe it, herself . . . myself. I can say anything on the page but that doesn't make it true. I wrote that I■ lay down. "Full prostration," she said, and so I■ became I. I lied. It had taken almost twenty years to get to those lines even though they can be written or read in an instant—like dying—a lifetime to get there, and then—there she is—and then—there she's not. Pfft. A lifetime to get to those lines and then, everything, everything! that mattered is disappearing into the great maw of this lie that is consuming the colossus before her eyes . . .

Here is the entire confession. 19 years worth. She had asked him not to come in the window; it was another way of saying she certainly wasn't going to leave the door ajar.

There it is. All of it. A shambles. I wasn't going to open the door to something I would have to believe in. Believe in and act upon, then live with. Life on the page, it's a breeze. You don't like the weather? Bring on the sun. I seem to have written an entire book about you that I was intending to scuttle at the last moment, by saying I just couldn't work it out. As if the book was the point of it. As if the point of it wasn't always to see how things are, to stand before it, how it is, the is-ness of it all, and the book, well, her attempt to tell a story that documents what can't be put in words.

I've hit a brick wall, I says, to no one who is around to listen. M. is upstairs, not, as she incorrectly expects him to be, full of earnest, useless advice about the literary process and the spirits who come to him regularly, and how easy it is, but praying for her. Praying for her. He knew she would come to this moment, but he hadn't expected her to fail.

I've hit the brick wall, she thinks, marveling at what it must have taken for the photograph to capture the exact moment when *El Mago* burst through from the other side. We think he's looking at us and that we've done it, we have called him across to us, but that's after the fact. What was he looking toward when he pulverized those stones?

The one who wants to come in, the one who is *Over there* is waiting to enter, the J.C. guy, a musician, she writes, when she wants to write magician, even though she's writing so carefully, one slow, slooow, word after another, because the words aren't words any longer, not if they are going to be inscribed in the holy memory of what is, what is coming to be, but "Kind of Blue" is playing, making a corridor in the air.

She's talking about the dead, you understand. She's not talking about a sonnet or a prose poem, we're talking about the dead. The living dead. But she means something else by that phrase than what is commonly meant. She doesn't mean the living are dead. She means the dead are alive and they are on their way. They are coming through the door.

This one, who wants to return, he's not coming in the desert route, you can be sure. No wine, crosses, candles, not even feathers for him, no gospels or testimonies, no I was there, no belief, no believe, no heaven, no hell. No bullshit. We're talking about the dead. He drifts into the city, mr. nobody, mr. no one, mr. i'm not the one, pants rolled, no shoes, no signs, no high signs, no nothing. His words of power are. . . .

Magician enters from *Over there* and makes things real. Magician enters from *Over there* and makes things real. That's his theme—magic makes things real. Magic makes things real. Does she get it? That is what magic does, it makes things real.

She ponders this:

Magic makes things real.

I was prepared to write about spirit, but I wasn't prepared. I wasn't prepared, Julio, to admit that she believes in you, herself. She was prepared to admit to you, to herself, your little secret, that you exist, but I wasn't prepared to say it aloud. Not here. Not on the page. Not to the world. Before the cock crows three times. O cock o, o cock o, o doodle-doodle-do. The hell. It's real.

And there he is, seated on the floor, CDs spread out like tarot cards in the inscrutable patterns of his mind.

There are the two of them. She is living and he is dead. What's the difference? What's the big deal? The question hovers between them. Tehuti has come to interrogate her heart:

> they rise to appear at the edge of night
> like those voices you hear singing somewhere
> . . . what song you can't make out,
>
> . . . pale shades . . .
> when the vortex threatens to suck me down
>
> The dead speak louder . . . [64]

What are you going to tell him, I? Are you going to say you made up the dead, that they're figments of your imagination and, even so, death doesn't exist? Are you going to advise him to find another ghost writer because the last years have been a lie? How about a divorce? After all, it's been twenty years and dissolution comes hard after such a time.

Julio, *querido*, I confess to you before Tehuti, the Master of Divine Words, and the 42 Assessors. I knocked on your door. I almost broke your door down. Then when you answered and came toward me, I locked the door against you.

I lied.
I refused.
I betrayed you.

Silence. No thunder. No lightning. No hell and brimstone. Not even admonishment. No response. Their book. At the last moment, out of exquisite courtesy and fear of humiliation, she had intended to deny him. Isn't that what confession is—admitting evil, admitting failure, admitting ill will? But her final ruse doesn't work. The 42 Assesors are still waiting for the truth.

She doesn't know this place. She has never been here where everything is at stake and the flourish or facility of the phrase won't save her. This is the moment on the horn that's to be like no other, her solo, no one can save her, no fuck the solo bring on the band, gonna save you. She can't shave the grace note off this edge and make it right. She is reaching, she's gonna give it whatever she's got; she's got her breath extended just so, and steady. It has a long way to go, maybe to the moon and all the marble steps of light in between, not an up and then a down, but the magic formula that no number reveals, stated once and then again, but in another form, so fish to bird, night to dawn in sacred increments, a rapture of hills, endless and unending plains that jettison themselves into valleys and then rise up in great granite peaks, puncture the night; only an angel can manage it. Whatever self there is, blue suede shoes or alligator, gold chain around your neck, ankh, oudja, nothing can help her here. When she steps out, she must step out, no net under the high wire to catch her, pale umbrella twirling on hope, the note is all there is. Are you ready for the next one coming, and the next? She's not ready, but who asked? She's heard the music in some dream she longed to enter at least once, and here she is on stage, spotlight, shadows and all, she can't falter, not for an instant, so she lifts the horn as she bends slightly forward, the golden arc as it meets her golden lips, one brass body, and it's a one . . . two . . . three. . . . She brought herself to this moment; she, herself, called to the moment of truth, called, called, calling . . . two perfect notes:
Welcome   Spirit.

Magic makes things real. He has found out her heart. Her fears and exultations. This is real. There is a spirit in the house. She's afraid. This is real. There are things she can't understand. This is real. It doesn't matter what she writes, there is a spirit in the house. This is real. She calls him Julio. He is Julio and he's not Julio. This is real. Julio is dead. This is real. There is a spirit in the house. This is real. Julio once knew this spirit. Julio wrote about him, and wrote from the spirit's divine intelligence, and wrote according to the spirit's ability and willingness to mediate the worlds, to open the path between *Here* and *Over there*. This is real. A human being is not a spirit. A spirit takes whatever shape it pleases. This is real. The spirit has come to get her. There is a corridor. The call goes out and the spirit descends. This is real. The notes spiral up and then they spiral down. Words. Words. Words. Spirit descends. This is real.

Am I sitting on the floor alongside your couch or am I not sitting on the floor?

You are not sitting on the floor. That is not how the dead deport themselves. They do not act as if they have a body. When I say you are seated on the floor listening to CDs, that is not what I mean. It is just a manner of speaking.

What do you mean?
I mean that you are here, she says.

And then she speaks again of what has always been real between them. Her ladder across the gorge, her land of is.

Thewomaninthecellar, Julio, what can be done for her from *Over there*? Shall we have a funeral? How many horns do we need to open the way? Listen, Julio.

They listen together. They go to the window. They look down onto the street. And here come the drums. The wake up drums. The wake up on the other side drums. The long snake, skin shedding, people, coiling and uncoiling, under the golden curl and twist, the plaintive cry of trumpets. It's the jazz funeral, the *belonga* at last. The final opening of the way, the spin through the eye of the needle, the dead dancing toward the *Over there*, reaching across toward *On this side*.

May there be no impediments. May her soul fly free into your hands.

She looks to him, at that moment, to assist her with the exact language for such an unprecedented alliance, but he is silent. She changes the CD. *A Love Supreme*. What else?

He is extending himself toward shaping her so that she can do what is needed to be done while *Over there* he is creating lament at the open end of a long golden horn, the corridor, the passageway from *Here* to *Over there,* from Here to *Over there*, from *On this side* to *Here* and back again. Unimpeded is the goodness of the heart. The beat and the drum, the heart beat and the drum, the wind and breath, the cry of the golden horn continuously passing between them.

Swear!

It is time to swear the oath by the great serpentine waters of Styx that by their very gloom disallow lies. He looks at her, the way men do, searching out the place he can get a handhold so that, finally, he can take her down. It's what she wanted, isn't it, the six white or black horses, the pigs squealing as they fall into the hole in the ground, the smell of styx and sulfur, the dancing figures on the old walls, the invocation of the drums, the call of the flute, the trumpet's announcement, the wind whistling, the old ones waiting, the underground waters running so fast . . .

Swear!

On the swirling blue green waters of the river Styx, Iris, herself, the young one, the sweet one, swears the inviolable oath.

I swear, I will not deny you even when the cock crows.

Oh Hermes Trismegistus, I will not deny you even when the cock crows, oh thrice great Hermes.

Now it's his call. She has opened the door and he has, she admits, come through the wall.

And, there is, as I had secretly dared to hope, the Advent, the unassailable presence of spirit, an ever-flowing fountain, words pouring companionably into the eternal blue-green waters of silence.

· · ·

Welcome Tehuti, Hail Thoth, Architect of Truth . . . We stand before (you) who witness the judgment of souls, who sniff out the misdeeds, the imperfections, the lies and half-truths we tell ourselves in the dark.

Hail Thoth, architect of truth . . . Who Creates the World through Words. . . . Give us the words of power that the heart of our story may beat strong enough for a wo/man to rise up and walk in it.

Hail, Thoth, architect of truth. . . .

ЛІ

O vanidad de creer
que se nace o se muere,
cuando lo único real es el hueco que queda en el papel,
el gólem que nos sigue sollozando en sueños y en olvido.[65]

Tuesday, August 26, 2003 6:17:04 PM
Mt. Pinos, California
Happy 89th Birthday, Julio Cortázar

Notes

Part I:

1   Cortázar, Julio. "To a Woman." In *Save Twilight*, trans. Stephen Kessler. San Franciso: City Lights Books, 1997: 123.

2   Cortázar, Julio. *Hopscotch*, trans. Gregory Rabassa. New York: Pantheon, 1966: 53.

3   Ibid., 243.

4   "Get a Move On." In *Save Twilight*, 37.

5   Ibid., 41, 43.

Part II:

6   *Hopscotch*, 64.

7   Cortázar, Julio. "Press Clippings." In *We Love Glenda So Much and Other Tales*, trans. Gregory Rabassa. New York City: Alfred Knopf, 1983: 85.

8   "Get a Move On." In *Save Twilight*, 43.

Part III:

9   Cortázar, Julio. *A Certain Lucas*, trans. Gregory Rabassa. New York: Alfred Knopf, 1984: 16.

10 *A Certain Lucas*, 16.

11 "Get a Move On," In *Save Twilight*, 41.

12 "Get a Move On." In *Save Twilight*, 45.

13 *A Certain Lucas*, 96.

14 "Get a Move On," In *Save Twilight*, 37.

15 *A Certain Lucas*, 96.

16 *A Certain Lucas*, 97.

17 *The Book of Hags: A Radio Play in the Form of a Novel*, dramatized by Everett Frost. Produced for KPFK Paficica Radio, Los Angeles, 1976. Published on cassette, Washington DC: Black Box 1977.

18 All references to the *I Ching* are based on the work of Stephen Karcher, who has recently revisioned the *I Ching*, adding to the familiar Wilhelm/Baynes [Bolligen] translation, new interpretations and translations of the original texts which originated in China's pre-Confucian, shamanic past.

   Karcher, Stephen. *How to Use The I Ching: A Guide to Working With The Oracle of Change*. Massachusetts: Element, 1997.

   Karcher, Stephen. *Total I Ching: Myths for Change*. United Kingdom: Time Warner, 2003.

19 Amando, Jorge. "Tres temas para Julio," In *Queremos Tanto a Julio: 20 Autores para Cortázar*. Alegria, Claríbel and Darwin J. Flakoll, eds. Managua, Nicaragua: Editorial Nueva Nicaragua, 1984: 130.

20 Skármeta, Antonio. "Tall Story." In *Queremos Tanto a Julio*, 107.

21 Randall, Margaret. "Conversación realimaginaria." In *Queremos Tanto a Julio*, 74.

22 Ibid, 65.

23 Gelman, Juan. "Carto a Julio." In *Queremos Tanto a Julio*, 19.

24 Galeano, Eduardo. "Una casa de palabras para Julio Cortázar." In *Queremos Tantos a Julio*, 18.

25 Alegría, Claribel, and Darwin J. Flakoll. "Julio, cronopio y palafiscio." In *Queremos Tanto a Julio*, 57.

26 *A Certain Lucas*, 50.

27 *A Certain Lucas*, 17.

28 Cortázar, Julio. *A Manual for Manuel*, trans. Gregory Rabassa. New York: Pantheon Books, 1978: 9.

29 *A Certain Lucas*, 5.

30 *A Certain Lucas*, 27.

31 Cortázar, Julio. *Cronopios and Famas*, trans. Paul Blackburn. New York: Pantheon Books, 1969: 25.

32 *Hopscotch*, 1.

33 Cortázar, Julio. "Blow-Up." In *Blow-Up and Other Stories*, trans. Paul Blackburn. New York: Pantheon Books, 1985: 114.

34 *Hopscotch*, 437.

35 *A Manual for Manuel*, 11.

36 Ibid., 3.

37 *Hopscotch*, 555.

38 *Cronopios and Famas*, 111.

39 *A Certain Lucas*, 96–97.

40 Eight days before World War I broke out, the Count Begouen and his three sons discovered the Trois Frères at Montesquieu-Aventes (Ariège) in the Pyrenees. And later, Herbert Kuhn wrote of it.

   Campell, Joseph. *The Way of The Animals Powers, vol. 1*. San Francisco: Alfred van der Marck Editions: 1987, 75–76.

   Kuhn, Herbert. *Auf Spuren des Eiszeitmenschen*. Wiesbaden, West Germany: F. A. Brochaus, 1953: 91–94.

41 *Hopscotch*, 306.

42 Ibid., 281.

43 Once the world was formless and empty with night until found by the light and filled. Under a moon both dark and bright, man grew half-obscured, while olive branches bent toward the light and roots dug deep in clay darkness. We create ourselves in the forms we imagine. Years pass. We are what we have spoken.

 Awakening Osiris: The Egyptian Book of the Dead. Trans. Normandi Ellis. Grand Rapids, MI: Phanes Press, 1988.

44 *Hopscotch*, 257.

PART IV: THE KING'S WITCH:

45 "Even the smallest of you is able to resurrect the dead," is said of the Tanaim, the Sages of the Oral Torah.

 Ginsburg, Rabbi Yitzchack. *The Alef-Beit*. New Jersey: Jason Aronson, Inc, 1995: 131.

Part V: Riff:

46 "The Pursuer." In *Blow-Up and Other Stories*, 239.

47 Pirozhkora, A. N. *At His Side: The Last Years of Isaac Babel*, trans. Anne Frydman and Robert L. Busch. South Royalton, VT: Steerforth Press, 1996: 114.

48 Ibid., xxxi.

49 Ibid., xxviii-xxxi.

50 Mandelstam, Nadezhda. *Hope Against Hope: A Memoir*, trans. Max Hayward. New York: Atheneum, 1970: 352.

51 Ibid., 372–373.

PART VI:

52 Cortázar, Julio. *The Winners*, trans. Elaine Kerrigan. New York: New York Review Books, 1999: 331.

PART VII:

53 "The Pursuer." In *Blow-Up and Other Stories*, 209.

54 *Hopscotch*, 361.

55 The higher functions of the brain—the memory and the reasoning faculties- are explained, according to Hyden, by the particular form of the protein molecules which correspond to each type of stimulus. Each neuron in the brain contains millions of different molecules of ribonucleic acid (RNA), which are distinguished by the disposition of their basic constituent elements. Each molecule of (RNA) corresponds to a well-defined protein, the way a key is perfectly adapted to a lock. The nucleic acids tell the neuron the make-up of

the protein molecule it is to form. According to Swedish researchers, these molecules are the chemical translation of thoughts.

56 Crick, Francis. *Astonishing Hypothesis: The Scientific Search for the Soul*. New York: Scribners, 1995: 3.

57 "For example," the impulse which corresponds to the note 'mi' as picked up by the ear, will slide rapidly along from one neuron to another until it has reached all of those containing the molecules of RNA corresponding to that particular stimulus. The cells immediately construct molecules of the corresponding protein which that acid governs, and we have the auditory perceptions of the note." *Hopscotch*, 362.

58 Cortázar, Julio. *62: A Model Kit*, trans. Gregory Rabassa. New York: Avon, 1973: 34.

59 Cyrillic character.

60 *62: A Model Kit*, 15.

PART VIII: RETURN

61 Cortázar, Julio. "To Dress a Shadow." In *Around the Day in Eighty Worlds*. Trans. Thomas Christensen. Berkeley: North Point Press, 1986, 249.

PART X: CONFESSION:

62 "Get a Move On." In *Save Twilight*, 41.

63 "Get a Move On." In *Save Twilight*, 130.

64 "Friends." In *Save Twilight*, 89.

65 "To a Woman." In *Save Twilight*, 122.